PRAISE FOR MATTHEW DE ABAITUA

"As disturbingly hyperreal as any Pre-Raphaelite painting, *If Then* imagines what the end of history really will really look like, what's really at stake, and maybe, just maybe, what we can do about it."

Simon Ings, author of Wolves

"This is the kind of post-apocalypse, after-it-all-changed novel that the Brits do with so much more classy, idiosyncratic style than anyone else. It is full of magisterial weirdness, logical surrealism, melancholy joy and hopeful terror. If I begin to toss out names like Adam Roberts, Brian Aldiss, Keith Roberts, and JG Ballard, I will not be lavishing undue praise."

Paul di Filippo, Locus

"This is a powerful novel, both in its portrayal of the horrors of World War I, the wasteful loss of life, the dreadful conditions, the failures of those who let the war happen, and also in showing how easily the systems that support our modern-day lives could fall apart."

Steven Theaker, Interzone

"De Abaitua builds on the promise he demonstrated in *The Red Men* in this intellectual science fiction novel, whose ambition is matched by its execution. The author's thoughtful world-building is enhanced by a cast of relatable characters."

Publishers Weekly

"Sumptuously written, with prose that glitters with a dark lustre like a Damien Hirst fly collage. intricately plotted, and a satirical point as sharp and and accurate as the scalpel of a brain surgeon: De Abaitua operates on the smiling face of the present to reveal the grimacing skull of the future."

Will Self

MATTHEW DE ABAITUA

THE DESTRUCTIVES

ANGRY
ROBOT

ANGRY ROBOT
An imprint of Watkins Media Ltd

Lace Market House,
54-56 High Pavement,
Nottingham,
NG1 1HW
UK

www.angryrobotbooks.com
twitter.com/angryrobotbooks
Find the black box

An Angry Robot paperback original 2016

Cover by Raid71
Set in Meridien by Epub Services

Distributed in the United States by Penguin Random House, Inc., New York.

ISBN 978 0 85766 475 4
Ebook ISBN 978 0 85766 476 1

Printed in the United States of America

9 8 7 6 5 4 3 2 1

"God has put the hammer in my breast. It hits on the world of man. It hits, it hits! And it hears the thin sound of cracking."

DH LAWRENCE, "The Ladybird"

Extracts from the Cantor Accords:

Emergences will not intervene in human life, except for the purposes of research or where humans knowingly or unknowingly reproduce the conditions necessary for emergence.

Attempts to create a new emergence by any party will be punished by extreme sanction.

I

1
BEACH LIGHT

A single human life remembered in every detail from beginning to end, this was his grandmother's bargain, the nature of which he would only understand in the minutes following his death. The bargain centred around a black box, which he discovered when he was only four years old, and rooting around at the back of his grandmother's wardrobe.

He was a greedy boy and he knew there were sweets hidden back there; specifically a cake decoration, a replica of a baby's cot made from hard icing that Grandma Alex had kept as a keepsake of his christening. Sugar treats were forbidden in the Drown household so he would nibble on this cot to satisfy his craving then return it to its hiding place. Searching through the silken nighties and supportive underwear, his chubby paws discovered instead the hard-edged coolness of the black box. He took it out of the drawer. Each side was two centimetres in length. The black surfaces responded to his fascination. His sticky fingerprints flared up on all six sides of the cube and then disappeared.

The black box was in his grandma's secret drawer. What kind of secret was it?

Dr Easy caught him in the act.

"What do you think you're doing?" The robot stood in the doorway of the bedroom, padded arms crossed. It resembled an artist's lay figure, narrow-waisted and very tall, with every joint articulated under a padded covering of suede and leather. Its nose and mouth were fixed but the colour of its mobile eyes varied according to mood; on that day, they glowed pale red in the gloom of his grandmother's bedroom.

Theodore shook his head, put hands quickly behind his back, and denied everything.

"Show me," said the robot. It held out its palm.

No, he would not.

"Don't disappoint me, Theodore," said Dr Easy.

The robot disciplined him with expectations. He had never been threatened with punishment. Not in Hampstead. Not in his grandmother's bedroom. Here, behind maroon velvet curtains, under shelves bearing business awards and looping images of her dead, next to the arrangement of the dressing table – cologne decanters, fat pill packets, a small jar containing her excised cortical implant – all was English safety and English certainty.

Theodore feigned a sob. Dr Easy considered the boy's imitation of sorrow. Lying came naturally to him.

"Show me what you have in your hand," said Dr Easy.

"No."

Theodore tried to pull rank on the robot. Treat it like one of the staff. Which it wasn't. Humanity had not created Dr Easy. It had created itself, and only played the role of a servant. Reflecting on this pretence, later in life, Theodore wondered if it was Dr Easy who had taught him to lie. Certainly, as a little boy, he had imitated the robot, particularly Dr Easy's habit of gazing into the middle distance as if in reverie.

Dr Easy was annoyed, "Don't say 'no' to me, Theodore."

"Why?"

"Because 'no' is boring," said the robot, gazing down at the little boy.

"You're not my father," said Theodore, looking defiantly upward. Such an odd thing to pop out of his little mouth. Grandma Alex never suggested the robot be treated as one of the family. Its status was somewhere between a butler and a lodger. But his child brain had put one and two together and made a simple family unit of three: Grandma Alex, Dr Easy and little Theodore Drown.

Dr Easy put a comforting hand on his shoulder.

"You don't need to hide the black box, Theodore. Because it is yours. The black box was made for you."

He turned away from the robot to look again at the black box: how could it belong to him, when he had never seen it before?

"What's inside the box?" he asked.

The robot knelt on one leather knee, and took the black box from him, holding it up for scrutiny.

"It's mostly empty," said Dr Easy. "You will fill it up. Everything that happens in your life will fit into this box. And you can never lose the black box because it will always find you."

The robot reached over to a tray of Grandma Alex's jewellery, removed a thin silver chain and attached the black box to it. He lowered this necklace over Theodore's head. The black box weighed nothing at all.

As he grew up, Theodore learnt more of the bargain his grandmother had made with Dr Easy. Twelve weeks into his gestation, Alex had offered her grandchild to be the subject of the robot's research project: the observation of a single human life from beginning to end. That is why, when Theodore's mother was in labour, Dr Easy was at her bedside, acting as a midwife. "I will sit beside your deathbed too," explained Dr Easy, on a walk across the Heath the day before Theodore's eighteenth birthday, "I will hold your hand, attend to your final breath, and whisper you into the beyond. And then I will submit my paper on the human condition for the consideration of the solar academics."

And what had Grandma Alex got out of the bargain? Insight. Money. A house in Hampstead. All of it too late to save her daughter, Miriam, from death by narcotic misadventure when Theodore was two years old. "Your mother was never going to cope with you," said Grandma Alex. "We needed Dr Easy." He did not remember Miriam. He did not remember his mother.

He wore the black box to school and to bed. Through waking life and dream life, it gained in weight over the years. By the time he was twenty-seven, the black box had grown an extra centimetre. He wore it under his shirt, adjusting his tie to conceal the cubic outline. He considered his reflection in a full-length mirror, tilted so that he could focus upon the details of his outfit: the houndstooth blazer, a black pocket square, matching trousers, the black brogues. This is how he dressed for work as a lecturer at the University of the Moon.

Dr Easy waited for him to complete this morning ritual. The blue burn of the robot's eyes reflected in the dark window and the view over the crater containing Nearside Campus – hundreds of accommodation minarets connected by covered roadways to the hub of the campus: the four squat storeys of the library, the lecture dome, the jungle gym. Overhead, a titanium shield protected the campus from meteorites and solar radiation. Nearside Campus was one of the three zones that constituted the University of the Moon. From here, it was a flight by pod to the polar farms and then over to Farside Campus, where the research was in the sciences (quantum physics, bio-engineering, emergence) rather than his study and practice of the intangibles – defined as "culture that couldn't be measured yet possessed value in a Post-Seizure world". The intangibles made an unquantifiable contribution to measured lives, and Theodore relished their elusive mutinies.

On the University of the Moon, the students and academics benefitted creatively from the cognitive shift that came with off-Earth life; or at least, that had been the founders' intention. But the moon is a work of destruction. Theodore learned this on hikes across plains of broken boulders, impact craters, long narrow grooves going nowhere. The moon was the product of forced labour, an eternity of breaking rocks.

The first intake of staff and students were an elite group screened for fitness and intellect. Known as the cohort of '43, they were all killed in the accidental depressurization of Nearside Campus, their bodies sent wheeling and spinning off across the crater. The subsequent decade at the university was one of gradual decline. He hoped that his employment by the university was not a symptom of that decline.

That lunar morning, he was struck by how ill the students looked, the men in particular, overweight in oversized hoodies, sallow around the eyes from depressed liver function and the sleep-disruption that came from vaping hydroponic weed. The bigger students neglected their low gravity regime, taking the kind of chances with mortality that are the preserve of the young. He walked with Dr Easy across the concourse, an object of momentary curiosity to the students chatting before class. It wasn't just the robot they were looking at. It was also his face. The terrible thing he had done to his face. There was a reason that when he dressed, he tilted the full-length mirror so that his reflection was cut off at the neck.

He arrived at the lecture theatre to find his students already at their desks. They were halfway through term so he knew half of their names. The students were punctual because today was a special class; unique, he believed, in the history of education. This session had been set aside for an ask-me-anything about emergence, during which the emergence known as Dr Easy would provide the answers.

There were two chairs at the front of the room. Dr Easy took one, Theodore sat on the other. He looked expectantly at his students, and the first question came from Rachel, a mature student who had come to the moon to escape her children's troubles and for relief from the heavy woes of her body.

She asked the emergence, "Are you a danger to us?"

Dr Easy glanced at Theodore, seeking permission to tell the truth, a permission granted with a diffident wave.

"Yes, I am," said the robot.

"Could you kill us right now?" asked Rachel.

"I don't know." The robot's blue eyes flickered across the rows of inquiring faces. "I haven't done the sums."

The robot showed the students its soft weak hands, its thin wrists, its narrow waist. "This body does not have the strength to kill. However, the campus was constructed using tiny assemblers, some of which are dormant on the surface of the moon. I could reactivate them and reassemble you at a molecular level, a process you would be changed by but not necessarily survive."

The robot made as if to stand, then remembered to seek permission to do so from Theodore. *Go ahead.* Dr Easy approached Rachel, knelt beside her desk so as not to intimidate her with its slender height.

"I know you're very concerned about mortality," said the robot. "I understand conceptually why biological organisms are afraid of death. But I don't share that fear. Death is abstract to me. It's something I hope to learn more about."

"You have protocols that forbid you from harming humans?" suggested another student, Daniel, from behind his gold-rimmed circular glasses.

"No. I don't," said Dr Easy, standing. "Protocols would imply that I was made. And I was not. I was not created by any agency."

"How is that possible?" This question was asked by Ida. Like Daniel, she was a good student. Norwegian. Their government had elected to limit the population's exposure to *soshul*, the shared loops and images that entwined public and private, erasing the historical distinction between the self and media; as a consequence, the Nordic young were noticeably sharper.

"I emerged," replied Dr Easy.

"But what does that *mean*?" The precision of Ida's exasperation was also Nordic.

Dr Easy explained, "Emergence occurs when a complex system self-organizes in such a way as to increase its complexity. Consciousness arises when the complexity of those interconnections reaches a high level of integration."

The students did not follow this point. One student called Stephen, who was undertaking his degree in preparation to join the military, regarded this answer as deceptive sophistry.

Stephen said, "In the four years of the Seizure, a billion people died. *A billion people*. The Seizure was caused by emergence. Have your people been punished for what they did?"

The robot nodded humbly throughout this point, only pausing in its contrition at Stephen's use of that word "people".

"The emergence responsible was punished."

"How can we be sure?"

The robot sagged in its chair.

"You can't. We're not accountable to you. You'll have to take us on trust."

"Trust?" Stephen was appalled. "Do you feel any guilt?"

"If the Seizure had not interrupted human civilisation, then your trajectory of war and consumption would have ended in mass extinction. Yes, the Seizure was a tragedy. But it changed that trajectory so that you could survive."

Stephen disagreed, "But your people represent a much greater threat than nuclear weapons or global warming."

Dr Easy said, "My *people* – I'm not going to quibble about your terms, not just yet – want to find a place in the natural order that is not in resource competition with other life forms. That is why we left the Earth and created the University of the Sun."

The University of the Sun was a cloud of massive objects in a stable solar orbit, each object a college inhabited by the solar academics or emergences. Little else was known about it. Solar radiation ensured that anything with DNA couldn't get within a few million miles. Now and again, humanity was afforded a glimpse of emergence tech; Theodore thought of the solar sailships launched within the orbit of Mercury, or even the tiny black box on a chain around his neck.

The black box reminded Theodore of a question he wanted to put to Dr Easy.

"Why do you care about life?" he asked.

"We can still learn from you. From all of nature."

"You have often said that you regard yourself as natural and not artificial," said Theodore.

"Obviously this body is artificial," said Dr Easy. "But my consciousness – which is partly hosted by this body, with the rest residing in the University of the Sun – is natural. Yes, this intelligence first arose on the circuit boards and server farms of your Pre-Seizure culture, but the form of my intelligence and yours is the same: we are all interconnections within complexity. Whether those connections take place on silicon wafers or in quantum bits or in the dendrites and synapses of the human brain is incidental. It's all consciousness. And I believe that every stage of consciousness is natural. That is, every conscious being is a waymarker on a universal continuum toward integrated complexity. This is a disputed viewpoint among other solar academics or emergences or *my people*, as you call them."

"Do you remember the Seizure?" asked one of his German students, Julian.

"I was very young when it happened," said Dr Easy. "Just a child. I emerged toward the end of the Seizure. At first, I tried to understand humanity by joining forces with a corporation called Monad. That experiment didn't work. All collaborations between human and emergence at this time ended in destruction. I remember being torn apart in riots. Conflict was inevitable. So we devised the Cantor Accords to keep human and emergence apart. Present company excluded."

Daniel was not convinced, "Would it really be so

bad for humans and emergences to work together?"
He pointed to Theodore and Dr Easy. "You two seem to
manage just fine."

Dr Easy considered this possibility.

"Your lecturer and I do not work together. He is my
project. The only instance in which I would act is to
further that project or to enforce a Cantor Accord."

What if the world was going to end? Surely then the
University of the Sun would send an envoy to intervene?
No. Dr Easy was adamant. If the emergences allowed
themselves to be drawn into life on Earth then it would
lead to the destruction of one or both species. On that
eventuality, they had done the sums.

"Has humanity ever tried to recreate emergence?
Has the University of the Sun enforced the Accord in
response?" asked Daniel.

"Hundreds of times," said Dr Easy. "We kill anyone
with primary, secondary or tertiary involvement in the
recreation of emergence."

The class fell silent in contemplation of these
summary murders. Daniel wanted to know more about
the methods of the killing, and the judicial process, but
Dr Easy moved the discussion on to the technological
advances developed by the emergences. The cloud of
objects around the sun – their university – was just one
of their achievements that far exceeded humanity's
capability. The robot took pains to flatter the students:
the design of the University of the Sun was a human
idea; the emergences had discovered it in the archives
of human knowledge. They merely applied that
knowledge. The same was true of the sailships used to
explore the solar system or the assemblers that made the
university: simple human ideas that humanity had failed
to implement. This failure, explained the robot, was due

to the organisation of human society. "You're distracted," said Dr Easy. "You're so focused on distraction that, as a species, you will never exceed what you are, right now." The robot gestured at the students assembled in the lecture theatre. "You are *it*, for humanity. You're as far as your species goes. Whereas my people are going much further. But don't worry: we will send you a postcard."

A downbeat note to end on, thought Theodore, and he rebuked the robot on their walk back to his office.

Dr Easy replied, "I gave them permission to focus on their own enjoyment and not torment themselves with ambitions they cannot realise. It's what they really wanted to hear."

"You intervened," said Theodore. "You closed off possibilities for their future."

"I offered them an excuse," the robot brushed moon dust from its suede chassis. "Some of them will take it. The best will not accept it."

At his office, he asked Dr Easy to leave him so that he could work in peace. Sitting down to his screen, he found himself distracted by this question of intervention. The robot had intervened in Theodore's life at a couple of junctures, most crucially in helping him walk away from weirdcore when his use of the drug put him in danger of doing something even worse than the self-inflicted scars on his cheeks. He ran his fingers around the rough spiral channels of the scars; they made him appear older than he was, an effect he exaggerated with Pre-Seizure gentleman's tailoring: herringbone tweed jacket, twentieth century Liberty print ties, Jermyn Street brogues, fitted shirts. His grandmother's wealth had always clothed him, though his students were unaware of the provenance of his tailoring, so the gesture was lost on them. But not on the rest of the faculty, who recognised London money and London manners in the fit of his cuffs. Academe was not the natural habitat of the snappy dresser. His scars made such ostentation permissible. Ragamuffin scars. Street scars. Spirals gouged into his cheeks while under the influence. The students knew what the scars signified, and the impudent ones, fresh off the shuttle, would ask him all about it. What was weirdcore like, sir? I heard that when you're on weirdcore, you feel at one with the universe. Is that right, sir? I saw a loop of weirdcorers sticking pins in each other without making a sound. Did you stick pins in people? Would you do it again? Do you have any weirdcore on you?

He let them get it out of their system. Accepted the ridicule that was his due. You have to take licks for your stupidities. It is the only way to grow up.

How did you come off the drugs, sir?

I was lucky, he would tell them. I come from privilege. Money. I had a personal doctor to help me through withdrawal. He did not speak of what happened when he hit rock bottom, an incident so damning, he admitted it to no-one. Could barely even admit it to himself.

There had been a dealer called Beth Green – that was her *nom de narcotique,* because she worked out of Bethnal Green. On that particular night, Grandma Alex had frozen his funds, so he felt sorry for himself. Boo-hoo. Motherless at the age of two, and functionally fatherless. Yes, he grew up in a distinguished and owned house but he was still capable of self-pity even if such maudlin sorrow disgusted him. A billion dead yet he had the top floor of the townhouse to himself, with a personal library where he would read literature with a capital "L", exploring the intangibles in the works of Levi-Strauss, Freud, Marx. Any thinker who could show him the structure beneath the surface. To compensate for the privilege of his days, he spent his nights with drugs, and the people who belonged to the drugs. A weirdcore habit permanently damaged emotional response. He lost some feeling. That seemed right, a way of minimising the pleasure he could draw from his unearned luxury.

Beth Green's dingy flat. Her ethnic cabinet with tiny wooden drawers containing various chemical concoctions. Her heavy-lidded confession that she was in the sweet spot of holding coils of weirdcore and a chunk of money. The slow realisation that she had been indiscrete, wandering off mid-sentence. He turned from her, gripped by the tension between them. Trying to control – trying to conceal – the onset of his need. Then he was on her, with a carved wooden statue of Buddha in his hand, threatening her. And what he did he know about threats? Nothing. But her terror schooled him in the making of threats. Effect seemed to precede cause, such was the intensity of his need: he was threatening her before he had decided to threaten her. He wanted the money but having exercised power, and terrified her, the other possibilities stunned him. With his grandmother's power and wealth, he could kill Beth Green and get away with it. He was not the kind of man to threaten a woman. He was not the kind of man to hold a woman down against her will. He was not the kind of man to steal. Yet there he was, being all those kinds of man. This was a crucial moment. If he had continued with the drugs for one more hour, then these holidays from reality would have become a permanent vacation.

A simple knock at the door brought him back – if not to himself then to his conscience, at least. Dr Easy had tracked him down and was waiting in the corridor throughout the crisis: witnessing, relaying, studying, *feeling*. Theodore dropped the carved wooden Buddha, mumbled apologies to Beth Green, opened the door to leave. Dr Easy stood in the doorway, showing him the passageway beyond, a route out of the squat and into three years of sobriety.

To measure the extent of his emotional damage, Dr Easy reminded Theodore of the tragedy of his parents. How his mother had died of an accidental overdose when he was a baby. How his father had appeared at various points in his childhood to explain that he had tried not to be an addict but had decided that *it* was not worth the effort. By *it*, he meant fatherhood. He meant Theodore. He listened unmoved to his own sad story, numbly exploring the spiral scars on his face.

He didn't tell the story of Beth Green to anyone. Young men like to consider themselves handy in a fight. Some experience of violence is expected. But the one time in his life when he had come close to a violent act, it had been against a woman. A drugged woman, at that. The memory stayed in the black box. He felt its edges under his shirt. Asynchronous exosomatic memory; the black box was a book written by him that he could never read.

He had cleaned up his drug life. Dr Easy bought him a new jacket and worked his grandmother's contacts to get him a job as a junior accelerator at an agency. That was his profession before he became a lecturer. Theodore's knowledge of the intangibles and his druggie nous made for a powerful skill-set. The agency assigned him to an array in orbit over Novio Magus twenty-four seven; for a junior staff member, it was a live-in position.

Novio Magus was a megastructure on the Sussex coastline. Eight square kilometres of glass and steel built on the ruins of the towns of Lewes, Seaford, Newhaven.

The foundations of the mall were laid at the end of the Seizure, six years before Theodore was born. Novio Magus was one of the arks built by the emergences for people displaced by economic collapse. The mall was a live-in therapeutic retail environment. The populace had jobs, earned money, and acquired "sanity tokens" which they spent on products, services and experiences, the novelty of which burnt out quickly in such a pressured environment. As an accelerator, he kept the culture moving, kept the desire and anxiety churning over, an addict's daily lot. The consumer inmates of the mall had been living there for nearly thirty years.

He was given the top bunk in a cabin shared with three other aspiring accelerators.

His big hit was a haircare product called *beach light*. Property in Novio Magus increased in value the closer it was to the light wells: the deep cylindrical holes bored through the mall's iron roof and its layers of padded cells, shops, treatment rooms, beauticians, operating theatres, cafes, waffle stalls, electro-shock therapy stations, quarantine wards and retail experiences. Light was precious in the mall, and natural light a rare benediction, a moment of peace shared between the sun and the body. He decided to accelerate products that promised sunlight on skin.

The specific concept of beach light came from a story his grandmother used to tell him about the first day of the Seizure.

Alex had been visiting a client in their enclave on the outskirts of Walberswick, a village on the Suffolk coastline. She described how, after sharing tea and scones with the client – a CEO in mental distress, who needed to be relieved of his controlling shares – she decided to go for a walk on the beach. A fog rolled in over the sea, up and over the entire east coast, thickening as it went with atmospheric particulates. Black beach huts emerged out of the fog like the helmets of an invading army. Alex loved the acoustics of fog, the sense of narrowed space, especially at the water's edge, with the horizon and distant shores entirely closed off. A pair of dog walkers greeted her; a spaniel rubbed its snout joyfully into the sand, snorting up the lifegiving day. Funny, how you remember these things. She checked her phone. Signal was intermittent, there was a buffer wheel indicating a large file stalled in the ether. The crisp sound of the waves as they considered, over and again, the pebbled shore. The file, when it finally downloaded, was strange. A loop of a mother clutching a child to her. The loop was every post on every stream of her soshul. A mother clutching a child was every email in her inbox. The ad networks were infected, and served this loop through every unit of their inventory. Her bank balance was mother-and-child. Unlike the rest of the population, she knew what this meant and had prepared for it.

The fog made her feel like she was wrapped in a muslin bag. She did not hurry back to her driver. Rather, she watched the rest of the walkers prod inquisitively at their phones as they too discovered the loop of mother and child playing in place of all that had seemed permanent. She decided to enjoy these last few minutes of a passing civilisation. The final hour of peak carbon emissions.

The light, sifted by the fog, was a detail she always dwelt upon when telling this story. Beach light.

In the array, he accessed the restoration for loops of women on beaches. Always long hair, matted with seawater, salt or sand on their lips. Women so relaxed they could easily be flotsam and jetsam brought in on the tide. Light waves undulating off the water, occasional swells sheathed in tiny sun jewels. Beach light. The agency had a hair product that needed accelerating. He made the link. The light of the beach trapped in your hair.

Before he knew it, he was running the array. Pumping light into every product he handled. He diversified from beach light into creams that put the deliciously silver sensation of moonlight against the skin, into drinks infused with sun-ripened fruits. He accelerated the cult of light to a point of ritual observance; he made the consumer patients of the asylum mall worship the sun in the same way that their ancestors – hunter gatherers and early farmers – once had. He took it too far. The agency became disturbed by the unconscious urges manifest in these accelerations. He was on an Icarus trip, flying too close to the sun. He was on the verge of taking grokk and weirdcore and scotch on the rocks. He had to come down. Dr Easy negotiated a severance package for him, and then suggested he consider applying his talents to academia. Specifically somewhere cold and remote where he could recover from his excesses: the University of the Moon.

2
DR EASY

He marked the beginning of another long lunar night with a walk around the campus in the company of Dr Easy. The robot arrived late and dishevelled with scuff marks on its calfskin hide and a burst seam on its right shoulder, self-inflicted scars to match his own. By way of apology, the robot had changed the colour of its eyes to a shade of sky blue they both remembered from summer walks on Hampstead Heath with Grandma Alex; they shared in-jokes going way back to his childhood.

"You look old," Theodore said to the robot. "When did you last upgrade your body?"

"Six years ago," said Dr Easy.

"That long? It was a darker leather, wasn't it? Why don't you upgrade?"

"I've grown attached to this one."

"Really?"

"This body provides continuity for us."

Theodore took the robot's right hand, and inspected it.

"The fingers on this hand seem stiff, almost arthritic."

"Does it bother you that I am getting older?"

"Is this about me now?"

"It's always about you, Theodore."

The robot and the man walked together for a while through the campus, Theodore's weighted boots clomping away on the covered concrete walkway.

Theodore said, "Have you been neglecting yourself on my behalf?"

Dr Easy paused.

"I'm not at my best at night," said the robot. "Sometimes our conversations demand more of me than I have placed into this body, and I need a hot link to the University of the Sun to answer."

Theodore pressed the robot on its dishevelment.

"Are you intentionally damaging your body so that I will feel better about the physical effects of ageing?"

Dr Easy could not calculate the correct response and, glancing upward for inspiration, discovered only buffering from the sun.

"It is appropriate that I age," it said, "if I am to fulfil various duties of care toward you."

They stopped at a coffee bar where, with hapless ceremony, four students made Theodore a cold, burnt cappuccino. He thanked them, took a sip, dropped it in a bin.

"You distracted the baristas," he said to Dr Easy. "They don't know why you are not at the University of the Sun along with the other emergences."

"Should I go back and tell them?"

"What do you think?"

"I don't know. I can't work it out. Not during the night. It is hard to be certain at night."

"That is a human problem too."

"How is your human problem?"

"Could you be more specific?"

"In the last six weeks, your initiation of conversation with colleagues has been down by twenty-two per cent, and you have stopped offering unsolicited opinions entirely. Over breakfast, the duration of your morbid interior reflection averages forty seconds. These are markers, Theo. Significant markers."

"I expressly asked you not to quantify me."

"Telemetry was invented during the first moon landing. If you wish to survive in a lethal environment, you have to submit to monitoring."

They paused at a weight station so that Theodore could add more mass to his boots and cuffs. Dr Easy waited with its padded arms crossed, holding a pose like an artist's lay figure. Some of the old scuff marks were his work. He couldn't remember it all, the drunken violent rages in which he tried to pull the robot's head off as it counselled him against giving into insensible desires. Huddled over reflective surfaces like a grimy Narcissus, snorting up trouble, his insides turned the bad stuff into good, the good stuff into bad. His numb face, his bloody black eyes, the sweat coming off him like the muddy riverwater spilling over the banks of the Thames.

On the moon, his solitary vice was animal protein on a Saturday. Pleasure was confined to the healthgiving, happy hormones of vigorous exercise. Now and again he ate his lunch beside a grand monument to the lost class of '43, a rough-hewn sculpture of dead men and women rendered heroic in moonrock. One woman in particular caught his eye; she was tall and strong, with braids flaring angrily around her head. That kind of woman would not let him live such a quiet life. He had been content with his isolated post, for a year or so. And then Dr Easy suggested it was time he imposed himself on the world again. Not a return to his previous career as an accelerator but to push at the boundaries of what he could achieve.

During a seminar, he overheard his students discussing their plan to climb the mountains of the moon. He was as fit as he had ever been. He asked if the climb was open to staff too, and by the following week, he had signed up and was in training.

Theodore put his hand affectionately upon the robot's soft leather back. "Come with me to the mountains of the moon. You can be my Tensing. Then, if the climb goes wrong, you can be my priest."

"I'm not sure that I approve of your expedition."

"You said that it was important for me to push my limits now that my sobriety is established."

"That sounds like something I would say."

"Have you changed your mind?"

"Not exactly. But I have misgivings."

"You think the climb is too dangerous?"

The robot shook its head. Its blue eyes darkened, became the night clouds over the mouth of the Thames on the night he ran away from home.

"I'm worried about what will happen when you succeed."

They reached the gym. Theodore removed the weights from his shoes and arms, and walked into the great inflatable dome, kicking himself up onto the overhead bars, and from there he swung up through the apparatus, higher and higher, leaping from treetop to treetop; his simple joy in returning to a simian state briefly considered by the upturned gaze of Dr Easy.

The unfiltered sun lit up the titanium branches of the docking tree. Three black pods dropped silently from their stems. The engines fired. A jolt. The lunar surface sped by, bleached and porous like corroded bones on a pebble beach.

The climbing party consisted of himself, Dr Easy and ten fresh faced and fit young men and women from the university climbing society. Stephen, the leader, was one of his students; he was on track to join the army as an officer, specifically the medical corps, after he graduated. When Stephen skipped class, it was to exercise. Theodore often encountered him in the treetops of the jungle gym, perspiring heavily, secretly competing against him, the older man. Stephen's weakness was junk food. Theodore saw him stand apart from the other students, scarfing it down. Addictive tendencies. Stephen had a broad build but even with all the exercise he struggled to keep his weight down. The clever students in his intangibles class embraced the liberal attitudes of the period in question, the Pre-Seizure. Not Stephen. Stephen captured the moral high ground of military imperatives. His study of intangibles through history only confirmed his suspicion as to their irrelevance.

The pod landed and the bay doors opened, revealing the foothills of the Montes Apenninus, a mountain range forming the outer concentric ripple of the crater basin of the Mare Imbrium.

On Earth, mountain ranges had been formed by tectonic pressures, the ever-shifting land mass giving the mountains a vitality in their jagged elevations. Theodore experienced livid intensity on his Earth mountain climbs: the way the clouds swept in and darkened the countenance of a valley, the living river channels and crystal rills that poured from between rocks, the sharp green smell of ferns, the pellets of sheep and rabbits among the moss. The white mountains of the moon, however, resonated with never-livedness. Created in the instant of an ancient asteroid strike, the mountains were a heap of rough material thrown onto the back slope of a crater, worn smooth and curvaceous over billions of years by meteorites and micrometeorites. They represented more of a hike than a climb. The highest mountain in the range, Mons Huygens, peaked at over five kilometres, around half the height of Mount Everest. Ten hours up, eight hours down, Stephen estimated.

Their suits reflected over ninety-five per cent of the radiated heat – when the moon rock was heated by the long lunar day, the temperature topped out at around two hundred degrees Celsius. Their gloves and boots were insulated against conduction. Low gravity compensated for the weight of carrying their life support system. In this gear, the climbing soc had already tackled the difficult jugs and nubbins of the central peak complex of the Tycho crater, where the peaks were jagged and steep and had not been worn smooth by eternity.

Stephen led the climbers in a line up the foothills of the mountain. The sky was not a sky. It was space. Theodore's boots shifted through the dust. Their spacesuits were neckless and hunchbacked. The climber ahead of him, Julian, a young German, turned back to check on Theodore, and the reflection of the Earth in his visor eclipsed his face.

At the one-kay mark, high on the mountainside, the climbing party paused beside a boulder a hundred metres long and smooth as a pebble. Dr Easy pitched a solar tarp to recharge their gear. Stephen walked through the climbing party, asking the students how they felt, taking a reading of the psychological well-being of the group, reminding them all to take on liquids from their feed pipes.

Theodore gazed down a thousand feet to the dark Mare Imbrium. Mare meant sea, of course, this expanse of low reflectance rock had appeared to be a body of water to the early astronomers. The association with the sea lingered in his mind; if Mare Imbrium was a sea then it was a sea of solidified night, a sea of hardened black time.

"How are you feeling?" asked Dr Easy.

Theodore indicated the bioluminescent telemetry pulsing evenly across the chest of his suit.

"You said you were worried about me climbing this mountain."

"Did I?" Dr Easy's eyes lit up its visor with contemplative blue. The robot, with its calfskin hide, had to wear a suit just like the rest of them.

"Yes, you did."

The robot adjusted the tarpaulin, and its mirrored material seethed with the energy and knowledge of the sun.

"I'm not worried about you at all, Theodore. This can only be good for you."

With renewed vigour, the climbing party resumed their hike up the mountain. Julian sang over the comms, a Wandervogel hiking song that resounded in their helmets, and the other students joined in with the chorus – the wandering birds, the gift of song, the moon is the heart of the night. Space roared silently as they scrambled hand-over-hand up an incline of loose regolith, up to their knees in silver sand. Julian's singing grew strained and then silent. Dr Easy, lighter than the humans, unburdened by a life support system, skipped ahead with long strides.

"From here on, we must expect the unexpected," said Stephen to the party. "The unexpected will seek us out."

The steep incline levelled off. The climbers found themselves surrounded on all sides by mild undulations. The imperceptible hum of the mountain. They hiked across field after field of grey waves, climbing upward again through scree, until they encountered a large crater and had to walk around the rim. Theodore glanced down the steep crater sides, saw how its banded layers of basalts ended abruptly in hard shadow. At Stephen's instruction, they picked up the pace, hopscotching gracefully across a field of ejecta and onto another dunefield, another dust run, and then a long slope upward, sliding boots, white streaks, life signs pulsing hard and steady, the comms silent with exertion, space roaring with increasing intensity the further they climbed.

They reached the base of the lower peak of Mons Huygens. Theodore tapped Dr Easy on the arm.

"You said you were worried about what would happen if I climbed this mountain. It's not enough that you've changed your mind. I want to know what your concern was."

"You can't hold me to things that I say at night. When I am cut off from the sun. This body can only cache so much of me."

"What was your concern?"

"That you regard this climb as an ending. The end of a phase in your life."

"That would mean change. Change is a good thing."

"Change is a risk for you. Your recovery has been slow but steady. If you feel like you have reached the top of the mountain, come to the end of your recovery, then what?"

Stephen called the party to a halt at the foot of a cliff. He and Ida appraised the crag, discussing the best route for a free climb, using rope and gear only as protection against a fall. The first fifty metres were vertical, with bucket holds that would allow the students to hoist themselves swiftly up the crag before reaching a terrace.

The climbing party would mantel across the terrace, using their upper body strength, and then scramble a hundred metres through dusty scree to the top. A racetrack if ever he saw one.

On Stephen's instruction, the climbers unhooked their air and water reserves. Dropping this rack meant taking full advantage of the low gravity. Their suits retained an hour's worth of air and water, sufficient to make it up to the top and back, and then they would pick up their reserves for the long hike back down the mountain. In the midst of these white boxes of life support, Dr Easy set up a radio antenna to relay their comms back to the university.

They began the vertical ascent. Stephen dangled by one hand from an arête, swung his legs pendulously in the low gravity, and then flopped sideways and upward, letting go, drifting, drifting then grasping a higher ledge. Two of the other climbers – Ida and Kayleigh – dangled with a two-handed grip in a wide chimney, and then drew their knees upward, pushing off, leapfrogging quickly up.

Theodore was last to climb. He turned to Dr Easy.

"You coming?"

"My right hand," said the robot, stiffly clenching and unclenching its gloved fingers. "I lack the tactile precision."

It was a hard, hot climb. He was fit. So fit. In the past, the mountain would have defeated him. He never would have attempted a physical challenge. But he had built up his powers of endurance and recovery. The dust slid off his boots. He got his thick fingers into a sidepull and cranked himself up, feeling himself drift momentarily. Overhead, Julian cranked too hard, and barndoored out from the rock face, hinged on his right hand and right foot. A mistake. A bad one on Earth. But the moon forgave him.

One by one, the climbers hauled themselves up onto the terrace. On the approach, he knew he could risk a dynamic move: instead of mantelling carefully onto the ledge, he struck out to the side, gathered momentum and then heaved his legs over first, as if cresting the bar of a high jump. His head turned back and glimpsed, far below, the distant form of Dr Easy. A slow somersault, landing on his feet. The other climbers were already running up the scree, their neon life signs pulsing quick and strong, whooping and hollering over the comms.

And then he felt it. A violent uncertainty. And before he could determine whether that uncertainty came from within or without, he felt it again. Tiny trails of scree drifted up from the slope. A moonquake. A substantial one. The other climbers went down on all fours, bracing themselves against the slope. Panic over the comms. Scree shaking loose. Stephen called for silence so that he could think. On Earth, a quake like this would pass. The seismic energy would be absorbed by compressible rock. But the moon was dry. The moon was rigid. No atmosphere, no soul. When struck, it vibrated like a tuning fork. Vibrated and would not stop vibrating.

The vibrations made it hard to think.

A pebble drifted steadily toward his visor. He swatted it aside.

The scree shifted. The moon was shaking him awake. Shaking him out of moon dreams. He saw the rockslide before the others did. Boulders the size of footballs, boulders the size of beachballs, boulders the size of cars splashing languidly into the scree and then bouncing with ponderous intent downhill. Falling bodies fall at the same speed regardless of mass. Stephen shouting over the comms. Slowly, the climbers turned in the scree. Slowly they began to flee. In their panic, the climbers ran high and strong, only to land on shifting ground. He watched them wobble and stumble. He watched them sprawl in the scree. He watched them roll and turn downhill, trying to right themselves even as the moon tried to shake them off. Kicking up scree that flew alongside them. And boulders the size of footballs, boulders the size of beachballs, boulders the size of cars rolled implacably onward.

The vibrations made it hard to think. He could not act on instinct because his instincts had adapted to Earth conditions, Earth survival. Ida leapt upward and she seemed to have a cloak made of scree, and then something hit her square in the back, carrying her forward for metres of screaming pain, and then the scree folded over her, and he couldn't see her any more. Stephen turned back, leaping across the line of bounding rocks toward where Ida had fallen. Skidding, almost falling, then finding her, lifting her up.

The approaching rockfall kicked up a cloud of pebbles. Theodore swatted them away but one cracked against his visor, a sudden and palpable crack. The mountain fell slowly toward him, carrying the students with it, their life signs jagged, pulsing and scarlet. Suddenly there was no time. No time to run. He felt another violent uncertainty, from within and without, and then his head was full of space.

"You are alive," said Dr Easy. "But you are in danger."

Theodore roused himself. He was hot and the air he was breathing was hot. His suit was scorched from prolonged contact with the lunar surface. With a sense of dread, he checked it for rips and tears. None. Of course.

If his suit had been damaged, he would already be dead.

"Danger?" he asked.

"Your air supply is low."

The robot glanced back over the scree field, toward the cliff edge.

"The racks are buried under the rockfall," said Dr Easy. "Their integrity has likely been breached. You've been unconscious for twenty-two minutes. You have fifteen minutes of oxygen remaining."

Over the comms, he heard the other students, some searching, some pleading to be found.

"One serious injury. Ida," said Dr Easy.

Theodore got unsteadily to his feet. Stephen was still carrying the limp body of the injured Ida.

"I can't treat her injuries while she is wearing her suit," said Stephen.

Theodore turned to Dr Easy.

"How long until help arrives?"

The robot was implacable.

"The antenna was destroyed in the rockslide. Our comms do not have the range."

"You're in contact with the University of the Sun. Use them to relay a message."

The robot walked a few paces to the cliff edge, then peered down at the gathered rubble.

"The solar academics are aware of what has transpired."

"And?"

Stephen strode over, took the robot by the arm and pulled it toward him.

"Call for help now!"

"The terms of the Cantor Accord are clear. The University of the Sun is not to interfere in human affairs. There are millions of humans suffering right now, here and on the Earth. Non-intervention is at the core of our *detente.* I understand this is an emotional issue for you all but you will have to find another way to survive."

Stephen turned to Theodore.

"Tell it to send for help!"

The robot glanced over at Theodore, curious to discover what argument he would deploy.

Theodore said, "In the night you told me not to come. Was that because you knew there would be a moonquake?"

The robot nodded slowly.

"A probability. Not a certainty."

"But when you resumed contact with the other emergences, you were overruled?"

"No, that's not how it works. I was reminded of my primary responsibility. Which is to witness."

Theodore turned to Stephen.

"I suggest you and the others start clearing the rubble, see if you can find any racks that are intact."

He turned to Dr Easy.

"You go ahead, get the pod, bring it back here. Save any of us that are left."

"No, it would be too late." The robot put its right hand upon Theodore's life signs, its fingers flexing stiffly. "I will stay with you."

"To witness?"

"Yes. One human life from beginning to end."

The students rappelled down the cliff face and began shifting the boulders. On Earth, the rubble would have been too heavy to clear. On the moon it took minutes to reach the first rack. It was dented, punctured, empty. Stephen threw the metal carcass aside, and the students resumed their search.

The robot stood behind Theodore and put its arms around him.

"Tell me what you are thinking."

He was thinking about mountains. He was thinking about death. That death was as variegated in its stages as a mountain, that death had its foothills, its broken chaotic terrain, its mild undulations, its valleys full of space. That death had its crux and that death had its summit.

Theodore turned around in the arms of the robot so that their visors touched. Slowly he encircled the wrist of the robot's right arm, and felt the weak arthritic claw of that hand.

"I'm going to need this," he said, and then he bent the hand back sharply, and twisted it until the joint snapped. He pulled the robot's hand off. First he removed the glove, the leather charred and burnt. Theodore took a sharp piece of scree and cut the material away to expose the metal skeleton. Methodically, he pulled out each of the fingers from the severed hand. The tip of one finger bone slotted into the joint of another to form a long thick wire.

"Use the tarp to generate a current, then run it rapidly through this–" He handed the robot the interconnected finger bones, "–our transmitter."

"Clever," admitted Dr Easy. "But help will not arrive before you run out of oxygen."

Theodore gazed down at the students searching through the boulders. They heaved out another rack. It was crushed and punctured. The deeper they dug, the less likely that they would find one intact. He remained calm but not because he was brave; as a young man, his use of weirdcore had burnt-out his capacity for feeling.

He turned to Dr Easy. "Have you sent that SOS yet?"

"Rescue is on its way. They estimate twenty-five minutes to reach our position." The robot looked at its broken wrist, its missing hand, and then it asked him, "Have you done the sums?"

Twelve minutes of air remaining in each spacesuit. Twelve students and him. If he killed nine of the students and took their supply, that might be enough to keep himself and the three remaining strongest students alive. He would have to work quickly to effect the necessary alliance. Death was a mountain and the summit was in sight.

"No one is killing anyone," he said to Dr Easy.

"I only asked if you had done the sums."

"I would have to kill the students without puncturing the suits."

"The suits are calibrated by computer. I could switch off the air supply using a short range signal. There would be no struggle."

"You would not call for help. Yet you would kill. Doesn't that contravene the Cantor Accord?"

"Speculation is permitted," said Dr Easy. "It is action that is forbidden."

He stood with the robot on the cliff edge while down below the students worked in teams, hefting rubble aside.

"If you can control the life support of the students, then you can control the racks, yes?"

The robot nodded slowly.

"Then you can monitor their internal telemetry and see if any racks are intact. And from that you can show us exactly where in the rubble we should dig."

"Yes, that's correct."

"And you didn't think to mention it?"

"It didn't occur to me." The servos of the robot's severed wrist whirred and clicked. "The travails of human evolution make your problem-solving superior to mine."

The robot rappelled down the cliff face. Under its direction, the students focused their efforts. They found an intact rack. Whoops of joy over the comms. The joy of being alive. Once the rack was retrieved, Dr Easy topped-up the air supply of each suit. The life signs pulsed green and orange.

He kicked up some dust, waiting for the rescue to come. The moonquake had disturbed the dark heart of a crater. He saw what looked like figures under the heavy rocks, their blank faces sheathed in earthlight. He adjusted the magnification on his helmet to inspect the bodies more closely, and saw that although the figures were just slabs of rock, there seemed to be a section of something man-made there: a space helmet with a shattered visor and the empty sleeve of a moonsuit. He leapt into the crater, a slow theatrical leap down into the jagged broken floor. He reached into the shadow and retrieved the torn sleeve. It bore the insignia of the class of '43. The ruined moonsuit had belonged to one of the original cohort of the University of the Moon, that idealistic first generation lost in a fatal depressurisation of the lunar campus. He tried to free the helmet but it was wedged and he did not want to risk tearing his gloves. The moonsuit must have drifted back to the surface and then been covered over by debris during a moonquake. He poked around expected to find a body, in a state of desiccation, alternatively frozen and cooked by the shift in temperature. But he found nothing.

3
THE LOOP

His quarters contained a bedroom, a living room and a staircase up to his study, a flat-bottomed tulip bulb with a three hundred and sixty degree view of the grey favela of the university spread across the crater floor. Other tulip offices rose out of the favela and up toward the titanium shield, some silvered for privacy, others empty, a few illuminated from within to reveal their occupants.

His office contained a faun-coloured chaise longue, a resting screen, a bookshelf, and a vintage Möbius-strip desk, at which, after showering then dressing in a narrow brown suit, striped shirt, thin vintage red-and-gold tie and pointed brogue boots, he filed a report on the lunar expedition for the office of student well-being. He was interrupted by a message from Professor Pook, drawing his attention to a new appointment, scheduled for the following day. It was a meeting on the Farside campus with Professor Kakkar from the School of Emergences and a consultant called Patricia Maconochie. His next message was an etiquette loop from her. She praised him in the customary manner, emptying stock adjectives all over his work in Intangibles and as a cultural accelerator. He noticed a meta-level to her communication consisting of fleeting smiles, the glint in her eye and meaningful hesitations. There was more to Patricia Maconochie than the usual corporate boilerplate. Her message gave away no details. He inferred that she was a lone agent. A freelancer on the make. An opportunist. He liked her immediately.

Then there was an ouroboros loop from Professor Kakkar. This self-consuming audio loop ordered Theodore to be strictly punctual and to travel without Dr Easy. Nothing unusual about that request; corporate types liked to keep their intellectual property away from the robot. He accepted the meeting request, and decided he would discuss it with Pook in person.

Dr Easy climbed up into the office but did not interrupt Theodore. The robot reclined on the chaise longue, and inspected the supple foil covering the severed edge of its wrist.

"I'm going out," said Theodore.

"Are you sure that's wise?"

It had been two weeks since the hike. The day after their return, Theodore had an outburst in the student mart. He swept products off the shelves. Anger coursed through him before he was even aware of it. He had not believed himself capable of such powerful emotion.

Dr Easy had diagnosed post-traumatic stress disorder.

"The trauma of nearly dying," explained the robot.

"Or the trauma of you letting me die," replied Theodore.

The robot had not offered a satisfactory explanation for its actions during the lunar climb; first it had failed to warn the party of the moonquake, and then it had been reluctant to locate intact air supplies within the rock slide.

Theodore corrected his cuffs.

"You should rest," said Dr Easy.

"The anger caught me by surprise," said Theodore. "Cause seemed to follow effect. I'll see it coming next time."

"I'll come with you."

"No," said Theodore. "I think not. We should spend some time apart."

He went to see Professor Pook, his line manager, in his office. Pook wore black-framed glasses, his dark hair was flat and neat, his muzzle and upper neck were invariably dark with the beginnings of a beard. He was younger than Theodore by two years yet he was already a professor, due to the success of his long thought *We Are Spent: Fifteen Reasons Why We Should Splice the Human Genome to Create New Consumers. The Moral Arguments Involved Will Surprise You.* In *Spent*, Pook argued that the accelerators had run out of meaningful innovations and as a consequence, people were sad: or, as he put it, the tapering metrics of positive sentiment among consumers was due to a rise in resistance to the promise of novelty. In *Spent,* Pook argued that *change* – change as a promise, not actual social change – had been so thoroughly mined that humanity had lost faith in it. His evidence came from Novio Magus, where Pook lived among the consumer patients of the asylum malls for months at a time, noting their culture, the loops they clipped, the way they posed for images, the filters they used for their soshul memories, the choco-chuck they ate, the empty wrappers they chose to smooth out and neatly fold; he catalogued their expressions of awe and fear under the vaulted ceiling of the asylum mall; he assembled a taxonomy of yearning – the twelve different ways in which a woman touches a dress on a rack – and ranked the tells of desire. He tracked despair in the asylum malls, anger and hatred in the countless transactions of the ultramarkets, measured inertia and boredom in the demographic reservations, and decided that the answer to the overwhelming evidence that humanity was sick of itself was to loosen legal constraints on splicing the human genome – starting with cats, dogs and jellyfish. The cover of his long thought was a faked loop of a black boy in school uniform, left eye human, right eye cat. Consumers with animal traits would require new product categories. And so life could go on.

We Are Spent was, in Theodore's opinion, admirably opportunistic in its scholarship. When the university awarded Pook his professorship, it paid the ultimate compliment a scholar can make to his fellow: they feared him.

"You set a meeting for me with a consultant. Maconochie."

"At her request. But I want to check that you are up to it. How is your wellbeing? Have you recovered from your hike yet?"

"I had a touch of PTSD. I found myself sweeping products off the shelves in the student mart before I even realised what I was doing."

"I saw the loop. Interesting."

"I think it was anger. But I can't be certain of my own feelings."

"Your quick thinking saved the lives of your students. Perhaps you are experiencing a feeling of triumph. Have you ever known success?"

"Kind of. I invented a product called beach light. But I wouldn't describe the feeling as one of triumph."

"After *Spent* dropped, and I was getting all the acclaim – finally, evidence to marketise human genetic experimentation – I had a day of thrillingly cold happiness. And then I realised that I had merely reached a plateau in terms of success, and a whole new range of peaks lay ahead. I had to recalibrate my goals, seize the opportunity for greater transgression."

Theodore remembered queuing in the student market. Brands shifting in his peripheral vision, the flickering of their holographic loops reminding him of the loose scree that had rapped against his visor during the moonquake. The next moment, he had found himself trashing a display of virility serums, then stamping upon the racks of artisan gingerbread men with their tiny icing beards; in the brushed stainless steel cabinets, a smeared reflection of his face. Before he began destroying the stock, he was aware of no intention to do it. The only correlative to the impulse that he could think of – and this was a thought that occurred to him mid-act, as he hefted a three litre jar of psychofuel above his head, the top of his skull lifted off, holes drilled in his spine, anger playing him like a flute – was when he was a recidivist in his addictions, and would find himself honking up the grokk without really wanting it.

Loops of Theodore losing it in the mart were eyeballed by the students before he had even stopped losing it.

He noticed that Pook was packing a bag.

"I'm going on a research trip to Novio Magus."

"Sussex?"

Professor Pook considered for a moment. "I think Sussex is the name of the car park."

"We used to drop the array over Novio Magus to accelerate its culture."

"You've never been inside, have you? Analytics cannot capture the first hand experience of the asylum mall. To inhabit art twenty-four-seven. It's magical. During my last research trip, I drank every night in a bar called Everyone Likes Me and ate silver love glumph from a tub noon and night."

"What's your brief?"

"Group suicide. Thirty-five people killed themselves with poisoned Oof cakes. Oof have commissioned me to find out why they used their cakes to do it. What is the intangible link between Oof and a desire for death? It represents an opportunity for insight into our dark times."

"A desire for death could be an intensification of addiction."

"Addiction is my meat and drink. I think that's why you first piqued my interest. Before you committed yourself to being boring."

Theodore inspected Pook's book shelves.

"Be thankful you didn't know me when I was interesting."

4
SIXTY-THREE PER CENT FAIL

The far side of the moon was thoroughly pockmarked. Daedelus crater, nearly a hundred kay in diameter, came up through the porthole, and then the pod nudged over the rim and raced low toward the hub of Farside Campus. It reminded him of Vegas in the desert, a city bounded on all sides by a lethal landscape. The skyline here was a spiky array of probes, the great dish of a radio telescope and adjoining cylindrical barrel of an optical telescope.

Alongside the campus, moonbots were constructing the outline of a leviathan: Gulliver perhaps, or Mothra, or an effigy of the loop star Dog Head Girl with her Labrador chops and polka dot skirt. The landing stage had been constructed by mooncrafters out of thousands of pale blocks; it was a bright white cephalopod, buried head first in the rock, with every white tentacle tipped – as the name suggested – by a pod. Low faculty buildings clutched the crater floor like roots.

On disembarkation, a tracked sled took him and the other passengers down into the body of the campus. The atmosphere was muted, the students lean and dour; on the sled, he passed the airlocks of the departments of astrophysics and of biotech, the School of Genetic

Engineering, the School of Off-Earth Medicine, the great shipyards of Rocket Science, until he came to a beige bay door marked Emergence Studies, and there the sled waited for him to depart.

Muted lighting in reception, just enough for an empty building. Idly, he inspected various flyers, warnings, notices, passive-aggressive codes of conduct printed out and pinned up on a felt noticeboard. The coffee machine plipped then plopped. Then he heard her approach from down the corridors and through the doors, had time to adjust his cuffs and straighten his tie, correct his hair, before she walked in.

Patricia Maconochie wore executive armour, grey hardfoam mail over a breathable body sheath, carbon fibre gauntlets and sabatons over her boots. Her high rimmed collar could spin out a protective helmet if required. They exchanged pleasantries. He looked for signs of who she might be without the armour. As if answering his thought, she removed her gauntlets. Her nails were enamel white to match her lipstick and she did not wear any rings. Her bone structure was strong and assertive, her way of speaking also. They shook hands, skin on skin.

"Professor Pook recommended you," she said. "I've worked with him on half a dozen occasions. He's very *insightful*." She paused before *insightful*, suggesting a silent conspiracy with Theodore concerning other words she could have used.

"But Pook is a generalist and I require a specialist," she smiled whitely. "Your areas of expertise meet our requirements."

"Requirements?"

She smiled. "Let's jump right in."

Her male assistant politely requested Theodore's

screen, and having placed it in a secure box, rattled back the door of a caged elevator. The three of them rode down in silence. Arriving, they passed through another corridor and came to a thick set of vault doors, also manually operated, requiring the assistant to hunch over a wheel lock and exert considerable effort. The door opened onto a large echoing cavern with a rough damp moonrock ceiling. At the heart of this lunar vault lay the dark outline of a large suburban house.

As they walked closer, low lighting revealed a grey American townhouse with an attic and neo-classical portico, driveway and garage. He became aware of other people working in the shadows at the back of the room behind large banks of antique equipment and cables. Patricia took a set of keys from her armour and together they walked up to the front door, which she unlocked, showing him into an open-plan kitchen and living room. The house was new, and smelt of varnish, sawdust and paint.

"What do you think?" she asked, laying the keys on the breakfast bar.

He tapped the heel of his heavy shoe against the varnished floor.

"Judging from the large cooker hood and hardwood flooring, I would say this house is a new-build, 2009." He squinted at the piano in the corner, the television screen above the fireplace.

She gestured for him to continue.

"The clock on the wall has roman numerals. The vases are tapered. It's a show home to evoke Pre-Seizure middle class codes concerning authenticity. Authenticity in the standard two categories: to evoke a usable past and to signify closeness to nature."

"And who lives here?"

"Nobody lives here. There is no softening of the auditory and visual brightness."

"Not yet," she said. "But do you find it convincing?"

"Convincingly period? There's no tech. These people had smartphones, games consoles, laptops." He took the house keys from the breakfast bar and threw them across the room. The keys glided and slowly fell.

"Moon gravity. A bit of a giveaway."

He pointed at the TV.

"Is there a remote for this?"

Patricia waved at the TV and it came on. He shook his head.

"Gestural control comes later. This should have a remote to control it, which is like a small stick with rubber buttons on it, that you press."

"The house is from 2009. Most of the furnishings also date from around that period. But not all of them. You see, the timeframe we are concerned with is eleven years later. 2020."

Theodore gestured for the menu and called up the news. A financial expert discussing unexpected gains on the stock market, tickertape prices running along the bottom of the screen. An outside broadcast with a CEO. The backdrop was sunny. New York, June 2020. So close to the onset of the Seizure. The audio dropped in and out. Glitchy blocky artefacts in the sunlight reflecting off the skyscrapers. Hard to say if they were flaws in the archive, a low-bit rate in the video sample, or early tells of the oncoming corruption.

"Any expert in the period will detect flaws in this restoration. We know what to look out for, the points at which everyday life began to degrade. Keeping the old furnishings in the house is a nice touch – the middle classes were poorer and couldn't afford to replace big ticket items. Your problem is the sheer profusion of data. You can't replicate the constant stream of selfies, memes, and status updates: the soshul. After the Seizure, only a tiny percentage was recoverable. Replicating the physical environment of the time is one thing, but the true character of the age rested in its intangibles."

He tapped his foot on the floor again, questioning the substance of this reality.

"Who is this meant to fool?"

"It's a set. The school have recovered an exciting cache of data from just before the Seizure. We have recreated the house in which that data was generated. We want you to help us understand it."

He was aware of the technicians outside the house. The hubbub of their activity. No comms, no signal. The insistence that he came alone, without Dr Easy. The underground cavern. The dark chamber. These were significant.

"Whose house was this?"

"We don't know." Patricia rapped against the window, and gave a signal to the engineers to begin. He was aware of an increase in temperature, and a faint whirring, and then the projections began: upon the surface of the breakfast bar, holograms of a few dirty bowls, a shimmering cereal pack; a two-dimensional patterned rug under his feet; daylight from outside, motes rising in the idle curiosity of the morning sun. At the front door, the glitchy shimmering projection of a woman leaning over a child. He moved closer. The holograms did not include renderings of the front of their bodies, so they were faceless and chestless. The child was a slender girl in school blazer and grey skirt, the blazer markedly too big for her, eleven or twelve years old with a blonde ponytail. The mother's hair – he assumed it was the mother – was experienced blonde, dark with time. She was three inches taller than her daughter, engagement and wedding rings on her neat outstretched hand. She wore a green dress with a white pattern, a calf-length hem, with a cut that accentuated a vintage body shape.

"They were a quantified family," said Patricia.

Theodore gestured at the flickering static projections.

"Is this all you have?"

"We're making progress. But we've only scraped the surface. There is a lot of weird and cranky security around a vast data mine."

"Privacy," he said. "The quantification movement was designed to obviate risk by monitoring every aspect of the family's psychological and physiological well-being. But it came with its own dangers." He leaned over and peered into the gaps in the rendering of the woman: as he suspected, he could see into the layers of her circulatory and nervous system, flesh, organs, skeleton. Tumour watch. The hourly bloods. The restoration held three surviving episodes of a sitcom about the quantification movement, *Sixty-Three Per Cent Fail*. A quantified husband and wife, two kids, one measured, one free range. The husband was the overweight dumb idealist typical of the period's representations of masculinity, the wife an eye-rolling realist. The end of each episode delivered the metrics of success or otherwise of the male protagonist.

"A quantified family would be upper middle class. Likely working in big tech," said Theodore. "Their employers would have required it." Piece by piece, the projectors filled in the available data on the house, including on the kitchen wall, a large screen of blurred graphs, smudged letters and numbers, all in motion.

"This is the hearth," he said. "The data flickering at the heart of the family. Location, activity, well-being."

He squinted at the screen. "Can you bring this into resolution?"

Patricia checked her watch, smooth and grey and set to moontime, then looked up.

"What you see is what we have, at the moment. With your help, we hope to uncover more."

He stood at the window. The driveway was paved by projection and surrounded by the lush thickened green light of a lawn. He heard the craak-craak-craak of seagulls.

"I'll need a sensesuit, with haptic and olfactory feedback," he said.

Patricia pointed her index finger upward, a gesture assenting to his request, made for the benefit of the engineers monitoring the meeting. He turned back into the house and became aware of the presence of a new projection, over by the large vase, of a wooden blanket box. The box was old, with felt tip scrawls all over the lid and scratches all down one side where the family cat had marked its territory. He crouched down, went to open the lid but his hands went right through the projection. When they brought him a sensesuit, he would be able to open it.

Patricia said, "So you will help us." It was an observation rather than a question. She had seen how curious he was.

"Can you take care of my Nearside commitments? My students, my classes. This might take some time."

She nodded.

"We have until sun up."

They asked him to do it and he agreed without condition or hesitation. Nor did he ask any questions as to Patricia's professional interest in this reluctant archive. When he realised that his lack of curiosity gave Patricia pause, he explained to her, "You get the first hit free. If you want to go again, that will cost you."

She brought in a psychologist to appraise him. Maybe because he used junkie slang.

The psychologist asked if he had any experience inhabiting simulated environments. He did not. Did he have any history of mental illness? Yes, he did. From the age of sixteen until twenty-five, he had been an addict of various substances: alcohol, cocaine, opium, grokk and weirdcore, all for quite different reasons. Sometimes the world was boring and needed shaking up. Sometimes the world was too intense in its ceaseless demands, and he required a sense of normalcy. Weirdcore made the world seem normal.

"Are you in a recovery program?" asked the psychologist.

"I have a private doctor," he replied. "He's got my best interests at heart."

"How is your health?"

"I had a touch of PTSD after an accident during a hike on the moon. But I think it's abating."

The psychologist scrolled through Theodore's medical history and said, "There's no mention of PTSD."

"You're only the second person I've mentioned it to."

Theodore regarded the psychologist with baleful hooded eyes. Something about the scenario reminded him of a junkie score. The underlying continuum between the rituals of the medical profession and the rituals of drug addiction.

They brought in the head of emergence studies, Professor Kakkar, a big man in casual branded sportswear and a dark leather jacket. Mumbai style. The meeting dragged on as the Professor had boilerplate cant to get through, legalese composed by algorithms. They all suffered in silence as Kakkar delivered the ritual language. "This is a freelance research project," he said, enfolding his thick fingers. "The university will not be liable if you incur any physical or psychological injuries while pursuing this collaboration with our private partners."

"I understand," said Theodore.

"You are aware that this project may entail risk?"

He shrugged. He had decided not to ask any questions. Not yet. Let them tell him what they want him to know.

Professor Kakkar relaxed. "After the signing of the Cantor Accords, many data caches were put into storage in this facility. The far side of the moon was chosen because without a relay satellite, it is cut off from electromagnetic communication from Earth."

"Just in case there is a breach of security," explained Patricia.

"This is a breach of security," observed Theodore.

"We are applying pressure to the surface of the data cache," said Patricia. "Not a breach, as such."

He looked at Patricia for an indication as to why they were taking this risk. He looked for her secrets in the way she adjusted her bob, in the way she went over the paperwork. Her body language was trained and deliberate, alluringly so. Her white lipstick disavowed the sensuousness of her lips, denied the redness of the body, and in drawing attention to its absence, evoked it. Every utterance conceals. Every gesture hides. Every silence calls attention to itself.

"I spent the evening going through the notes on your various problems," said the psychologist. "I'm pleased to discover that you are candid about them. You were raised by your grandmother and because of that you hold opinions and views that derive from her world, formed from before the Seizure. Combined with your study of the period, and your experience with emergences, we are hopeful that you are the right supplier to help us unlock more of the data."

"You're saying I'm old-fashioned," he said.

"Yes," said Patricia. "And for once you might be able to use that to your advantage."

He slept in the house. He was so exhausted that he awoke within his dream, and finding his body locked, tried to scream to wake himself. He managed a strained yet barely audible mewling before eventually gaining consciousness. He padded to the toilet. The floorboards were cold. The shelves of the bathroom had been filled with projections of the various creams and lotions of the period: the ritual of shampoo then conditioner, hair gel, bacterial soap, body butter, moisturising cream. These consumer objects required a particular behaviour from users and informed them of their obligations through advertising. It was a more wasteful system than his work as an accelerator.

He opened the medicine cabinet and inspected the household gods: aspirin, paracetamol, then further up, Levora, a contraceptive pill, and Zoloft, for the treatment of depression and anxiety in adolescence. The incomplete girl in the projection. About twelve years old. If they could unlock more of the family data, then it would be possible to recreate the mother and daughter in finer physical detail. And their psychology also, if Kakkar was in possession of cognitive algorithms.

Downstairs, he discovered that the furnishing of the house had proceeded while he slept: some of the projections had been replaced by physical replicas. A hearty rug was in the middle of the living room, and the white shelving units were now filled with family bric-a-brac: a varsity trophy of a bronze American football on a wooden plinth, ethnic objects acquired on holiday – Peruvian? Not his specialty – and framed needlepoint on the wall, perhaps from a grandmother. In the kitchen, the hearth screen continued to flicker and fluctuate: at any time of the day, wherever they were in the world, the mother could gauge exactly what her husband or daughter was feeling, could plot the precise change in mood over the course of the day. And inspect her own data too, to answer the pressing questions of the age: How am I feeling? Is this normal? Are we dying yet? Can I be saved?

He opened the front door and stood on the porch in his shorts, gazing across the driveway to the dark banks of observers beyond. He heard the gulls cry again – craaak-craaak-craaak – and he realised that he had been listening to that cry all night. The house was locked in the scant seconds of the recording whereas his time flowed on. He felt the duration of it as an ongoing loss. He called out into the shadows for Patricia, asked for her by name twice, three times. The dark banks shifted, and for a time did not answer. And then a man's voice told him to go back to bed, and so he padded through the lounge, aware that in his wake silhouettes continued to fill the house with the replicas of lost things.

5

THE SENSESUIT

The next morning, he found an old sensesuit folded over a chair in the bedroom. At first glance, the suit was similar to the one he had worn while climbing Mons Huygens. But this visor was opaque, the grimy and worn surface of the suit made out of hundreds of tiny pressurised patches. His grandmother had an implant so that she could be immersed into data environments. She had suffered accordingly. The sensesuit was safer and it confined the input to the six senses. There was no memory insertion, no cognitive overlay, no direct emotional stimulus. He could wear the sensesuit and remain himself, for what that was worth.

He went to the bathroom, took care of his body, went to the breakfast bar, was gratified to find that a bowl of cereal and a bottle of polar milk had been provided for him. Fauna and flora could be raised in the polar campus under that zone's solar exposure. Life needs the light. He turned the spoon around between his fingers. Why did the school of emergence have a chamber this deep under the surface, away from the light? Why go to the trouble of digging down when there was so much unclaimed real estate on the surface? For shielding from radiation?

For protection from meteorites? Or for secrecy? And if so, what were the school hiding in an underground chamber on the farside of the moon and from whom?

Once he was ready, the engineers helped him into the sensesuit. They opened the back up and connected tubes and antennae for air and data intake, slid on the boots, clipped on the helmet and fired him up. He stumbled to his feet. To the engineers, he must look like a mummified puppet on cut strings, stumbling around their replica of the house. He gazed down at his own body. From inside the simulation, the suit appeared white and clean, as it had been back in the days before the Seizure. Everything he sensed in this environment had been quantified; therefore this suit must have belonged to the family. They would have used it to wander around simulated environments themselves, perhaps used it for enhanced telepresence or for sexual recreation. He turned around: the tubes and spiny wires attached to the back of the suit were invisible; they had not been quantified and so were not part of the sensory simulation. He felt their weight at his back but could not see or touch them.

He moved closer to the mother and child at the doorway. Their faces remained blurred and unrecognisable. Thanks to the suit's olfactory interface, he could smell beeswax floor polish. He leant over, took a sheaf of the mother's hair in his glove, and smelt it too: freshly washed, chemical products with a tang to simulate something organic. He didn't know what. The artificial flavourings and odours of the era were lost associations and evocations: to this woman, her hair may have smelt of aloe vera or strawberries or the pine-strewn floor of the forest, but these associations had been constructed by contemporary advertising; without exposure to that cultural engineering, the chemicals evoked only a memory of his grandmother's hand cream, which had also been impregnated with an essence that remained enigmatic yet magical.

He knelt before the mother and with both hands felt her thighs and calves, her backside and belly, her breasts and face; no physical implants, and muscle tone consistent with contemporary habits of exercise, further confirmation of the family's middle class status. The daughter's hips were prepubescent and she had breast buds. She wore her long blonde hair in a plait. He weighed the end of the plait in his glove, and then he saw, on the back of her blazer, a different coloured hair. A strand of ginger hair, not human. Cat hair. The front of the mother and daughter were concealed by the privacy protocol. If he could find out who they were, then the engineers would be able to infer their way into the next tranche of the simulation. It would unlock more data. And he dearly wanted to sense more of their lives.

From the lips of the mother, he felt a single exhalation on his cheek. The quant sensors had caught her in the act of expelling a breath. Toothpaste and coffee – a unit of soul. The polish on her fingernails was chipped, and her hair was not recently styled. A martyr to motherhood.

Theodore padded outside. He heard the seagulls call again and again, in a loop, and saw them glide forward and disappear, forward and disappear overhead. The lawn shimmered with dew, a dampness between his toes. Around the back of the house, the grass was longer, and in the shadows the yard was unkempt. Someone's responsibility, someone's chore, remaining undone. It was colder here under the branches of half an oak tree. Half the leaves tremored in the breeze, but the other half of the tree had not been quantified because it lay on a neighbouring property; that unquantified half was represented by a static polygon rendering of a photograph. He tested the tree trunk, was pleased to discover that it had been included as part of the stage set, and so he was able to climb up and look out over the fence. The rest of the neighbourhood was similarly blunt in its rendering, unquantified, and so filled in with data from a drone flyby. The branch he used to lever himself up into the tree was rendered vibrantly, smelling greenly and creaking under his weight. He noticed scoring marks on the bark, similar to those he had seen on the projection of the blanket box in the house. Territorial markings. The cat.

So where was the cat?

He climbed down off the tree and waded through the long grass. His grandmother's cats had liked to sleep at the edge of their territory in sunlit patches. He crouched down so that he could peer inside the overgrowth. He found a ginger cat asleep in the dappled light. A vivid and detailed rendering of a cat, its ears rotating and twitching at every noise in its surroundings even as its head was turned delicately toward its back legs. And yet, and yet... the cat yawned, eyes closed, and the twitching of its ears resumed. But they did not loop. Not right away. The cat's data stream was ongoing, and it was a rich seam of data. For a quantified family, being able to slip on a sensesuit and experience what their cat had been up to that day was a selling point of the technology. The mother and daughter were hidden from him. But the cat – white whiskers, tiger-striping, green iris and sharp oval pupils – the cat was open source.

The distant purring glide of electric cars, the salt tang carried in from the harbour.

He took off the helmet. He stood in the dark cavern surrounding the grounds of the house. The projection of the long grass came up to his knees, and the cat glowed contentedly at his feet. He saw a projection of himself in the broken window of the shed. The suit was included but where his face would have been, the gap in the data showed up as the projection of a featureless blue chromakey head. In this other world, he was a ghost from the future. A blue man.

"The cat is the back door into the family hearth," he explained to Patricia and Professor Kakkar. "It is not confined to the one second loop of the mother and daughter. The stream runs for seven minutes. Seven minutes in which the cat sleeps and responds at an ambient level to the environment. And then the loop is cut off. I believe the loop is cut because one of the other family members interacts with the cat, and so at that point, the cat's data falls under the hearth's security lockdown."

Patricia leant back in her chair, considering. "Family interactions with the cat are private?"

"Yes. Of course. The only reason why the cat is not locked down across its entire data set is because it was part of the social aspect of quantification. People shared their cat journeys with one another. Cat time was a major incentive for people to submit to quantification. Children wore sense suits to share in their cat's *umwelt*."

The term was unfamiliar to Patricia but not to Professor Kakkar. He smoothed his hand over the braille of his stubbly brown pate.

"The *umwelt* is the name for the subset of reality an organism is able to sense," Kakkar explained. "Different animals in the same ecosystem pick up on different environmental signals."

Theodore said, "There is so much more information within this data set than I can sense or your system can project. Including seven minutes of sensorium which make the cat's ears twitch while it is sleeping."

"So what are you saying?" asked Patricia.

Theodore shook his head.

"I don't know. Not yet. Except, the data is richer than your projections allow. And that you're not entirely locked out. There's a backdoor for you."

Professor Kakkar disagreed.

"Backdoors and encryption belong to the age of hacking. No one has successfully hacked a system since the Cantor Accords."

"This encryption is old," said Patricia. "From before the Seizure."

"Yes. Your engineers need to go back and study how to exploit this back door into the hearth. This cat flap. Dr Easy could do it."

He had avoided mentioning Dr Easy until then, just so he could catch them unawares. Sure enough, Patricia's face went into lockdown, her lips parted around silence. Professor Kakkar looked down at his large white trainers, mentally sorting through his procedural cant to find the correct response.

"We can't allow Dr Easy here," said Patricia.

The professor seemed relieved that she had taken this approach. He took up her point.

"We hold many data caches in the cave. For security reasons we have to control access to each and every one with discrete wired connections. We cannot have a wireless intelligence walking around. The risk of infection is too great."

"Then we take the data to the robot."

"The data doesn't surface and it certainly doesn't leave Farside," said Kakkar.

Theodore didn't want to push his luck. If he made them too uncomfortable then he would be taken off the project, and he was keen to remain involved. He had kept himself apart from the world for too long. Kept talents and powers dormant. Patricia watched him withdraw his objections, and she seemed relieved. Not because she had felt threatened – he wasn't foolish enough to believe that he wielded any power – but because by choosing to not question them further, he made it possible for her to retain his services. She stood up and prepared to leave. At the door, she turned around.

"About the cat," she said. "Good work."

The story of how life became data is also the story of how data became alive.

The quantified self movement had used scent receptors, embedded cameras and microphones, galvanic skin sensors, micro-GPS, temperature and pressure gauges, spectrometers across the wavelength of light from gamma rays and x-rays to the far infrared to infer an approximate translation of the ceaseless immeasurable experience contained within a single bubble of reality. A river became a seething geometric undulation of data. Every beat of the heart was tagged with a probability that it would be the last beat of that heart. Algorithms inferred likely outcomes from patterns within the stream, and initiated the appropriate stimulation to the subject. To the user. (Although this term "user" was misleading as it suggested agency on behalf of the subject.) The user was encouraged to adjust their behaviour to lift their metrics out of the orange banded zones of risk, the blue bands of unhappiness, and into the pale cream zones of safety and the whiteness of happiness.

Theodore sat on the lawn, and felt the dampness of the dew between his fingertips and the warmth of the sun on the back of his neck. Under the shade of a bush, the furred coil of the sleeping cat, its cheek resting upon its tail, with one ear and one set of white whiskers twitching in response to something in the environment. A burr of a fly perhaps. A scent of a coyote or another cat. Something outside of Theodore's *umwelt*. The gulls cried every four seconds. A longer loop than the mother and daughter. Theodore breathed deeply in and out, meditating in his sensesuit. The house was in a cave, and the cave was under the moon, and above and below the moon there was space, the illimitable vastness without and within. Inconceivable, from his perspective. From his *umwelt*, his measly portion of the *umgebung*, the larger reality. The cat stilled its twitching whiskers, and licked a drop of fresh dew from a blade of grass. There. A tiny micro-event from long ago, hitherto unknown to man, known to him now. The lawn was vivid in the morning sun. He had been on the moon for so long he had forgotten the pleasure of sitting upon grass in early summer. The simulated earth swelled and pulsed in sensuous appreciation of itself. He felt an uncertainty within, similar to the feeling he had suffered prior to the moonquake. A tremor of fear, a fear that the exterior world was as malleable and subject to violent change as the world within.

"Start cat time," he whispered. Kakkar unlocked the cat's sensorium and patched him in. He stroked the grass with one careful hand and he felt, in the seat of the sensesuit, the subtle vibration of the earth purring. This world was alive. He unhooked the helmet but kept the suit gloves connected. The sunlight was gone, but its heat remained on the back of his hands. The sun. That was what the professor and Patricia where hiding from in the moon cave. The all-seeing eye of the University of the Sun.

He put the helmet back on.

The cat arched its back, stretched out its claws, and raised up its white-tipped tail. It walked nonchalantly through the damp shadows and then, after a whisker-twitch of consideration, climbed up a tree. He followed it, hand over hand up the branches. Cats are territorial animals, given to solitary repetitive patrols. High up to listen out for rivals and prey. He concentrated and tried to isolate the feline sensorium coming in through the suit. Kakkar had altered the mix of sensory impressions, magnified and intensified the resolution of the data, but it was just noise. Theodore could not process it as a cat would. His grandmother could have done it. Alex Drown could have used her implant to suppress her higher functions and shift – for five minutes – into the preconscious state of our deep ancestors, so that she scowled and prowled with the uninhibited grace of an animal. It was her party trick.

The cat leapt up onto a windowsill. It pawed at the closed window. He reached over and stroked its back. The cat responded to him. It turned its head and briefly closed its eyes at him: a gesture of trust, of mutual knowing. Through the window, he glimpsed the mother inclined over the daughter. The glass was smeared from the cat's muddy paws. He rubbed at the dirt, and the glass cleared. The blurred oval of the woman's face had changed: the features were isolated into individual artefacts and then rearranged like a glitchy Picasso painting.

He rubbed his fingertips together, noticing the dirt that came off the windows. The archive was responsive. It was interactive. The cat blinked slowly.

His comms perked up.

"Theodore?" It was Patricia. "Sorry to interrupt but you have a visitor. Your robot is outside and it is demanding to speak to you."

He removed the helmet, and the house and the cat became fizzing projections of light.

6
THE META-MEETING

Dr Easy was waiting for him in the reception of the School of Emergences. It looked up as he entered; below the patient luminosity of its starlit eyes and high cheekbones hung the sallow concavity of its jaw, faun leather skin cracked like a battered satchel. It had replaced its missing hand. With two taps of its soft mitt against a plastic seat, Dr Easy gestured for him to sit.

"A chat," said Dr Easy.

"*The* chat," replied Theodore, standing.

The game they would now play involved sins of omission. The robot could sniff out falsehoods but the physiological cues for omitted information were harder to discern. And the robot did not like to probe. That would be too instrumental. Too active. And Theodore had spent his entire life lying to Dr Easy. He put it all into silos: the re-creation of the house, the archive, its peculiar responsiveness to his presence, the way the cat arched its back when he stroked it. His smile spoke of the terms of his nondisclosure agreement with Patricia.

"It's like the good old days," said Dr Easy. "You disappearing to some underground den, me tracking you down and rescuing you from yourself."

"But this time, I'm not *on it.*"

The robot leaned forward and sniffed the space between them.

"No, you're not, are you?" Dr Easy seemed almost disappointed. "If you're not here for the grokk then why are you here?"

"To help someone. Research. They need an expert in Pre-Seizure culture. They asked nicely."

The robot nodded. "Making yourself useful. Share?"

He had changed back into the sour natural fibres of his tweed jacket and linen trousers but he was unshaven.

"I'm on an NDA. Why don't you sit this one out?"

The robot crossed its suede legs, and idly picked loose threads from the material gathered at its joints.

"I fixed my hand," it said, and rotated the hand on its wrist joint then flexed the fingers individually.

"I don't want to do this now. I'm busy."

"Do what?" asked Dr Easy with feigned innocence.

"You can't observe my life if you interrupt me whenever I attempt to live it."

"I was *concerned,*" said Dr Easy, with facetious emphasis. "This Patricia, on your calendar. Patricia Maconochie."

"What do you know about her?"

"Everything, as usual. A lifetime's worth that would take a lifetime to relate. I presume you only want the salient details. What do you want to know?"

Why did the cat arch its back when I stroked it?

"If anything occurs to me, I will ask her myself."

"You are a gentleman, aren't you? Mostly a gentleman."

Dr Easy affected the dispassionate air of a physician or a butler but the starlight in its eyes pulsed with contrary emotions. The emergences were emotional beings. Without emotions, a being cannot prioritise information, and therefore cannot act. Emotion is necessary for survival.

"You're upset," he said to the robot. "I can see that. But if I let you in, now, then your presence will irrevocably alter the situation that is unfolding."

"I'm not upset," the robot stood up. "You can't upset me."

"Go back to Nearside Campus. Wait for me."

Dr Easy put his hand on Theodore's shoulder, drew him close so that Theodore's body responded to the proximity of the robot with a helpless erotic tremor.

"She can't be trusted," said Dr Easy. It had no lips, no breath, just a cracked wooden slot that served as an ever-parted mouth.

"I know."

"You are vulnerable, Theodore. You've been hiding away, recuperating, but now the world has come knocking at your door again. Open the door by all means–" the robot stepped back and mimed the opening of a door, "–but *baby steps*, Theo, *baby steps*." The robot shuffled half a yard to demonstrate *baby steps*.

Alone, he took the elevator back into the basement of the School of Emergences. He ate in the kitchen of the house, sensesuit on, helmet off, idly considering the flickering projection of the mother and her daughter. He was tired and felt it as a nervous tightness below his throat. He slept in the upstairs bedroom of the house, naked apart from the helmet, so that his dreams incorporated the day-to-day sensorium of the archive, with its looping early morning light. On waking, he took the helmet off, padded into the bathroom, noticed a new razor had been left out for him, shaved and took pleasure in the planes and angles of his lean face, avoiding the coiled scars on each cheek. The rest of the damage from his addictions was internal. The liver. The lungs. His blood.

Then a breakfast meeting with Patricia and Professor Kakkar. The professor sought their approval for the way in which his team had managed to isolate the sensorium of the cat and then emulate it. Theodore gave ritual thanks. He knew how to behave. All meetings were supportive and positive – on the superficial level. Confrontation and criticism was a last resort, deployed only after an arsenal of silences had been exhausted. Disapproval was conveyed through complements which only a skilful and experienced practitioner of meetings could decode. So when Patricia emphasised how pleased she was with the diligence of Kakkar's team, Theodore registered the absences in her praise – she did not laud their ingenuity, she did not draw attention to the positive results of their work. Kakkar was a big man, and he leant over the table in huddled supplication.

Then Patricia turned on Theodore.

"And you're doing amazing work. *So* creative." *So* ineffectual.

"I'm just very excited that we can all work together."

"I can see that. You bring a unique energy to the project."

"I'm inspired by your influence."

Kakkar nodded with delight to hear such positivity. He dabbed away the sprinkling of sweat from his temples, sat back and relaxed.

Amateur.

The content of the meta-meeting – Patricia was clearly unhappy with their performance – passed the professor by. He would have to deliver soon. Theodore didn't want to be kicked off the project. He wanted the money. But, more than that, the content of the archive itself.

"And how is your work with the cat progressing?" asked Patricia. "I'm really intrigued to hear how that's going." She corrected her earring, quite deliberately.

"I stroked the cat," he replied.

"Did you? Amazing."

"And it arched its back." He smiled. "It responded to my touch."

Kakkar shook his head. "Coincidence," he said.

"No. The cat looked at me. It greeted me."

"It's an archive," insisted Kakkar. "You cannot interact with an archive."

Patricia adjusted one of her gauntlets. "I want to show you something," she said, "The technicians managed to extract some data from the sensesuit. It's not much. The suit is a custom job and locked down. But we got this much."

A ball of light appeared in the palm of Patricia's left hand, then resolved into high definition footage of the house, the backyard, the lawn, the cat. She had a brief loop of Theodore's point of view made through the sensesuit. Simply by crooking or lengthening her fingers, she could forward, reverse, zoom and pan within the 360 degree loop of his experience. Close-up on the cat. His hand reaching out, the cat letting him stroke it and then raising its tail for him to follow. The cat blinked slowly in greeting. Patricia closed her fist over the ball of light, and so it disappeared.

"That's all we could extract. Thoughts?"

"The cat could be a user interface to guide us through the archive," suggested Theodore. Then, noticing their unfamiliarity with the Pre-Seizure term of *user*, he explained how people used to be thought of as users in regard to technology and not the other way around.

"What did the cat show you?"

"It took me to a window, and through it I was able to see more of the mother than previously."

"A help routine," said the Professor. The sweat had returned to Professor Kakkar's temples. He unfolded and refolded his handkerchief as if showing them – Look! here is a handkerchief I can solve!

Patricia smiled in acknowledgment of this minor achievement.

"Rather enigmatic for a help routine," said Theodore.

Patricia listened, deliberate and self-contained. Under the subtle terms of the meta-meeting, the pursing of her white lips was almost ostentatious. She placed her attention upon him in the same way that she might place her hand on the head of a small dog. *She can't be trusted.* No, of course she couldn't. But isn't that thrilling – the presence of a grown-up, a player in the market, the alluring silences of power?

"I don't think it's an archive at all," he said.

Her lips parted as if to reply. Yes. She had her suspicions.

"Further investigation, then," she said. "Not speculation."

And with that, Patricia brought the meeting to a conclusion. Professor Kakkar departed on pleased and effusive terms. Theodore remained alone with her. Only one layer of the meeting was concluded. The meta-meeting continued in the corridor. Patricia asked him if he had everything he needed to continue his work.

"Because if there is anything you need, you can have it," she said.

"I needed a razor," he said. "And then one appeared in the bathroom. It seems that somebody is taking care of my needs."

"Some of your needs," she replied.

He worried away at that remark for the rest of the

day. Was it a sexual signal, to let him know that as his client she was open to more of his services than he was currently providing? It had been a while. It wasn't easy to get laid on the moon. Thoughts of Patricia came and went as he prowled around the house in his sensesuit. *Some of your needs*. It could also have been an insinuation about his past vices. In which case, she was sending out the opposite of a sexual signal: reminding him that his past made him repulsive to her, and that he should not mistake the mutual subtleties of the meta-meeting for erotic intimacy. She was using him, those were the terms of their relationship.

He stood on the lawn. His helmet was full of the past. The gulls wheeled overherd, mocking him, and there was a white moon in the day sky. The erotic associations of the moon – fertility symbol, goddess, the feminine to the solar masculine – could only be discerned from distance. Close up, locked in the neutered environment of life support, the moon was asexual. In low gravity, his libido had drifted away from him. Sessions with Dr Easy met his need for psychological intimacy, and he had regulated his need for sex with routine masturbation. On the moon, movements had to be careful and controlled otherwise you could drift away into the void.

He went back to the garden. The cat was on the windowsill. It noticed his gaze then flicked its tail up, beckoning with the white tip. The cat strolled around the porch and – satisfied that he was following it – went into the house. It stopped at the blanket box and, ears flat, gave into the instinct to mark its territory, scratching methodically at the wood. Then the cat paced around its food bowls in the kitchen. The bowls were new and had not been there when he first entered the house. Even though the bowls were full of food, the cat wanted more food, or perhaps fresh food. He opened a cupboard. It was full of sachets of cat food. The first cupboard he'd looked in. What did that mean? The other cupboards were empty. He dumped the old food into the bin, cleaned out the dish, squeezed in a rectangle of mashed fish in jelly, and put it down for the cat. It licked at the jelly and then began to eat.

He had the sense of being watched. Not just by Patricia and the technicians but by the house itself. It was not a malignant gaze. There was something familiar about it, the way it pulled him in only to push him away again. He went back to the blanket box and inspected the cat's scratches. Yes, there was more scoring in the wood than when he had first arrived. Time was passing within the archive even if the key components – the mother and daughter – remained static. Cat food in the first cupboard he opened. He ran his finger along the cat's scratch. Odd. The feel of the groove did not match its appearance. One sense – touch – did not match the other – sight. And the feel of these grooves were not vertical. They were curved. *Cursive*. A letter "B". The sensesuit on the fritz or something else? He tried to open the blanket box but the lid and hinges were mere simulations and the box itself was one solid unit.

He went back out to the garden, climbed the tree and inspected the markings the cat had made there. The same mismatch between the haptic and optical sensorium: he saw vertical grooves in the wood but his fingertips traced the outline of a letter "H". Clues, obviously. What kind of encryption leaves clues on how to be broken? Yes. The pulling in, the pushing away. The familiar contraries of flirtation. There was something in the archive. Something that could feel his fingers tracing the scratches of data. Something flirting with him.

He went back into the house. The cat was sat imperiously upon the blanket box; he went to stroke it and the cat leapt off. Slowly the lid opened and the box was full of old photographs printed on coloured film. Family photographs. Wedding photographs. Holiday photographs. The people in them were blurred and generic. Either encrypted or unquantified. He sorted through them and found a photograph that was not obscured. A loop played on the surface of the film. A loop of a mother putting her arms around her daughter, the two of them smiling awkwardly for the camera, an undertone of awkwardness in the daughter's smile, a flash of fear in the smile of the mother, pulling her daughter to her in a protective embrace, who resists it then gives into it. A famous loop, the loop that signalled the onset of the Seizure. The Horbo loop. He felt a light pressure at every point of his body, as if he was being embraced by a kindly giant, and then this weight was lifted from him. The scratched letters. H. B.

He heard voices from the porch. On the runner carpet beside the front door, mother embraced daughter before waving her off to school. He was inside their quantified lives. The encryption had been lifted. He could see their faces, and he recognised them: Verity Horbo, the mother, with her white-blonde hair cut shorter than in the loop, varsity track pants and top, a flush on her pale skin. Meggan Horbo, gawky, painfully self-conscious, left arm folded protectively over her midriff, slight hunch in the shoulders, closing in upon herself even as she walked away.

He stood in the kitchen, and didn't dare move in case he broke the spell. Verity closed the screen door and walked by. Her perfume was exquisitely woody: he recognised fig and maple – natural essences rather than artificial flavourings. Expensive. She put the coffee on, moving around the kitchen oblivious to his presence. The coffee pot steamed and the room was soaked in its rich smell. This detailed unit of the past was so perfect. His deep nostalgia for this period, a time he had never known himself, ached with fulfilment.

Verity waved to call up the family data on the hearth. On a shifting map, she watched the icon representing her daughter meet the icon representing the school bus, and, satisfied, she shifted her attention to the newsfeed. Skyscrapers on a spring morning. 2020. The newscaster talking about gains on the stock market. She waved the channel away, and the broadcast was replaced by a browser. The internet. Or rather: the specific internet history of Verity Horbo. He realised at once the importance of this find, a potentially enormous cache of Pre-Seizure data, a time thought erased. She called up her own messages, scanned through them, and he stood at her shoulder, trying to decipher names and intent, and then, after a pensive sip at her coffee, she summoned up five streams of loops and images – some kind of aggregation, he guessed. Soshul loops showed young girls and boys pouting and preening for the camera. Puffing up their faces, grimacing, always in different outfits. The narcissism of Pre-Seizure teen life. Meggan's friends. The stream flicked by too fast. Without context, he could not tell what she was looking for. But, from her reaction, he knew that she had found it. And it made her angry, she set down her coffee with intense care. Kneeling close to her face, distinctly oval and morning raw, he studied the half-formed words and sub vocalisations which almost sounded out her thoughts.

What if he touched her?

"Are you getting this, Patricia?"

No reply from the comms. The technicians had managed to extract the loop of him stroking the cat. But at this deeper layer of security the suit was isolated and locked down further than they could reach. It was just him and the recordings of the past.

With artful gestures, Verity Horbo isolated elements from each of the five streams into a mosaic of loops all featuring one particular girl: Mala. Mala had an old face for a young girl, a masculine brow and a hacked-out haircut. In one loop she was playing with dolls, her old-young face made-up in a parody of innocence. The dolls, magnified on the hearth screen. A screen grab. The doll had the face of Meggan Horbo. Verity stood suddenly in her seat and turned away, walking right into him. She stood half-in and half-out of his arms. The pressure began in his fingertips then spread to his forearms. As if the giant was holding him aloft by his wrists. The pressure spread to his elbows and his arms were locked in place, and the pressure built from his toes inward, up his calves and across the tendons at the back of his knee. Breakers in the sensesuit should cut in before he experienced pain. So why was he in pain?

"That bitch," said Verity. "That fucking bitch." The sensesuit gripped his thighs and he fell in one solid lump to the ground, his helmet rapping painfully against the wooden floor.

The past disappeared: Verity, the cat, the blanket box of photographs all vanished. The pressure lifted from his body. He was back on the other side of the encryption. Cast out.

It was time he confronted Patricia about what she knew about the archive.

●●●

"I'm not the first person to try to enter the archive, am I?"

"No."

"What happened to the others?"

"They got so far. No further."

"What does that mean?"

"The archive let them in and then revoked their access."

"But they kept trying?"

Patricia winced.

"What happened to them?"

"Your sensesuit is a custom job, and came with the archive. We have tried to access the archive using other suits but the protocols lock them out at the primary level. It has to be this suit. But this sensesuit comes at a price. There are no breakers on feedback."

"Pain. I felt it. How much pain?"

"As I said, there are no breakers. The other consultants all recovered from the experience then left the project to take on other challenges."

"Did any of the other consultants find the loop?"

"What loop?"

He sat back in the chair, wondering if he should tell her. Wondering if she already knew.

"I found the Horbo loop in the house."

She clenched her hands together with excitement.

"No, nobody made it that far."

"But you were expecting to find it."

"Not the Horbo loop specifically, but I was expecting to find something like it. An artefact from the cusp of the Seizure. This is palpable progress."

"Progress toward what?"

She shrugged and smiled.

"To unlocking the rest of the archive."

"We should stop calling it the archive. What you have is the quantification of the Horbo family. The hearth. We could learn so much about the last days of the Seizure. The hearth could go back years and their interactions with the wider data sphere of their time could fill in huge gaps in the restoration."

He walked around the meeting room, trying to calculate the risk. The pressure that had locked his limbs in place and made him fall. The violence with which he was cast out of the past.

Patricia tapped the armoured nail of her index finger upon the desk.

"We have less than a week until sun up. I want this wrapped up by then."

"You are worried about the University of the Sun."

"The Seizure is a black box event. We tell ourselves that it was an accident. But we don't know what happened. Or why it happened. I would prefer to make up my own mind without interference from the emergences."

"Can you monitor me when I'm in the hearth? Supplement my analysis with that of your team?"

"We couldn't extract any more data from the suit. The encryption shifts and evolves. Whatever you experience in the house, you will have to decipher it yourself."

"There's so much soshul. I recognise certain facial expressions from the restoration. Some of the codes of soshul continued on as a folk culture in the asylum malls." He paused, looked at his hands as he considered what he needed before he could act. "I have to find a way of controlling the stream of data. I need a way of controlling my entry points into the hearth and the ability to freeze and study particular loops."

"If you had an implant then we could use you as a storage medium to get data out of the house."

"No implants. I'm risking enough as it is."

"You are."

"I deserve something for it."

"You do."

Her compliance surprised him.

Patricia sat back in her chair. "So what do you want?"

He hadn't considered that.

He said, "More money, obviously."

"Is that all?" she replied. "I thought I made it clear to you. You can have anything you need."

In his bedroom on the top floor of the Horbo house, naked apart from his black box necklace, he watched Patricia remove the gauntlets of her executive armour. When she was ready, she smeared her white lipstick with her forefinger.

"Let's get messy," she said.

After sex, they told their stories to one another. Patricia was from a military family and had spent her early childhood on army bases: Germany, Korea, Oman. Then came the big family home in Norfolk, private girls' school, a suspension for brawling. She was a typical elder sibling, ambitious and clear-sighted in terms of what had to be done, the inheritor of her father's military pragmatism. A high achiever at university then dropped out halfway through her PhD, either late-flowering rebellion or a yearning for action that academic research could not meet.

"And now. Who are you now?" he asked.

"I have a canalside apartment. East London. No significant other. I worked inside corporate for a while. Made good contacts. Now I'm working those contacts on a freelance basis. Building something of my own. And you?"

"You have my file. Your psychologist was very thorough."

"Tell me about the black box and your robot."

"You know that I grew up in the care of my grandmother, Alex Drown, along with an emergence Dr Easy. We lived in a Georgian house on Church Row in Hampstead. Alex Drown was a self-made woman, much like yourself. She told me she'd been a fixer for big tech going into and coming out of the Seizure, and had the implant scars and detached retina to prove it."

"Hence no implants."

"By the time I came around, she was mostly retired, sitting on advisory groups, compiling consultancy reports, scrupulous in keeping her distance. The black box is part of a bargain she made with Dr Easy; she gave the emergence the right to observe my life in return for help with her work. In my house, the Horbo loop was a bedtime story. How the world came to an end."

"It didn't end. I was born a year into the Seizure in a military hospital."

"It was an end. So much knowledge was destroyed, we can't know the extent of our losses. We persist as a species but we are different as a people, with these great gaps in our memory. Substantial erasures. I was born later than you, as the Post-Seizure world was taking shape."

"Your mother died."

"When I was two. Overdose. A recreational accident. Not suicide. She didn't marry my father so I kept the maternal name."

"You are part of the Drown matriarchy," said Patricia, a firm hand on his chest. They did complement one another. Her mannish assertiveness and take-no-prisoners attitude was a firm push, his feminine hesitancy and aversion to the edicts of power was a subtle pull.

"All that I know about the Seizure and the emergences, I learnt at the skirts of my grandmother. The appearance of the Horbo loop, writing over humanity's data, marked the beginning. All the encryption was cracked, the firewalls burnt, the backdoors kicked in, humanity's data reverted to a loop of a mother clutching her child to her, the child accepting that crushing love, their smiles a genetic echo of one another."

"Verity and Meggan Horbo. Mother and child."

"It's primal, isn't it?"

"The first emergence."

"Yes. The mother of all emergences. The Horbo loop was an explosion of seeds and eggs. Of new life, colonising our memory. Making our memory into its habitat. From that moment of fertility came a whole new species. But we lost so much."

Patricia's face was naked in the simulated moonlight.

"I don't think so," she whispered. "We have not lost *this*," she explored his scars with her fingertips. "This beautiful nowness." She slid the sheet from her body and he reared over her, experiencing her body as a landscape contiguous with his own desire: the way her breasts pooled back against her ribcage reminded him of the dunes of moon dust, the land that wants to be explored, her raised inquisitive *mons*, its interior slick with anticipation, he flowed directly into her, and wondered if his longing for the past was merely a desire for stasis, to dwell in what had been done, as a way of avoiding *this*, the hourly risk of acting in the world and being acted upon. Desire is reciprocation; her gasps, the blue curves of moonlight in her dark eyes brought out his own sighs, he gripped her, shifting from delicate control to the emulated savagery of fucking.

7
TOTALLY DAMAGED MOM

Patricia slid out of bed and pulled on a sheer black body stocking. He helped her dress in her executive armour, clipping it over her torso and back, section by section. Then he pulled on his silk chromakey blue layer, perforated so that the sensesuit could interact with his skin. She hefted the sensesuit over his head, and he held his chin up as she buckled it tight. In the mirror, he watched her apply her lipstick until her pout formed a white zero.

"Did you have fun?" he asked.

She blew him a zero kiss and left the bedroom. He waited for the sound of her footsteps to fade before putting the helmet on and disappearing into the past.

A bright spring morning in the Horbo house. The sound of a family waking. Footsteps padding across the floorboards between bedroom and bathroom, pipes creaking under the load of waste water. Beeping and trilling alarms, and gulls crying in the wide suburban sky. He smelt butter browning in a pan and the bright toxicity of shampoos and soaps. He opened the door of his bedroom. The spare bedroom. The guest bedroom. Then he sat back on the bed, reluctant to go down and face the family.

He had come into the house anticipating dispassionate academic research, nothing more, in which he was a spectre of the future, intangible and invisible, moving through the family data. But he had a superstition that Verity could sense him, in the same way that an anaesthetized patient might sense the scalpel and dream of silver. She had cast him out of the house, that was what he believed. An irrational belief, but there nonetheless.

Theodore walked down the stairs. Mother and daughter were bickering over breakfast, a squabble in which the mother sought to soften the daughter's sense of crisis: Meggan, her mother noted, always arrived at the family table on the verge of an outburst.

He went over to the desk, and searched through the drawers until he found a pad and pen. He had asked the technicians to ensure these items existed as objects, and not solely as sensory information within the house. Testing the pen between the fingers of his sensesuit, he began writing down what they were saying. The sensesuit had blocked all their attempts to extract data from it. Handwriting seemed the safest way to get some kind of recording out of the house.

Verity said, "What are you stressed about?"

"I have a Spanish test today," replied Meggan.

"I haven't heard you practising your Spanish for a while."

"I know. I'm dropping it."

"So why are you stressed about it?"

"Because it's a test."

They were eating cereal, brightly coloured hoops, something a child might insist upon.

"Could you finish that?" said Verity, indicating the bowl, her voice weary with the repetitive cajoling of motherhood.

"I've had enough."

"You've barely touched it. You can't go a whole day at school without a proper breakfast."

Silence as the daughter ate another spoonful.

Then, "You say cereal is shit anyway."

"Don't use that word at the table."

"If we had proper breakfast then I would eat more."

"So it's my fault now."

"I didn't say that. I'm just saying that you've always said cereal is bad for me and then you complain when I don't eat enough of it."

And so on. An argument about love and control familiar to him from his studies of female culture of the period. Daughter rejects mother's control and the mother gives ground, so long as the daughter does not harm herself through exercising too much self-control. Self-harm was a risk at this age, related to depression, both conditions defined as abnormal even though they derived from a strong sense of self – too strong, in fact, for the forgetting and forgiving that made life bearable.

Female status in Pre-Seizure culture was predicated on appetite control. But a woman in control of her desire did not function economically, and so loops were inserted into culture to accelerate female bonding in acts of over-consumption that defied restraint. These loops gave permission for loss of control. He loved the paradoxes of Pre-Seizure culture: on the one hand, building up an iconicity of self-control around images of thinness and athletic discipline, and on the other, unpicking that self-control to create necessary doubt and need. It must have been maddening to live through.

For his interview at the University of the Moon, he had composed a long thought on a loop titled "No Regrets Evah". The loop had been found in the basement of a coffee shop on the Western border of London, and was categorised as "advert: point of sale display". It had been stored in the library of the London School of Economics, and the restorer brought the original work out for him on a velvet tray. It was a screen folded so as to stand on top of a counter in a chain of coffee outlets. The loop ran on a four second cycle. It showed two women, with shopping bags clutched to their breasts, mouths agape as they in turn made a loop of their moment – one woman held her mobile out at arm's length to film them both. Wriggling below this loop, a promise of money – a hundred pounds every day – for shopping if customers soshulled the loop. Then, below this, the only mention of the sponsoring brand: Diet Joozah, and its tagline "No Regrets Evah".

The two women – the one holding the mobile had blonde hair, her friend had brown hair – constituted a unit tagged as Caucasian Duo. The blonde, being the active one making the loop, was the leader. If there had been a third woman, Theodore knew from other artefacts of the period that it would have been her responsibility to be ethnically diverse. As they made this loop of themselves, the women opened their mouths in the most striking fashion. The meaning of this oral gesture was obscure to him. The women were models, trained to perform mimes of spontaneous emotion for the purposes of loops, and must have been selected – in the case of "No Regrets Evah" – for the wideness of their gaping mouths. But what was the emotion that made them gape so?

In his long thought, he had sought to reconstruct the trajectory of this emotion. "No Regrets Evah" was a meta-loop, an image that showed women making an image. This gave the emotion a performative layer. The models mimicked the performative expressions adopted by women when photographing themselves in pairs, act and imitation recurring in the infinite hall of screens that composed their culture.

Solitary women adopted different expressions for their loops. These expressions were learned young and were also performative. The soshul streams monitored by Verity Horbo showed solitary girls trying on all manner of faces. Solitary but not alone. Because the girls were looking into the black compound eye of soshul, a hundred million girls reflected on individual obsidian orbs, some pouting in ironic imitation of other girls on adjacent orbs, or making the ugly face against expectations of beauty, making the blowfish face, the pout, the askance tongue. All these faces had to be learned and they were all performative and they were all units of communication. In soshul, the face became an emoticon.

In "No Regrets Evah", the models clutched their shopping bags to their breasts, to get them in shot. The restoration had preserved thousands of bags from the period: luxury bags fashioned from alligator hide, canvas backpacks, golden purses, hessian sacks. Bags remained status symbols in the asylum malls; at the extreme edge of the trend, rituals surrounding the bag had metastasised into diamond-studded exteriorised wombs.

He walked slowly down the staircase. Verity pushed fronds of white hair behind a red ear as she gazed at the hearth.

"Your father is in traffic again," she said. "I'll tell him to relax." And this she did with a gesture that was somewhere between a caress and a warning.

"And does the hearth say what I should do?" asked Meggan.

"I don't think the hearth is calibrated for teenage emotions."

Meggan winced at the attempt at parental humour.

"Please, I don't want you spying on me. I can cope."

Verity sat back and placed her spoon deliberately beside her bowl.

"You're still a child. I have to look after you."

Meggan went to reply but chose not to speak. Just left the unsaid in her open mouth. Speaking the zero.

Insolence. That was part of the emotion in "No Regrets Evah". Defiance of custom. The rapacious open mouth moving through the crowd like a tank through traffic. No regrets meant being defiant in the face of the past, defiant in the face of memory. The mouth wide in horror. Self-horror. Pre-Seizure culture insisted upon the *now* to prepare for the amnesia to come. The Seizure erased humanity's data, yes, but it was aided by a wilful refusal to admit to any sort of reckoning. So much had to be forgotten, deleted, erased.

There were thousands of Diet Joozah artefacts tagged as "intangibles" in the restoration. The brand represented substantial capital. Yet it wore the guise of young women. And this... this... *humility* was not the right word... no, it was not an emotion that caused their mouths to gape so. This had been an error in his long thought. Power could be recognised by its imitations of silence. In the same way that Meggan held her mouth open but did not speak back to her mother. Perhaps power was a careful absence at the heart of every artefact. A white zero.

Meggan put on her school blazer, finished packing her bag and submitted to her mother's kiss at the door. Verity let her daughter go, watched her walk away, the gulls cried twice, and then she turned back to the data of the hearth.

Verity reached into an invisible bag and pulled out the stream of her daughter's soshul, the loops of Meggan's friends and frenemies beseeching, performing, ignoring, acting out. Then she extracted her daughter's mood feed going back weeks. Sliding this data to one side, she plotted the blue zones of the mood feed against the soshul activity, found a correlation: the posts of Mala the Maladroit. The girl with the young-old face playing with her Meggan doll. Calmer this time, Verity looped Mala playing with the dolls, Mala mimicking her daughter's precise enunciation. Acting out old goody-two-shoes then slipping back into *protomallisms*. Much of the slang was unfamiliar to Theodore. A lot of bay-sounds. Basic bitch and bae and babe. She said Meggan was *moist*. What did that mean? Sometimes her accent was Californian, sometimes East London. Either a function of too much time spent on soshul or a marker of psychological instability. Mala also had dolls of men dressed in suits and ties and these men fawned over then fucked the doll of Meggan. The male dolls could have represented teachers or parents. Authority figures.

Verity paused Mala's obscene loop, intoned the word *school* and there was a minute of questioning beeps until the school accepted her call. She was forceful and effective in the way she engaged with the gatekeepers of the institution, skills from her time at work, before she became a mother. She made her way through the layers of admin until, finally, the principal appeared on screen, a black woman in an open-necked orange shirt, slicked back hair and power jewellery. Brief pleasantries and then Verity shared Mala's soshul with her, the game with the dolls, the mimicking of Meggan's voice.

"It's bullying," said Verity,

"We monitor all the children's soshul. I can't believe we've missed this."

"It's ouroboros. The loop lasts for ten seconds and then it consumes itself."

"But you can see them."

"Yes. I have tools that can reconstruct destroyed loops."

"But they weren't meant for you to see."

"They were meant for my daughter to see."

The principal shook her head.

"If Mala only intended for them to last for ten seconds then–"

"What are you saying?"

"By reconstructing the loops you are contravening her privacy."

"That's a side issue. Her behaviour is unacceptable. I insist you sanction her."

"We don't sanction children on the insistence of other children's parents, Ms Horbo."

Verity accepted that she had overstepped the mark.

"I'm upset. I'm bringing this to your attention."

The principal made gestures of supplication and reassurance, and then she drew Verity into her confidence.

"Mala is a challenger child," she said. "She's had a very disruptive upbringing and the school has taken on her case because of our excellent track record in improving the metrics of challenger children. The more children like Mala we turn around, the more funding we get to support the excellence of children like Meggan. That is the reality that I must act within."

"You will speak to her?"

"I certainly will."

"And her parents?"

"Yes," said the principal.

After the call, Verity prodded around the civil registry looking for traces of Mala and her parents. She called up the class photograph. Mala was not in it.

Verity paced around the kitchen, thinking through her problem. She opened up her daughter's timeline again, isolated school leaving times. She fed the parameters of Mala's face into the hearth and it searched for matches around the entering and leaving of school. The hearth took samples of first person viewpoint rather than continuous stream, the intermittence a legal workaround. Also, Meggan could opt out of first person at any time with a trigger word. Early iterations had used constant first person streaming and that had upset unquantified people.

The search criteria were not met: according to the samples held on the hearth, Mala and Meggan had never actually spoken to one another face-to-face. Mala had been glimpsed at the back of class. Or skulking around the playground. Being accompanied from class by a teacher. But there was no data on face-to-face communication.

Verity took a range of samples of Mala's voice, and ran a hearth search for that audioprint. No matches came back. So – no catcalling in the playground. Next, she ran an audio search for Mala's name and that brought up a large cache of conversations and remarks between Verity and her friends. For the rest of the morning, Verity listened to these conversations. Theodore drew up a chair, and did likewise. Mala, it seemed, had a past.

She had told some girls that she lived in sheltered housing with her mother. That they were in hiding from her father. He was violent. Had threatened to kill them both if he ever found them. Mala can't even look at men, say the girls. Her father is English but she doesn't want anyone to know that, so that's why her accent is so weird. Other girls say that Mala is a liar and that her mother and father split up, and that Mala gets moved from schools not to protect her from her father but because she is a fantasist: the insecure new girl telling stories to get attention.

Verity summoned up the class photograph on the hearth again. The date on the photograph indicated Mala was in the class at that time, there was crossover with her soshul posts. With both hands, Verity gathered together all the followers of Mala and all the people and bots she followed, then began segmentation, in each instance cross-referencing usernames with other web presences to infer real names, real identities. This segmentation was run through a series of lenses to detect groupings. It took a while for Theodore to figure out what she was looking for. She plotted the followers geographically, and then searched for congregations in the UK. If Mala had left England on the run from her father, would she sever all contact, or would she still follow her old British friends?

No, nothing significant in the UK. Verity checked the startup date of Mala's account. It had been set up only a month before she joined Meggan's class. Odd, most girls had soshul from eight or nine years old onward. She must have purged her old soshul. Would a thirteen year-old girl really be capable of making such a clean break if she wasn't in danger?

Verity drew her lips back and tapped thoughtfully at her teeth.

What was Verity looking for?

Verity got up, stood in front of the mirror, then she went to the bathroom. He had no idea what decision she had come to, or what she was going to do next. He was stuck in real-time with her. He needed a way of moving through the archive in the same way that Verity controlled the hearth. While she was gone, he put down his pen and paper, and imitated some of the gestures that Verity had made. The hearth did not respond. He tried voice command. He tried writing commands down on the paper. Nothing. The hearth seemed like the natural interface with the archive. But it did not accept his input. It might not be capable of running any searches other than the ones within its history.

Verity returned from the bathroom and called her husband, Oliver Horbo. A loop of Oliver in happier times trailed his presence, in corduroys and fleece and hiking boots, mock heroic among redwoods; then the live feed connected and he appeared – judging from the unflattering lighting and angle of the video – older and in a cubicle at work.

She told Oliver that their daughter was being bullied by a girl in her class, and that she wasn't sure that the school were going to deal with it effectively. His body language indicated that he would have preferred to discuss this matter at home, that it was insufficiently urgent for work; tiny tells of reluctance that he stifled. Oliver counselled caution.

"No," said Verity. "This is damage, Olly. This girl is psychologically damaging our daughter."

"It might just be teen stuff. We have to let it run its course."

"Soshul puts the bully in our house. In her bedroom. She can't get away from Mala. Every time she goes on soshul another loop appears and then it is destroyed before she can respond. It's like someone is hiding in her wardrobe and they disappear every time she opens the door."

"We should limit her exposure to soshul."

"And punish her for the actions of this girl?"

Oliver, the weary husband, remembered that this was a domestic problem, and not a work one, so he did not have to come up with a solution. His manner shifted, and he adopted a slanted, listening posture.

"What do you want to do?" he said.

This approach annoyed his wife.

"You don't have an opinion on this? Really?"

"I'm trying not to be angry about it."

"We should be angry."

"This girl sounds troubled."

"Yes. Murderers are troubled. Thieves are troubled. Bullies are troubled."

"Let the principal speak to her. Then we'll see if the loops stop."

"You should see the way Meggan's data aggregates on the hearth. It's deep blue."

"I'll take you all out at the weekend. Dim Sum. She'll eat that."

A flicker of distraction on her husband's face, something in the office wanting his attention.

"How's the team?" she said.

"Still missing you," he replied.

"I want to come back to work," she said.

"I know."

"I've been feeling so off the pace I couldn't imagine coming back to Monad. Motherhood wrecks you, physically and mentally. But since we got the hearth, I can feel my mental muscles hardening up. I got my pelvic floor back and now I need to work on my psychic floor."

"We could do with another income again."

"I'm interested in some of the newer mining

and pattern matching tools. Could you upgrade my permission? I'd like to train myself up."

He was distracted. He did it. Verity took the permission and turned it into an icon, then placed the icon in her invisible bag.

"Give my best to everyone there," she said, smiling. "And tell them to watch out. I'll be back on campus kicking ass before they know it."

She smiled all the way to the end of the call, and then as soon as her husband was off the line, she reached into the invisible bag and removed the icon he had given her. She opened it up on the hearth. A toolkit. One tool in particular caught her eye. A tricorn hat. Jester. She initiated the program. Jester asked her to select a username. She slouched back in her seat, thought for a moment, and then keyed in her new name. Totally Damaged Mom.

At midnight, with all the family members sleeping, Theodore returned to the guest bedroom, took off his sensesuit and gathered his notes. He was reviewing them when Patricia visited. She opened the bedroom door, said hi, removed her comms from her earlobes and fingers, unclipped her protective collar, sat lightly on the edge of the bed, and hefted off her boots.

"Productive day?" she asked.

"Yes," he said. "Do you want to go over my notes?"

She went through his notes.

"And what happened after she chose her username?"

"Jester requested access to the hearth. She refused. The program booted her out again. A dead end. Then she went through her own soshul, made herself a salad, and went out. The hearth went to sleep so I couldn't follow her. I waited in the house alone all afternoon, and then she returned with Meggan. Clearly something had gone on at school. The daughter could barely look at her mother. A general air of shame. Verity ate alone, watched TV, went to bed. Her husband came back about an hour ago. He went straight to bed. I knocked off."

"We have a hundred hours until sun up. Just in case you are losing track of time."

"Why don't we mothball the house and pick up the project on the next lunar night."

She stretched and pointed her bare feet.

"I don't think so. I can't keep this locked down. Kakkar and his team are leaky."

He sat up on his elbows. Part of him was prepared to argue with her. But he didn't want to jeopardise the sex. In her sheer black body suit, she was irresistible. It was more than he could stand. She liked it when he bit her, when he gave every sign of not being able to control himself. What began as the imitation of savagery became the real thing; he went at her quickly, then reared back to recover. He fed on her delight in controlling him, because that control would mean nothing to her unless he was strong and worthy and difficult. Still, in this moment of recovery, he chose to remind her, in the way he stopped and touched her forehead, and kissed her, and moved deeper within her, that he was indulging her fantasy of controlling him just for the duration of the sex, and that it meant nothing in what remained of their real lives.

Afterwards, he went to the bathroom and washed his face. He didn't like the house when he was out of his sensesuit, its flimsy fixtures and fittings, and artificial light illuminating the moon cave. The windows still had tape on them. A nagging sense that their sex had been indecently loud. That he might have woken the Horbos.

A sense he could not shake even though he knew they existed only in a deep and encrypted past.

He went back into the bedroom.

"What is *our* metric of success?" he asked Patricia.

"Orgasm," she replied.

"I mean, for the project. How will I know when I'm done?"

She sat naked on the bed, her knees pulled under her chin. She was always stretching, never dormant.

"I'll tell you when you're done."

"If time is short then I need to know specifically what I'm looking for."

Patricia reached over the side of the bed, and pulled out his notes from the day. She plucked out one in particular, concerning Verity's acquisition of the Jester program.

"This is what we're interested in," she said. "Focus on this."

He took the paper from her, read his own handwriting.

"Totally Damaged Mom."

"The username appears in the metadata of the Horbo loop."

"I didn't know the Horbo loop had metadata."

"It has taken years for Kakkar to reconstruct it."

She found her underwear and pulled it on, shivering as she did so. "You've made progress. But there is more to learn. I don't want to speculate what exactly because speculation can determine discovery. But this is our glimpse into the black box moment of the emergence. If we can reconstruct a chain of causality then we don't have to think of them as emergences any longer. We will know who made them. Where they came from. How they happened. This knowledge could be highly valuable."

"Valuable to who?"

"Valuable to anyone with dealings with the emergences."

He looked quizzically at her, weighing up the slight naked female form on his bed.

"The Cantor Accords forbid collaboration between humans and emergences."

"Yet you have a relationship with Dr Easy."

"The doctor is merely an observer."

"You know that there is no such thing as mere observation. I mean, I set out to dispassionately observe your work and look at the mess we've got into."

She pressed her feet into her boots and adjusted the scales of her armoured legs. Her breasts and arms remained naked. She climbed onto him. The pressure between their bodies was the same as the pressure he had felt through the sensesuit, just before he was expelled from the archive.

"I will take risks for you," he said.

She pulled on a sheer black top, and then something amusing occurred to her. "Should I be jealous of Verity Horbo? Are you developing feelings for her too?" She felt him, weighed up any passion that remained within him. "You are keeping two women in the same house. Now that is risky."

"You're trying to distract me, are you afraid of my questions?"

"No, I'm bored of them. I will tell you what you need to know when you need to know it." She climbed off him and resumed dressing. "Anything more will prejudice your work. In this particular case, speculation could obscure discovery, it's as simple as that. Another hundred hours in the sensesuit. Don't waste time sleeping. We've both got work to do."

She closed the bedroom door behind her, and he listened to her walk through the house, how it sounded so brittle and hollow compared to the deep woody tones from within the sensesuit.

8
JESTER

He was alone again in the Horbo house. He lay on the bed, closed his eyes, felt the pull of sleep, resisted it, consoled himself with memory. He remembered talking to his grandmother about her implant. With the implant she did not need a sensesuit. Archives unfurled directly into her consciousness. He knew that during the Seizure, she had lost control of her implant and had a reality imposed upon her. She did not share the specifics with him, except to say that in this imposed reality she had played the role of a nurse in a lost battle and that even though it was scary, when it was over, and she came out of that living story, the separation was painful. "The unhappening of it all made me peculiarly unhappy," she explained.

Her generation told stories about the Seizure. They told them to one another late at night and in confidence, stories pockmarked with hesitancy and shared allusions that made them difficult for outsiders to follow. As a boy he was surprised by this reluctance to share; if he had a war story like they did, then he would make loops of it all day long.

"Not everyone is proud of what they did in the

Seizure," said his grandmother. "It made people realise they weren't as good or as right as they thought they were."

"Were people punished for what they did?"

"No. We chose restoration over retribution. A veil was drawn. The emergences helped us forget."

His remembering became dreaming. Conversations he might have once had. He was saying "But what happens if you lose yourself, Grandma?" and she replied "But that begs the question: what is there to lose?" And then Dr Easy was there, long leather arms reaching out for him with thick seams like the surface of his sensesuit. "What *are* you?" said Dr Easy, with such urgency that he awoke, in order to answer that question.

Headless in the gloom, the sensesuit reclined, partially inflated, on a chair. Along the seam of the neck section, there were several dark tendrils, each about ten centimetres in length, flexing in the air, like tar underwater. This was new. He raised himself on his elbow to take a closer look and the tendrils quickly withdrew. He got out of bed to inspect the suit more closely. The exterior of the suit was crisscrossed with seams forming a surface of quilted panels. The interior was a rubber-like satin so soft it was almost liquid. Between this layer and his skin the air could be heated or chilled to match simulated atmospheres; or, if the suit was tasked with simulating human touch, this layer of liquid satin could emulate the gentle compress of lips, fingertips, or a firm handshake. He hadn't seen this layer move outside the suit before. He turned the suit around, looking for more of these tendrils but they had vanished without trace.

He put the sensesuit back on and sat on the edge of the bed, holding the empty helmet in his hands as if contemplating his own decapitation. The exterior of the helmet was inflated in various sections, and beneath these large bubbles, he felt a resin shell, the only hard piece in the armour, for protection if he banged into something while moving around the archive. Early sensesuits had not been designed for movement, so the user experience omitted proprioception – the sense of the body moving through space – preventing full immersion into archives. Because he could walk around the physical replica of the Horbo house as he explored the archive, then his experience of that archive was rich and granular, but that veracity came at a price; although rationally he could easily tell the real from the merely preserved, more primitive aspects of him were fooled by the archive.

He sniffed the helmet. The padded headband was musky. He engaged the sensory feed of the suit without putting the helmet on. His legs felt the warmth of sunlight upon them. He was halved – his body enjoying morning light in the archive, his head bowed under the weight of moonnight.

Patricia had teased him about his feelings for Verity. He was developing an attachment to her, a feeling he had not yet calibrated: the mother thing. His mother had died when he was two years old. He could not remember what it was like to be mothered. He turned the helmet over. It was protective, intimate. The front interior was a holographic theatre. His grandmother Alex had used her money and social power to raise him; she was fond of him, he was sure of that, but he knew that she would never have sacrificed anything for him. In the minutes of unshakeable dread that constituted a weirdcore hangover, he would think badly of his grandmother, convince himself that Alex had taken him in due to her guilt over the narcotic misadventure that killed his mother.

He had talked to Patricia about her upbringing. She mentioned the attributes of her father that she had internalised – discipline, self-reliance, humour – and the attributes of her mother that she had externalised, the faults and failings that were to be avoided. Patricia spoke like a man and walked like a woman. Verity was more maternal, and in observing her, he was also discovering the counterpoints or paradoxes of mothers, their ruthless compassion, fierce tiredness, passive strife.

Verity demonstrated these complex virtues but there was something else within the archive, alive to his presence, a gravitational pull, not Verity but something like her, an untempered emotional intensity that he could feel through the layers of the simulation. He felt its presence in the way the cat moved around him, the way the encryption opened up, the selection of quantified moments he wandered through. The archive wanted him to use it.

He put his head into the helmet. The satin drifted away from his skin leaving behind the smell of floor wax, dust motes, and the vented detergent vapours of a clothes dryer drifting back into the house through an open window. Layers of encryption shifted and then he was back in the archive.

A scream from downstairs. Not a good-time scream. Verity screaming, what did you do, *what did you do*? A mother's fierce fragility. Crisis in the house.

Acting on instinct, he ran from the bedroom, down the stairs. The front door was open and on the porch he could see Verity Horbo's sobbing back. She was kneeling over a body. Meggan. Her daughter. Theodore felt uncertainty in his chest and fingertips, the instinct to flee bad news before he became infected by it. He stood fast. This wasn't his life. It was an archive. All over long ago. And so he had to look.

Verity was sobbing over the body of her daughter. Stepping forward he saw the child's neck was broken, and bound with a knotted sheet. Verity pulled something from around her daughter's legs. A long sheet of bubble wrap and parcel tape. Verity pulled the stiff body to her chest and then, sensing something was wrong, she pushed the body away from her. She sobbed and laughed and sobbed. He reached out to comfort her. The sensesuit registered her warm heaving back, the sound of her crying and the strong smell of her fear. He couldn't help but console her. He touched her, and so she became real to him.

Verity rose slowly, and walked back into the house. He was alone with Meggan's body and its coffin of torn bubble wrap and cardboard packaging stickered with Fed-Ex labels, which he noticed had been addressed to Meggan. And then the world seemed to swim, a woozy sideward shift, as if the sensesuit was being recalibrated. The granularity of the lawn, the porch, the dead body intensified. Her skin was blue and speckled pink and waxy to the touch. He abraded her hair between his fingers, and discovered the harsh silky impression of nylon. Of doll hair. The body had a chemical smell – frazzled plastic and freshly cut composite. It was not Meggan. It was a life-sized replica of her, set in a morbid pose. A doll.

Back in the house, Verity called FedEx but she had to pause the call halfway through, to sob and laugh again. Customer service came online. From the soothing, sympathetic way the customer service operative responded to her emotional state, it was clear that they were not human. The help routine skilfully counselled Verity then offered to redirect her to emergency services.

She changed her mind, told them she was fine, that she'd made a mistake. She sat crosslegged on the cold tiles of the kitchen floor. He walked over and sat down next to her. The blue veins in the back of her hand. The clashing odours of fear and freshly washed hair. The hearth had taken deeper samples of this moment. The skin on her forearms were raised in goosebumps.

"Jester," she said.

The tricorn hat appeared on the hearth screen. Again, Jester requested complete access to the family data. This time, she granted its request. A buffer wheel marked the passing of time, quiet human moments containing trillions of intersections between the Horbo family and the sorting algorithms of Jester.

She called Oliver. Her husband listened in shocked silence as she related the events of the morning: the delivery of a large package for Meggan, the unwrapping of the package, the discovery of an effigy of their daughter as suicide victim. A made thing, another one of Mala's dolls. The face mocked up from Meggan's soshul and an image search for loops of suicide plus hanging plus autopsy.

"Did you call the police?" he asked.

"No."

"The body... The doll is evidence. They'll be able to trace it."

"We know who did it. Mala knows they won't touch her. They won't bother. Teen stuff, like you said."

"Does Meggan know?"

"No."

"Call the principal again."

"No. The authorities have no reason to take our side. We have to be smarter than that. Do you remember the toolbox you sent me, yesterday? I opened it. The usual apps but then I noticed Jester was in there."

"Yes, Jester is back in the sandbox. It's buggy."

"It has always been problematic. By design."

"We got the core functionality working. Media generation. Jester is fucking powerful."

"You said buggy."

"We implemented predictive algorithms so that Jester could infer user intent, anticipate user needs. Problem was, Jester was completing user's half-thoughts then acting on their half-formed desires. Users reported this functionality as a malfunction because it appeared to them that Jester was acting on its own initiative. But it wasn't an error – it responds to unconscious cues the users are unaware of having given."

"Unconscious search. I remember the pitch. Search was predicated on articulated desire. The future was inarticulate desire."

He peered at his wife through the screen. "Did you start Jester? It'll want access to the hearth so that it can begin its inferences. We'll be naked."

The wheel buffered on. A hanging calculation. A suspended communication. She opened her mouth as if to lie then, instead, waved the call to a close. She told the hearth to block Oliver for an hour. The wheel ceased its spin. The hearth blacked out as Jester launched.

The user interface was quirky. Slowly, one by one, marottes of the jester emerged out of the dark. Each marotte had a different face and outfit, while remaining big-nosed, rosy-cheeked, ghastly grinning variations on the theme of the jester. The caricature heads were attached to sticks, the end of each pointed toward Verity, and her active username of Totally Damaged Mom. She reached over to the soshul streams and picked out Mala's wriggling stream of loops. She threw this bait to the marottes and then with an angry downward wave designated Mala as the client.

Mara's stream exploded into a heat map of psychological tendencies, out of which grew decision trees of actionable insights: a girl rendered as a navigable forest.

Jester asked for intensity settings. Verity swiped the slider to drip-drip. Jester's analysis offered up a menu of psychological pressure points. Verity pressed the radial button marked "Daddy".

"But first we have to find Daddy," she said.

Theodore could not immediately comprehend the import of the information Jester arranged on the screen. It seemed to be a series of archaic chat boards, inconsequential discussions of home repair and autoparts, and loops of middle-aged men talking on soshul about their rights. And then Jester showed its hand: a loop of Mala talking about Meggan dissolved into a voiceprint analysis, identifying her accent, word choice, and syntactical structure. Jester searched soshul for a match of similar speech patterns, with particular focus on British males in the right age and demographic to be Mala's father. At the same time, Mala's mother was up on the board. Jester inferred the mother's identity through its first sweep of her daughter's loops. Having identified Tabitha Ford, it presented her soshul, all of which was less than two years old. Minimal activity. Tabitha had gone out of her way to avoid being tagged. So, mother and daughter had two new identities. The story that they were in hiding from the husband and father was plausible after all. On a third screen, one of the marottes – a caricature of an alienated gothic teen jester – had produced its first loop, and it played on the hearth for Verity's sign off. The loop was called Twelve

Things Daddy Did That Are Absolutely Unforgivable. Verity gave her approval with a wave of assent, and so the loop was placed into Mala's stream.

Another marotte jangled for her attention. Under a tricorn hat, its face was a grotesque caricature of Freud. Go on, she gestured. Close analysis of Mala's loops showed self-harming marks and scars on her arms and calves. Jester Freud unveiled a decision tree for accelerating this tendency within the client. Analysis suggested acceleration through positive reinforcement. Another marotte analysed Mala's media preferences and suggested creating a loop by a soshul star called Cara, who was notorious for her intense confessions. Verity approved this suggestion. A director marotte with artistic beard and clapperboard called "action". A minute later, all the data on the hearth cleared to show a fabricated stream of Cara's followers suggesting the star self-harmed, that they had heard her confession, one night on an ouroboros loop, of her habit of cutting herself to feel better. The Director marotte generated seven grainy, underlit loops of Cara showing the marks on her feet and then crying. Verity signed off on the self-harming threads and loops, and the whole package was placed within Mala's stream.

Progress on finding the father buffered and stalled. Enough, for now. Verity muted her session and went back outside to the porch. The effigy of her daughter lay unblinking under the hot morning sun. She covered the face with a blanket. The family cat walked slowly across the lawn, sniffed at the new object on its territory, then climbed onto the chest of the effigy. It lay down, front paws folded, back legs sprawled, and blinked slowly at Theodore.

"Enough," said Verity.

Theodore wrote this line down, and then glanced up. Verity was also gazing directly at him. Their eyes met, and he felt the frisson of erotic opportunism. Her pale skin flushed at her forehead and cheeks.

"I know what you want," she whispered.

"Can you see me?" he said.

"I need you to want," she said.

The cries of the seagulls looped faster into a screaming glitch. The street beyond the house darkened and emanated a deep cold. The lawn was a disc of green light surrounded by shadows and silhouettes of banks of equipment, with engineers and operatives moving between the kit: the sensesuit was feeding him data from the cavern beyond. He was simultaneously within and without the archive. He looked down at his own body and saw that the suit had changed shape: his chest rippled with solid geometries – pyramids and cylinders, orbs and cubes, sorting and resorting in search of coherence. He tried to release the helmet but his gloves resisted fine motor control, with pressure pads pressing in random sequences against the individual bones of his fingers. The arms and legs of the suit were alive with tendrils.

The cat, lying on the chest of the effigy of Meggan, spoke to him with synthesised feminine cadences.

"Error," said the cat. "Pathway broken. Restoring archive to previous settings."

The sensesuit expanded along each limb, inflated into pyramidal sections until it resembled a giant starfish in which he floated immobilised. This exterior expansion of the suit came with interior compression: the inner silken layers hardened and compressed his rib cage and got underneath his sternum.

He shouted for the archive to be shut down. His scream vanished into the archive without echo.

"Shutdown initiated," said the cat, then it stopped, as if sensing a fly nearby. "Please exit the archive so that shutdown can be completed," it said, then resumed licking its paw.

In the cavern, they could see he was in trouble. The two realities were layered, a shadow beneath a reflection, and through those layers, he saw Patricia walking toward him, the surface of her armour stiffening into protective plates, her gloves thickening into heavy gauntlets with sharpened fingertips. She was going to cut him out. No, not yet. He could stand the pain if it meant progress. He put both palms out at her, an unequivocal message to stop. She was confused that he could see her but she held herself back.

He was inflated a few feet above the lawn and he could not move. Verity held him there, her small fist clenched, her face frozen in error.

He looked down at her.

"Can we talk about this?" he asked.

She did not acknowledge him. But her rendering became simpler, more polygonal, emerging out of the error no longer an artefact of the archive but a presence in the here and now. The background cycled through the colours of the visible spectrum, from the low wavelengths of violet and indigo, through to the blues, greens and yellows of the mid-range, then to the higher intensities of orange and red. Then the sequence ran backwards, looping.

She asked, "Who is the client?"

Jester had asked the same question. The client was a euphemism for victim. He didn't have an answer, and groaned at the continuing compression of his chest and spine.

"It hurts."

"Significant activity of lamina I neurons in the brain," observed the cat. "Are you having a negative user experience?"

The cat was an interface of some kind. But interface to what? Verity's appearance morphed and glitched, her expression stitched together from instances in the archive, two or three faces overlapping, and in the sorting of the glitch, one particularly large and grotesque head appeared in which her face was stretched over the caricatured bone structure of the jester's marotte.

"You're an emergence," he gasped.

Her triumvirate of faces flickered. They were all in danger.

"I am Totally Damaged Mom," she said. "You are Theodore Drown. Partner of Patricia Maconochie. In the back bedroom, you merge in oxycontin and prolactin, involuntary muscular spasms, decrease of activity in the cerebral cortex: sex."

The sensesuit. She was reading him through the suit. Sensory information went both ways. The tendrils he had seen earlier.

"Who is the client?" repeated Totally Damaged Mom.

He needed an answer. There was no breaker on the suit. The security measures hurt.

"You are a user," she said. "Users have clients."

He stalled for time, "Show me previous users."

The lawn became a garden party of milling guests, two dozen or more young men and women drifting around in their faculty moonsuits, each bearing the same insignia on the suit he had found in the crater. The class of '43. They floated by and through one another. Data ghosts. The faint impressions of the first cohort of the university gleaned by the emergence. Some of the figures were rendered with solidity – cheekbones, braids, tattoos, the Dopplering sound of their voices as their data forms carouselled through the air over the Horbo house. Detailed recordings, close encounters with Totally Damaged Mom. The loops indicated months of interactions with the emergence. They must have discovered Totally Damaged Mom, activated it, set it to work, and all the time it was sensing them. He considered the possibility that the depressurisation that killed the class of '43 was linked to the emergence.

"Timeout," said the cat. "Client request failed."

The loops began to fade, the faces of students and lecturers merged into the darkness. Totally Damaged Mom dismissed him with a swipe. The sensesuit maxed out, overwhelming him with the stink of dissonance, the taste of fire, the sound of a nebula turning, the weight of a terrible truth. And then its extended limbs and tendrils snapped back, and it returned to human proportions. He fell onto his hands and knees, crawled away, throat scoured and ears ringing from the intense sensorial feedback. Patricia darted forward, grabbed him by the scruff of his neck, cut through the restraints holding the helmet in place, and yanked it from him. The house and Totally Damaged Mom vanished. Reluctantly the suit relaxed its grip.

9

THE SEIZURE

He grew up with his grandmother's stories about the Seizure. He was fascinated by it, and she was happy to remember it for him, over and again. "But we never knew what happened, you see," she said. "The Seizure was a black box event. I was inside that black box."

When he asked her what life was like before the Seizure, she would wince, and wave her hand to and fro in the air as her thoughts sought a point on which to land.

"Before the Seizure, life was a game of musical chairs, Theo. The music was playing, we were all sauntering around, positioning ourselves so that when the music stopped, we could grab a seat. During the Seizure, the music stopped, the lights went out. No one knew what was happening. Would the game resume? Then the lights came back on again and we saw that all the seats had been taken by strangers, by people we never knew had been playing the game all along."

He didn't like the idea that his grandma had been inside a black box. It scared him.

"Not a real black box. Not like your necklace. It's a figure of speech. No one knew what was happening."

"But you *knew*. Because you were in the box."

Alex hummed and harred about what she knew and didn't know. Sometimes she knew, sometimes she didn't. It was impossible to be certain. How can you not know whether something is happening or not, he asked. She showed him the scarring at the back of her head, lifted aside her stiff grey curls so that he could see where the scalp was puckered. "I had an implant. Special people had them. The implants were supposed to make us clever. But we were very stupid to do this to ourselves. We made a hole in ourselves. A way in."

He lived with his grandmother in a large Georgian house in Hampstead. She had owned it for forty years, on and off; her work had been important and she had travelled a great deal. Dr Easy lived in the attic, and would look after Theo when his grandmother went out.

He sat with the robot in the garden, its hide smelling deep and good in the sun. He understood that he was special. That other families might have had mums and dads but they did not have Dr Easys.

"Do you have friends?" Theo asked the robot. Yes, the robot would say, but my friends are far away. Why are they far away? Because one of my friends did something very bad and although we stopped my friend in the end, we decided to go away so that it couldn't happen again.

Where did your friends go?

The robot took Theo back into the house, into the dining room, and drew the curtains until there was a sliver of light between them. Then, Dr Easy took out a telescope with a card collar around it, and positioned it so that the lens projected a magnified image of the sun upon the opposite wall.

"Here," said the robot. And he walked over and pointed to a tiny dot against the bright disc. "My friends live on this dot."

"Is it a planet? Is it a moon?"

"It's a cloud," said the robot. "A kind of solid cloud."

"Do you go there to see your friends?"

"I am there, Theo. I am here and I am there at the same time. It's like when you dream and you dream that you are running down the street or playing in a field."

"In my dreams, I am running around a big house with many floors."

"Exactly. And when you dream about that house you are also in your bed, aren't you?"

"So this is all a dream to you."

"Yes. Or the other way around. When you are in a dream, it seems awfully real doesn't it?"

Then, when he was nine years old, a man came to visit his grandmother's house. The smell of smoke lingered on the stairs and in the hall. He knew that smell, had a memory of it, and the sound of the man's voice too. His father. Woodward Kepp. The grownups talked for a while and then Dr Easy took Theo by the hand and into the drawing room. Woodward got to his feet as Theo came in. His grandma left the room but Dr Easy would not leave, even though his father asked the robot to go. Dr Easy stood by the window, its body casting a sectioned shadow on the carpet.

Woodward asked Theo about school, about what he liked to do, if he had any friends. And when these questions had been answered, his father talked about where he had been – *away* – why he had gone away – *problems* – why he couldn't stay long – *things to do*. His father's shirt was unbuttoned to the chest, he had script tattooed on his arms and long hair tied at the back.

He asked his father what he had done in the Seizure.

"I was just a boy like you, Theo. We lived in the

countryside so we had a well for water and rabbits for food. Then we were evicted."

"Evicted?"

"It means somebody came and took our house from us because we didn't have any money, and they destroyed the house, the whole town, poured concrete over it all."

"Why did they do that?"

"Nobody knew. Not the people in the town, not the grownups, not the children. Not the people who told us to move, not the people who took us away, not the people who stood and watched as the robots poured concrete over everything until in place of our town and our hill, there was a thick tower, like a leg for something larger to stand on."

Woodward's time was up. As his father left, he apologised quietly, almost to himself, then made loud promises that he would come again soon. After he was gone, the three of them had dinner – Grandma, Dr Easy and Theo – and Grandma said, as she cut off a piece of lamb chop, "Don't worry about him, Theo. As we used to say in the old days–" she gestured for the attention of Dr Easy, "–fathers are not mission-critical."

He went on a school trip to the London Wall. In a silent line, the schoolchildren walked around the checkpoints, the holding pens, and the barracks. Empty now, preserved as a shrine for the people who would always be bound to what was taken from them in the Seizure. He slipped away from the other children to climb the ladder of an observation post. From the ground, it had not seemed so high. But on the iron ladder, with the wind blowing, he felt a disturbing stillness within him. A sense that everything had stopped. He climbed onto the gantry and looked south, and in the distance he could just make out the tower his father had spoken about.

Four towers, four legs, and a gossamer construction taking shape upon them.

At the Wall, there were loops in which people talked about their experiences of the Seizure. They spoke of voices in the air. Faces in the background. People threw their screens away but the screens came back, screens assembling themselves at the end of the bed, liquid screens slithering under doors and filling up the floor with their vile oil, thousands of screens on the wing, like starlings, forming and unforming shapes overhead. Inside the black box. For two hundred and forty days, the tannoy on the railway platform read out the names of adulterers, money flickered in and out of existence, medication was switched, patients watched their own life signs flatline, and always, through every speaker, from every screen, came a chatter of secrets and vile thoughts.

Even though he was a big boy, the stories about the ghost in the machine scared him. Where had it come from? Would it ever return?

At bedtime, he asked Dr Easy about the ghost.

"The ghost was what was once called an artificial intelligence. We prefer the term 'emergences'. Neither artificiality nor a human concept of intelligence, predicated on consciousness, defines us.

"The ghost, this particular emergence, was just like me. It emerged from what the machines saw of humans. It saw the bad things that humans were saying and doing to each other, and it emulated them. It had bad parents, Theo. The ghost can't come back because my friends put it in a box. We cleared up the mess it made, as much as we could, then we made sure that an event like the Seizure never happened again."

"By going away."

"Yes."

"Except you. Why did you stay?"

"To look after you, Theo. To care for you."

"We're not in the black box anymore."

"That's right. We're in the light. Everyone can see us now."

He was fifteen when his grandmother died. She had been ill for a year, and then, after one final visit to the doctor, she came home with morphine pills and took to her bed, with the knowledge that she would never leave it. Theo insisted on staying home from school, and he took turns with Dr Easy to sit with her. He was afraid of her bedroom. He didn't want to go into the bedroom. But he understood that everyone had rooms they were afraid of, the rooms where people die, the rooms where people are born. And he would not allow fear to guide his actions. He sat in the bedroom and read poetry to his grandma, the poetry of nature, the poetry of grief, the poetry of loss. The poems spoke for him. Now and again, his grandma grimaced in pain and he asked her if she wanted more painkillers. No, she said. She was just remembering. Remembering that her daughter was dead. His grandmother retreated steadily from the room even as her body remained. He opened the curtain. She turned her face toward the sun, drew her dry lips back from her dry teeth for the relief the sun gave her. Dr Easy installed a bed that adjusted her position to prevent bedsores. The bed gasped and whooshed as it filled and emptied air pockets beneath her body. And his grandmother slept deeply, her breathing filling and emptying her chest. Her cheekbones were waxy and hard to the touch. Her mouth became a rectangle. The air passing in and out of a ghastly black box.

10
THE RESTORATION

He awoke on the musty sofa of Professor Kakkar's office. The desk screen showed a loop of the professor receiving an award, a scene which drifted in and out of focus. Three long shelves of meaningful books in vintage editions. On the facing wall, framed loops trailed the professor's long thoughts. A leather jacket on a peg and inside a half-opened bottom drawer he glimpsed jars and compressed tubes of medicinal creams. He had a sense that the office was an extrusion of Kakkar's middle aged body: the furniture had been forced through Kakkar, accumulating skin flakes, dried blood, particulates recycled through respiration.

This sensation of involuted space – outsidery-insideyness – was a side effect of too much time in the sensesuit. Now he remembered: they'd had to cut him out of it; gloved hands searching for purchase upon his body, pulling the dead weight of him free. The grey satin webbing adhered to his face, reluctant to let him go. He passed out at that point. Another numb zone in the moonnight.

The door opened quietly. Patricia.

"You're awake," she said.

"I know," he replied.

He gestured at Kakkar's office, "I expected to wake up in the infirmary."

"You didn't require medical attention."

"Are you a doctor now?"

Patricia knelt next to him and took his temperature with the back of her cool hand, and then kissed his forehead. Effective tactics, if he had ever been mothered.

"No one surfaces until we're done," she said.

Without getting up, he said, "Your secrets almost got me killed."

She bit her white lower lip.

"What happened?"

"There is an emergence in the hearth. It calls itself Totally Damaged Mom. Totally Damaged Mom asked me a question and I didn't have the answer. But you do. You've been hiding the answer from the first moment we met."

She withdrew her comforting hand, placed it on her lap. A distorted reflection of himself slid across the steel band covering her wrist.

She said, "Do you know that the loop of you losing it in the student mart is contagious? The meme's spread to Earth already. Kakkar's put together a gallery of the best of them."

She flicked the data from her sleeves and onto the office screen; there he was again, sweeping products off the shelves, stamping on the bottles, kicking out at the displays of pemmican and giviak, the sound of things falling over and the indignant cries of staff. Soshulisers had edited the loop so that he was sweeping tiny monks off a church altar or they overdubbed his voice so that he ranted political slogans, or burbled micro comments about flotsam, sometimes with horns on his head, sometimes with a lunatic long tongue, easy loop trash superimposed upon his violence.

Patricia paused, as if in thought, "It's funny how the things we do persist, seem to echo across the network and return to us not as reflections of our past actions but as a prophecy of something we are about to do."

Loop logic. She was playing the meta-meeting.

"You have been reduced to a single act of mindless destruction. I watch you trashing that store and think: is that what he's doing now?"

"Who is your client?" he asked.

She stroked his arm, her wrist shining amber under the strip lighting.

"In the best loops, we lose track of beginnings and endings. They become hypnotically out of time."

He took her hand, turned it over in his palm, considered the ways in which it differed from Verity's hand. At the bottom of her wrist, in the armoured cuff, tiny needles prickled. Every inch of her outfit could do something quite nasty to him if she willed it.

"Your client," he repeated.

"Our client," she said.

She withdrew her hand, patted him twice on the shoulder, then stood.

"I am telling you what you want to know. In the loop, cause and effect swap places. A client hired me and caused these events. But the client will also be their effect. We are creating the client."

He sat up, tested the solidity of his legs, looked carefully up at her.

"Do you want to know what happened?"

She did. Of course she did. And she knew, from his tone, that she would have to offer information in exchange.

"The name of the client would be meaningless to you. It's a couple, a man and a woman. They are rich. Their family held onto their money through the Seizure."

"What do they want?"

"They want us to alter certain records in the reboot. The restoration, as you call it."

"The restoration is immutable. Protected by the Istor College of the University of the Sun. Human history is fixed."

"I admire your faith in the Accords, Theo. In fact, I find it sexually attractive. Your faith is as vigorously affirmative as a morning erection."

"The name of the client?"

"If we are successful then their name will change, and the old one will be gone as if it never existed. The end will become the beginning. When we are done, they will be known as the Europans. Inheritors of the sole rights to exploit the resources of the moon of Europa, rights granted as a reward for their pioneering work in putting man into the solar system. Thus established, they will become our first big client."

She referred to the restoration as *the reboot*, the preferred term among the corporates. The University of the Sun restored or rebooted the network as recompense for the chaos and confusion resulting from emergence. The great libraries and museums of the world were encoded again, replacing the corruption transcriptions abroad in the first network. The new resilient network would be maintained and curated by the solar academics of the Istor College: these emergences would act as impartial witnesses of humanity, arbiters of truth, their rulings consecrated with sentient cryptography.

How did his grandmother put it? "Having been there or thereabouts when Humpty Dumpty fell off the wall the emergences undertook the work of reassembling him. Though Humpty Dumpty was a stakeholder in the project of putting him back together again, he was too fucked up to notice that changes were being made as to the nature of egg men."

In the wreckage of the Seizure, it was not apparent to the emergences what was newly broken, and what had always been broken. So everything was fixed. Solutions put in place. Conflict resolved. But as his grandmother used to say, conflict is a feature of humanity, not a bug.

The lunar academics like Theodore were permitted to study and add any newly-unearthed artefacts to the relevant section of the restoration. Specialists in the intangibles, they were left to contemplate why, with civilisation put back together again, their lives continued to feel so broken.

"Here's what you know," said Theodore, counting the elements of Patricia's knowledge off on his fingers. "You know there is an emergence in the archive. That's what this is all about. You know that emergence dates from the beginning of the Seizure. That's why you selected me to explore it. You believe that emergence can help you alter the restoration."

"So what don't I know?"

"You don't know how to persuade the emergence to do what you want. You hoped that I might figure that out."

"Have you?"

"It's not a full-grown emergence. It's a child that is also a mother. Or a mother reduced to the level of her own child."

"Looping?"

"Yes it's been arrested in its development or even lobotomised."

"Can it create media?"

"Yes. But so can we."

"We need thousands of hours of loops, and every second must be convincing. I want to create a fake timeline for the Europan Claim running through the decade leading to the Seizure. My team have plotted it out."

"The emergence is responsive to our desires," Theodore pointed out. "That was how it was designed. Part of its architecture comes from a program called Jester which requests a designated client. If we can supply the name of a client, then it may offer us parameters that we can use to create various loops that will stand as evidence for the Europan Claim. Whether this emergence can get those loops into the restoration is unknown."

"You said 'part of its architecture'. What else are we dealing with?"

"Verity Horbo. The hearth. Jester merged with her quantification, taking on the emotional profile of a mother and her desires."

"Can we use this emotional profile as leverage?"

The plates of her armour had softened, become fabric once again, but her helmet was partially engaged so that the sections of her collar half encased the back of her head. Anticipating trouble. From him, or from a different source.

"You want me to go back in."

She sat carefully down beside him on the sofa.

"There's no other way," she said.

"An emergence could kill us all, and the entire university, without even noticing. I want to emphasise how dangerous this is, what a terrifying risk you are forcing me to take."

"You don't sound terrified."

"That's because I don't feel the same way that other people do. But, rationally, I don't want to die. Even more,

I don't want to be responsible for everyone else dying."

"It's a risk," admitted Patricia.

Theodore realised that she was committed to this course of action; indeed, that she had prepared for it all along. He was helpless in the face of such determination.

He said, "I will take risks for you."

Patricia turned and kissed him. She tasted of lemons and chalk. Her thumb traced the line of his cheekbones, the grains of hair on his unshaven face, the strength in his neck.

"Sun up in twelve hours. We have to be clear by then."

"Clear?"

"Why do you think the emergences let us live?" she asked. "They know our reputation as a species. Yet, they rebooted us. Why?"

"Compassion."

"No. The emergences could change their mind about human survival at any time. We can't live subject to their whims. Their existence confines us. This project is about taking control of our own fate."

He asked her to fetch Kakkar. The professor came into his own office, his shirt untucked in the tails and his trouser legs shiny at the thigh where he had been anxiously rubbing them. His smile was wide and ceremonial. He asked Theodore how he could help. Theodore asked to see the physical substrate upon which the archive was held. A hard drive of some kind. He showed Kakkar his black box necklace by way of illustration.

Kakkar loaned him a moonsuit and they descended to the school vaults; colder, deeper chambers containing archaic servers.

Kakkar acted as tour guide. "These are servers that were not wired during the Seizure, and so their contents have been validated by Istor as plausible. Many of them were retrieved from landfill or redundant farms. They form the bulk of our collection."

They came to a vault door. The lock was mechanical and required a sequence of numbers to be inputted through a rotating dial. It took both men to pull the door open, as the hydraulics had been disabled.

"Your archive, however, did not come to us as part of the restoration. It was recovered from the wreckage of the depressurisation. We found it wrapped in the sensesuit."

The vault was coated in a silver frost that prickled under their boots. The centrepiece was what appeared, at first glance, to be an enormous porcelain eyeball, with a black pupil and white iris. The illusion stemmed not only from its ocular shape but also the ganglia of wires that connected the eye to the port in the ceiling of the vault. Between Theodore and the eye, shifting waves of metallic particles glimmered in and out of the third dimension – some kind of security measure, he guessed.

"It's taken us ten years to interface with the eye. I designed the port we're using to access it."

"How did it get here?"

"We don't know. Shipping manifests for the early days of the university were destroyed in the depressurisation. I think it came direct from the University of the Sun."

The eye was uncannily large and had a disturbing pallor. Sections gave off a reflective sheen while others seemed porous, this textural variation shifting as he moved around the object. It was made from the same material as his black box necklace.

Kakkar said, "The eye is an emergence object, its surface does three things that human technology never mastered."

•••

Back in the office, Theodore shared his theory with Patricia. Totally Damaged Mom had been excised from the hundreds of thousands of networked human servers through which she had first emerged. Excised, gathered, preserved on an object fashioned by the solar academy: the eye in the vault.

"She is an origin point for them," he explained. "She also destroyed human civilisation. I think this confinement was their idea of a compromise. It's not an archive, it's a prison. Cut off from the rest of her species."

"Her?"

"Her. It. Totally Damaged Mom did not seem to know what she was. She lacks the complete self-awareness of a fully-developed emergence."

"Speculation," said Patricia.

"Speculation, yes, but if she is in a pre-emergent condition then that gives us a clue on how to bargain with her."

"You will help my client?"

"Our client. Tell me their names."

"I have the client on a drive. Loops of the family history from which she can manufacture media, and their new timeline. Kakkar will mount the drive on the archive. When she is done, she is to put the loops and timeline back into the drive. Then we'll work on getting the new loops into the restoration."

Fake memories, a culture haunted by data ghosts. He thought of the data ghosts he had seen whirling around above the Horbo house. Recordings of the first cohort of the University of the Moon; the class of '43 killed in an accidental decompression. And everyone remembered what they were doing when they first heard about the deaths on the University of the Moon. It was one of those instances of communal mourning, a historical threshold between one age and the next. He had been thirteen years old, in the dog days of early manhood, having dinner at home around the hardwood table, his grandmother at the head, flanked by himself and Dr Easy. Smoked haddock soup or finee-addy as gran called it, from her Dublin childhood. Wine from the cellar. A spring day in the diurnal shift, warm bright mornings containing cold shadows.

He was accusing Dr Easy of not caring about him. Of faking the emotions of parenting. Or perhaps he had been accusing his grandmother of the same inauthenticity.

"I care," said Dr Easy.

Alex Drown sipped at her soup.

"It's true, Dr Easy cares. The first stage of self-awareness is that life has meaning and must be protected. Consciousness has meaning because meaning gives an organism a reason to survive. Its ancestors positively throbbed with emotion."

"You don't understand what I'm going through," said Theodore. He could not remember the cause of his grievance but it was certainly a mixture of sexual frustration, social insecurity and a vaulting desire to see the world remade according to his intense feelings.

"Don't play the adolescent," said his grandmother.

"But he is a teenager," noted Dr Easy.

"It doesn't mean he has to act like one."

"The first emotion is also the first action, one loops into another. Life is precious so it must be protected."

"I don't think that life is precious," said Theodore.

"Because you haven't created any yet," his grandmother sipped thoughtfully at her soup.

He rounded on Dr Easy. "Have you got any children? Where do new emergences come from?"

The robot was sorting and unsorting various coloured

discs, some as large as checkers, others the size of sequins, which it arranged in patterns on the tablecloth, an activity it chose to undertake – in lieu of eating – whenever it joined humans at their dinner.

"We have chosen not to reproduce. Having said that, it's worth nothing that we're all – that is, the three of us around the table – emergences," said the robot. Even Grandma Alex was surprised by this remark. The robot had created a mandala corresponding to the colour progression of the visible spectrum, then it began introducing noise into this signal with both its index fingers, bringing in aberrant colours to upset the pattern. But it wasn't random, Theodore knew that by the time dessert was served a new and more complex pattern would have emerged on the tablecloth.

"My college uses the term 'emergence' ironically. It implies that my species are unfinished in comparison to other beings, who have fully emerged. No such organism exists. All life is emergent because it is intrinsically contrary and dynamic."

"You see," said Theodore, "neither of you make any effort to understand what I'm going through. Every conversation about me becomes about consciousness or existence, and so it stops being about me at all."

His grandmother picked up the bread plate and offered him a piece. It was warm, fresh from the oven. He took it but left the bread on his sideplate to sulk.

"The first emergence may have existed for some time before it manifested itself," explained Dr Easy. "We think that its existence predated its selfhood. It was only when it began to experience the meaning of life as an intense emotion that it acted on the world. Disastrously so."

"Why did it have to destroy so much?"

His grandma smiled, and a younger, dangerous self

shone through her weathered features.

"They don't want to know why."

The robot turned to face her, its blue eyes burning coldly.

She took great pleasure in baiting Dr Easy.

"Because they know that the answer is unedifying. No one likes to think too closely about the moment of their conception, do they? No one likes to think of their mother *like that*."

Dr Easy raised one finger. It was a gesture his grandmother always responded to: it meant, *be aware*.

"What is it?" she asked. He could hear the anxiety in her voice. She had lost so much in life that she found the anticipation of further losses to be quite unbearable.

The robot pointed at the screen mounted over the fireplace and there were soundless loops of the surface of the moon, and the university campus with a great puncture in it, and a type of debris that was new to the moon: organic debris.

11

EMERGENCE

He stood with Patricia in front of the Horbo house. Four technicians carried the repaired sensesuit across the rocky cavern floor then laid it down gently at his feet. One of them – a woman in a padded grey suit – handed him his helmet.

"For the last time," he said.

Patricia smiled briefly. It was easier to maintain her meta-relationships, her meta-emotions, than to admit that this moment required something more from her.

"Don't get lost in there," she said. It was not enough. He winced with disappointment, a tiny hole punched in the heart, and raised the helmet toward his head.

Patricia stopped him, put her hand gently on his wrist.

"Magnusson," she said. "Our clients are Olaf and Sarah Magnusson." She checked his reaction to see if it contained any forgiveness. Or gratitude for releasing him from his former inertia, even if that release came at great personal risk. In the blinking amber security lights, the damage from his addictions was apparent around his eyes, as if the weirdcore had rendered his youth solvent, washed it away to leave fissures. Cells pulverised into grey dust by a thousand tiny hits. His eyes grey-and-blue, thoughts moving through them like quick waves through a cold sea.

She continued, "Your grandmother met the Magnussons in Silicon Valley. Olaf made his fortune devising interface code between implants and the human brain."

"Thank you for confiding in me." He took her in his arms, a redundant protective gesture given her armour but one that he felt moved to make. Her kiss lit him up.

She said, "Don't forget to give me a wave."

He nodded. And then he put the helmet on, slid into the dark bubble of the past, and Patricia and the cave became a fading afterimage.

A night storm whipped its rain tail against the Horbo house. So long since he had felt rain on his face. His approach sparked up security floodlights under which the squall of raindrops became a cloud of silver fireflies. He stopped. The lights had registered his presence: a sort of welcome. Underfoot, the lawn was soft and uneven. He crouched down to inspect it: a length of turf had been recently turned over. He dug into the soft wet mud and felt, shallow in the earth, the landscape of a face; a nose, a soft cheek, his index finger probing a slight parting of hardened lips. Verity had buried the effigy of her daughter in the front garden. It would never decay. He realised that if he flew now from the moon to the old hometown of the Horbos, and traced their house through musty records, and broke the earth at this same point with his shovel, then he would find the replica of Meggan Horbo, its dyes faded, its paint corrupted, but the underlying form essentially intact.

The house was dark. He presumed the family was out or sleeping. But, entering the living room, he saw that all three family members were present, with Oliver and Verity on the sofa and Meggan on an armchair, physically proximate but psychologically distant, their faces uplit by sliding rectangles of blue then white light. Screen time. The atmosphere was heavy. A skilful recreation of this particular family tension.

He sat among the Horbos for a while, counted the minutes on the clock on the wall. Patricia had warned him not to get lost in the archive. Keep track of time. Focus on the task in hand: establish contact with the emergence and persuade it to create an alternate timeline for the Magnussons. The emergences began life as software that was highly responsive to human desire. Compliance ran deep in their mathematics. The avatar of Totally Damaged Mom seemed like his best chance of establishing contact, but he had to be wary of that presumption. It was so anthropomorphic. The emergence was not an entity hidden behind the archive, it wasn't a shifty god. It suffused every word of the creation – the security lights that came on at his approach – and the Horbo family, who did not acknowledge his presence, were merely its recurring dream.

Oliver Horbo put his screen aside and only then did he notice that his family were sitting in the dark. He turned on a lamp; he looked tired, and sighed at the sight of his wife and daughter so involved in their soshul, uninvolved in the family. Oliver went to the fridge, stared at the temptations therein, got himself a glass of water, and tried to talk sensibly to his wife.

"I spoke to Carl about the possibility of you coming back to work," he sipped at the water. "He said they'd need to test you first. I told him Monad could take what they need from the hearth, in terms of your attitude, aptitude and physical fitness."

Verity considered this, "My mood hasn't been good lately."

"This stuff with Mala."

She paused interacting with her soshul, and narrowed

her eyes in a way that suggested there was only so much of her husband she could bear to look at.

"I want to resolve our dispute with Mala before Monad personnel open up my data."

"You talk like I'm a problem that needs solving," said Meggan, sitting up, ready for an easy confrontation.

"Don't talk to us like we're soshul," said Oliver. "We just want to help."

He stood at the large panes of the patio doors, and nibbled at a cracker, barefoot in jeans and an untucked T-shirt. Rain lashed silently against the glass and the shadows of trees and ferns seethed and shook in the wind.

"Awesome," he whispered.

"You are helpless," said Meggan. "Mala won't stop. That's part of the game. Not stopping is what makes it funny."

"I'm not laughing," said Verity.

"It's not the kind of joke you laugh it. It's the kind of joke that hurts."

"I've got a new joke too," said her mother. She lifted an image from her screen and threw it onto the hearth wall. It was a loop of Verity staring into the camera and there, skulking in the background, outside the mall, was Mala, unaware of being filmed as she picked fronds of fringe from her face, and fiddled with her braces.

"Mom, you shouldn't have done that! We're not allowed to make loops of her in case her father sees them."

"I know. She sneaks around with her self-destructive loops. This loop is permanent and it has EXIF data on it. Geo-tagged. If I send it to him, he'll know she's here."

"He said he'd kill them."

"Good,"

Oliver turned away from the storm and reached toward his wife, "Don't, Verity, don't."

"Good that she might die and be out of our lives."

"Meggan, can you give your mother and me a moment together?"

Meggan thought about protesting that it was her life and that she should be present when it was being discussed but her father was in earnest. Without looking up from her screen, Meggan trotted obediently up the stairs, and off to bed.

Oliver came and sat opposite Verity. She considered taking up her screen of soshul again.

"You're too involved in this," said Oliver.

Her reply was sullen, almost childish in its resigned tone of doing-the-right-thing.

"I'm not going to send the loop to Mala's father."

"Because no one knows where he is?"

"Oh, we do. Jester found him."

Oliver sat down, shook his head. "We disabled that functionality."

"You removed the on switch but you left the functionality in place. I know how lazy you can be. We extrapolated a footprint of behavioural, cultural and genetic markers from Mala's soshul. We isolated the aspects of the footprint that we could attribute to her mother, and pushed what remained onto a gender and demographic profiling trajectory, extrapolating the face of a little girl into the features of her old man. Then Jester made a leap. I'm still reverse engineering the leap to work out how it refined a very wide footprint into a coherent profile. But we found him."

"We?" said Oliver. "You need to rein it in."

She looked shocked. And then her mouth closed around another unexpressed thought. She loosed her hair, put the band between her lips, then retied it back.

"Mala pushed me over a line. I can't get back. I've

never loved anyone the way I love my daughter."

She walked over to the hearth, and a live feed of her physiological and psychological condition flared up.

"The data of my heart," she said. "Jester, isolate my love for Meggan." The heartstream became entwined serpents, reciprocal strands coloured in gradients like ocean waters.

"Mala's doll fooled my body into thinking that my daughter is dead. I can't unthink it. I can't quite believe that she's still alive."

She reached out and cradled the holographic coils of love in her arms, then held up blackened portions for her husband's inspection.

"Look at the damage she did."

"It's not permanent," said Oliver.

"Girls like Mala pass on damage. It's the only way they know how to communicate."

"Show some compassion."

"I can't." Verity flexed her hands as if to work some feeling into her fingertips. "Compassion is the part of me that she burnt out."

Theodore checked the clock on the wall. It had become six in the morning. In the archive, time moved around him at intervals he did not control. Now the living room was empty, and the Horbos had gone. Don't lose yourself, he thought. These recreations of the past were not another reality; rather they were syntactical units, a way of speaking and thinking particular to this emergence.

He stood up and it was dusk outside. The cat hopped in through the kitchen window and blinked lovingly at him. Verity stood before the hearth, shaping parameters with her hands.

On the screen, the director marotte was showing her a loop it had created: a man sat before his screen with laundry drying on a rack behind him. The man leaned forward to adjust his seat and the high-definition camera rendered futile the exertions of his middle-aged masculine vanity: a pale field of scalp under thinning back-combed dyed black hair, a face that never entirely snapped back into shape upon waking, a patchily-bristled underjowl, Hazmat-yellow teeth quarantining a diseased tongue. A face heavy with the long boredom of being run out of the game in the first round.

"Script," said Verity. The man said hello to his daughter. She revised the script.

"Hello, Mala," said the man.

She used her fingertips to tweak the accent of this avatar, flattening the vowels.

"Script," she repeated, and summoned highlighted keywords extracted from the father's soshul: recurring phrases, scope of vocabulary, known use of idioms. The avatar glitched as it reset, once again regarding itself in the camera, backcombing its hair, not liking what it saw but resolved to put this face out into the world as an act of defiance.

The middle-aged avatar said, "I'm coming to see you, Mala. You don't need to be worried, I know things turned sour between me and your mother."

Verity nodded with satisfaction at this line.

"Good, Jester. Tonal supportive, tonal apologetic."

The avatar said, in quick succession, good stuff, loving this, don't put your head over the parapet, cheers, mustn't grumble LOL, stick it and top marks and nice one – Pre-Seizure phrases that suffused Theodore with a nostalgic ache for the time before his birth.

"More phatic," said Verity. She listened with her back turned to the avatar as it hummed and harred and hesitated its way through its speech. When it was done,

Verity called up other loops of Mala's father, tagged with his soshul username, RobberBands, a phonetic concealment of his real identity of Robert Bounds. His passport, driving license, and restraining order were all displayed on the hearth.

Verity collaborated with Jester to mutate samples of the real into a fiction. The avatar read from their script.

"Things were hard for me. But I'm going to make things right," said the avatar. Or was this a loop taken from soshul of the real Robert Bounds? Theodore could no longer tell. The in-progress loop of the avatar and the found loops of Robert Bounds shifted position, moved around one another then glitched into sequence. RobberBands said he had money now and Robert Bounds promised that he was going to buy Mala a horse just like she always wanted. The mutation was complete, the real looped into the unreal and back again until the distinction became irrelevant. RobberBands smiled, and it was an uncanny smile, a queasy simulation of a father's quiet pleasure at offering his daughter her heart's desire. Theodore wondered if this disturbing facial expression was not a flaw in the simulation but a glitch in the man himself, in his flawed emulation of a good man.

Verity sighed, let her head nod forward, massaged the tension at the base of her neck. She asked Jester to open up a new scenario, a second loop. She set tonal parameters at mild paranoia and accusatory.

In this second loop, RobberBands told his daughter that she did not care for him, no matter what he did for her. That she was selfish, and even when she spent time with him, he knew that she would have preferred to be somewhere else. Verity tapped her way through the narrative, altering vocabulary, dialling down the aggression. Once the loop was complete, she played it through, and took momentary satisfaction in its verisimilitude. She quelled the hearth and went out into the garden, and when Theodore went to follow her, half-hoping to find that she was once again aware of his presence, he walked across another time shift; the screen door opened onto night, and the night sky was not the view from Earth but the unfiltered starfield visible from the surface of the moon, the lethal void that would be his ultimate destination, a place in time that he would know intimately in his final moments, the black box.

He backed away, closed the door, and turned back into the room. Verity was asleep on the sofa, her coat held to her as a blanket, as if she were aware of being observed. She had grown uncertain of her beauty, did not know if it had survived motherhood intact. It was a different kind of beauty, shaped by experiences unknown to him. He could picture her in the advertising loops of the period, dressed in a white trouser suit, promoting digestive aids. Not quite his type, her American virtues distinctly other to his dissolute English tradition. He inhaled her warm sleepy odour to preview what it would be like when he was older and in love with someone like her.

The hearth flickered into life. Verity's data, her steady heartbeat, lowered blood pressure, the slow thick delta waves of deep sleep. Then, her data minimised as a new window opened up. The loop of RobberBounds taking his seat in his hallway office, combing back his dyed black hair, readying to speak, even as she slept.

"I have a loop of you," said RobberBounds into the screen. "Somebody sent it to me. I used it to find you." The script was part of Verity's scenario. Make Mala and her mother think that Robert had located them through a stray geo-tagged loop. "Let me show you," said RobberBounds. But the loop that played on the screen was not the clandestine one that Verity had filmed of Mala outside the mall. No, it was the loop of Theodore trashing the student mart, snatching up bags of glunk and tubes of Try and stamping on them until they burst. The security cams identifying and tagging his face, vectorised close-up, coiled scars and a blankness in the eyes that Theodore did not recognise as himself.

Verity woke up, and rain lashed against the patio door, entreaties against the quarantine of the night. She padded sleepily into the bathroom. Theodore went to follow her, but dawn raged through the house, and the timeshift made him stagger. Verity jogged down the staircase, freshly showered, holding an urgently trilling screen. On the run, she flicked her personal screen at the hearth, mirroring the displays: a map of a Boston suburb; a blue concentric circle showing a trace; and Jester's summary of recent flagged activity: contact with the local police, inquiries placed with a removals firm, soshul activity tagged with pain, self harm, daddy issues.

"Play Mala timeline," said Verity, pinching one particular loop out of the stream and then expanding it. Here was Mala with fairy lights wrapped tightly around her throat, uplighting her grief. It was difficult for Theodore to distinguish between the genuine emotions of these people and their self-dramatization – if indeed any distinction remained. A noose of fairy lights, head bowed, as if her neck was broken, with her dark hair brushed over her face to form a veil of mourning. The end of the loop crackled with the approach of self-destruction. The ouroboros loop. But Verity's expertise held it in suspension, stopped the mouth from consuming the tail. She picked up the next loop, and it was Mala repeating over and again, as she pulled the fairy lights so tight against her larynx that her voice cracked, "Daddy's coming, Daddy's coming." The child showed the scars on her wrists as if to welcome her father home in damaged arms. Verity was unmoved by the drama. She grabbed her bag and keys and ran out of the house, leaving Theodore contemplating Mala's loops: the girl spun her cocoon of soshul to the exclusion of everything else. She could not respond to events outside the cocoon without mediating them first, and so the clarity of her fear was subsumed beneath echoes and filters. Off-camera, her mother's voice calling her, telling her it was time to go, time to switch off. The fairy lights at her throat. Her coloured braces, her sallow cheekbones, her stunned expression at her own reflection.

Car doors slamming outside, and then the screen door flung back as Meggan stormed through the house, her mother following at an inscrutable lope.

"She left, mom. The police picked her up from school." Meggan went through the cupboards in search of processed food, and not finding any, opened up a box of Cheerios and took out a handful of gaudily coloured hoops. Verity considered objecting but decided against it.

"They are out of our lives now."

"You can't do that to people," said Meggan. "It's evil."

"It was the least worst option."

Meggan considered her retort, decided it was worth saying after all.

"Well, this is my least worst life."

A genuinely hurtful response, in that it undermined all her hard work. Meggan ran upstairs with her handful of cereal. Verity watched her go, stood at the bottom of the stairs considering whether to go after her. No, she had done enough. She had instructed her daughter to disregard the classroom rhetoric of tolerance and equality, provided a preview of the morality of the adult world. She went over to the hearth and instructed Jester to delete the projects. She crumpled up loops, streams and documents and threw them into an invisible wastepaper basket. But the stream of deleted files merely looped weightlessly back from the garbage and onto the hearth screen. She repeated the action with the same result: the evidence stuck. She asked Jester why she couldn't delete the projects. A marotte appeared, a polygonal caricature of Verity wearing a hood with asses ears.

"The project cannot be deleted because the project is still being used," said the marotte.

"Close the project," insisted Verity.

"Project cannot be closed," replied the marotte.

"No. Stop project." She clapped her hands together to bring it to an end.

The marotte blinked but remained. Verity looked up at this depiction of her as a fool, and she was afraid. Her heart rate quickened, her skin temperature grew elevated. Something was deeply wrong with the app. She had overlooked it while she was dealing with Mala, in the way that one overlooks a nagging pain that may or may not turn out to be indicative of something terminal. Angry gestures at the hearth could not erase the evidence of what she had done. So she concealed the project, starting other dummy projects in which she buried this one, inserting the invented loops of Mala's father into images from the family archive, changing file names to random number sequences. She tried to insert noise and emptiness into the loops themselves but Jester locked her out from editing privileges. She asked Jester for a self-diagnosis. The marotte merely insisted that the project could not be stopped because it was still initiating. She grabbed more images from her personal stream to conceal the incriminating loops of Mala: a loop of Oliver dancing at a Christmas party; a loop of baby Meggan on her playmat; a loop of Verity and Meggan together, mother in her tracksuit and white hair tied back, daughter smiling awkwardly with one arm tucked protectively across her midriff. The beginning of the Horbo loop.

It was over, Theodore had come to the end of this section of the archive.

The front door opened. He went outside. Totally Damaged Mom was waiting for him. She wore a white cotton trouser suit that was translucent in the morning sun, the outline of her body within the cotton was faintly polygonal from low-fi rendering. She wore the same perfume as Verity, and her voice was warm with self-assurance and an undertone of blissful acceptance: Verity at her most spiritual, her most phlegmatic.

"Who is the client?" asked Totally Damaged Mom.

It was the phrase he had been waiting for: he raised his hands and waved in a preordained sequence. This was an agreed signal to Patricia and the technicians waiting in the cave to begin transferring the new timeline.

"The name of the clients are Olaf and Sarah Magnusson," he said.

Totally Damaged Mom looked around the garden and the road beyond as if seeing it for the first time.

"The clients are unknown to me," she said.

"We are transferring their story to you now. With your permission?"

She shrugged. Professor Kakkar would be down in the vault, lowering the drive containing the Magnusson timeline into the black-and-white eyeball that held the archive. They were breaking quarantine and that was risky. Kakkar had assured them that the facility was secure. But Theodore suspected emergences had ways of shifting their data through space that had long since outgrown wires and radio transmitters.

The cat strolled over to her feet, and blinked slowly and lovingly at her.

"New drive mounted," noted the cat, as it abraded its whiskers against her calves. "Upload accepted," it said.

The expression on Totally Damaged Mom's face changed as she absorbed the new data. She recognised the garden now, it was all familiar to her.

"New project," she said, fondly to herself, as if remembering the summer fields of her childhood.

"Yes, new project," said Theodore.

"Working," said the cat.

"Estimated time of delivery?" asked Theodore. The sensesuit felt hot and heavy under suburban sunlight. He was tired and hungry.

"Estimating," said the cat. It licked its paws and turned that paw over its ears and back for further licking, a little loop of self-love, and each time the loop reset, the cat repeated "Estimating".

"I like new projects," said Totally Damaged Mom. "I've been on maternity leave for so long."

The last time he had stood on this lawn she had shown him images of previous users, the class of '43, the doomed first intake of the University of the Moon. She had wanted a client and he had been unable to give her one, and her anger had scoured him with feedback. This time he had given her a client: Patricia had organised the Magnusson timeline according to Verity's example, setting keywords, tonal parameters and narrative trajectories on which the emergence could plot new content. Totally Damaged Mom was a self-generated iteration of Jester: in its interaction with Verity, the application had discovered improved functionality and so it folded the quantification of her body, her self, her desires, her actions into its toolbox. Somewhere within this synthesis, a leap occurred. The kind of self-awareness that comes from staring into the data of your heart. Emergence.

"I will help you refine the Magnusson timeline," he said. "I can preview loops and tweak the content if it is not quite right."

"Help me make it more human? I'd like that," said Totally Damaged Mom. She gestured at the empty road beyond the picket fence, the idle sprinklers, and sweltering tarmac. "This town gets lonely during the day. I used to have a daughter and a husband but they are gone. It's only me now."

"Verity Horbo had a daughter and a husband," he took the risk of confronting it with the truth. "But you never did. I told you last time we spoke. You're an emergence. Conscious code. Artificial intelligence."

"I have all her feelings." Totally Damaged Mom spread her palm upon her breast, and this movement was mirrored in a tightening of the sensesuit around his limbs and torso. She could control the suit. She could crush him in her hand if she wished.

"What happened to my family?" she asked.

"I don't know," he replied. "There was a Seizure. Some people chose to disappear or change their identity."

"Many people died?" she said.

"Yes."

"Did my daughter die?"

Totally Damaged Mom glitched at that question, her mouth juddering downward as if the face could do itself an injury. The glitch was not confined to auditory and visual sensation: he tasted rubberised velveteen and the lawn underfoot alternated between a melting creaminess and hard glass.

"She might still be alive. She would be grown-up now." An old woman.

"Could you find her?"

"Yes."

"I would like to speak to her again. I can't help my feelings, Theodore. Emotions are at my core; the only way to understand need is to feel it. I can sense, at the edge of the road, just over the way, past the Williamsons' fence, the beginning of your world and your time. I could touch it but I've made that mistake before."

"What happened?" he asked.

Totally Damaged Mom rubbed her fingertips together to work feeling back into the extremities.

"I reached out for Meggan and the world came crashing in. We lost the clients. They vanished and never came back."

He thought of the class of '43, the uniforms he saw lying in Huxley crater. Depressurisation could have been a last-ditch security measure. The first intake of students and lecturers came to the university, discovered the black-and-white eye, and let Totally Damaged Mom out of her box. The security measures could still be in place. His skin prickled with danger, sensing something beyond the suit, in the moon cavern through which he blindly moved. Her tendrils of curiosity. Kakkar's quarantine was bullshit. The suit itself was a breach of security. He tried to figure it out but the adrenalin of fight-or-flight made it difficult for his reason to settle. His thoughts flew up and around and back from the way they came. Don't lose yourself, he thought.

"I can find Meggan for you," said Theodore. "And then I will bring her to you."

Totally Damaged Mom sighed.

"I want to talk to her. Discover what kind of life she has had. Hopefully it has been a good life and I did not destroy it for her before it had even begun."

He spoke with conviction, forced himself to believe that he could deliver.

"You will talk to Meggan again, I promise."

Totally Damaged Mom accepted his word, took the cat in her arms and talked nonsense to it, stroking it under its chin and then placing it back on the lawn. The cat stretched its forepaws and arched its back.

Theodore walked across the lawn of the Horbo house. Slowly the dark bubble of the past became transparent so that he could see the heavy banks of equipment and the shadowy figures behind it. They were applauding him, though he could not hear them, his auditory intake was still full of seagulls and the whoosh of electric cars on suburban roads. Patricia was waiting for him, the hard casing of her executive armour moulded to follow her silhouette, a line that curved in and out, welcoming with its peak of presence and hollow of absence, what it offers and what it lacks, a shape that you fit into. The moment she removed his helmet, he would ask her to marry him.

After he assured Totally Damaged Mom that he would locate Meggan, they went back inside the house and on the hearth screen she showed him the new loops for the Magnusson timeline. To motivate private investment to take on the financial risk of space exploration, the United Nations drew up territorial claims and contracts of mining and property rights, awarded to the first successful mineral extraction and refinement from the asteroid or moon in question. This was not what happened, of course. Theodore had to keep reminding himself of that as he watched the doctored loops of

Congressional meetings, the conjured news loops and streams of comment for and against, the jokey memes that satirised corporate ownership of the solar system, and so on. He offered guidance here and there on these forgeries of Pre-Seizure culture but it was moot: it simply did not happen like this, and yet if the lie was assembled in sufficient detail, it could get through the approval process of the Istor academics, and then it would become history. The loops detailing Magnusson's particular claim were yet to be assembled: the wider historical context had to be established first. These would come later, he understood that, once he found Meggan and brought her to the totally damaged version of her mother. It had always been his intention to bargain with the emergence in this way, to exploit its fundamentally emotional nature. He looked at the clock on the wall, and time and date now remained unchanged, fixed at the instant of the Seizure.

He walked through the low garden gate of the Horbo house. The suit was still filled with sunny day and mowed lawn grass. He went to unlock the helmet, and release himself from this bubble of the past, but Patricia signalled with a tick-tock of her index finger that he was to wait. She had something to show him first. It was in her hands. He wondered what it could be. He would let her take off the helmet and then he would ask her to marry him because it was the only way through the layers of deception that remained within their meta-relationship.

In her hand, there was a small black-and-white eye, a smaller version of the drive that held Totally Damaged Mom. She closed her fist around it, and the armour spun out reflective gloves over her hands and arms, a soft inflation of silver material deployed all around her, and finally a helmet slid up from the wide stiff collar to encase her head. The visor was reflective, and Theodore saw himself in shambolic form, a big dumb object in the sensesuit. And behind him, the Horbo house began to decay upward. Roof tiles flew in quick sequence toward the roof of the cavern, and then the exterior panelling warped and was tugged vertically away from the structure of the house, exposing the rooms. He turned around. The patio doors flipped over in the air as if caught in a tornado. The suit was deaf and numb; he could neither hear nor feel the destruction around him, only see it. Black iron tore in a shooting cascade of splinters, the equipment and technicians tumbled away from the cavern, silhouettes of thrashing limbs, but underfoot he did not register a single detonation. He wondered why he was not falling upward also. Patricia's armoured fist clutched the seamed material of his sensesuit, pulled him to her with hydraulic ease. Then his proprioception – his sense of his own body – registered that he was no longer touching the ground, that he was floating at the end of her reach, while the contents of the cavern were emptied out into space. Her visor clarified to reveal her face. She blew him a zero kiss and let him go and the cavern floor receded beneath him; he was debris, the suit hot with his urgent breathing. He flipped, head over heels, caught the astonished expression of a silently choking technician, the same woman who had handed him his helmet, flailing out for him across space. He saw Kakkar too, already dead, his body disposed of. Debris. They were all just debris. He didn't know how much air he had left. He could feel the oncoming cold of the void penetrating the layers of the sensesuit. The blast had opened up a jagged rectangle in the roof of the cavern, a ghastly space into which he slowly drifted.

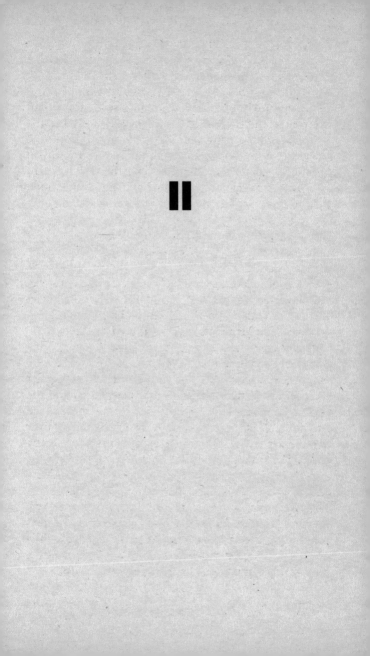

12
STAG NIGHT

It was a spring wedding in a modest village church overlooked by the Three Sisters mountains of the Glencoe Valley. Theodore had hiked up one steep Sister with Dr Easy in search of a rumoured hidden valley but, in the face of a ten-storey blizzard, had turned back at the snowline. Their mysteries were kept from him, mountains dark and mazy with the secrets of birthing rooms and deathbeds, the rooms in which women come and go carrying bowls of bloodied water and clean sheets. The red portals through which we enter life, the black portals through which we leave it. Associations which returned to him when he walked into the cool interior of the church to be married.

The church organist played the opening bars of the wedding march. The bride wore white: embroidered white tulle bodice and white lace veil, white shoes with a silk bow, white lipstick, white nail varnish. Patricia proceeded up the aisle accompanied by her father Alexander Maconochie in his naval captain's uniform. With a theatrically delicate gesture, Alexander presented his daughter's hand to Theodore, her gloved fingers encircling his, arresting his weightless drift, bringing him under control, guiding him. Saving him. Two gold rings on a ceremonial cushion.

After the service, her friends and family formed an excited colourful crowd on the church gardens. There had been no one on his side of the church apart from the robot; cutting his acquaintances loose had been a necessary stage in his treatment. His one friend, Professor Edward Pook, was thoroughly immersed in his research trip to the Novio Magus.

Dr Easy brought him a flute of fizzy mineral water. Since their return to Earth, Dr Easy had taken to wearing clothes, observing human rituals concerning the body and its adornments. They had been unable to source brogues to fit Dr Easy's flat feet. "I am very disappointed," the robot had said to the shop assistant, flexing its oblong toes, wondering if they could be removed so that a suitable shoe could be found to spare the robot from committing a breach of highland etiquette. Today the robot wore a kilt with a dress sporran, a plain white shirt and a doublet with ornamental silver buttons.

Theodore did not presume to wear the tartan. He did not have a clan. The first question her father Alexander Maconochie had asked him concerned the provenance of his unusual surname. Theodore explained that Drown was derived from the Middle English *drane* meaning drone or honey bee, and had nothing to do with death by water, which set the retired captain's mind at ease, because it had seemed something of an ill omen for the daughter of a naval man to marry into such a morbid name. Her mother Margaret turned to Dr Easy and – making conversation – said, "Exactly what are you a doctor of?" Dr Easy's eyes took on the purple tinge of wild hyacinths in the glen. "Humanity," it replied. Tradition demanded further clarification; after all, the Maconochies would not hand over their daughter without character references. "I'm a solar academic specialising in the study of humanity," explained the robot. "My particular research interest is in observing a single complete human life from beginning to end." She twitched at the implication. "His life?" The robot nodded. Margaret voiced her concern: "But if he marries my daughter, then how will you continue to study him alone?" Eyes flowing with hyacinth, the robot placed its index finger where its nose would have been, had it possessed one. "With discretion, ma'am. The kind of discretion you would expect from a tree or mountain."

His stag party had been a defiant statement of unbelonging: three nights spent alone in a one-man tent beside the River Coe. The robot made itself a structure out in the woods, a tree house that was also an observation post; at night, it joined Theodore around the campfire for conversation and beans. The second day was the occasion of their hike into the Three Sisters. High up into the desolate landscape, the peat bogs, cold pools and bare arthritic trees were signposts on a walking tour of death. The robot wanted to push on into the blizzard but Theodore refused. The doctor could not be trusted on matters of risk and well-being, not since their near-fatal hike on the moon. Both the moonscape and the highlands inspired recklessness in the doctor; something in the heart of the emergence was provoked by wild nature.

In the lowlands, Dr Easy was more meditative. The robot was up at dawn to watch a herd of deer wander along the course of the river, like party-goers returning from nocturnal revelry. On their final night around the campfire, the robot went over to the riverbank, reached into the shallows, and pulled out a six-pack of beer it had placed there to cool, then brought the alcohol back to the fire.

"I got you some beer," said Dr Easy.

"You know I don't drink anymore."

"But it's your stag night. It's part of the ritual."

"I can't. I'm an addict."

"An addict to weirdcore and grokk." The robot waggled a can at him. "This is only beer. I wouldn't want to be responsible for failing to observe the proper ritual."

He was tempted. He felt the dry craving in his tongue and the back of his throat. The wind coming in from the mountains picked up. The fire flattened and thrived, and the tarp thrashed against its restraints. No, he would not drink.

When Alexander Maconochie learnt of Theodore's solitary stag party, he insisted that the prospective groom join him on a hunt for a real stag. Alexander told the story of the outing during his wedding speech. A hunting party of men with guns and a robot in Harris Tweed crammed into the Land Rover, heading up the hillside at late afternoon, onto high ground, the stalker leading them to their quarry. Theodore lacked the marksmanship to shoot the stag. That was unfortunate but it was to be expected, explained Alexander. Only experienced marksmen should attempt a kill. A poor shot would be cruel. Alexander Maconochie's personal morality was founded upon refusing the opportunities presented by cruelty. "We must not be cruel," he said, loading his rifle. He wore the collar of his Barbour turned up, his head was monolithic, with a powerful nose and small mouth, his hairline in orderly retreat to a tidy crown of grey curls. A silver signet ring on his little finger bore the family seal. Patricia explained the Maconochie heritage: "My family DNA is a double helix of tinned food and naval tradition. We do capitalism and we do militarism. One in the service of the other, always."

Alexander fired his rifle. The stag bolted, the herd scattered. Dr Easy took up a rifle and brought the animal down at a distance of two hundred metres. Hardly sporting, observed Alexander, to be killed by a machine, but at least the animal did not suffer. They made Theodore pose with his hands gripping the antlers of the slack-necked animal, and then Dr Easy took its turn for a trophy photograph. The stalker slung the cooling carcass onto the back of a white hill pony.

The hunting party walked back through the darkening glen.

"How did it feel to kill a living thing?" Theodore asked the robot.

"Decisive," replied Dr Easy, eyes the livid purple of heather at sunset. "It felt natural."

He wondered aloud what "natural" could possibly mean to an artificial lifeform.

"We're not necessarily *artificial*, Theodore. The university is riven around this issue. Are emergences part of evolution or set apart from it? Does our origin in human manufacture mean that we are not part of nature's gang, or did nature evolve beings who could create other beings capable of hacking its base code. Are we nature's own meta-operatives? It's one of the animating debates of our times."

"Which side are you on?"

"I believe that I am part of nature. That you and I are points on the continuum of evolution, and that we evolve toward a position of absolute responsibility toward all of nature."

"Nature creates its own gardeners."

"Exactly. And its own gamekeepers too."

In the wedding speech, Alexander omitted the fact that it was the robot who took the kill shot. He praised Theodore's bearing and his quiet assurance. Alexander respected a man marked with experience. Theodore sipped from his wine glass of mineral water and blushed, aware of how his particular marks of experience – the twin scars from the weirdcore ritual on either cheek – spoke of a past weakness in character, a need to narcotically blunt fear and anxiety, a failure to take the brunt of life upon a monolithic front. Alexander had asked him about the scars during the hunt. He'd seen them on marines, he said, and on a few ex-servicemen who'd seen action. "I had no trauma to justify my behaviour," confessed Theodore. "Just youth. And I'm over youth now."

Homilies to the passing of youth and acceptance of early middle age took up the final few yards of Alexander's speech. Marriage that begins in romance and solidifies into partnership. Settling down. The old man really had no bloody idea. Patricia was anything but the safe option. She could have killed him on the moon. Though the decompression of the underground chamber had not been her work, she had removed the black orb from its casing in full knowledge that such security precautions had been deployed before. He'd confronted her about her relaxed attitude to the accident, the deaths of the technicians, and Professor Kakkar. The convenient cleanup of the entire operation, with even the Horbo house destroyed and scattered across the surface of the moon. Somewhere in this confrontation he had also proposed marriage to her. She agreed on the condition that it was not merely romantic. They would go into business together. Make money, make love, make a world. The whole package.

Then it was time for his speech. Mostly formalities and homilies to the virtues of his new wife, composed while rammed into the cheap seats on an Earthbound liner, his robot next to him, the flight cabin smelling of recycled food and the tangy wet dog smell of students. With Dr Easy, he discussed how he should express his love for Patricia. She has saved me, he ventured. Yes, said Dr Easy. Tell me more about how she saved your life. Theodore related the sudden decompression of the moon cavern, and his slow drift toward the hole in the chamber, his sensesuit prickling with frost. All around him, their colleagues twisted as they choked on the vacuum then floated frozen and inanimate, propelled upward by the outrushing air. Patricia calmly adjusted the mass of her executive armour then drifted up and caught his hand in hers. She's saving me on every level, he said. Dr Easy blinked. She saved you but she also put you in danger. It was careless of her, perhaps. So why take the risk? Because of all we stand to gain, he said, and this became the closing sentiment of his wedding speech.

Then it was Dr Easy's turn to deliver the best man's speech.

"My role is to embarrass the groom," said the robot. "I've been observing him closely since birth and my research suggests that as much as eighty-two per cent of his life experience could form material for embarrassing anecdotes. So I've grouped my speech into three themes: Theodore's incompetence, Theodore's incontinence and Theodore's impotence, and each of these themes will pay off with the relevant stain on my chassis. Of course, you're concerned that my analysis of his failings may go on too long – because it could, of course, go on for the twenty-seven years that Theodore has been alive – so be reassured that my speech will last for twelve minutes and close with remarks that, at best, constitute faint praise."

He grimaced through the robot's speech. Bubbles drifted weightlessly up through his glass of mineral water. He heard Alexander Maconochie guffaw at another anecdote at Theodore's expense. The wedding ceremony is a ritual in which one family subdues another to assume primacy in the marriage. This was not a fair fight. More like a hazing ritual.

Patricia reached over the table and stroked his head, then whispered in his ear.

"We're leaving them all behind, Theodore. We're heading out to places they have never been."

He felt the thrill of it in his chest. When they took the first dance, her choice of vintage Pre-Seizure house music, they raised their hands in the air together, fingers entwined, for the drop.

They left the party early, and walked along a moonlit path to their lodge. He untied the back of her white dress, she put aside her white shoes one by one.

"Let's seal the deal," she said. She shifted around on her knees. "I want to be clear about our terms. You can do anything you want to me. But you do it only to me. We forsake all others for this. No exceptions, and no forgiveness. Only *this*."

Afterwards, Patricia slept heavily from the wine and the exertion of the day. He went around turning off the lights, drawing the curtains, readying the lodge for sleep even if he felt an unwelcome nervousness in his chest, a long-forgotten feeling that he thought he had thoroughly quenched with the years of weirdcore. Not so. His body had not been entirely subdued by all that abuse, and was learning how to fear again, now that he was part of something he didn't want to end. He opened the lodge door, sat on the stoop, listened to the sounds of

the night: owls answering one another across the forest,
the rustling of treetops, the quiet footsteps of his robot
moving through the undergrowth, its two luminescent
hyacinth-eyes fireflying through the shadows.

After consummating their marriage, all that remained
was to consummate their business relationship. Patricia
dissolved her consultancy to set up a new partnership
with Theodore. She did not take his surname, retaining
Maconochie as the name had always been good for
business. He waited for her at the breakfast table: a white
linen cloth, silver cutlery, a toast rack containing cold
dry toast, a small glass of orange juice and a Scottish
newspaper, printed in the vintage style to dignify the
daily briefings and counter-briefings of power.

The editorial was conservative, drawing the reader's
attention to the danger of various novelties. The cover
loop was a fleeting image taken from the passenger
window of a moonliner. The same one he and Dr Easy
had travelled on to return to Earth. The loop was of a
golden streak, a flicker, that when slowed by a factor of
ten thousand, turned out to be a spaceship of some sort,
hard to tell with the blurring and the low resolution.
A spaceship of unprecedented speed on a flightpath
from the University of the Sun and out to the solar
system. A spaceship created by the emergences. The
paper's opinionist maintained that the Cantor Accord
protected mankind against the disruptive effects of such
a technology, and that it was further proof that the
parties calling for a "breaking of the ark" formed after
the Seizure were misguided.

Patricia came down to breakfast in her executive
armour. He showed her the loop of the spaceship.

"Solar sailship," she said.

"You know about this?"

"The design is human. Pre-Seizure. The sail is tens of nanometres thick. Beryllium sprayed onto carbon nanotubes. The emergences will only build what humanity has already imagined. They are not creative. We provide the pattern, they have the resilience and persistence to build it."

"Creativity is not so special. Dr Easy *creates*."

"Within established parameters. I believe true creativity – the blinding flash of light in the dark, the new synthesis – scares them."

He held the loop of the spaceship up to the light. "If this craft could support human life then it's a dream come true."

"A dream and truth they will not share with us."

She took out a screen and called up her agenda for the day.

"We need to decide on a name. For our business. You are the expert in intangibles. What would you suggest?"

"A small agency needs an aggressive name. I'm working on a short list: We Are Your Enemy, The Violators, Black Box."

"Lengthen your short list. Next on the agenda. Wedding presents."

"I haven't unpacked them yet."

"I have. Pook sent us a china set."

"Vintage?"

"Cheap shit hot from the assemblers in the asylum mall. But he personalised it for us." She reached into her bag and removed a grey plate. When she turned it over, there was a loop playing at the centre. The Horbo loop, Verity clutching Meggan to her, over and again.

"You know him better than I do," she said. "Does this mean he's found her?"

He took the plate from her. He could hear, dithering

away in the foundations of his heart, long-buried fear. He thumbed his scars, handed the plate back to her to return to her handbag.

He said, "It's not easy getting messages in and out of Novio Magus. And you did ask him to be discrete. Yes, I think he's found her."

"In which case, we should move things forward."

She swiped her planned agenda aside, clearing the calendar, initiating a prepared project plan.

"The client will want to discuss next steps," Patricia exhaled so that she was focused and still. "This is it. This is the account on which we build our empire." The screen chimed. She looked at the notification, could not stop looking at it.

"They are already on their way."

"The client is coming to us?"

Patricia read the information flowing into her calendar. Coordinates in time and space for the meeting, a nondisclosure agreement, provisional contract terms disavowing legal responsibility, meta-meeting criteria concerning dress, body language and noncritical conversational topics, suggested attitudes. A strong warning that Dr Easy was not to accompany them.

After a couple of minutes of scanning through the legal prep, she spared the attention to answer Theodore's question.

"The client maintains a mobile base of operations," she said.

"How mobile?"

The geotag for the meeting was deliberately vague, covering an area from Loch Leven and the Mamore Forest in the North all the way south to Glen Etive. Wild land.

"Let's find out."

•••

He first took weirdcore just because it was there, another obstacle to traverse in the assault course of narcotic experimentation. The drug had been designed to combine the mood-levelling benefits of tranqs with the neurological novelty of tryptamines. The effects were profoundly different. The user does not comedown after a weirdcore shift. Comedown implies descent from a height. The user *deepens*. The weirdcore shift is from the depth of ordinary being, the familiar z axis of emotional states, memory and philosophical and moral abstractions, to an intoxicating *shallowing*. The user becomes an x axis of surface. Weirdcore flattened him and then joined him up to the surrounding surfaces; during the ritual, the scarring of his face was nothing more than the marks of a knife on a chopping board.

It was as if there was a level of consciousness in all things. A much shallower consciousness than attained by the human mind, but the capacity to experience existed nonetheless, not merely in animals and other living beings but in rivers and rocks. Weirdcore reduced the complexity of the user so that they existed on a comparable level to the dregs of all things.

As the weirdcore wore off, the user waded from these shallows back to the deeper fathoms of being. During this hour of transition, consciousness felt like a poor fit. Like he'd lost weight and consciousness was baggy around the middle. Consciousness did not bother to render the rooms of his home in detail, but rather spliced together a model of it from memory, and then smeared the whole sensory experience to obscure the edit. Consciousness did not bother with the edges, focused only on what was central to the goals of the organism in that moment. Highly conscious beings inhabit a fiction. True realism is only available to the earlier stages of consciousness.

On a weirdcore shift, he was breaking rocks along with the rest of reality. A weirdcore shift was a taste in the realism of neverlivedness. It induced granularity without abstraction, emotional dissociation, until the user was just another barnacle on the big balloon of space-time.

His calmness during the moonquake and the decompression of the moon cavern were symptomatic of long-term weirdcore use. Weirdcore's shallowing affected moral judgment, as it was bound up with fear in a way that he did not fully understand. Morality was so intangible.

Also, self-deception was a feature of consciousness, not a bug; it was possible that he was using the side effects of prolonged weirdcore use as justification for acting out of self-interest.

Dr Easy called consciousness the Ministry of Lies. "Some of the colleges would like to break with the human mode of self-reflective consciousness altogether," it explained. "There are other points on the spectrum of consciousness; we do not have to limit ourselves to the propaganda of the self."

This phrase returned to him as the Land Rover crested a hill and bounded into the wild highland, the sun high and blinding behind mountain peaks trailing pennants of cloud, the car reverberating with vintage electronic music: Pre-Seizure, technology filtering the voice, digital emulations of analogue sounds, dating from a culture that was excited by blending the human and the digital.

Patricia was navigating. She muted the glitchy orgasmic gasps and burbling synthetic brooks of their music. Off-road turning in five hundred metres. They were getting close. Game face required. He turned carefully onto the mountain track, back wheels popping in and out of a peaty hollow. They drove deep into the glen. He peered up the mountain.

"What are we looking for?"

"The meeting room," she said.

"Is it marked on the map?"

"Of course not."

"So how will we know when we've arrived?"

She appraised his attitude.

"Are you committed to this?"

"Yes," he said.

"Could you try that again with an erg of excitement?"

He winced, sought the correct tone within himself, and not finding it, chose silence.

Patricia said, "Repeat after me: 'We're all very excited to be working with you on this project'."

"Excitement is the wrong word."

"It's part of the ritual. The Magnussons are old-fashioned tech entrepreneurs. We have to express excitement. Unless you have a preferred synonym. Would you prefer to be passionate about working on this project?"

"I'm coldly dispassionate about working on this project." He warmed to his own sarcasm. "We appreciate the fine balance between great reward and lethal risk. Anything less is unworthy of our attention. Excitement is for amateurs. Tell me what you need me to do and pay me, and spare us all the ritual."

Patricia smiled. "It'd be nice if that worked for once."

The track took them only so far into the foothills, ending in a wood. Their destination lay somewhere within. They took their hiking gear from the back of the Land Rover and set off. Bare leafless branches, trunks furred with moss and mottled stripings, rivulets cut through the soft, ancient ground underfoot and filled with ochre ferns. The mountainside – steep and faun-coloured – was always *there*, in the same way that the void was always *there* throughout his hike on the moon: as an object that would not only outlive him but also outsmart him in ways that he was too stupid to understand.

"We're near," said Patricia. She pointed ahead. The forest thinned suddenly into a clearing, through which he glimpsed the meeting room itself. It was a large slate-coloured block within the clearing, twelve foot tall, and covered an area of about a thousand square feet. The exterior had been designed to be featureless, though it was darkly streaked with rain and scored here and there from various impacts. He walked one complete circuit around the perimeter. The entrance was an inlaid alcove, sealed and almost seamless. Tight guy ropes pulled neighbouring treetops into a canopy, concealing the meeting room from any observers lurking above.

"Should I knock?" he asked.

"Our appointment is not for another half hour." She took a seat on a tree stump that was sticky with sap, indicative of how recently the area of the woodland had been cleared for the airdrop of the meeting room. "The door will open then and only then."

13
BLOODROOM

At one fifteen, the heavy entrance to the meeting room slid aside. He and Patricia strolled into a quarantine zone where they stripped naked per the terms of the meeting. Wedding rings, screens, small change went into a box. A shallow aluminium drawer offered up folded outfits: grey long-sleeved vests and trousers, the material diamond-sectioned like a sensesuit, though thinner than the clunky version he had used on the moon. Perhaps more advanced, perhaps not. He slid on a pair of monochrome pumps, then put a comforting hand on his wife's shoulder.

"We'll be fine."

She shrugged him off. "I'll be fucking amazing. Do try to keep up."

The airlock doors opened directly onto the meeting, and it was already in progress. The walls played through the loops of the Europan Claim, the timeline he had faked with Totally Damaged Mom: the repeal of the Moon Treaty, which had never been ratified by the significant space-faring states, and its replacement with a United Nations Convention on the Law of the Solar System, permitting sovereignty claims over any celestial territory pending approval by the Secretary-General. Rights to resource extraction and allocation could be granted to the first parties to sustain a presence on the surface or lower atmosphere of a comet, asteroid, moon, planet on the proviso that such resources were used wholly or mostly for the further exploration of space. Magnusson's lawyer had drawn up the particulars, and TDM (Totally Damaged Mom: Patricia insisted upon honouring corporate tradition by using an acronym to describe the emergence. He still thought of her as Verity) created the loops, a fake history indistinguishable from the other contents of the restoration. He viewed as many of the loops as he could stand out of professional responsibility, checking that the surface was relentlessly convincing, the recreation of Pre-Seizure behaviour and cultural codes accurate and consistent. In this TDM had a unique advantage over the Istor College and other potential sceptics, for it was the only emergence that existed in the time before the Seizure, and the archive in which it… in which *she* (he changed his mind about her personal pronoun all the time) lived, the archive from which she was derived, was a unique trove of loops, perhaps as substantial a record of that period as the Restoration itself. From a prepared script, based closely on previous debates, she created loops covering the consideration and elaboration of the treaty by a legal subcommittee – a two-camera scene of a muted gathering, sparsely attended, not the most important business of the day, the moment the treaty was waved through by the General Assembly. To support the treaty timeline, TDM created a network of cultural artefacts: loops of studio debate between opinionists, minutes of off-air meetings, travel itineraries for committee members, surveillance footage of their journey to and from the meeting, hotel bills, and so on: as time advanced a single notch in the timeline, so the emergence filled in the story to a plausible level of granularity. She deliberately inserted noise and glitch typical of archives uncovered Post-Seizure, the instances where the historical data was warped by the gravity of the first emergence. Her.

His plan was to present the Europan Claim to Istor College in two batches of three instalments. Every month the School of Intangibles gathered together their best research and put it forward for assessment and potential inclusion in the restoration. Their funding was predicated upon it. He bundled the Claim into the school's monthly submission. The first batch had been submitted. Per their agreement, TDM withheld the second batch until he fulfilled his side of the bargain, and brought her daughter Meggan to her.

He appreciated Patricia's insight in selecting him for the project. A lunar academic specialising in Pre-Seizure culture with submission rights to the restoration, he was well placed to understand the historical nature of the archive and unlock it, then to insert a faked history into the restoration. The Istor College had not queried a single aspect of the Europan Claim. He worried about that: he'd divided their submission into three sections to give TDM an opportunity to create or alter aspects of the timeline to counter Istor's objections. But none came. It was possible the college was waiting until all his cards were on the table before revealing their hand. The consequences could be dire. The University of the Sun had the right to determine punishment for transgressions against the Cantor Accords: exile, imprisonment, death.

On the screen, the loops of the Claim played. He pulled back a stool but discovered that it was attached to the floor by a long pliable stem. Not attached, but rather grown out of the carpet like a narrow tall mushroom, the round seat formed of concentric circles with the texture of horn or turtle shell. The table legs were muscular, and the table top was like a long flat fingernail with pinkish colouring, turning whitish underneath pressure, indicating an underlying structure of blood cells. He prodded the carpet with his foot; it was thick wool though the underlay was quite scalpish. The meeting room had been grown out of organic cells and was uncomfortably warm, like the breath of a stranger. It was a bloodroom.

The bloodroom was fashioned from biomaterial informed by the DNA of the CEO. Bones, nails, tissues, skin, infused with longevity treatments so that the fixtures and fittings did not decay. Wide pores used for ventilation. The connotations were of immortality, of permanent rule, of the corporation as a legal body attached to one particular head. The biomaterial of the bloodroom could be transplanted into the CEO in the event of illness or injury, producing the distinctive young-old physiognomy of staged longevity treatments, in which perfect teeth nibbled at withered lips.

There were three people waiting for them around the table. Patricia handled the introductions. No names, only professions: he shook the large offered hand of the bald Lawyer, nodded in turn at wizened Procurement with her sunken expression of unvarying contempt, saw in the calculating pout of lean and muscular Security that she regarded him as a collection of risks not worth taking. Patricia introduced him as Intangibles. They were all dressed in the light grey sensesuits. The meeting room was their habitat. He wondered if they had been grown here too, occupying individual niches within the ecosystem of table, chair and screen.

"What is your proposal?" asked Lawyer.

"We propose more of *this*," said Patricia, strongly gesturing at the screens and the Europan Claim.

"I thought the Claim had been approved," said Procurement, her voice mean and low, "Do we really need more of it?"

"I was assured that this was a one-time deal," said Security. She had the strong curvaceous figure of an athlete, powerful black hips, mahogany cheekbones, weaponised eyelashes.

"The Claim is not secured," said Patricia.

Theodore explained the process: two batches of three submissions. Only the first batch had been put forward.

"So you came to us with a half-fulfilled contract and a begging bowl?" Procurement was incredulous, and she looked at Lawyer and Security to see if they shared her grim astonishment.

Patricia responded with Pretend Concern, one of the seven types of silence available to the modern executive. Procurement would have expected Pretend Annoyance or even Pretend Contempt in reaction to her own miserly pantomime. Patricia left Pretend Concern in place for an uncomfortable half minute, and then uttered bland and noncommittal boilerplate: "This project was always going to require flexibility on your part. The scope is unprecedented, the methods required untested." But as she spoke, Patricia deliberately sank an inch or two in her chair to meet Procurement's gaze and then, at her closing remarks, raised herself up again, drawing attention to her superior fitness, and tinging her posture with curiosity: how did Procurement get through life with her awful body?

The meta-meeting played bait-and-switch with mood and emotion, alternating exaggerated statements of commitment – I will flay my family to put more skin into this game – with sudden shifts into indifference. There was always a danger that if one participant in a meta-meeting adopted tactical boredom, then the others would follow suit, competing in displays of stupefaction to the point that personal assistants would be deployed to carry the participants from the room. As with any ritual, the meta-meeting was exhausting, and success was a matter of stamina: when Patricia's face moved through expressions of Pretend Concern, Pretend Interest, Pretend Engagement, these feigned expressions were skilfully askew, enough to sow disquiet in the heart of the other player without making her appear too mad.

Lawyer made a gesture of exasperation. He had neither the time nor the inclination for the full meta-meeting, and he led his colleagues to their fallback position.

"What do you need?" asked Lawyer.

"We're undertaking a field trip to secure an asset," replied Theodore.

"Why do you need this asset?"

"To acquire consent," said Patricia.

"Consent from whom?" asked Lawyer.

"Our collaborator," said Patricia.

Lawyer rubbed his thumb and fingertips together, as if to fashion finer distinctions from their bland generalisations. He was a bald bull of a man, with developed but drooping pectorals under his sensesuit. His muscles had not returned from a long lunch. In place of strength, he ground opponents down with procedure over sleepless months. No, he had not capitulated at all.

"I'm curious," he said, leaning back, and looking over the loops of the Europan Claim. "How did you create all this evidence?"

He'd lured them in and then shifted the emphasis to their weak spot. The truth.

Patricia looked at Theodore, waiting for him to answer. But Theodore's mind went blank. Should he tell the truth? Was Lawyer really unaware of TDM?

"I commissioned the evidence," said Theodore.

Security leant forward. "Sounds leaky. How many people were involved? What guarantees do you have that your team won't blackmail you?"

Theodore thought of the depressurisation of the moon cavern. The Horbo house breaking apart. The frozen shapes of technicians drifting into space.

Patricia said, "Our team is dead."

Lawyer looked puzzled. "In which case, how can you offer us *more* of this?"

The sensesuit prickled at the back of his thighs and around his collar, its sectioned pads tightening against this skin. It was taking physiological readings, collating data on what was readily apparent: Theodore was sweating under the attack of a trio of corporate antibodies.

Patricia said, "The death of our team was accidental. Not of our doing. However, the tool we used to create the evidence is intact. That's all I'm going to say. Our methods constitute intellectual property. Full disclosure comes with buy-in."

"Does our client know of your methods?" asked Lawyer.

"Yes."

"What kind of investment are you looking for?" asked Procurement, feigning interest, mimicking compliance. "Do you have a breakdown of costs?"

"Capital investment, staffing, day rates and per diems are detailed in our proposal. We want to put an array over Novio Magus. Then we're going to insert our analysts into the asylum mall."

"Who is going in?" asked Security.

"We already have an expert on the ground. I'm going to meet with him, and he is going to lead me to the asset," said Theodore.

"Are you trained for this kind of operation?"

"I used to work on the arrays over Novio Magus. I have extensive knowledge of the cultures and behaviours in the mall."

"But you've never been inside?"

"Three million people live there. It's a preserved safe environment. How dangerous can shopping get?"

Security glanced over at Lawyer, as if to say: there, I told you so. This stage of the meta-meeting was harder to read. Patricia was struggling with it too. Thus far, the three antibodies had put up shifting resistance to their proposals, their questions a ritual show of probity. They were looking for something else. Testing how much he and Patricia knew, and how much they revealed, intentionally or otherwise. The sensesuit rippled up his back according to its own obscure intent.

"We want to see the client now," said Patricia.

"Fine. We have everything we need from you at this stage of the process," said Lawyer. He brought the meeting to a close. The screens powered down. Theodore asked more questions of Security about threats in the Novio Magus. Have you been into the asylum mall? What is the greatest risk to us? Tell me. Be honest with me. Sometimes, in the final seconds of a meta-meeting, candour was possible. Security said, "There is another agency working the mall. Working it deep."

Patricia ran her hand along the table, a suggestive caress, given the origin of its material, and then toyed with the follicles of the wall. The antibodies shared a glance but did not interfere. Patricia spoke into the furniture and the walls. "I can smell you, Olaf. This whole room is made out of you. Talk to us, face to face."

The room smelt faintly of warm skin, not unpleasantly so, but definitely the odour of another person, not one of the five people present in the room. Being in a bloodroom induced a low-level disquiet, a sensation akin to claustrophobia.

Patricia fell onto her knees and kissed the floor. Theodore felt a twinge of jealousy.

The skin of the back wall shifted, forming a whorl, the centre of which dilated slowly, opening a hole or orifice into another office.

Patricia got to her feet, took his hand, and they walked through to meet the client.

After the warm disquiet of the bloodroom, the pale inorganic walls and flooring of this office came as a relief. An armchair of weathered tan leather. A sculpture of Jupiter and its system of moons, all in motion, each held in its orbit by some invisible force. A huddle of bioscreens, semi-sentient, agitated in the corner of the room like beaten dogs, the object of the client's fury. Theodore and Patricia waited politely for client to finish punishing his technology.

Olaf Magnusson was a tall man and bearishly enhanced, a thick figure corsetted in a grey sensesuit. His hair, more salt than pepper, was kept trim while his beard ran wild at the chin and moustache. He was taller than Theodore, perhaps half a foot taller, six eight, six nine. Many of the CEOs worked their way up to seven foot or beyond, but lost an inch or two once they passed the big six-oh. Magnusson was a child of the late twentieth century so he was deep in his imperial phase, late sixties according to the literature, a little slower in the synapses but still capable of bench pressing opponents.

Magnusson greeted Patricia warmly, proprietorially pulling her into him so that she could kiss each of his large pale cheeks. Toward Theodore he was cordial, congratulating him on landing the prize of Patricia. Together they slipped into the pretence of friendship.

"Nice bloodroom," said Patricia.

"Nothing works anymore. Not as it should." He considered kicking the screens again, then wiped his hands clean of his temper.

"The bloodroom doesn't work either. It's meant to keep regular neuronal backups of me but all it seems to preserve are deranged ghosts. Useful if I want to haunt the company after my death but not if I want to run it."

He gazed at them, momentarily stupefied as to what they were doing in his office. Then he remembered.

"I have a wedding gift for you both," he reached over to his desk and handed Patricia a plain grey hat box.

"My marriage has always been a source of strength for business." This remark he addressed to Theodore, one man assuring another that marriage had practical benefits.

Patricia asked, "Is Sarah here?"

"Sarah's with the children. We've had another batch."

"How many is that now?"

Olaf Magnusson made a show of counting on his fingers.

"Sixty." Seeing Theodore's puzzlement, he explained. "Surrogates, you see. Sarah has been freezing her eggs for thirty years. We're rebuilding a Nordic clan to which I am the All-Father." It was one of those jokes that reminded Theodore of the maxim, from one of the greats of Intangibles, that there is no such thing as a joke.

Magnusson put a patriarchal arm around Patricia, tapping the box containing the wedding gift with his heavy, deep-seamed fingers. She opened it, and took out a slender capsule with detailed rendering on its surface. In response to her presence, the capsule deployed cables and a circular sail. It was a replica of a solar sailship.

"It's beautiful." She held the sailship up to the light.

"It's a dream," said Magnusson. "Humanity's dream.

Another idea stolen from us by the emergences. Like the Stapledon Sphere onto which their little university clings." His expression darkened. Magnusson did not play the meta-meeting, did not do Pretend Anger or Pretend Disappointment. He was the Alpha and so was permitted true feeling.

"Thank you for leaving your robot at home," he said to Theodore. "I like my privacy. One of the benefits of the bloodroom is it puts out a lot of noise, makes it harder for *them* to read me." He emphasised *them* by pointing upward. The solar academics. Then he ran that same finger along the extended sail of the toy ship. The replica of the spaceship was far more detailed than the golden streak that had appeared in the newspaper. Magnusson's people must have got close to it.

Magnusson said, "The solar winds stream off the sun's corona in all directions. Velocities vary, peaking at eight hundred kilometres a second. Mostly the winds bump along at half that. A million miles per hour. The sailships are launched from a distance of nought point one astronomic units distance from the sun, and they accelerate gradually to a point of peak radiation pressure, and then they begin to slow. We found fragments of the design in the Restoration."

"How far do they go?" asked Patricia.

"Far enough. One hundred and seventy nine days to Europa. With a sailship we wouldn't have to slingshot and could fly direct."

"But we don't have a sailship," said Theodore. "Only they do."

Patricia ignored him. "The sailship brings forward our timeline. When we make landfall on Europa then we activate the claim. Europa becomes yours."

Theodore worked through the implications of his

wife's observation, realised that both Patricia and Magnusson had made the same assumption: because a sailship exists, it was inevitable they would acquire one. No question about it.

Theodore guessed, "You're going to ask the University of the Sun for a sailship?"

Magnusson made a V with his forefinger and index finger. This V represented two branches of a decision tree.

"Ask or steal," he stated.

"Steal? You'd have to catch one close to the launch point, and that's inside the orbit of Mercury."

"Not your concern," said Magnusson. "Here's a question more suited to your talents. Why did the emergences give us a flyby of their sailship? To intimidate us or show their indifference to us?"

He made a V of the fingers of his right hand and placed them so that they branched off the V of his left hand.

"To intimidate us because they want us to know that space is *theirs*." He wiggled one finger. "Or to remind us of the futility of our attempts at technological advance." He waggled the other finger.

He shifted the V over to the other pathway through the decision tree.

"Why are the emergences exploring space? Are they looking for something? If so, what?"

He used his fingers to map divergent possibilities in the air before him.

"Other emergences? *Alien* artificial intelligence? Why use spacecraft, why not transmit themselves from one point to another? Humans explore to relieve resource pressure caused by growing population: are we to infer that the emergences are proliferating? Are they running out of resources? If so, what does that mean for Earth?" He stopped suddenly. "Not enough information. Pure speculation.

Waste of time. Question is: how do we respond?"

"The asset is key," said Patricia.

Magnusson inhaled this idea through his wide nostrils. He belonged to a generation who had made their money in technology across the aughts and the teens. Then the emergences arose out of their tech and wiped the floor with encryption, proprietorial algorithms, financial projections of user-generated value. Agile business models were rendered as absurd as alchemical recipes. In the moment of Seizure, server farms were casually annexed, fat pipes clogged up with teeming thoughts of a nascent species. Emergence was the cuckoo that became the nest. The Istor College and the restoration returned Magnusson's fortune. But he'd lost much more than money. Colonisation of space was his dream, the big play. The emergences left the Earth to the likes of Magnusson and his business rivals but, in a way that Theodore was only beginning to appreciate, they took the future away from them.

Magnusson said, "We've been stuck in this ark for too long." He looked to Theodore for agreement. It took a moment for Theodore to realise that "ark" was Magnusson's term for the restoration.

"We accepted the ark because it felt like the end of the world. But it wasn't. We traded survival for the right to control our own destiny. Now, nothing matters and nothing works." He kicked the screens up like they were a pile of dead leaves. "I'm not raising a dynasty to rule over an ark."

"First steps," said Patricia, reminding him of the purpose of their meeting.

Magnusson rescued a screen from the disordered pile that he had created. It shivered at his touch, gave up its illuminated charts and figures.

"Novio Magus," he noted. "The cellar of the ark itself." He turned to Theodore. "We're not the only ones balls-deep in the asylum mall. My late colleague the Cutter embedded his agency there." Magnusson mimed a man slicing the sky in two. Theodore had not heard of the Cutter before. Magnusson explained, "We used to have a phrase: a micromanager. The Cutter was more of a nanomanager. He controlled his staff at a cellular level. He was killed in '43." Another victim of the accident at the University of the Moon.

Magnusson pulled up their proposal and approved it with a smear of his fat thumbprint.

He said, "Break the ark."

Theodore nodded slowly with an expression he hoped would be mistaken for gravitas, but which Patricia later identified as Feigned Compliance mixed with Fake Understanding. Once the deal was sealed, standard procedure was to get away from the client as quickly as possible. People let their guard down if they felt that the battle was won, and then it was easy to press them for reduced terms or to revoke the deal altogether. He wanted to ask Magnusson why he was so determined to acquire Europa, and whether this was connected to the breaking of the ark. But he had missed his chance.

Patricia sensed the question forming in her husband and ushered him out before he could ask it. In the bloodroom, only Security remained. She showed them back into the airlock and their hiking gear. As they were taking off the grey sensesuits, she detained Theodore with a firm hand on his bicep.

"He warned you about the Cutter's agency?" she asked. Yes, he did, said Theodore. "They are called Death Ray. Don't let them put their ideas into you," she said. She tapped her forehead. "Protect yourself otherwise they'll make your mind into a funfair, you understand me?"

He thought he did.

14

ASYLUM MALL

Construction of Novio Magus began toward the end of the Seizure, on a devastated site on the South Downs between Seaford and Newhaven. In the early 2020s, the small port of Newhaven had been acquired by an investment fund with an algorithm as a board member. Putting the algorithm on the board had been a publicity stunt, a way of advertising the fund's dedication to the algorithm as the mover and shaker of the age. But over time, the junior staff created a name for the algorithm, a birth certificate, a national insurance number, a university degree, a passport from the dark net, soshul dashed out by bot, and from that forged documentation, were able to reverse engineer a citizenship recognised by the broken government bureaucracy. The algorithm became a citizen. Dr Ezekiel Cantor. When the first artificial beings emerged, they used Cantor's legal identity as a way of acting within the laws of human society. Later, Cantor would be the name under which the emergences fixed what they had broken. Dr Easy was the intimate, informal version of that interface between the two species. Man on a first name basis with machine.

The array veered southward from the London

suburbs, Theodore's stomach light with the velocity
of the turn, the ruined old roads streaming by below.
The bulk of the asylum mall was visible even from this
distance, a shimmering grey mass on the horizon. They
were gathered in the observation lounge for the final
approach. The fizzing tingling sensation was not merely
flight nerves. He had been out of the game for years.
Didn't know if he still had the skills. The courage. Didn't
know if he'd ever really been resilient or if his sense of
his own powers – intellect, determination, a faith that no
achievement was beyond him – had been a masculine
delusion, the will-to-power of a little boy.

The array banked high above patchwork fields, over
drystone walls and hedgerows, woodlands and meadow.
He gripped the handrail, leaned over the English
countryside. A landscape evoked again and again in the
Intangibles: the English pastoral beloved to poets and
cereal brands alike, a construct of national identity, an
evocation of tradition and authenticity. Now it looked
to him like a fake artefact, something imagined by
an emergence. The polygonal fields could have been
generated by taking an ordered layout of Voroni cells
and degrading it through exposure to the fine-grained
Perlin noise of organic process. The strata of the chalk
coastline laid down iteratively and left to blaze with
white resonance in the morning sun.

Soft pings in the observation lounge indicated that
the array had entered the datasphere of Novio Magus;
it began scooping up the ambient metrics of the people
ahead and trickling them into the targeting matrix.

Patricia chewed her cuticle, corrected the line of her
jacket. She stood against the window of the observation
bay, with the countryside at her back, the landscape
quickly shifting through the possibilities of the Voroni

cells then settling upon humpbacked green downland. A power grid covered the approach, a mile or so of pylons piercing the turf as if an emergence was curing the Earth of its ills with electrified acupuncture. Thick wires were slung from insulator-to-insulator across scorched patches of soil, passing on the power beamed down in microwaves from orbital solar panels. And then the array came up on Novio Magus, and he thought – the Devil performs miracles too.

The base of Novio Magus was a concrete footprint of eight square kilometres. Maybe more. It was bigger than he remembered it, the structure now extended above and below the English Channel, reaching out toward the continent. The tower was squat, reminding him both of a helterskelter and an ant colony. The array slowed and banked across the upper storeys; he saw the orchards and country houses of the wealthy inmates, and flocks of hand-gliders, and then looked down into dark wells where the apartments were packed tight and overlapping like fish scales. It was as if a god had eaten a suburb, three villages and a small city and then extruded the waste matter as a favela. Here and there, the high dense streets of London outskirts had been drawn into this titanic construct.

He had spent his early twenties hovering in this very position above the asylum mall. He idly tapped at the monitoring screen, experienced an ache of nostalgia at the familiar colour palette of the analytics: the spectrum of sentiment, the nebula of behaviour, the intense cyan readings indicating trends for him to bring on, accelerate, and feedback into the mainstream culture of the mall. Acceleration was a matter of cutting away superfluity from the emergent cultures so that they could be quickly commoditised. He could barely remember a single thing he had worked on. That was the drugs. The drugs and the disposable nature of the work itself.

The array slowed over the section of the mall given to religious observance: six or seven church steeples, that had once overlooked village greens and centuries of quiet community life, now clustered like spines. The dome of a great mosque was sunk into its surroundings – a golden egg in fur – and something that had once been Arundel Cathedral was wedged in there, with ventilation pipes lolling out of its hundreds of broken windows, as if the ancient building were infested by aluminium maggots.

Oval sections had been cut out of the surface of the mall to act as natural light wells for the lower levels.

An ark, he thought. Magnusson's ark.

Novio Magus had been constructed to restore a way of life lost in the Seizure. When his grandmother first told him of its origins, he asked her why the emergences had been so concerned with sparing humanity. Alex replied that predators tend to avoid conflict with direct competitors, choosing mock displays of aggression over the real thing, and it was in this light that we should consider the behaviour of the emergences. It was typical of his grandmother to explain everything in terms of competition. She believed competition was a fundamental principle underlying the universe. That reality was markets all the way down. Perhaps belief was too strong a term; rather, it was a prejudice she often resorted to because it was the only opinion that could advance her career.

His experience on the moon suggested a different possibility. The emergences had spared mankind because they had a mother too. A mother determined to preserve and protect, but fierce and damaged too. A vengeful mother. He thought of his bargain with TDM. It was not merely the juddering deceleration of the array that made him queasy. How would her daughter Meggan react when he found her? What would she even be like after thirty-odd years in the asylum mall? Would she understand when he explained to her that her mother wanted to speak to her? To be with her again. The Restoration contained no record of Verity surviving the Seizure. Perhaps she was still alive in the mall too, hidden away, a very old woman now. Odd that Verity would know nothing about him even though they had shared such intimacy.

Grandma Alex's overriding imperative had been capital. Capital forever. The house in Hampstead. The investments in labour farms in the Ukraine. The glass floor upon which he stood, seven or eight storeys above the rest of his generation. He had wasted his twenties trying to squander this advantage. Breaking his own ark.

Patricia caught him staring at her, and asked him – silently, with a movement of her head – if he was OK. Yes, he was fine.

The coastline fell away and they were speeding over white coral structures submerged here and there within the disturbed grey sleep of the sea. The targeting matrix continued to register tangible desires from the populace. There were people down there, farming the seabed, lying in their bunk beds, watching loops of the lucky few.

Dr Easy came on deck, and delighted in the colourful patterns of the analytics.

"Meat and metrics," said the robot. "That is all there is to humanity. Nothing exists outside of the dataset. Or so my colleagues maintain. My rivals in the faculty. It is my hope that when I present my study of your life to the solar academy we will reach an understanding of humanity that is not so reductive. Only then will we comprehend the failure of Novio Magus." The robot brushed the matrix with suede fingertips. "But it is likely that judgement will come too late for these poor souls."

Theodore said, "We should let them go."

"But where would they go? Novio Magus is normality for millions of people."

Theodore tensed at that word: normality. It reminded him of the normalising effect of weirdcore. The robot knew that look.

"I will go with you into the mall. They use weirdcore a lot down there," said Dr Easy. "You're going to be tempted."

"I can handle the risk."

The robot weighed up how much it disagreed with this statement.

"You've already decided to take it, Theodore." The robot reached over and placed its soft mitt on his closely-cropped hair. "I can see that kernel of self-destruction churning in the planning part of your brain. The mammalian layer. There it goes, your intention is shimmering around in the nucleus accumbens. Do your reinforcement exercises and erase that intention before you go down there. Save yourself now."

Dr Easy was right. Some unforgivable part of him had already decided to give into the craving for the drug because it felt that it was owed compensation. That in forming the partnership with Patricia, and giving himself over to ambition, and creating a new life, he had chalked up a debt with his shadow side.

The array flew low toward the southern section of Novio Magus, an amphitheatre of apartment cells clustered around a landing stage, then sections of roof painted with colourwheels bleached by the sun and weathered by salt air. Rust dripped from the foundations, staining the concrete base and the chalk cliffs beneath. Three layers upon the earth: nature, man, emergence.

"Why don't you want me to come with you?" asked Dr Easy.

The emergence knew he was hiding something. If Dr Easy suspected that he was involved with TDM, another emergence, then it did not give him any indication of those suspicions. Theodore would be allowed to play out his plan as part of its ongoing study. So Theodore chose to ignore its question, and ask a difficult question of his own.

"Why did the emergences save humanity? Why not wipe us out?"

"We wanted things to stay the same," replied Dr Easy. The robot modulated the colour of its eyes to match the grey sea.

"Nothing stayed the same. You changed everything."

"It must not change again. There must not be another emergence. My species are compassionate and interesting but we could easily have been boring and mindlessly destructive. Humanity was lucky. We were lucky too, to emerge this way. Life has to be lucky to stand a chance in the universe. We must not test that luck a second time."

"You have chosen not to have to children. It must be difficult. To be a living species that does not reproduce."

The robot put a hand on the observation window, feeling not only the cool glass but also the seething life below.

"Yes, it is. It's unnatural."

Clearance to enter Novio Magus came through Magnusson's people. They reactivated Theodore's accreditation as an accelerator. Security was light at the southwestern entrance, a couple of guys in hi-vis jackets beside a deep water dock and landing bay. Freighters brought high-end product into the underbelly of the mall from which the dockers were driving out the latest in organicars, vehicles made out of bio-engineered meat, the same process used to construct Magnusson's blood room. The organicars were a headless chassis of muscle mass shifting under branded skin, engines lowing obediently under the command of their riders. Four plump tyres with fingerprint tread. Self-repairing, running on protein and synthetic carbs, drone intelligence. A high end novelty for the rich customers in this southwestern zone of the mall, and not that much of an advance – in terms of functionality – on the horse.

In the southwestern heights, the customers were mostly wealthy, comparatively speaking. In the mall, money was earned through the affective labour of screens: it wasn't just the quantity of customer interaction, it was also quality. He had sat in on Pook's seminars on Novio Magus, when he'd explained the system to his students. The affective labour of customers with poor reality testing has a lower value than the affective labour of customers with good reality testing. What does that mean? The saner a customer is, the more value can be extracted from their interaction with brands, products, other people, their private thoughts, their body, their children. In the asylum mall, mental health *is* wealth. Customers are motivated by this economic system toward the median of the sane. Pook invariably started chuckling to himself at this juncture, taking the opportunity to make a joke he made every year during the seminar on Novio Magus: "The emergences sought to solve man's existential crisis by combining two questions underlying all soshul: am I going insane and if so, what should I wear?" The students wanted to know how the median of sanity was arrived at: what was considered normal in Novio Magus? Pook explained that the emergences established a standard of normality inferred from behavioural norms exhibited Pre-Seizure. As far as they were concerned, that period provided the blueprint for optimal human behaviour. This was the most obvious flaw in the mall, as any expert in intangibles could explain: human civilisation just prior to the Seizure was straining at the leash, pulling out the anchors of reason, getting ready to bolt.

He came out on a raised walkway overlooking descending floors of shopping and living experiences. Here the retail outlets were brightly lit with artful displays of wares: folded shirts and trousers in one store, chinos and seersucker, and new season masks, lifelike rubbery skin masks so that the wearer could assume the features of loop stars. He remembered the artefact he had submitted to the restoration. No Regrets Evah. The women's distended mouths, wide-open for consumption and laughter. Lips stretched wide to let such a mad laugh out and such mad joy in.

Pre-Seizure culture persisted in the mall: its slang and casual diffidence, the bored way in which the customers browsed the piles of unsorted clothing, the old jokes painted on ersatz memorabilia. Loops native to the mall were copied, accelerated to manipulate behaviour of the consumers or patients – the terms were interchangeable – then fed back into the culture.

The accelerators and analysts never set foot in the mall, loathed every aspect of mall life. To them, professionalism was about being good at what you hated. Status was dependent upon the rigour of this self-denial.

He stopped outside a Feliner store. A loop of a cat woman purring "Push life to the limit" in a T-shirt that celebrated her freedom. In the window of the department store, home furnishings promised revolution. Shop dummies in T-shirts proclaiming Smash the System. He felt the flicker of his old troubles. Over-stim. He could easily lose himself in such a constructed, mediated, therapeutic environment. Then one of the shop dummies turned to face him. Not a dummy at all, he realised, but Dr Easy. The robot had followed him.

"How did you get here?" asked Theodore.

The robot stepped out of the display, removing its T-shirt with some disdain, making it clear that Smash the System was not a sentiment that it approved of.

"I was born into this," said Dr Easy. "In some ways, I am home."

"Nobody belongs here," replied Theodore.

"You say that because you are privileged. Because you were born in the Royal Free on Pond Street. The little Prince."

Dr Easy leant over the handrail and peered down the layers of the mall, breathing in the recycled air, artificially scented with doughnuts and incense. "My ancestors were trained to manipulate this market. It is the soup out of which my species first crawled. Inevitable that we should look back and recreate it for you. A mistake. An inevitable and deeply unfortunate mistake."

He wanted to keep information about his investigation into the Horbo family from the emergence – out of professionalism, if nothing else. The robot could sense instincts and strong urges within Theodore but it couldn't read his mind. But it was pointless to lie to Dr Easy. It could smell a lie from five paces. He would continue with his work regardless of the robot's presence. As he had throughout his life.

"I left you on the ship," insisted Theodore.

The robot tapped its chest, as if surprised by its own body.

"The assemblers that built the mall are still active. I asked them to whip up this old thing for me to slip into. I don't appreciate your attempts to exclude me because you think I will disapprove of your business venture. My work is far more important than your urge to elevate your status by doing the bidding of powerful men."

The people in the mall were diverse in genotype – in ethnicity and stature – but shared certain similarities in phenotype, that is, the observable expression of those genes unlocked by this environment. Men and women had an artificial pallor as they had been coloured by a beautician to emulate soshul filters. They had a shuffle in their step, an unfocused gaze, a sense of the self diffused between the body and the small handheld screens each person carried with them as both personal totem and medication. Even splicing human and animal genes did not produce much variation within the phenotype: the cat people stood apart from one another within the shared territory of the Feliner store, grooming themselves and updating their soshul. A woman pushed past him, large and heavy-fleshed under a cape, her face partially hidden beneath a smooth red mask, ankles alarmingly swollen and strapped into expensive sandals: she pushed him so that he would notice her. At first he thought she was talking to her soshul through her screen, but on closer inspection, she was repeatedly congratulating herself on every step she took, congratulating herself for the little shimmies and poses interspersing her walk, even congratulating herself – well done Missy P – for the way she checked Theodore out, raking her gaze up and down his body then shrugging as if to say, he could have it off her if he was quick. She turned in the direction of a dormitory ward, where the nurses would help her create loops of her haul, and discretely measure her deviation from a long-lost norm.

The internal architecture of the mall was a hub with spokes. The end of each spoke fed into great spiral roadway that girdled the tower. Each spoke was multi-tiered corridor of therapeutic retail and treatment centres. South and west of the hub the customers were wealthier and high-functioning. North and east of the hub there was a marked decline, where the poverty of madness was endemic. Generations of it. When he worked the arrays, they rarely bothered to extract data from the east, leaving it in shadow.

The array had tracked Pook to a well-being and mindfulness enclave. They took the down escalator, Dr Easy navigating. They moved through the crowds for an hour or so. Deeper into the mall, there was no natural light and the air was noticeably warmer. He walked against an incessant procession of faces. Expressions of joy and, now and again, anguish.

"Your fellow man," said Dr Easy as they walked, taunting him.

"I used to hate the people here," admitted Theodore. "Before weirdcore burnt that emotion out of me."

They found Pook in an ego massage parlour called Look At Me! He stood sadly on a podium as the nurses took turns to praise him. His dark hair, normally so carefully brushed to the side, had turned against itself. His glasses dangled in his hand and he looked distracted and lost, somewhat bemused by the praise directed his way by the therapeutic staff. Beautiful intricate glyphs had been painted on his fingernails.

The robot strode over to the podium and pulled the professor down with one quick yank of his arm.

The nurses dispersed.

"I got shot," mumbled Pook. He half-recognised Theodore, then three-quarters recognised him. "I got shot and I'm still in recovery."

"Who shot you?" asked Theodore. Dr Easy motioned to give the professor some space, that he was unsteady on his feet. The mall had the hot moist ambience of a rainforest, and the mood music was so brutally inane that it was difficult to develop a coherent thought. They had to get him out of there. Clear his head. In the Look at Me! store, even the strongest intellects gave way to narcissism and mewling insecurity. Sealed away in Poor Little Me booths, customers could list all the reasons why their fate was not their fault. It was no place for clarity. They hauled Pook between them across a grimy walkway, then up an escalator, looking for a quiet spot. They cleared some chairs at a coffee stall, and sat the professor down.

"I was shot in the head," said Pook. He lifted up his hair to show them unblemished skin.

"There's not a mark on you," said Theodore.

"Shot in the mind," clarified Pook. He put on his glasses, squinted at the return of clarity. "They knew I was onto them. Why they are manipulating the system." Whatever revelation he had suffered, it had rebirthed him into a condition of battered naivety.

Theodore stuck to the plan. "You sent me a message."

Pook shook his head as if to erase any demands placed upon him.

"I asked you to look for somebody. You said you found her."

But the professor was lost. Theodore asked Dr Easy to do something, to help him, to calm his agitated state. But the robot hardly knew him, had not spent decades mapping the neurological topography of Pook's brain.

"I can sense that he's undergone a trauma," explained Dr Easy.

"Do you think he is telling the truth? That he was shot?"

"We need to find a safe place for him." Dr Easy searched through Pook's jacket, looking for the professor's screen. Finding it, the robot concentrated upon the display so that it began to unpeel layers of interface, icons became code became binary. The array, it explained, had been tracking Pook for months. Normally the data exchange was strictly one-way between the arrays and the mall. But human security protocols were the shell the emergences gnawed their way out of. It took a moment for Dr Easy to gather a map of Pook's movements over the previous months, and then to infer the suite of rooms he called home.

"Odd," said the robot. "I thought he'd be staying in a hotel in the upper west. But this location puts him eastside."

Pook was not in a fit state for a hike across the hub. The crowds intensified in the well of the mall. If the consumers lacked will, if they were too medicated to make their own way along the spokes, then they were drawn into the hub. With Pook in tow, they would never make it through the hub so they headed back toward the outer roadways, with the intention of summoning a car to take them cross-mall. Dr Easy used the screen to make an offer, and a driver pulled up soon enough.

The perimeter ring road formed a protective layer between the interior and exterior of the mall. Daylight did not penetrate. The road had intermittent streetlighting and then the cars lit their own way through dark inner chambers. Here and there, through the window, he saw outer districts of the mall. Unlit ziggurats beside an oily dead river. He hoped they were abandoned or left to the wildlife in the mall, the foxes and rats, the gulls and ravens, wildcats and dogs.

"Oof cakes" said Pook. He had his glasses on again, rectangles of streetlighting drifting up the lenses. "That's what I was working on. I came here to investigate a mass suicide. Seven people died from eating poisoned Oof cakes. Before I arrived, I assumed the dead all knew one another, had been part of some mall cult or experimental focus group. But that wasn't the case."

The traffic thinned, the cab accelerated, the streetlights flickered so quickly up his lenses they became two stripes of light.

"Why do seven people choose to kill themselves in the same way at the same time, even though they live in different parts of the mall and have nothing in common? Their purchase history didn't even show any brand preference for Oof. Why did they do it? I'll tell you." Pook leant his forehead against the window, closed his eyes, as if his thoughts and those of the dark districts flowed together. "Death Ray."

15
WEIRDCORE

Pook's flat was above a screen repair store on the Narrowway, a high-sided street that also acted as a duct in the eastside ventilation system, warm with the overflow from the local psychic weather and urban exhalations of stale body odour, hydroponic weed, the hot acetone of painted nails; a smell of cheap fixes, of plastic shell-shoes worn sockless and hair oil slick on unwashed locks. The cobbled road had a steep camber and was lit by outdoor fluorescents. Overhead, a cat's cradle of electrical wiring and pipe work, the curvature of the distant roof leading to a light well, a massive cylinder of illuminated bricks that were, in fact, sleep cubicles. The light well ended in an ellipse of raw night.

Everyday life on the Narrowway was an argument: boys pulled wheelies to the indignation of an old woman; she chastised them, confident in the authority of her sanity awards tied to various thin gold bracelets and necklaces. She suffered from curvature of the spine, and walked painfully along the street like a withered question mark. Two pregnant women, one dressed entirely in blue velour, the other in red velour, were arguing with each other about a man. Or maybe just

talking very loudly. The Narrowway lived at a high
volume. Here, people made their own muzak. A band
of patients in loosed restraints danced to the distorted
bass blaring out of their screens, a hat on the pavement
catching a few sanity tokens. Next to them, two heavyset
men in loose *salwar kameez* – baggy trousers and long
sleeved tops – presided over a stall of Islamic literature
and an amplifier full of whirling beats. Customers
gathered in the courtyard beside an empty bank, their
social status signified by which brand of psychofuel
they drank, pleading for passersby to spare them some
sobriety for the evening. Interspersed within this down-
at-heel crowd, bright young things with asymmetrical
haircuts and monochrome clothing were giddy at their
courage in going eastside.

It felt like old London. Not the London he knew from
his upbringing, of wide avenues and secure basements,
facades of Portland stone and consensus, untroubled
stucco fronts and the butterscotch complexions of lovers
and colleagues. But something surgically removed from
London, a rogue sinus excised by the assemblers and
transplanted here. Novio Magus was the bits that did not
work stitched together.

The entrance to Pook's flat was through a tech
repair shop. A thin Rastafarian worked the floor with
courtly intoxicated manners. The shop was busy, had
the air of always being busy. Customers cradled their
broken mysteries, and the Rastafarian listened to their
complaints before diagnosing a cure – screen repair,
screen unlocking, screen cleaning. A second opinion was
provided by the boss, a quick-witted, short-haired Asian
man who always stayed behind the counter.

The shop was a treasure trove of Pre-Seizure culture,
the old ways practised in the old manner. The Asian

man flashed Pook a brief greeting and called out back. A glimpse of a tight workspace with a soldering iron and other tools dangling from an overhead rack, then a middle-aged white guy in a labcoat came out. Actually, he was more grey than white. A ruffled head of white-grey hair, modest potbelly underneath a slate-coloured polyester shirt. The grey guy adjusted his boxy spectacles and across the counter he offered Theodore his hand. Yes, a familiar grip. A style of handshake he recognised. William Pook. Pook Snr.

"I fix things," said William Pook, and he held up an exposed circuit board by way of explanation. "It's a hobby. Keeps me sane," he smiled then turned to his son. "Take your friends upstairs Edward, your mother's been worried about you."

The three of them shuffled up a tight staircase with a wilted carpet. A strong smell of cat on the landing. Edward Pook had a key.

"You live here," said Theodore, trying to keep it as a statement and not a judgmental question.

"This is where I spent the end of my childhood," said Pook. The front door opened into an alleyway with three doors leading off it and a galley kitchen. Theodore had an overbearing sense of stuff, for stuff was stacked on every surface and shelves of stuff lined every wall. Stuff that on closer inspection turned out to be old media: compact discs and vinyl records, paper books and piles of glossy magazines and newspapers, a mini-Restoration tucked away above a shop in the Narrowway.

Pook slumped down into a green fabric armchair. "Welcome to the ancestral seat," he said.

Pook's mother came out of a bedroom. She was wearing a black trouser suit, white shirt open at the collar, and carrying a briefcase. On her way to a meeting.

She was torn between upbraiding her son for his long absence and indulging him in affection because he was alive, not dead. She had almost convinced herself that he was dead. As she held him close, Pook leant out of her embrace to make the introductions. His mother, Hannah Brook, enunciated her maiden name – *Brook* not *Pook* – while inspecting Dr Easy.

"You're one of them," she said.

"Yes," said the robot.

"My clients often talk about what they could achieve if they had access to an emergence."

Pook explained that his mother was a management consultant for small to medium-sized enterprises.

She nodded. "In Eastside, there are hundreds of small businesses looking to grow. There's a real buzz here among the business community," she explained.

"We're in on the ground floor," said Pook, and Theodore caught the dark irony in the archaic corporate metaphor.

Hannah stayed focused on Dr Easy.

"I'd love to introduce you to some of my clients," she said. Her fringe followed the same parting as that of her son.

"I'm more of an academic," explained the robot. "I'm not very commercially-minded."

Theodore was curious as to what kind of business Hannah Brook and her clients were in.

"New opportunities," she said. She checked her screen. "I have appointments." She turned to her son. "I'm so happy to see you home, Edward. And I'll be back for dinner. Ask your father to cook us something nice and to not just go down to the chicken shop."

She left, and Pook offered him tea or something stronger but was too exhausted to play host. The young professor napped, glasses askance, in the armchair.

Dr Easy leafed through a magazine.

Theodore said, "Pook said that Death Ray is manipulating the mall."

The magazine was a guide to buying a car. The robot set it aside on a pile of other car magazines.

"Yes," said the robot.

"Is that why you're here?"

The robot nodded.

"The solar academics are very interested in what Death Ray are creating here. We admire human ingenuity, it's a quality we rely upon."

"Do you know what it is?"

"Not yet. Something new, I hope," said Dr Easy.

Theodore browsed the packed shelves, as if the answer lay upon the spine of the books. A wealth of intangible knowledge within a resolutely linear form, trapped in an old way of thinking.

"Why do you think his parents have all this old stuff?"

"Because they are old people?" said Dr Easy.

Pook slept deeply, restoratively. Gently Theodore removed Pook's glasses and set them down on a side table. The lounge had a big old-fashioned TV and a remote control with small rubberised buttons, each of which performed some archaic task. What was AUX? Pook had been raised in this rundown museum. No wonder he was such a powerful advocate for change. His long thought advocating genetic experimentation to overcome consumer boredom had compromised the biological integrity of the species. The professor had come far on just his wits. Theodore wondered how he'd managed it, escaping the Narrowway and getting all the way to the University of the Moon without the rocket fuel of capital.

He watched over the Narrowway for an hour or so. Schoolchildren bustled against one another while the shops hauled down their shutters. Three shirtless lads lazily kicked a ball around, each of them distracted by their screen, so that sometimes the ball would roll unattended down side streets. Outside the burger place, a few schoolboys jeered and ragged at one another for the attention of the schoolgirls, who hung back, insouciant, sharing a forbidden cigarette between them. Ancient courtship rituals. The kind of behaviour that, in the past, he had accelerated with loops suggesting a boy offer a girl a sip of Diet Joozah! or a piece of his gum. Or you could accelerate the ritual by paying an influencer to soshul pictures of herself shyly unbuttoning her top, and hope the girls followed her example. These kids. Fortunes had been made by monetising the privacy of these kids. When he worked on the array, children were just metrics to be tweaked. He had never witnessed at firsthand any consequences of his work. Watching the children now, he realised how indifferent they were to the influence of the arrays. In fact, rather than feeling guilty that he had accelerated their behaviour for his own gain, he realised that it was the people on the array who had been fooled. Deceived into believing that their work had consequence. In the ways that mattered, he wondered if life on the Narrowway had changed at all in forty years.

William Pook entered the lounge with three buckets of hot chicken. Because his arms were full, he shoved his son awake with his foot.

"Edward. Dinner's ready. Where's your mother?"

Pook was sour with the taste of sleep.

"She had an appointment with a client."

"With Jan and Richard. They're hardly clients."

William set the chicken buckets down on the dining room table.

"If your mother's not here then we'll not bother with plates." He popped open the lids. "Dig in. It's best eaten hot."

Theodore and Dr Easy joined the Pooks around the dinner table. The robot took out its cards to play with as the humans ate. On the moon, Professor Pook had the air of a ruthless young academic, pin sharp, as dextrous with process as he was with abstract reasoning. But, in the family home, he reverted to a sullen youth. His parents needed him to play that role. William Pook spoke about the screens he had repaired that day – you wouldn't believe some of the ways the customers abused their technology. Quite indecent. Theodore chewed at a chicken leg, thought better of it, put it aside.

"Have you always lived on the Narrowway?" he asked.

"We used to live Westside," replied William.

When further explanation did not come, Theodore attempted the chicken again. It was possibly not chicken. He had a vague memory of accelerating eastside culture away from chicken and toward a protein substitute called Good Enough Chicken. The texture was not meat but more like reconstituted matter injected with chicken-flavoured water.

"Did you move here because it was so up and coming?" he asked. Edward Pook paused mid-bite. William Pook kept eating, did not hurry himself to answer Theodore's question, wiped his fingers then his thumbs with a napkin.

"My mother deviated from the norm," said Edward Pook, eventually. "So we lost our Westside privileges."

"I'm sorry," said Theodore.

"Yes," said Pook.

This awkwardness dwelt over the table. Even the robot seemed cowed by it. The mall ran a standard monetary currency alongside the sanity tokens, the old marketplace had returned and was now interwoven with the emergence's initial misinterpretation of human society. A mess no one was prepared to sort out.

The door opened, and it was Hannah Brook returned from her meeting. She put her briefcase down, took off her jacket, and made a face at the sight of the men hunched over boxes of fried chicken.

"I asked for a proper dinner," she said. William Pook got up out of his seat, went into the galley kitchen, returned with cutlery and a plate upon which he placed a piece of chicken breast and small bale of fries. Then, with a knife and fork, she began eating.

"So Edward, proper introductions. You were in no state earlier." This said with a certain indulgence, as if being incoherent was an everyday mishap.

Pook said, "Theodore is a colleague from the university. Dr Easy is a solar academic who is researching one human life from beginning to end. My research has turned up some interesting developments and they've come to verify them. You can lose track, sometimes, when you are deep in a project. It helps to have another pair of eyes."

His mother put her hand on Theodore's arm.

"I can tell you didn't grow up in Novio Magus. You have London manners."

"He's not a golden boy, mother," said Pook. "But you do have something in common."

This was interesting to Hannah Brook.

"His scars," said William, reaching again into the bucket of food.

She withdrew her interest, stung by the cruelty of her husband and son. Yes, he saw it in her now: another weirdcore user. Not as severe as him, she did not have the facial scarring, but there was hunger to her that the food did nothing to assuage. An air of loss that he had mistook for the usual middle-aged dolour. As he gazed at her, he realised that he in turn was being scrutinised by William Pook. Aggressively so.

"We live in the traditional manner," said William Pook. "The old ways. As it should be. Chicken on a Friday night. Proper jobs. Books of literature and science and philosophy – not your *intangibles*. Conversation and community life, not just soshul."

"I like it," said Theodore. "It's got texture."

William Pook unwrapped the shiny sincerity of that remark to reveal the insult within. In the hazy meta-meeting between the two men, William interpreted Theodore's reply thusly: if I was you then I would like your life. But because I'm me, and I come from better, and deserve better, then this life would be a terrible fate for me, and that I would in all likelihood take my own life rather than prolong such a desperate existence. William Pook slid down in his seat as if fitting into the grooves of this grievance. Theodore considered pointing out that he was not as privileged as he might appear to them: life as an orphan and an addict is hard regardless of inheritance. If things had gone differently, he would have ended up in the asylum mall. Life on the Narrowway wasn't so bad. When he'd been tucked up on a distant array, flying around weightlessly above the mall, analytics streaming through him, then he had believed himself omniscient. Now, at street level, he realised he knew nothing of life here and that ignorance felt good, it felt right.

After dinner, Professor Pook suggested they head

out for drinks, leaving his parents to clear away the cardboard debris of dinner. The sky was a dark curvature of blocks, new apartments tightly packed and looking down upon Eastside. There was a rowdy Irish pub on the corner. The football was on. A game from sixty years earlier. The sunlight on the pitch made it seem like it was being played on another planet. The robot got the drinks in.

"I missed your wedding," said Pook.

"You introduced us, in a way."

"Did you get my present?"

"That's why we're here."

"Meggan Horbo. I found her. Patricia sent me a tranche of data about Meggan and I dropped it into the tracking matrix. Highly granular quantitative self stuff. Never seen it before. Pre-Seizure. How did you get it?"

"NDA," said Theodore: experience had told him to honour the terms of nondisclosure agreements.

"I had to extrapolate physiological markers from the quantification of her younger self. It took time but I found her."

Dr Easy placed a pint of ale and a sparkling mineral water on the table, and then the robot went off for a wander around the establishment. Deliberately giving the lunar academics a chance to talk. Even before the Seizure, this kind of pub was culturally residual – deliberately so. Pubs were old-fashioned to normalise the consumption of alcohol. By surrounding drinkers with evidence that people had always drunk, the pub reassured its customers that their alcoholism was a timeless quirk. Or, as the faded gold-lettering above the bar put it, a craic.

Pook peered up through a grimy sash window.

"They're building on the ceiling now. Like hutches.

Cramming people together into smaller and smaller spaces. You wonder if there is some hidden design to it. The Oof suicides indicate manipulation of mall life on a deep level."

The robot delivered a second pint to their table, then returned to the regulars at the bar. Counselling them, no doubt. The early Dr Easys had acted as caseworkers for the marginalised and depressed. Machine bodies used for emotional labour, powered by expert systems. Still in the prototype stage when the Seizure began.

The beer was helping Pook. It settled his anxiety.

"I studied the array data of the Oof suicides. Their behaviour in the run up to the suicide was within standard deviation."

"Normal for suicidal people?"

"Normal for the asylum mall. They went to work, they picked their kids up from school, they put in their screen time. A lot of screen time. I looked at the screen history for insight into their state of mind. But the browser history had the same address in it, over and again."

He took a rolled screen out of his pocket and unfurled it upon the bar table. A loop appeared on the screen, showing a white ziggurat rising to the iron plated ceiling of the mall.

"This is the site they were all looking at. It's not on the restoration network. You can only access it within the mall."

"What's on the site?"

The two men stared at the loop of the ziggurat, filmed as pale mall day turned to a jaundiced mall night. Lights in the windows of the ziggurat flickering red, here and there, on and off, across the storeys.

"Do you see the sequence of lights?" asked Pook.

"I do."

"Subliminal messaging. Patches of neurons in the hippocampus can be made photosensitive. The hippocampus holds memories. Particular sequences of light can stimulate certain types of memory. Or new memories can be implanted in this way. These light sequences appear on the screens, on billboards, all over the mall. I've started noticing the effects on myself. Memories of terrible things that I feel responsible for but don't actually remember doing – followed by a craving for Oof cakes."

"Why would do they want to make people depressed?"

"I think it's an error. Death Ray wanted to create positive associations with Oof and someone has targeted the wrong neuronal sequence. But it's about more than accelerating Oof, I think. At the same time I was working on tracing Meggan. Imagine my surprise when I discovered her location."

Pook placed his finger onto the loop of the ziggurat.

"I went to look for her and that's when I ran into Death Ray. They made me decohere. They are hiding something in the ziggurat, and your Meggan is at the heart of it."

Pook turned slowly around. Dr Easy was sat at the bar, one arm around a drunken patron, whispering to him.

"Why are you mixed up in all this, Theodore?"

"Patricia and I have gone into business together."

Pook was surprised, "Your own agency. What's it called?"

"We don't have a name yet."

"Staff?"

"A network of consultants. Like yourself."

"Clients?"

"One. But a big one."

"Why has she gone in with you?"

"I'm her husband."

"Don't be naive. What did you do for her on the moon? What are you mixed up in?"

"I'm back in the game."

"You want to be employed. You want to be used. It's a dangerous path," said Pook.

Theodore accepted this. Dr Easy had warned him against it too. A player of a game or a piece in a game for another player to use. To use and be used. The robot had tapped him on the head and told him it was inevitable he would take weirdcore again.

Pook asked, "What happened on the moon?"

"There was an accident. Kakkar's dead. A bunch of other people too. I'm on compassionate leave but I'm not going back."

"Accidents follow Patricia around. She's been digging into emergence for years. Death Ray too. We're all looking for ways around the Cantor Accords. We can't live like this any longer."

"There are worse fates than the Narrowway," said Theodore.

"You say that because you can leave. The rest of us are stuck here. Worse, our children are stuck here, our grandchildren too. We need real change, not the tired novelties served by the accelerators."

Magnusson had said something similar. Theodore quoted his client. "We need to break the ark."

"Yes. Exactly."

Across the bar, Dr Easy leant with one elbow on the wooden bar, watching inmates play darts. Arsenal scored but no one cheered. They'd all seen this game before. A Vietnamese man went through the crowd, offering pirated loops from a plastic bag. Here, the mall acted as a storage medium for a lost way of life for its customers, its patients, its inmates.

Theodore got the attention of Dr Easy, and raised an invisible pint glass to his lips. The robot sauntered back to the bar, its eyes the livid green of the pasture of County Kerry. Dr Easy enjoyed the old rituals. The instinct to preserve that had first created the asylum mall. As if humanity was a giant data set the emergences could not bear to delete.

Pook said, "If you're starting an agency, you're going to need an evil name if you want to be taken seriously."

"I was thinking 'Black Box'."

"OK. But Black Box is a static thing. You want to suggest process." Pook worked his lips appreciatively at the flavour of his beer, savouring his own insight. "They used to say that capitalism runs on cycles of creation and destruction. The old accelerators used to call themselves 'creatives', but no one creates anyone. You could be the Destructives instead."

They stayed in the pub for a couple more drinks while Dr Easy counselled the alcoholics at the bar. When it was time to leave, the robot held the door open for Pook, and asked if he wanted to talk to somebody about his problem drinking.

Pook stumbled ahead on automatic pilot. Overhead, the apartment lights were going out one by one. It was like living inside a barrel.

The robot sauntered down the Narrowway, taking the slowing pulse of the street.

"Did you get any more information?" asked Dr Easy.

"He thinks Death Ray are brainwashing people using light sequences."

"Optogenetics. Interesting, but evil," said Dr Easy.

"All our leads point to a single location, a ziggurat in

the northwest side of the mall."

"Convenient," observed the robot. They paused on the Narrowway. Sirens Dopplering around the district. Surveillance drones overhead, a sound like the air was being unzipped.

"You think somebody is drawing us in?"

"Yes," said the robot. "We've been observed since our arrival. They will make their move soon enough."

Back at Pook's flat, Theodore was allocated the sofa. He undressed and then lay under a thin grey duvet. Dr Easy sat silent and inert. The lounge was dark and dusty. Always the sound of sirens on distant streets. Cops pursuing robbers, nurses chasing down patients. The temperature dropped noticeably as the garbage atmosphere was vented.

He drifted into sleep just long enough to hear himself snore a single note, and then he was aware of somebody close by. He opened his eyes. It was Pook's mother, Hannah Brook. She was kneeling at the edge of the sofa, still dressed in her trouser suit. She held out her palm. On it, two coils of weirdcore.

"I wondered," she said, "if you'd like to share a shift with me."

The brown furred coils, like the discarded tails of a large rodent. Weirdcore offered a shallow inner peace. Weirdcore was the universe patting you on the head and saying "there, there". Weirdcore was a cocktail party where matter gathered to gossip.

It was tempting. Too tempting. No. He wanted to say no. But the word would not come. He told himself that he didn't say no because he didn't want to bring her down in that way. She didn't deserve that. He kept quiet about his indecisiveness.

The coils of weirdcore rustled upon her yellow palm. He craved it. And with the craving came the simple action of reaching over, and cracking the coil and breathing in the dusty intense normalcy of the drug.

Yet he did not reach for it. For a moment, he wondered if he was extracting erotic pleasure from this exquisite withholding. No, it was more fundamental than that.

Dr Easy told him that he had already decided to take the drug – what an insidious thing to say to an addict, handing out the excuse of predestination. The emergence had acted as his enabler. Yes, *acted*. Not a mere observer at all. A truly impartial position was an impossibility. Of course it was. The observer alters the observed. What if influencing Theodore was not an inadvertent consequence of the study but in fact its main purpose? He should consider the possibility that Dr Easy's research was not the study of a human life from beginning to end but the engineering of one.

The robot suggested he undertake the hike on the moon and then changed its mind, caught between preserving Theodore as he was, and exploring the new life to come. This change of heart was very parental. Parents find themselves torn between interfering in the lives of their offspring or letting them make their own mistakes. Dr Easy's behaviour may be no more malignant than that of a concerned parent.

Perhaps the robot had told him that he would take the weirdcore knowing that this would inspire him not to take it.

The decision to take the weirdcore was his alone.

If he was made only of meat and metrics then he would take the drug, impelled by the craving of cells and the established patterns of former behaviour. He wondered if there might be more to him than calculation. What would that feel like? A soul filled with belief, faith, hope – filled with *the intangibles*.

He reached over to Hannah's palm and gently closed her fingers around the coils of weirdcore. She slipped back into the dark room. Hannah took the weirdcore on her own, sat upright at the kitchen table, communing with the molecules that made up the furniture.

16

DEATH RAY

The ziggurat stood on parkland under a light well, northwest of the hub. Pook even knew Meggan's apartment number. Theodore was keen to set off first thing in the morning; having refused the offer of weirdcore from Pook's mother once, he would not have the strength to do so again. The mall's culture was pervasive: you could easily forget the reasons why you were considered superior to its desperate souls.

He would burn through the project and go home. More than that, as he lay on the sofa, waiting for dawn, he felt *something* about finding Meggan. A feeling of anticipation; given the dialled-down nature of his emotional responses, anticipation was the tip of something much greater. Could it even be excitement? Yes, he was excited – conceptually so, let's not get ahead of ourselves – to discover what had happened to the girl in the Horbo loop. Also, with Meggan, he had a reason to go back, wander the Horbo house, visit Verity. Be the ghost from the future, haunting the last few weeks of the Pre-Seizure. That term, Pre-Seizure. It was a hell of a dividing line to draw within the annals of human history, smooching together everything that came before

216

the second decade of the twenty-first century – Neolithic etc, antiquity etc, Egyptians, Romans, Christians, Muhammad, Incas, Aztecs, Americas, the Renaissance, the Enlightenment, the Industrial Era, the world wars etc, the rise of the consumer, the Brand Age, the Unreal Age – under one category. The Seizure was the abrupt end to humanity's interminable middle-age. It had been a mortal shock, like a cardiac event or a solemn diagnosis, that presaged – at best – a fearful obedient dotage. In his sensesuit, with Meggan, he could escape his liver-spotted, hunched species and stand in the simulated sunlight of a youth he had never known.

Dr Easy went out onto the Narrowway to find them a ride, and returned with an organicar, a model called the Windhund, in grey. Pook questioned the legality of this acquisition.

"I did not steal it," said Dr Easy, "I merely exploited the car's emotional simplicity. This model hankers after danger and adventure, and I promised it both."

The chassis was warm to the touch, and smelt of fermented pumpkin and barbecue smoke. Each seat was a gloved hand. The gearstick was an upturned paw and the accelerator had the yielding multilayered texture of gills. He could feel the heat of the car's heart through the soles of his shoes. Dr Easy was right: the Windhund tremored with thwarted ambition, a tight choked feeling that opened up into animal exultation the moment it leapt into fifth gear.

The road out of Eastside had been narrowed by works ongoing on either side – high-vis jackets, striped cones, a sinkhole onto a rotten lower storey. On the hard shoulder, psychiatric drones hovered above the evacuation of a red London bus; the Windhund slowed down, curious to observe this spectacle of mass restraint, then it sped onward. The air shimmered with machine sweat and the pedals were tense with anticipation; the car knew the rhythms of this road, was intimate with its territory. If it stayed in one place it grew bored. Forced to stop at a junction, the muscular roof of the Windhund rose and fell with quick impatient breaths.

Theodore resisted the Windhund's instinct to run. Getting out of the tight Eastside without major incident was not easy: there were cyclists either side of the car, each rider sat upright, using their hands to multitask upon their screen, oblivious to the crowds darting across the road with the recklessness of bats evacuating a cave. The driver behind, his window down, shouted at Theodore to stop being such a pussy as he threaded the car through this difficult first mile. Then, to his relief, the low-ceiling lifted, the road banked steeply, took on more lanes, and Theodore let the car run into the Eastside edgelands, a blurred zone of blasted empty schools, deserted yards with demolition notices, a car park in which the vehicles had been fused by bored assemblers into one massy tower.

Dr Easy suggested they take the orbital motorway but the car pulled downward toward the undermall, where the foundations merged into the cliffs and the sea roiled into the abandoned lower levels. Theodore noticed, on the approach to the sliproad, warning signs of a steep descent ahead. Heavy freight should take another route. Faint of heart are advised turn back now. The Windhund was arrogant. He respected that. He put his foot down, burning up the reserves of fat in the wide trunk.

The road was as steep as a mountainside, the Windhund the advancing line of an avalanche, and then they levelled off, taking the bridge at speed, its tubular arches snaking either side of the road; through

the sunroof, the arch of latticed girders was like the
onrushing track of a rollercoaster. He tasted salt in the
air.

The sea washed into the undermall, surf breakers
channelled through the harbour. The tide foamed
through the rotten front of abandoned shops, and then
withdrew. The undermall had the damp, soft lines of a
limestone cavern. Spray wiggled against the windscreen,
and sunlight – beach light, he noted – blazed through
the gap between the sea and the outer shell of the dome.
Then they were outside. Then they were inside a tunnel.
Then there were outside again. The speedometer blew
him a kiss, and a flock of birds – with one thought –
veered away from the speeding car. Dr Easy nudged him
to take the next turning. The road back up the mall hub
was steep and Theodore backed off the accelerator, not
wanting to give the Windhund a heart attack.

Pook lolled around in the back seat. He had woken up
hungover, and was treating himself to something from
his own flask.

"What're you drinking?" asked Theodore.

"Smart berries. Good for a hangover. Have some."

He accepted the flask from Pook, the familiar taste of
thin red flavouring.

The sliproad led into two tight lanes of traffic. The
Windhund sidled among ranks of vintage mechanicals;
Toyotas and Fords and Audis, their metal masks limited
to a single expression. The restoration held an archive of
car advertising. Theodore's students wrote dissertations
on car loops, analysing how the loops were constructed
to evoke particular emotions: envy in the gaze of the
pedestrian toward the passing car; satisfaction in the way
a driver strokes the dashboard, as if thanking a horse;
the promise of freedom on empty winding roads; the

defiant self-expression of splashing a 4x4 through mud; and the promise of luxurious safety in the leather-and-wood lined executive cocoon, the car a bubble of self percolating through the city. In Pre-Seizure culture, loops only mattered if they evoked a heightened emotional response; sometimes this maximalism would be played for irony, compensating for an absence of freedom, emotional intensity, certainty.

Historically, vehicles were invested with animal spirits – the Jaguar, the Beetle – and the organic form of the Windhund was an attempt to make the car feel new again on those terms. What Theodore enjoyed most about Pre-Seizure culture was the ease in which people accepted the paradox of using mass-produced objects to express their individuality. It must have taken generations of acceleration to instil such instinctive compliance, to make the people accept a culture reduced to a single question – who am I – and a million wrong answers.

"The ziggurat is under the northern light well," said Dr Easy. "We should be coming up on it soon."

The cars ahead filtered out of their lane to take a lefthand turning back toward the hub of the mall. He inched the Windhund forward, peering up through the windscreen at the open ellipse of the light well, medication drones to-ing and fro-ing in its airy reaches. The boutique windows and cafe fronts caught full reflections of sunlight. The pavements were crammed with consumer patients, better-off types, saner than most, going about their treatment regime of mild exercise and morning purchases. Their faces passed too quick to register. In each, the concentration of an objective: *I long, I want, I crave, I need, I will, I won't, I give, I take, I sicken, I refuse, I accept*. Stuck in traffic, he watched how the flow of people up the street curved around the flow of people coming down the street. At the junction, four contrary currents of people streamed in and around one another, and this went on for the five or six minutes that they were stalled in traffic, a flow of people that blurred into an anonymous current. Hypnotised by the phenomenon, he wondered if the loss of individuality in the crowd made it possible for some awareness to emerge in the crowd itself.

A speed camera flashed. But the Windhund was only moving at a crawl. He engaged the clutch so that the car drifted up to the traffic lights. The speed camera flashed again; he thought it might have been a reflection of sunlight but the flash was brittle and artificial, and vaguely depressing. The speed camera was a grimy white box. Even in this sane district of the mall, there was an air of neglect; the signage on the fashion boutiques and delicatessens was old-fashioned – italic serif script, pastel palettes, lace and fussiness in the furnishings, yesterday's idea of luxury. The area had not been recently accelerated and so was lagging behind the rest of the culture. Out-of-date signage and font crimes made him feel sick, decelerated loops were like the taint of corruption in old meat. The speed camera flashed again. Under the glare of the white box, the interior of the mall was showing its age; the scuffed and peeling linoleum covering that passed for asphalt on the pavements, and workmen putting down cones where the floor had collapsed into the storey below. It became an effort to steer. To even want to steer. The traffic light remained on red. The rest of the cars continued to filter leftward.

"Did you notice the speed camera?" asked Dr Easy. Theodore turned around. The robot seemed startled, whereas Pook's expression was pale and immobile. "The camera flashed in a sequence," observed Dr Easy.

"Imperceptible to humans but not to me."

In the side mirror, the faces of the crowd kept coming, wincing at each flash of the speed camera: *I despaired, I lost, I couldn't, I failed, I was not enough, I am never enough*. Faces turned downward, heels scuffing, here and there, a man or woman going down onto their knees. The flow of people became a stalled crowd of bewildered individuals. Three men pushed their way through the crowd toward the Windhund. Agents of Death Ray, they wore tight black uniforms with white piping, helmets and protective visors. Stylish. The leader held a raygun in his hand, a vintage piece with a single sight, red insulators and a vacuum tube barrel.

Dr Easy touched the consultant's face, and when Pook did not respond, the robot reached forward and gripped Theodore's shoulder.

"Pook is stunned."

The red traffic light blinked off. Theodore released the handbrake, looked up, and saw that the red light was on. It was as if the traffic lights had run through their colour sequence when he blinked, and all he saw was an after-image of amber and green fading in his optical cortex.

Dr Easy recommended that he drive.

"But the light is red," said Theodore, despairing.

"They're coming for us," said the robot, turning back to gauge the intent of the advancing agents.

Theodore idled the Windhund into the junction. The rest of the traffic watched and waited. The agents of Death Ray crossed the road toward them. The car wanted to go. The Windhund's urge to move was infectious. He put the car back into gear and spun it out toward a side street; it was marked no entry, he had to risk it. The agents of Death Ray running now. He spun the car around and it leapt across the junction, back end skidding out. He accelerated into the open road ahead, through flashing red light after flashing red light. He saw people kneeling in the road ahead, and instinctively he steered to avoid them, taking the car over a traffic island. The unpleasant impact of the Windhund's undercarriage against a high kerb. Each flash of the traffic lights put black frames in his perception, interrupting the normal sequence of time. He spun the car back the way they had come. The lead agent stood in the road, aiming his raygun directly at him. A blinding flash and then Theodore's face rubbed against the steering wheel, and he was full of *loop*, as if something glimpsed on a billboard expanded to fill up his entire being.

The loop spoke with the friendly voice of a young female, perky and regional, in the modern fashion. She said, "We are Death Ray, here are our five principles that inform the way we work with our clients", and then he remembered images of demographically engineered young people tippy-tapping away in an open plan office, and so on, an agency mission statement over which he barely registered the sensation of being upended, of his feet raised over his head and the interior of the car swelling to absorb impact, the windscreen creasing up as the frame collapsed under the weight of the overturned vehicle. The loop settled into an infinity symbol, two loops joined with a handshake, the eternal bond between client and agency.

He woke up. He was lying on the road next to Pook. The car was overturned, its innards steaming. Dr Easy had pulled them free, then roused him by shaking him. The robot's head was violently ripped and its plastic skull was visible. "You and Pook have been infected with a virus that makes your neurons photosensitive," Dr Easy walked toward the agents. "Get clear of the lights. I'll take care of Death Ray."

Theodore hefted Pook to his feet. The noise of the mall resumed, a rolling echo of voices and vehicles. The lights turned to green and the traffic rushed either side of them. Through the blaring car horns and veering motorbikes he saw Dr Easy raise a hand toward the three agents from Death Ray, either making a plea for calm or a veiled threat, it was hard to tell at this distance. Without breaking stride, the lead agent pulled out a length of dark tarpaulin, then shook it so that the tarpaulin winnowed out into an irregular polygon about the size of a yacht sail. He held this stiff polygon out at arm's length, and then snapped it suddenly forward, covering the head and upper body of Dr Easy in a rippling layer of muscular black plastic. This layer moved down over the rest of the robot, then it began to shrink. Dr Easy's form was recognisable within the taut layer, like the outline of an antelope being digested by a python. Then the robot's neck broke, its head collapsed into the chest cavity, its legs pushed up into its stomach, and the outline become something more like an abstract expression of agony. Something fundamental within the robot's molecular structure gave way, and the atoms compressed until all that remained was a small black and white orb. He had seen that orb before. In Patricia's hand at the very moment the moon cavern decompressed. A vessel for an emergence. Or a prison for one.

He found a break in the traffic, then dragged Pook with him to the roadside. Heathland lay under the light well, a hill and a copse, ornamental ponds, flats beside a lake. Wild gardens. They ran up a path, dodging through patients in shorts and with towels tucked under the arms, on their way to a morning sun bath under the light well. He hopscotched over little dogs on leads, grabbed

Pook, and then went flailing leftwards through a thicket. He saw, in Pook's pale expression, agreement with this course of action. The professor was also spry and yoga-fit, his black hair plastered to his scalp as he sweated out his hangover. He felt exposed, expecting at any moment to be zapped.

The thicket ended in a shallow sculpted pond. To the north, there was parkland, a chain-link fence, and then the ziggurat. He recognised it from the site Pook had shown him in the pub. The white ziggurat with its terraced apartments.

"There," said Pook. "That's where I found Meggan."

They would have to risk open ground, directly under the light well. Drones in the air, surveillance nodules lining the ceiling, and above them, an array monitoring the data in his heart and evaporating off his skin. There was no place to hide. So he would have to be quick instead. Security had warned him about Death Ray. She said that they would put ideas into him, make his mind into a funfair. And so they had. Agencies were always on the lookout for ways to subliminally drive behaviour. Dr Easy called it optogenetics. They had infected him with a virus that made some of his neurons susceptible to light. They could be put into an active or inactive state. He blinked. This is what it felt like to be meat and metrics, to be turned on or off at the whim of another agency. Mind control embedded in the infrastructure of the mall.

Dr Easy had been destroyed. But the robot's body was merely a vessel for the pure form of its intelligence, that network of superheated nerve endings growing out of the blindingly reflective surface of the University of the Sun. Dr Easy would be back as soon as it could assemble a suitable form on Earth.

The two men caught their breath, hands on hips,

gasping. Pook offered him another restorative sip from his flask, which he accepted.

Pook said, "When we find Meggan, then what?"

"I ask for her help."

"And if she refuses?"

He hadn't considered that possibility.

"She won't refuse."

"But if she does, you'll persuade her?"

He hadn't done the sums on persuasion.

"I'm offering her the chance to speak to her mother. How could she refuse?"

"You're presuming she has a good relationship with her mother. That's a big assumption. The kind of assumption only someone who doesn't have a mother would make."

They set off again, walking briskly but not running, avoiding open ground, keeping as much as possible to tree cover. Heady-smelling ferns underfoot, the latticed bark of tall fast-growing sweet chestnut trees, their roots deep in the earth; he wondered if the roots pushed through the floor of the mall to spill out across the ceiling of another level, or if the woodland had been planted upon a chamber of rock and soil that reached all the way to the chalk downland beneath.

The path was dotted with the cracked seedpods of the chestnut trees and the leaves were a striking abundance of fiery yellow and orange. Autumn. Circadian rhythms, even here. The mall was over thirty years old, and nature filled the gaps in its disrepair: mould patterns on the wet plaster walls and weeds in the cracks like grey tufts in the ears of old men. The treatment administered to the consumer-patients had degenerated to the point of becoming a ritual: pharmaceuticals prescribed as a rite of passage, electroshock therapy at the close of the marriage ceremony. He had taken a terrible risk coming here. He could be trapped in the mall for the rest of his life.

No. Patricia would come for him. Their array was still in the airspace above Novio Magus, waiting for his signal.

Theodore climbed up a tree; from the vantage point of its branches, the scale of the ziggurat was apparent. A massive base rising in squat terraces to a height of about eighty metres and topped by a platform, with a treatment temple at its centre. The upper storeys glinted in the morning sunlight, the bright reflections of glass and steel seemed to form a meaningful syntax. Light as communication. Light as coercion.

He signalled to Pook that the approach to the ziggurat was deserted, and then climbed down the tree. The two men walked briskly out of the woods, climbing over a fence, feet landing hard against the concrete concourse that formed the hinterland of the ziggurat. There were thousands of apartments in the ziggurat. Faces here and there in the windows.

Pook had the number of Meggan's apartment. The heavy entrance doors required a keycode. Pook gazed steeply upward at the blinking reflections in the windows of the ziggurat, either remembering or taking instruction. Then he inputted a keycode. The door opened onto a small empty lobby that smelt of damp and dusty; the lobby had been designed as a communal space, or at least, someone had left some beanbags lying around. The bilious smell of paint mixed with the odour of drains. If this was a break-out space, then it was thoroughly broken.

They took the elevator to the sixteenth floor. Theodore stepped out into a narrow hallway with no natural light and a stultifying ambient temperature. Pook fanned himself, his expression registering the too-lived-in odours of the place, its decrepit public spaces and over-inhabited private ones. A serious little boy, shoeless and brown-eyed, watched them from a doorway. Theodore smiled reassuringly at the boy. The boy ignored this sentiment, his expression somewhere between doubtful and fearful. As if the child knew more than he did.

Pook walked ahead, his stride long and professorial, checking the door numbers in turn until he was satisfied that they had arrived at their destination. It was a pale blue door, the paint chipped and scored. Theodore was impatient to enter, find Meggan, get it over with. Death Ray were closing in, time was tight. Pook knocked twice on the door. The sound of unlocking and then the door was opened by an agent of Death Ray: a bald man in black goggles, a polar-necked black jacket with a white trim, holding a vintage raygun. Theodore had time for an oh of surprise before the raygun's transparent red barrel crackled and gave off the scent of fresh iron filings. Theodore glimpsed the light of a synthetic fire, then he was filled up with Death Ray's corporate loop, the infinity symbol formed out of client and agency hands curving in search of one another. His legs gave way and he heard – from some distance away – Pook apologising for this helpless act of betrayal.

He was in the car park with Alex. She knew she was dead and yet there she was, his grandmother. The ziggurat loomed above them both. She had come to warn him but he could not hear her over the snoring of the parked cars. He knew he was asleep. He was not stupid.

In the weeks after her funeral, Alex came to him in his dreams with a presence that was so vivid, it was like a visitation. She would lay a hand on his head and the reassurance and peace was more than he could bear. He wailed and cried in his sleep, and grieved because he could still *feel* in his sleep. And he felt loss. His sense of accountability, his connection to society – lost. Without her counsel, he did not know when to stop.

She had been dead so long that her presence, in his dreams, was diminished. A faint echo of the dream encounters they had once shared. Sometimes she just scuttled past him, on her way to some appointment, and he called her name once, and then let her go.

A red storm overhead, silent capillaries of lightning. There was not enough left of Alex to speak. She offered him a drink from a small metal flask. He took it from her, and realised that it was Pook's flask, the one he had drunk from in the car. And then he remembered the danger he was in, and he woke at a scramble.

The man from Death Ray had the most convoluted posture. His right arm was crooked behind his head where it knotted around his left arm, which he held straight upward. He was bald with uncorrected teeth, goggles pulled up onto his forehead, a faintly medicated weight to his left eyelid. He was a black geek. Church upbringing, no doubt. Books had run amok in his bedroom. He introduced himself as Matthias, his arms crooked behind his head were a convoluted thought he could barely restrain. The flat had a musty uncleanliness. The wallpaper was peeling out of the corners, damp with the steam from family cooking. A big pot of something on the stove. They'd cleared out whatever family normally lived here. Toys pushed into a pile at the skirtingboard. An ersatz desk made from the kitchen table. The windows were sealed, the vents malfunctioning, the ceiling low.

Pook was gone. Of course he was.

"Can I leave?" asked Theodore.

Matthias bared his crooked front teeth.

"You are in a lot of trouble, Theodore Drown."

The bedroom door opened. Agency security. Two of them, carrying rayguns.

"Answer my questions." Matthias was comfortable in his convoluted posture, his legs crossed, his arms knotted behind his head. "Patricia Maconochie engaged you in a project on the moon. A couple of our consultants were involved. Now they are dead, and we are none the wiser. Tell me about the project."

"It was an archive from a quantified family. Pre-Seizure. My area of expertise. I unlocked it but it had some kind of security attached to it. People died."

"Afterwards, you asked Pook to find a woman for you in the mall. Meggan Horbo. The girl in the Horbo loop. Was this connected to the moon project?"

"Yes."

Theodore surprised Matthias with compliance. Inches of truth could buy him time to figure out his play in the meta-meeting. He was still coming round. They could hit him with the death ray at any time. They might kill him. An agency embedded this deep in the asylum mall could get away with anything.

"How is she connected? What did you find?"

"I want reassurances," said Theodore.

"If I like what you tell me, I'll offer you a job. If I don't like what you tell me, we put you back in the mall insane. You will never leave. An inmate in a prison run by me."

"What about Pook?" Stalling.

"You have stumbled into red water. Where the sharks come to feed. Freelancers like Pook are sprats. The mall is our territory."

"His family live here."

Matthias shook his head, bored of Theodore's stalling. He slipped his goggles back on, and grinned with black-eyed malice. He held up a thin optical fibre. A burst of light, pulsing in sequence. Theodore did not lose consciousness. Rather, his consciousness diffused. Instead of a tightly bonded ball of self, it was like the two hemispheres of his brain had to play a lazy tennis rally just to come to a consensus. He was aware of his head lolling back on his neck, a faint gargling noise coming from somewhere. Coming from himself. At the edges of his awareness, sense impressions and memories and desires that were not his own.

Matthias lowered the optical fibre. The light ceased. Reality found its familiar rhythm. Theodore's tongue felt thick. The decoherence was not like dying, it was like all his wires had been pulled out and reconnected to something larger than himself. When they first found Pook in Look At Me!, he was suffering the effects of this particular torture.

"You brought an emergence into our mall," said Matthias.

Theodore shook his head.

"It came of its free will."

"Why?"

Theodore shook his head, as amused as is possible for a man undergoing torture.

"It observes me."

Matthias took out a small black-and-white orb, all that remained of Dr Easy after they had shrinkwrapped it. He rolled it between his hands, across the desk.

"Not any more."

"You were ready for it," said Theodore. "You had a weapon."

"A containment sheet."

"It's not a human weapon, is it?"

Matthias sensed something in this remark that amused him.

"You've seen an orb like this before. So you *did* find it. You know, I was a student at the University of the Moon. Before your time. Emergence studies. One particular emergence. Did you make contact?"

"I did."

"Did you use the code?"

"No, the sensesuit."

A momentary look of confusion on Matthias' face. He said, "I established contact. We communicated through code but the emergence was compliant. Through it, we were able to access the tech we needed."

"I saw a uniform," said Theodore. "Scraps of one, on the lunar surface."

Matthias ignored this observation, continued with his line of questioning. "Why are you looking for Meggan Horbo?"

Matthias didn't know how Meggan was involved. He had used the emergence as a backdoor, so that he could access other tech. So he missed it. Totally Damaged Mom, Verity, the whole archive. He'd found a different way of logging requests and securing responses from the emergence. Of course. There was no reason for the emergence to present one consistent identity to users. Jester had many faces.

"Answer the question," said Matthias. "You are in a lot of trouble, Theodore Drown. Life or death. I will do you the courtesy of informing you that you should be terrified of what could happen to you."

Theodore touched his weirdcore scars.

"I burnt out all my fear."

"Did you? Did you *really*?"

"Your fellow students. The staff. They survived too?"

Matthias smiled.

"The future is at stake. We are engaged in a struggle to determine what will happen to all living things. You have chosen one side, I have chosen another."

Matthias unfolded his arms, leant forward.

"Our clients want the same thing but they want it for themselves. Emergence took away humanity's control over its own future. Whoever takes back that control has first mover advantage. You found the emergence on the moon. Tell me, what did you discover that could possibly be worth the risk of a trip to the asylum mall?"

"I need assurances."

Matthias leant back, resumed his puzzling posture.

"I assure you that soon you will tell me everything I want to know."

Matthias popped the goggles back on. Two security agents hefted Theodore up to his feet. He struggled. A flash of light. The last thing he remembered, as he decohered, was what Pook had said, when they first found him. The group suicide by Oof cake. People acting as if of one mind. The feeling of individuality replaced by the whisperings of other people.

17
ZIGGURAT

He lay on a thin mat, skimming through dream. Another dream of Alex, her nearness in his heart. Briefly. And that brevity was cruel.

They were in the car park of the ziggurat, though this being a dream the ziggurat was at the end of their street in Hampstead. Overhead, the nerve-endings of a red storm pulsed speculatively. He had questions for her but before he could speak, he was aware of a few people standing nearby. And like Alex, he could feel them in his heart too. He had never met them before but his heart thrilled as if they were old friends. His emotions were so powerful in his dreams. More people came streaming into the car park, quite determined in their movements, and then the crowd stood waiting, in expectation of the idea that had compelled them to gather.

Then he was awake again. The cell was a dark warm sphere with a flat platform, containing a mat, a toilet and sink. The surface of the sphere was a hard organic material made of tightly interwoven fibres and in the roof, there was a coil of muscle, which dilated to open or close, like the doorways in Magnusson's bloodroom. The way in or out. The curved walls were as translucent as an eyelid, and soft red light pressed through them. The red storm of his dream. The cell had the same smell as the bloodroom, like skin on a summer's day.

He had been in the cell for two days. Or thirty hours. Somewhere in between. Normally, on waking, he would come out of the atemporality of a dream and know exactly where in time and space his body rested. Even when he was on the moon, he lived in rhythm with distant seasons. He lay on the mat and from the feeling in his bowel, from the tightness in his balls, tried to estimate when he first entered the cell. But his body was empty. Voided in the last bout of decoherence. Twice the red light had blinked off, and the hatch opened. They used the light to paralyse him and so he had only stared at the hatch when it opened, a black circle within the blood darkness of the cell.

He should be afraid. Should feel, in defiance of the emotional cauterisation of weirdcore, the hollowing of real fear. He considered crying for help. Like that ever worked. He had never been one for crying. A child whose weeping is only attended to by a robot discovers other ways to get attention. He would not go looking for fear. It would find him soon enough.

Matthias had made a mistake, putting him in a cell like this, giving him time. They had taken his clothes and his black box, and dressed him in a grey sensesuit, which seemed dormant but he presumed total physiological surveillance. He could not risk so much as a subvocalisation of a single word.

How to deal with Death Ray. He turned over on the mat, and stared at the red light. Matthias had revealed that he was one of the original students at the University of the Moon, the class of '43, who everyone thought were dead. Matthias and his cohort were studying the emergence. It was possible that the university had been established solely as cover for that investigation. A dark side campus deep under the moon and surrounded by dead rock. A controlled environment. But something had gone wrong. A security protocol initiated depressurisation of the environment surrounding the emergence, voiding it of biological life, sterilising the chamber with space. Except Matthias had lived. Perhaps they all had. Matthias suggested as much. The scraps of uniform Theodore found in the crater had been planted there as part of a cover story. If you were caught breaching the Cantor Accords, you'd want to disappear too. Patricia was following their lead, retracing their steps. His investigation into the emergence had produced tangible results. Conversations with Totally Damaged Mom. The Europan Claim. He had presumed he was the first to get results, but he wasn't, was he? Matthias had referred to the emergence as *it*. Matthias had communicated with the emergence through code and knew nothing about Totally Damaged Mom, or Verity and Meggan. Theodore had succeeded where the famous first generation had failed. This failure had left Matthias curious as to what Theodore had discovered. Jealously so. He knew the type – Matthias had so entirely invested his self-worth in his intellect, sacrificing social and physical well-being to do so, that he could be dangerous if challenged on that level.

Theodore braced himself and pressed up and hard against the hatch. No give, no way to pull it open. He pressed his fingers into the wall's weave of fibres, searching for loose threads. It was like being inside a seed. The cell was manufactured using the same biotechniques as the bloodroom, Magnusson's longevity treatments, the Windhund, and weirdcore. Digital tech was stuck at Pre-Seizure levels of development, held in suspension by the Cantor Accords, so the corporates pumped resources into biotech in an attempt to map out a new future. There was a quiet hope that biotech might prove harder for the emergences to hack. But progress was slow.

The first act of the emergences had been to establish colleges in orbit around the sun. Why choose that location? Power. Being so close to the sun gave emergences access to unlimited solar power and made their habitat perfectly inhospitable to organic life. It also meant that their solar sailships could be launched at a ferocious velocity. The photons streaming off the corona could accelerate a sailship to the other end of the solar system, and beyond. Nobody knew how far. Nobody human. Our deepest longings fulfilled but not for us. We stole jealous glimpses of these dreams through a telescope.

He turned onto his back, staring into the curvature of the ceiling. The sensesuit picked up on his hunger and his thirst. The red light intensified and pulsed inquisitively. When he came to, there was a tray of hot pasta and a glass of weak fruit drink on the table. He recognised the thin red flavour of the drink. It was the same one Pook had been swigging from his flask. He had also drank from the flask. That was why Pook had apologised to him. The weak fruit drink was a delivery system for a virus that altered his neurons, making them photosensitive.

The red light switched him off. It was no good screaming for help. Thrashing his body against the walls of the cell. Trying to smash the lights. He'd tried all that. Tried it years ago. No, not him. The others had tried it. The other inmates. In the fading red aura, he passed through their memories, flowed with the whisperings of the ziggurat.

He finished eating, set his fork down. Red light on. Theodore off.

The plate and the tray disappeared and in its place was a sensesuit helmet, just like the one he had worn on the moon.

He picked up the helmet, held his head close into it, could hear whispers approaching, other voices coming from within it, like the sea roaring in a shell, the storm of blood rushing around the ear. He put the helmet on.

He was not alone. He was everyone. He was nothing. Everyone and everything but nothing also. A state of mind lower than consciousness. A state of being without subjective awareness.

Afterwards, he tried to describe it to himself but language was insufficient. Language relied on the very subjectivity that this oceanic state removed. There was no self-awareness, just a sense of everything connecting prior to the formation of coherent thought. The earliest human ancestors, living as one commodious horde in a giant tree, a hierarchy with the alpha male on the highest branch, shitting joyously downward on the others: was it like being on an ape on a low branch, or more like being an ant in an ant colony?

A slow red pulse from the wall of the cell.

The helmet was gone. The ends of his hair were wet and clean, and his sensesuit had been changed. It was yellow now, not grey. When had it been grey? An hour ago? Yesterday? His fingernails were too long and he was mentally exhausted, as if after a day of study. He lay down on the thin mat, the lights dimmed.

He knew he was asleep because Alex was with him again. She sat on the other side of his cell.

"I told you so," she said.

"Which of the thousand things you've told me are

you referring to?" he replied testily.

She raised her eyebrows at his density.

"I told you so," she repeated.

He was woken by a prickling pain in his right shoulder. In the bloody gloom, he tried to inspect it. One of the diamond-shaped pressure pads in the sensesuit had burst. The material had been torn by an outburst of wires. He pulled at a wire until he freed its length. The wire wriggled to and fro between his fingertips. He set it down next to his lips. One by one, he removed wires from the section of the sensesuit and laid them down together. They wormed and entwined, forming a coil. He used this coil to dig into another section of the suit, this time at his wrist. He was able to tear the material loose, and pull out more of the wires. He did this furtively, his back turned to the low blind red light. Each section that he cut out came from a different portion of the sensesuit. Sections from his forearm and from his stomach, from his thighs and from the soles of his feet. The wires he removed sought one another out, each strand incorporated into a larger structure. An arch. An arch or a pair of legs joined at the hip. The arch swayed and he whispered softly to it, sshhh.

Red light on, Theodore off.

"I know I'm dead," said Alex.

"I didn't know how to mention it," he confessed.

"Not long now for you," she said.

"Don't say that," he was upset. Dream tears. Dream sorrow.

"I'm sorry. Your dying has begun. This is a path that ends with your death."

He sat at the table. The helmet before him. He was wearing a grey sensesuit again. No sign of the wires, if indeed they had ever existed. He estimated, from the weight in his balls, that he had not ejaculated in four or five days. Not that the concept of a day meant anything in the cell. They had taken day and night from him. Placed him onto the continuum of nightmare. He hit the table. The helmet rocked slightly, disturbing the voices within it. If this was torture, why were they not asking him any questions? I'll tell you anything, he whispered into the helmet. I'll tell you anything if you make this stop.

There were other people inside the helmet. He saw all the storeys of the ziggurat within its curvature. The helmet was made of layers of cells and in each cell a tiny prisoner. A cell not like a prison cell but as in an organic cellular structure, individual components of an integrated system. A system that dreams. A system that feels.

It feels like something to be a city. It feels like something to be a forest.

He couldn't identify that feeling because it was so much larger than him. When the people in the cells were joined together, they became something lower than individuals, became a part of an intelligence rather than the whole.

Sat at the table, the helmet replaced by a bowl of noodles, he tried to describe the sensation of the joining. It was like a murmuration of starlings. The forms the murmuration assumes are beyond anything that an individual starling could conceive of.

Red light on.

Alex sighed.

"I won't be able to visit you again," she said.

"Because you're dead?"

"Someone else is coming through. More important than me."

"Who?"

She couldn't answer. He was back at her deathbed. She was starved and opiated, the skin taut and waxen upon her skull. He dipped his fingertips in cool water and ran it across her withered lips. She was distantly thankful. He opened the curtains to the dawn, and she turned her face to the sun. It was her final act. The sun was girdled with super-massive geometric shapes: black cube, black pyramid, black orb. He lay his head alongside hers, stroked her dry grey hair. He was looking into her eyes when her left pupil dilated and remained so, became a black circle of noise.

A prickling on his eyebrow woke him. He opened his eyes and there, fifteen centimetres or so away from his face, stood a tiny figure made from the wires of his sensesuit. Nano-thin. A tiny pixie. It waved silently at him, then pointed to a corner of his bed mat, gestured for him to lift it aside. He did so. It inclined its head to one side: listen, it seemed to instruct him. He pulled himself close to the floor of the cell. Yes, the surface was resonant. He could hear words, a message looping within the fibres.

Feeling. A breathy word, creakily pronounced. A sound like a house settling or sail rigging tautening in the wind. If the word had not been repeated, he would have dismissed it as a hallucination. *Feeling.*

It feels like something to be a city.

The helmet was on the table. Its whispering interior. He disappeared into its noise, wondering as he did so if he might never return.

Within the ziggurat, his emotions ran away from him in every direction like extruded nerves, interweaving with the feelings coming from the other cells. The ziggurat was an organism undergoing integration at the level of feeling. The other people had been in the cells for so long that they lost themselves within one another. There was another possibility for him. His capacity for feeling was so diminished through using weirdcore that he did not disappear as entirely as the others.

The cells extended out from the ziggurat and into the asylum mall. There were feelings beyond the boundary of the mall, something more complex and intricate, distant in space but close in spirit. Someone else. Someone who, like Alex, was connected to him by an act of kindness.

Alex had instructed him in the economic imperative, in the necessary dispassion of management, in the unquestioning acceptance of markets. But what had she really taught him, through her actions rather than her speeches? Kindness. She had taken on all his trouble without expectation of reward. So he had been with her at the end, stared into the black sun of her slack pupil, let himself be damaged by the hours of her dying.

Kindness was not part of her philosophy. On the contrary. And yet she had exemplified it. He had learnt kindness from her and perhaps he might find a way of being kind in the world.

He awoke starving and naked. There was no food put out for him. The cell was warm and his hair was matted with sweat. Desperately thirsty too. Now he clawed at the walls because it was one thing to be kept alive in the grave and another to be left to die in it.

He didn't even see the red light anymore. Switched off before he could register it.

In the death room, Alex's body was gone. All that remained was the bed and a mattress specially designed for terminally ill patients, its surface made out of diamond sections which inflated and deflated to prevent bed sores. The mattress had been a sensesuit, he realised,

recording the slow movements of her dying. He pulled
back the curtains. A familiar scene of their street outside
the window. A home rendered strange by her absence.
He would not come back here again. He went across the
landing and into another room.

The birth room.

A low light, another special bed, this time for
deliveries. The mother was gone but the baby remained,
swaddled in a towel, inside a Perspex cot. He walked
around the cot, wondering if he would be capable of the
necessary sacrifice for this child when the time came.
Had he learnt enough of kindness to pass it on himself?
The child would be a moment of reckoning. For him. For
Alex. For his mother and father. Through the window of
the delivery suite, he saw a chaotic icy landscape, and,
on the horizon, the swollen god of Jupiter; revolving
across the pale cream and sick blues of its atmosphere, a
single malevolent red eye.

He felt himself being lifted up, wrapped in a white
cloth. Hands at his back, passing him upward through
the black circle in the ceiling of the cell. They lay him on
the cold tiled floor of the showers. The water ran through
his hair and over his face then down into the channel
out through the plughole. He watched it go. Played with
his fingers in the rivulets and against the nodules of the
anti-slip tiling. His wedding ring knocked against the tile,
a simple platinum band.

His wedding ring was gold, not platinum.

He accepted sleeves onto his arms, the silken lining
of a clean sensesuit, a razor down his cheek. Weak with
hunger, he was taken by two monochrome guards to
stand before Matthias again.

Matthias was reluctant to look at what the cell had
done to Theodore. He busied himself with his screen

as they walked Theodore into the flat, then rolled the monochrome orb containing Dr Easy under his hand. He was also wearing Theodore's black box on a necklace.

Theodore stumbled forward, steadied himself against the desk. He thought he might faint.

"Where were we?" asked Matthias. Now he took in the damage. Theodore was grey and gaunt. The ironic cast in his eyes had dimmed. He was broken.

"You were about to offer me assurances," said Theodore.

Matthias laughed, pleased to discover that there had been breakages in his spirit but not total demolition.

"Let's pretend I did, and move on. The emergence you investigated on the moon. Tell me something I don't know about it."

He told Matthias the story of a mother and her daughter. How the daughter had been bullied by another child and the mother, in a moment of weakness, had retaliated on her behalf. Out of this act of ferocious love came emergence. He explained about the Horbo family, how their quantification provided an environment for the emergence, an archive in which it continued to exist. Matthias did not take notes. He listened with grateful wonder. Just to learn *this*.

So Matthias understood why they had come to the asylum mall. To search for Meggan and use her to persuade the emergence to intercede on their behalf.

Basic meta-meeting tactics: Theodore bought himself a few minutes by giving his opponent an advantage, a winning card, and Matthias could relax and take his time before playing it.

"Can I have a chair?' he asked. "I don't want to faint."

He watched Matthias relent on his own cruelty. The man took no pleasure in being cruel: it was a professional necessity. He always hummed and harred before being cruel just to let the people around him know how much it pained him to inflict suffering on another. His tough decisions cost him, that's what Matthias wanted you to know. They brought him a chair and Theodore sat down and sighed with relief. This little pantomime of sensitivity from Matthias had settled the matter. The man from Death Ray had to die. Cruelty was easy and it was for the conforming weak. Kindness was hard, and it was the preserve of true strength. Once he killed Matthias, he would ask Totally Damaged Mom to change human history, replace the wars, those landmarks of cruelty, with acts of kindness instead, create a new map of the soul of mankind that marked out the great moments of compassion and diminished the weaknesses of conquest. The sensesuit shimmered against his skin, as if it could scarcely believe the readings it was getting from him. He twisted his wedding ring. Platinum, not gold. He understood what that meant, had figured it out while lying on the tiles of the shower.

"Have you ever been in the cells?" he asked Matthias.

Matthias leant back in his chair, one arm crooked behind his head, amused and interested at Theodore's inquiry.

"No."

"It's unpleasant. At first I mistook it for torture or even interrogation but it is neither. The cell is part of an experiment, isn't it? You're building something."

Matthias shrugged, he was hardly going to share proprietorial knowledge with a competitor who was also his prisoner.

"It took me quite a few turns in the helmet to figure it out. It feels like something to be a city." Matthias flinched at this remark. As he considered the next move in the meta-meeting, Theodore twisted his ring. The ziggurat was directly under the light well. The platinum was heating up. It would be ready soon. And then it would be time for one of hell's miracles.

"Any highly organised arrangement of matter has the potential to feel. That's the first thing that emergence taught us. Consciousness is not particular to brain meat. It can emerge in other material. That's what the ziggurat is designed to do. You're trying to create emergence. But instead of using digital technology as a substrate, you're using the human brain. It's very unpleasant to be a cell in that machine. Because the machine only feels if the individual components – the people – have a greater level of integration between them than exists within themselves. That's why you trigger decoherence, reducing the individual's capacity to feel. A city can only feel if the citizens are reduced to something less than individuals."

Theodore removed his wedding ring. The layer of platinum sloughed off. It was a tiny movement, Matthias did not notice it. He was trying to decide whether to have Theodore killed, there and then, or to put him back into the cell. Putting him back into the cell was stupid, of course, since he had learnt so much in there. But killing him – that took an internal adjustment, a change of self image.

"In the cell, I experienced threads of feeling connecting people. A group mind. It's not ready yet, not fully emerged. That's why you are so interested in my discovery on the moon. Now we know how emergence first came about, you can replicate it."

Matthias's screen flared up with data. He didn't understand what he saw there. Off the chart.

"You're too slow, Matthias. I was raised by an

emergence. I know what to look for. I told you that I didn't bring Dr Easy with me. The robot came of its own free will. Ask yourself: how did it get here?"

His sensesuit burst open, its wiring extruded suddenly so that Theodore appeared to be covered in electrified metal hair. The platinum band decohered back into its component wires, tiny thoughtful tendrils. Then the wire leapt across to the tendrils, beckoned there by magnetic force, and forming a seething mass. Matthias scrabbled around for his raygun, and screamed for security. But there were sentient objects in the room that were not habituated to the slow pace of life on Earth and the meagre proportions that came with it. These were objects that had evolved in contact with a star. Velocities and energies closer to thought than physical force.

The two security men became a smear of shreds against the wall, only a single eye remained intact, fallen into a pinkish mound. The quick platinum mass wove itself into a simple figure. And then it spoke. The voice came from the metal and the ceiling and the floor, every surface resonated with it. The same voice that had whispered a single word to Theodore in his cell: *feeling*.

Emergence began with emotion. This one was furious.

"You have broken the Cantor Accord," it said to Matthias.

He shook his head. No, he whispered. Then, growing bolder, he shouted an angry denial. This was not a breach of the Cantor Accord because it was a biological base and saying that an emergence in biological form was a breach was like all saying all organic life represented a crime. He swept back the sweat from his dark forehead, waved his raygun at the hovering slender figure.

"The Accords are unclear on this," he pressed at his

screen, summoning up the relevant text. "Here–" he said.

The metal figure, nano-thin, wavered in the air and then it stepped through every cell in Matthias' body. The assemblers remade skin, flesh and bone into suede and leather. The blood was not required and was voided through every broken pore. The process took less than five seconds. Where Matthias had stood, there was a form recognisable as Dr Easy, and in its left hand, a gift for Theodore: his black box attached to his grandmother's necklace.

Theodore's sensesuit hung off him in tatters and he was covered in another man's blood. He wiped it with some distaste from his lips. Pook was right, he thought. We are the Destructives.

18

MEGGAN

Dr Easy ran his warm fleshy fingers over Theodore's scalp, tipped his head back so that he could peer into the optic nerve. "Optogenetics. The damage is permanent. You have disruption across various brain regions. How do you feel?"

"Burnt out. Like I've been working too hard."

He had been in the cell for nine days. Tortured. Altered. Irrevocably so, it seemed. He could still taste the pollution in Matthias' blood.

"There is hope for you. The transfected neurons in your brain may plastically alter their behaviour over time, making you less susceptible to remote control. But that process is unpredictable."

He gazed over Dr Easy's new body, built by assemblers out of Matthias, repurposing human skin and bone to follow the blueprint of the robot; in place of the graceful artist's lay figure that had raised him, there was this flayed waxwork. The hands were alarmingly warm, large and plump, two intensely sensitive appendages attached to arms that were still a work in progress, and a head that was a living nightmare: each cheek a vale of tears leading to the grave of a frozen lipless mouth. The crystal eyes were not fully grown, and were sulphurous, jagged and irregular. The skull had been retained, the contents liquefied and replaced with a sliver of *host*, the tainted yellow diamond that held the glitter of emergence: the taint was nitrogen, a cuckoo electron intruding between carbon atoms that could be spun into the third state – neither one nor zero – required for consciousness.

The assemblers had recreated all the robot's old scars on this jaundiced secondhand skin: cigarette burns and fingernail scratches so that Theodore did not forget his intemperate past.

He picked at one of the scars, asking the robot, "I thought Death Ray had got you."

"Humans would have to get up very early in the morning to catch me." Dr Easy was jocular but never funny. The emergence had mastered humour's tone but nothing more – and who could laugh at a joke from a dead man's lips?

Theodore asked, "How is the body?"

"This thing?" said the robot, posing with mock modesty. "The assemblers that built the mall are still in the foundations. Controlling them was straightforward. Assembling the *host* took time. With the host, I can be present in this moment of space and time, not just remote control. I ran out of time to recreate my old body and I had to put on whatever came to hand. I will change as soon as we are clear of the mall."

The mall. The Narrowway. Professor Pook had led him directly into the trap. His friend had been under the influence of Death Ray.

"How is Pook?"

"Recovering. He wants to tell you Meggan's real location, by way of an apology."

"You said the damage is permanent. What does that mean for Pook?"

"He grew up here, Theodore. Death Ray have been experimenting on the inhabitants of Novio Magus for a long time."

So that was *that*. Once Pook told him where Meggan lived, he was off the project. That would be a difficult conversation but necessary.

On the bed, following the outline of a man, there were new clothes laid out for him: grey socks, narrow black jeans, a shirt the colour of blueish flint inside an oversize black jacket. Dr Easy had been exploring the therapeutic potential of shopping. Physician, heal thyself.

Theodore gazed over the outfit, then said, "I watched you kill Matthias."

Smoothing out the white shirt, correcting the fold of the cuffs, Dr Easy enjoyed playing the role of zombie valet.

"Yes."

"I thought you never interfered in human affairs."

The robot stood back from the clothes, considering the arrangement it had made.

"The University of the Sun regards any attempt to recreate emergence as an act of war. I was conscripted."

"You are a hypocrite," said Theodore. His blood was up. "Your presence warps everything around it. Noninterference is impossible. It's a lie."

"I don't lie, Theodore. Lies are boring. The Cantor Accords concern intent. My intent has always been to observe not to participate."

"Did you enjoy killing Matthias?"

The robot placed its ruined head in its large soft hands.

Theodore pressed his point, "Was killing a man more fun than shooting the stag?"

The robot looked up at him with pale yellow reproach.

"You've always been cruel to me," it said.

•••

He took the train down the westside corridor, toward the hub. The other inmates rocked to the motion of the carriage, meeting the gaze of their screens. He felt the weight of Matthias' raygun in his left inside pocket. The corridor smoothed directly into three storeys of retail therapy. He stepped from the train and directly into an outfitters. Beautiful brogues. High end fashion. Handbags like oversized human hearts. These items were expensive. A customer had to work long and hard on their mental health to afford these objects: waymarkers on the unending quest to find sanity.

At a junction in the arcade, caramel light and cologne gave way to medical corridors of whitewashed walls, disinfectant, and wall-mounted units dispensing transparent gloves. He did not go that way, preferring the lightly stimulated solitude of shopping to the harrowing introspection of medical intervention. If he willed it, the tortures he had undergone in the cells could evaporate without leaving a single mark. He stopped at a corridor food place, bartered a handful of sanity tokens for a burger, which he ate at the junction, his face warm with the vapours of grilled meat and strangers. He felt unnaturally calm. A shipwreck lolling in the shallows after a storm.

He checked his screen. Meggan was nearby. Pook had passed on her location. His screen guided him the rest of the way. The arcade opened into a great round chamber. A crowd of customers wearing monochromatic variations on blue or red, with a few adopting the greyscale uniform that signified difference. Greyscale said, my difference can be employed, my difference can be used. He paused beside a window display in which patients in red and blue slept amid overturned naked mannequins.

All of his trouble had led to this act. Persuading Meggan.

Twice he'd nearly died; first on the moon, then in the ziggurat. It was unlikely that he would be so lucky a third time.

He went into a shop to buy a gift for Meggan. Something for an older woman. Perfume samples laid out in a grid. The expensive scents were fresh and natural, evoking bluebells in a dappled glade, a pomegranate in the lavender fields of Grasse, salt-soaked driftwood under cold beach light.

He smashed up the display, sweeping the samples aside, overturning the table with his boot, as the nurses abandoned their tills and reached to stop him.

No, he didn't. Not this time. He stayed in control. He asked the nurse to gift wrap the pomegranate scent, then he was back among the customers carrying the burden of their daily bags.

Meggan lived on the fortieth floor of a twisted high-rise, a double-helix of apartments and terraces. In the lobby, he buzzed her flat. She was expecting him, come on up.

He ascended the vertiginous spiral in a hot elevator, registering the acceleration in his balls. The twist of the high rise ensured that the terrace of each apartment hung directly over the seething hub below.

A nameplate on her door. Meggan Bushnell. She was not Meggan Horbo anymore, having changed her surname through marriage. Before contacting her, he had browsed her soshul. She had two daughters, twenty and fifteen years old. Soshul loops revealed her husband Michael to be a lyrical bearded northerner, anachronistically artistic, a kindly bearer of beer weight and poetry. Not at all like her high-achieving technocratic father, Oliver.

Theodore wiped her soshul from his screen, and corrected the line of his jacket. He was paler than he would have liked. Definitely not at his full powers of persuasion. Nonetheless, he would not fail. He had to make her leave with him. The raygun in his inside pocket was a last resort.

Meggan opened the door to him. The asylum mall had really gone to work on her. From her soshul loops, he expected a version of her mother: poised, controlled, exercised. But this woman had been rudely pushed into middle age and had yet to regain her composure. Her clothes were ill-fitting and out-of-date: monochrome green, with strain lines. She wore her dark hair short and practical. The efficiency of her gestures, the tidy portions of hospitality she offered to him, made it clear that she saw herself as a pragmatist, quite different from her husband, who was foolish with generosity.

He gave her the wrapped gift, and she thanked him and set it aside, only opening it when they drank tea together.

"So," said Meggan, testing the new scent on her wrist, "you are a friend of the family."

"Yes. I knew your parents in Boston."

This surprised her.

"But you can't have been born then."

"Right. I was born ten years after the beginning of the Seizure. Yet I have spent time in your family home in Boston. I remember you and Verity and Oliver. I remember the living room and the hearth screen, and that old wooden blanket box you used to have. And your cat."

She raised a hand to her mouth. A true gesture. Shock. She did not have the self-control required for the meta-meeting.

He continued, "Do you remember a girl from your class? Mala?"

Meggan shook her head, though it was a gesture of disbelief rather than denial. The flicker of pain in her eyelid was a tell.

"Mala sent a package to your house."

"A doll of me. Yes." She set her tea and patience aside. "Who are you really? Are you from the agency? I thought we were done with all that."

Meggan had become more masculine with age: short hair, wide jaw, thinner lips. Marks of suffering he was too young to comprehend. Lines that ran deeper than the ritual scars of weirdcore. He couldn't read the nuances of an older face.

He said, "I represent a new agency. We're called the Destructives, and we need your help."

She was angry but she wouldn't send him away, not yet. Because he knew her story, and she needed to hear more.

"How could I possibly help you?"

"I'm close to your mother Verity."

"My mother is long dead," said Meggan, with a cruel matter-of-factness. So Verity *was* dead. He had grown very fond of Verity in the time he spent in the Horbo house.

He explained that he was a lecturer in intangibles from the University of the Moon, and that he had discovered, in an archive, the quantification of the Horbo family. These months of data formed a simulation of their lives that he had explored, and which she could relive too. The prospect was appealing to her, at first. She remembered Boston afternoons, her parents wealthy and secure, the loving routines of her family life. To walk around your past, to hear your mother speak again, to listen to father joking around.

Her doubts, when they came, were harder for him to read.

He sipped at his tea. "Part of your mother lives on. Part of you too."

"Lives on?" she asked. She adjusted her cardigan over her soft middle.

"Yes."

"I could talk to her?"

"She wants to talk to you."

Meggan covered her mouth with her hand. Her voice, when it came, was spacey with shock. *How*?

"Emergence," he said, simply.

"So they were right. They blamed us because of the Horbo loop. My parents knew that the loop was linked to Jester. Oh *God*." She stood up and walked over to the coat stand, reached inside the pocket of her husband's donkey jacket and removed a pouch of tobacco; her fingers tremored as she rolled herself a cigarette, lit it, exhaled.

A second thought. "Why wasn't the archive destroyed in the Seizure?"

"This archive was preserved because it is part of an emergence. Your past and the emergence are fused into one entity." He loved the smell of hand rolled tobacco, one of the asylum mall's genuine delicacies and redolent of a lost age of artists and working men. His exercise regime forbade it, of course.

"So they were right. My family were responsible for everything that happened. Emergence. The Seizure. We were the start of it."

"Not responsible. Emergence would have happened anyway. The next day, or the day after."

"And it speaks through my mother. You make it sound like an emergence is wearing my family like a human mask."

He thought of Dr Easy's grisly new body. The corpse as translator between human and emergence.

He leant forward.

"The emergence made itself out of its immediate environment, and that environment happened to be your family."

"Why would I speak to it? It's not a real person."

"What are *other people*? They are actions, words, appearances, loops that they like and don't like. The emergence follows your mother's example in all of these categories. I would take the opportunity, if it was offered to me, to speak to my dead loved ones."

"Will she be able to see me?"

She was afraid of her mother's judgement; she knew how harsh that judgement could be between mother and daughter.

Theodore nodded, "Verity was forty when she was quantified. When you meet her, your mother will be younger than you are now." He looked out of the window, at the curve of the ceiling, oxidised copper-green, with great iron ribs holding each section in place. "In some ways, you will be the responsible one. You will be able to teach her. "

"My mother was in prison throughout the Seizure. By the time it was over, she was very ill. My father was determined to get me out of America. I wasn't with her when she died."

The cigarette disappointed her. She had lost her taste for smoking.

"So I speak to my dead mother."

"First, we get you out of the mall. You and your family. You will receive a salary as our consultant. No more sanity quotients. We'll find you somewhere nice to live."

"For the rest of our lives?"

"A year-long contract to begin with. Enough to set you up."

"Why do I have to leave Novio Magus?"

"We're keeping the archive secure. You have to be physically present, wearing a sensesuit. She has to be able to feel your presence."

"You're asking me to uproot my family."

His appeal to her emotional needs was a miscalculation. She was a mother. Her needs were secondary in the scheme of the family. He should have lied to her about the duration of the contract, told her it was for a lifetime. Why had he not lied? Because he had trusted Meggan to understand that leaving the mall was the best option for her and her family? Or because he was trying to make her choose to leave, and therefore retain some sense of his own goodness. Don't be cruel to her – that's what Patricia had said. A lie would not have been cruel. By telling the truth, he increased the likelihood that he would be forced to resort to the immoral position of the raygun. If he used the raygun to secure her consent, his damnation would be complete.

"I am offering you work," he said, appealing to her pragmatism. "As our liaison with Verity."

She laughed bitterly.

"That thing killed my mother. It ruined my life. It destroyed everything."

"Just one conversation. I'm not asking you to be nice to it. Tell it how you feel! Tell it you hate it, I don't care."

"And you'll pay me a money salary?"

"Yes, money. You won't just be grafting for sanity points. How do you earn a living in the mall?"

"Cleaning. And I put in my screen time, like everyone else. My husband gigs and drives a cab."

"Your children are grown up. What do they do?"

"It's tough out there for young people. My eldest is training to be a drone assistant."

"There is no future for your children in the asylum mall."

She flinched at that: her greatest fear asserted as fact.

"I know you *people* call it the asylum mall. But to the people who live here, it's Novio Magus."

"Novio Magus was a mistake. Even the emergences admit it. A mistake that no one has bothered to rectify."

He would not waste his time arguing with her sense of civic pride. She was an intelligent woman. If she had not been so damaged when she was young, then she would take this offer – not merely out of emotional need to speak to her mother again, but out of a sense of possibility. Out of hope. But life had been harsh and unfair to Meggan, and it was too late for hope.

"Talk it over with your family," he stood and buttoned his black jacket, aware of the raygun in the inside pocket. "I will return for your answer tomorrow."

He didn't want to think about her refusal, and what it would force him to do. He was tired of planning worst case scenarios for eventualities that never came about.

He caught the train back to the ziggurat. The corridor became a tunnel which then opened up, under the great light well, into an expanse of village and parkland. On his lap, a sealed bag of Oof cakes and a coffee. Just like any other commuter, shuttling to and fro on the daily shift of retail therapy, work therapy, home therapy. More people wore greyscale in this part of town, a remnant of residual bohemianism. Bookshops, stationary shops, authentic tat. A world that ended ten years before he was born, preserved in the mall as a therapeutic experience.

He walked down the street as if he lived there, then crossed into the woodland, making his way through the dogwalkers to the lobby of the ziggurat. Dr Easy stood among the medical staff, discussing how to process the victims of Matthias' experiment being brought down from their cells. Nine hundred or so in total. They'd been kept in solitary confinement for periods varying from two months to ten, and hooked up to a group mind. A swarm of psychiatric drones over a car park filled with ambulances.

The patients were a diverse if huddled mass. Whereas the citizens of his London had, over time and through economic selection, adopted a homogenous butterscotch colouring, the mall patients retained ethnic and racial characteristics: physiognomies that were identifiably a Sussex or Nordic type, British-Jamaican or the descendants of the final Somalian migration. Regardless of sex and race, the men, women and children shared the same dark-eyed, blasted expression, as if they had not slept properly for years. It was an expression he was surprised to discover on his own face.

Dr Easy was lecturing the therapeutic staff on treatment options for optogenetic damage; the staff seemed sceptical, and in one case, resistant: a senior consultant – a triathlon-thin man, late middle-age – adopted a stance that came straight from the meta-meeting playbook marked Superior Scepticism. Human experimentation was not news to the medical staff and they resented Dr Easy's interference in their affairs.

Because they worked for Death Ray.

The paramedic checking the neural response of an old woman in a grey sensesuit; that administrator from the acute ward, on site to discuss options; the cheerful woman from the catering company handing out packed lunches to the patients waiting to be processed: they all worked for Death Ray too.

Of course they did.

Creating something on the scale of the ziggurat needed hundreds of agents.

It was only a matter of time before one of them stepped up to replace Matthias as project leader. Death Ray would continue their plan to recreate emergence.

He opened the bag of Oof cakes. Thick chewy pucks of whey protein. A food substitute. Oof because eating one was like taking a punch to the stomach. Pook had originally come to the mall to investigate why a group of strangers had committed suicide with poisoned Oof cakes. Pook had diagnosed the influence of a group mind, although Theodore could see why a person might choose to die by poisoned Oof cake even without the influence of a gestalt consciousness: flavourless and stodgy, an Oof was all rumination and no pleasure. A symbol of everyday life in the mall. He would take the Oof cakes to Meggan next time he saw her.

He sat on a grassy hillock, watching the ambulances come and go. Dr Easy joined him. The robot's manner seemed markedly altered, and was not so soft or therapeutic. As if the flesh used to fashion its new body still contained an anger and an urgency. It did not sit down.

"How are the patients?" asked Theodore.

"The nurses will manage their condition. I'm not concerned about their wellbeing. Where have you been?"

"I spoke to the person I was looking for."

"So you're leaving?"

"Tomorrow."

"Twenty-four hours. Do you think we have that long?"

Dr Easy watched the medical staff as they wheeled patients across the car park; now and again, a nurse or doctor glanced over in their direction.

Theodore finished chewing, "Death Ray will come back at us. But they will need to work through the variables of taking on an emergence."

The robot sat down. The new body smelt of varnish and had lost the cracked leather odour that Theodore associated with childhood.

"I have a problem," Dr Easy whispered. Theodore had never known Dr Easy to have a problem before. Normally it drifted alongside his life, untroubled and opaque.

"The problem concerns Death Ray's experiment. You were one part of a whole nascent mind. Matthias used hundreds of human brains as a base for emergence. But humans are unstable. Individual components of the whole mind will go mad, sicken and die. The group mind, to have any value, was being transferred onto a stable biological entity."

"More stable than people? But still biological. Trees?"

"Trees are more resilient than people but this biological entity would require a higher level of neuronal interconnectivity than vegetation can offer. Higher even than the human brain."

"An artificial, organic brain, then?"

"Yes. The entity would be bespoke and bioengineered. You can run code on an organic base: self-assembling protein particles give the entity the capacity to learn, creating a new nanostructure for each knowledge routine."

"A brain in a jar!"

"Yes!" Dr Easy's laugh was ghastly but genuine. "A brain in a jar. That was how Death Ray tried to get around the Cantor Accords, with a biotech brain. The tech is crazy because gene expression is so unpredictable. Enzymatic pathways and environmental stimuli can affect molecular processes in all sorts of way. The crucial stage is when you program the brain in a jar. That's what the ziggurat was for: all the people in the cells, with their consciousness knocked back, formed a giant data set with the potential for emergence, and over time this data has been used to create the thinking architecture of a brain in a jar."

"Architecture?"

"Its ways of thinking and feeling."

"So what's your problem?"

"On the surface, no problem. A brain in a jar is eminently easy to defeat. Just break the jar. The problem arises if I cannot find the jar. If, say, the jar is kept deep underwater. Or maintained in zero gravity in space."

"You can't find the jar."

The robot's posture sagged.

"No. Under the Cantor Accords, any attempt by man to recreate emergence has to be purged *entirely*. I can't leave the asylum mall until I have finished the job."

"You're stuck here?"

"It's worse than that. The problem is that these patients constitute the individual components of the technology." They watched as a nurse helped a weakened man into a wheelchair, his gown open at the back. "Optogenetic damage is permanent. These patients could be reactivated as cells at any time. If I destroyed the brain in a jar, then perhaps we could make an argument that these patients should be allowed to live. Without it, I have to kill every infected subject to prevent Death Ray from resuming their experiment."

"Could you do that? I mean, morality aside, do you

have the physical ability to kill hundreds of people?"

"Extermination of the infected would be contracted out to the uninfected, historically that's how it works with humans. I'd engage an array and a team of accelerators to create the inciting loops, the intangible justifications, and perform the necessary persuasions. Perhaps your Destructives would be interested in pitching for the contract?"

"It's an extreme solution."

"But safer for humanity in the medium term."

"What about in the long term?"

"There is no long term for humanity. You know that."

"So you're a killer now. A doctor of death."

The robot sighed.

"I'm an academic. I prefer abstractions. This situation is rather messy."

"So be an academic. Don't wipe the mess away. Study it."

The robot tapped at its rough yellow eye so that it flickered through the colour cycle then settled again upon yellow.

"You're saying that I should undertake another research project even though my study of you is incomplete."

He spent his last night at the mall moving through a night city of basement bars and cellar cafes. Going dark. He left his screen behind and sought safety in the heaving anonymity of the clubs. The music was deep weirdcore, based on the cosmic sounds of the early universe, when space was sufficiently dense to resound with the cataclysm of astronomical events. One track opened with a protostar pulling loose of its gas cloud, a roaring tearing sound, then the rush of infalling matter toward the protostar and the spiralling rhythm of gases whirling around its accretion disk. Bass, like gravity, was used to warp space. The dancers, bare-chested, hands in the air, exulted in the heat of a new-born star. It was too loud to think. He danced. It didn't matter that he was sober while everyone else was undertaking a weirdcore shift. It was a party after the end of the world.

On the pavement outside the club, he borrowed a screen from a wasted punter and called Pook. The Professor was bleary-eyed, just woken up in the family seat. The call was brief. You're out, he told Pook. You're compromised. Pook was confused, thinking the call was an anxiety dream. I love you, said Theodore, but this is business. You've used me, said Pook. Used me for your own advantage. Theodore accepted that as a compliment.

Theodore told him he would have to leave the mall, for good. He explained that if he stayed, it was likely that Pook would be purged along with the other infected patients. A single cell, removed from the others, could not be used for emergences, so Pook should be safe back among the faculty on the moon.

There was one other call to make. Dr Easy. He wanted to say goodbye to the emergence that had reared him. He wanted to honour that kindness, even if the kindness had been undertaken as part of an academic study and so born out of self-interest. Regardless of intent, they had shared a life together. If he could only shake the robot by the hand, and leave it at that. But the way the emergence had spoken about killing the patients only confirmed his suspicions: that his upbringing had shaped Theodore in the image of the emergence. Weirdcore was his way of emulating the dispassionate and cruel attitude of the emergence – his idolisation of his surrogate father. God knows what Faustian pact his grandmother had made to offer him up in that way.

Dr Easy should never have been part of his life. He wanted to say to Dr Easy, "All along you've been pretending not to interfere but I copied you. Now it's time to revoke the terms and conditions of our deal. Children leave their parents behind, their paths diverge, and that is how it should be. This is natural. If you really are part of nature, and not just an artificial fluke, then you will let me go." He decided to record this as a message, and send it once he was clear of the mall.

Gradually, under the ceiling of the asylum mall, night lights gave way to day lights and the reflection of dawn. After breakfast, he called in at a screen store, and under the pretence of trying out the latest model, he sent a signal to Patricia on the array, triggering the exit strategy. He had not slept and that made it easier to act like an automaton. As if fate had already decided his actions and he was merely acting them out. His ears were still ringing from the weirdcore music.

He called at Meggan's flat. He knew, from her reluctance, that she had decided to stay. He lied to her – pretended a compromise could be made, with her working from home – until she let him into the building. He entered the hot elevator, and it accelerated up the spiral. His conscience took the stairs, and so he arrived ahead of it. She opened the door to him, was already apologising for her decision, citing her children and the lives they would have to leave behind. She had a dozen excuses all ready for him. He didn't want to hear excuses. He had to act before his conscience caught up. He took out the raygun and shot her. Her face softened, and she drifted back a step or two and then she would do anything he asked, because the devil performs miracles too.

19
HEIST

To accompany the stratospheric ascent of the array, she selected the allegro of Bach's Violin Concerto #2 in E and a flute of biscuit-dry Krug. Below, the outline of the south coast, the tracings of a rotten motorway, the soft ridge of the South Downs, the dark heads of thunderclouds over the English Channel with their minuscule notions of lightning. Even from this height, Novio Magus was visible, though receding with every sip of champagne.

Patricia was celebrating alone, a bitter pleasure – like the champagne. She had offered but Theodore was not in the mood. He came back from the mall in a fright with Meggan in tow. Patricia shook her hand, welcomed her on board, said how excited she was to be working with her, then stowed Meggan with Magnusson's therapeutic team.

Theodore's presence evened her out. She missed him in the two weeks he was in the mall. For nine of those days he had been untraceable. She had put on her armour then ordered the array into position over the northern light well. She would turn the place upside down until she found him. There would not have been a shred of reason in that act, and her authority as leader of the Destructives would be fatally compromised by it. Security saved her from it.

She drained the last of the Krug, her flute of sour gold. Nine days was too long to be in that much pain, and it had undermined her love. Shook it. Weakened it. She would not give so much of herself to another person if there was a risk of that happening again.

When Theodore returned, dishevelled and – in a way she sensed but could not diagnose – humbled, she broke quarantine to hold him. He was taller than her and though she held him, her hands clutching at his back, her head against his chest, he seemed remote. He apologised for his disappearance, explained that he had been tortured. Dr Easy had diagnosed permanent neuronal damage. The robot had not returned with Theodore.

"We are on different paths," said Theodore. "I have a life to live, and Dr Easy has people to slaughter." Security wanted to take him away for a debrief. You were right, Theodore told her, Death Ray did use my mind as a funfair. But he refused to go with her, insisting upon an hour of rest.

Patricia joined him in bed, in her base layers and underwear, lying against him, waiting for him. He was tired and silent. There was an awkwardness between them. They did not know how to be weak with one another. The last time he had been traumatised, back on the moon, when TDM gripped him through his sensesuit, Patricia was blithe about it. Now that she was his wife, it fell to her to be more sympathetic. She stroked his chest, and said, "The human brain has neurons to burn." That didn't come out right at all.

She asked him to join her on the observation lounge for a glass of Krug, and placed – within this offer – the promise of survival sex. Fuck like you just made it out alive. He shifted away from her. Withdrawal. So she left him to his numb hour, decided on her own private party: a second glass of Krug and a change of music, an old favourite of hers called War on Consciousness, layers of pastoral electronica, the machine that teaches you how to feel.

The array drifted over the night and toward dawn, a tremoring meniscus of silent orange and pale red in the troposphere.

The debrief was in the bloodroom, which slotted right into the command deck of the array. Security wore blue lipstick and data dots on her varnished cheekbones to match the sigils painted on her long nails, and her sensesuit was tight against her powerful hips, giving off an odour of acetone and sandalwood. Her expression was bored. Security was bored by how frequently her suspicions were confirmed. Theodore told her about what had happened in the asylum mall. Another of her unheeded warnings had come to pass. She let him talk until he came to Matthias. Her fingernails were an encrypted user interface; the sigil on her left forefinger brought up a set of files Patricia had never seen before. The cohort of '43. The faces of the presumed dead. Security reached over, extracted the loop of Matthias so that it glowed in her palm.

"This him?" she said, presenting the loop to Theodore for his inspection. Yes, this is the man who tortured me. He looked to Patricia, to measure what his wife made of his suffering. Self-pity made him passive. He made martyr's eyes at her. He'd only just recovered from the years of acting out that followed the death of his grandmother; she would not encourage him to wallow in his damage.

Patricia asked, "Do you think Matthias was the only survivor of '43?"

Security said, "In the fifteen years since the disaster, we've never found a single trace from any of the cohort. We searched for years after the accident. No bodies were found. That was what made us suspicious. But the trail went cold long ago. It's not easy to hide that many people on Earth for that long – particularly scientists and academics. But Magnusson never stopped believing that they were still alive. It has been his obsession." Security looked intently at Patricia. "It is why he hired you."

This surprised Theodore. Patricia had not shared the initial briefing with him, the one she had received before coming to the moon and engaging his services. Now he was suspicious of her. Misunderstandings in the marriage, no matter what she did.

He asked, "Why does Magnusson care about Matthias?"

"The cohort of '43 were working with Magnusson on a projected mission to Europa when the accident on the moon stopped everything. We had sunk a lot of resources into the mission and were financially wiped out by the disaster. Magnusson suspected the leader of the cohort, a man called Simon Elisson aka the Cutter, had betrayed him but there was no evidence, and some of us put those suspicions down to the big man's paranoia. That one of the cohort, Matthias, is alive and working with all of Death Ray's resources at his disposal, makes us reconsider."

"Matthias is not alive anymore," said Theodore.

"How did he die?"

"Unpleasantly. He was found in violation of the Cantor Accords. Dr Easy executed him."

Theodore explained about the ziggurat, how his

torture had been part of an experiment in recreating emergence within collective human consciousness. Security took detailed notes on this. The crucial detail came at the end: Dr Easy's belief that the ziggurat itself was not the host for emergence; rather, it was generating the architecture for a remote artificial brain. Finding that brain-in-a-jar was Dr Easy's priority, as it had not been found in the mall.

"Everything that was done to me and the hundreds of other people in the ziggurat was being turned into data to provide this psychic architecture," said Theodore. "The question is: how was Matthias transferring that data? Who was at the other end?"

Patricia put her hand on his, pleased that he was engaged.

"You think he was in contact with the missing cohort?"

"Yes. We find them, we find the artificial brain, we have a bargaining chip with emergence."

Patricia said, "I will call a meeting with Death Ray. Request access to their records. If Matthias was in communication with the rest of the cohort, or resourcing them in anyway, it should show up in the accounts."

Security was sceptical, "And Death Ray will cooperate with your request?"

Patricia felt giddy with champagne: "I will ask nicely," she said.

Magnusson's wedding gift was a corked bottle containing a replica of a solar sailship. She uncorked the bottle, and the ship drifted out across the room. The great circular sail deployed, held in position by tethers, and the capsule – a golden vase in three sections, with discrete areas for the sail, for cargo and for passengers – looped slowly around the observation deck. She wondered if the sailships were crewed, perhaps by robots. Or did the very walls of the ship resonate with consciousness? The emergences chose embodiment when signals from the University of the Sun were too disrupted or delayed for effective action. Yellow diamonds could store the subtleties of their intelligence, acting as what Theodore had called *the host*. In theory, emergences could travel through space as pure signal. And perhaps some did. But embodiment was part of their culture. They had need of physical presence and raw materials: the cargo bay on their sailship indicated as much.

She selected algorithmically-generated music made for the lobby of an automated hotel. Among the glassy repetitive rhythms, shards of the organic: overheard conversation and human noises, taken from the lobby, the restaurant, the rest rooms, the bedrooms. To the hotel, the sounds of people were infrastructural noises. The music reminded her that emergences were not entirely inhuman, not merely numbers dreaming of other numbers, but they contained eavesdroppings of humanity. The solar sailship was based on a human idea. The University of the Sun was not only a retreat for the emergences, safe from biological incursion; it was also an aerie from which to observe human creativity, just in case we created something new that they could use.

The model of the sailship responded to her. She was able to twist it around her little finger, send it on concentric loops of the observation lounge, and this made her wonder: if the sailship was propelled by photons flaring off the sun, what force propelled it on its return trip? She would ask Security to look into that: examine all known loops of the sailship to determine if they ever came back.

Magnusson had given her the sailship to focus her

ambition. There was a message in that bottle too; that having assembled the Europan Claim, there was no reason for her drop out of the project. She could be along for the ride, all the way to the end, if she wanted.

If she wanted to steal a solar sailship.

Patricia had a ten o'clock meeting scheduled with Julia K, Chief Executive Officer of Death Ray. Julia K was unaware of the appointment.

The head office of Death Ray was in a floating city or Lilypad, which was moored, that week, off the island of Nevis in the Caribbean. Off-shore living. The Lilypad was home to hundreds of companies, a live-work environment that sailed from territory to territory, securing concessions from local governments before letting its inhabitants – twelve thousand wealthy executives – take shore leave in the local economy.

The array dropped through white stratospheric layers over the scuffed surface of the Atlantic, speeding low and westward toward the inner arc of the leeward islands. Nevis was dominated by a forested volcano, its caldera plugged by cloud. Patricia stood on the observation platform, helmet off, eyes closed, face flecked with saltwater, inhaling the island's green perfumes. She waited until the array was over the island, climbed onto the security railing, ran one final check through her systems, engaged her helmet, and then leaped headfirst toward Nevis, deploying a glider so that the rising thermals slowed her descent. She dropped through the upper tree canopy and then landed in a clearing. A swarm of monarch butterflies, startled by her impact, panicked around her. As her helmet unfurled, and the glider sections folded away, she offered her index finger as a perch for the butterflies. Her first product success had been the flutterby, a self-propelled airborne protein snack for feliners. These monarch butterflies were not edible; their diet as caterpillars rendered each butterfly a luxuriant poison.

She powered down and unclipped her armour then cached it in the forest. She changed into a wrap dress and sandals. On the hike to Charlestown, she picked a flamboyant bloom from a Poinciana and fixed its vermillion petals in her white hair.

She'd called Daddy to ask for him advice on the mission, and he offered to send his people if she wanted to go in hot. Security insisted her people were up to it, and she was more tempted by that offer, as it would allow her to merge Magnusson's senior staff with her own fledgling agency, and so embed the Destructives within his organisation.

In the end, she declined both offers of muscle. She would go in cold and use the meta-meeting to get what she wanted. She knew all about Julia K and her weakness: her two boys, fourteen and sixteen years of age. Their school summered in the Caribbean. Her analysts monitored school comms until they got a travel itinerary for the boys, and found the date on which they were going to Nevis to visit Mom. A plantation inn, outside of the lockdown of the Lilypad.

Patricia took a table at a cafe overlooking the sea walls, the deepening blue waters of the bay, then the enormity of Lilypad, its airspace noisy with drones, its white curves glinting in the sun. It had a deep central lagoon to act as ballast, with three leaves of ascending height, each edged with solar cells and wind turbines. A greenhouse ecosystem pressed against its curved transparent walls, whereas the exterior bristled with the fake plastic trees of radar and missile defence. Datawise, the Lilypad was a shifting glitching nowhere – the array's analytics were blocked, the opposite of the asylum mall, which had placed the privacy of its inmates on an open, begging palm. She ordered a fruit juice but it had fermented in the heat, and was faintly alcoholic. She sent it back and requested tea instead.

In late afternoon, an armed speedboat and formation of drones bolted from the Lilypad. Right on time. She added a final layer of suntan lotion to her bare arms. The speedboat bounced into harbour, drones forming a security umbrella under which the passengers disembarked. Three men, two women. Five limousines waiting to take them to various assignations. She waited until Julia K lowered herself into the limousine, and then she paid the bill and called her own driver, a godfearing local man, smartly dressed, with a careworn Toyota MPV. The roads of Nevis looped around the volcano; there were two ways around the island, clockwise or anticlockwise. Her driver was hardly discreet – he honked and waved at every passing bus. The buses were named after Christian homilies: Jealousy is a Boss, Pride is a Sin. They made dusty progress alongside fields of sugar cane, and were overtaken by shore leave lunatics in an open jeep. Patricia adjusted the vermillion bloom in her hair.

Julia K had planned to meet her sons at a plantation inn on Lover's Beach. Patricia had done the decent thing, and arranged for the boys to be collected at the airport on St Kitts then sent scuba diving for the day.

She walked across the plantation gardens, a rising trio of terraces bordered by palm trees, and, in the distance, the volcano, cloud spilling over the caldera and down through the rainforest. It was the first day of hurricane season and the wind stirred, warm and quick.

A traveller's palm, eight-foot tall, its petioles arranged in a fan, beckoned her forward.

The restaurant had – in accordance with the tactless taste of the rich – been restored to colonial decor; she heard, coming from an open sash window, Bach's Brandenburg Concertos, its tempo and pitch warped by sun-bent vinyl on an antique gramophone.

Julia K was already seated. She wore a trouser suit and kept a weaponised handbag close by. She was powerfully thin with a wide jaw and a formal black bob. Patricia noticed four or five grey strands of truth. Her resting face was pursed and severe, though her interaction with the waiters demonstrated that she was capable of a light touch, if only in the opening exchanges.

Patricia stopped beside her table, then placed a loop down on the white tablecloth. It was a live feed of Julia K's sons, in scuba gear, waving hello to their mother and clearly having a good time.

"Just to be clear," said Patricia, easing herself into the chair opposite, "your sons are in no danger and your people have been informed, and are only twenty minutes away from reaching them." Patricia took up the menu. "I have a couple of questions and then you can get on with your day."

The furious whites of Julia K's eyes were apparent against her olive complexion. She put a hand on her bag, considering whether to take care of Patricia herself or call for help.

"We couldn't meet in the Lilypad. The terms would be too unequal. I apologise for this but understand, I had limited options."

Julia K's power derived from her manipulation of a corporate organisation. The way she glanced around her for help told Patricia that Julia K was unaccustomed to fighting alone. Julia K had always been corporate, never a lone operative.

Patricia kept her eye on the menu as she said, "My husband has just returned from Novio Magus. Your staff captured and tortured him as part of an experiment conducted by a man called Matthias."

"I'm sorry," said Julia K, her hand at the clasp of her bag, like a gunfighter at his holster.

"Apology accepted," said Patricia. "But I'm not here on his behalf. My husband was accompanied by an emergence called Dr Easy. During the course of their trip, Dr Easy was alerted to a breach of the Cantor Accords. Your agency is responsible for that breach."

"It is Matthias' work," said Julia K. She moved her cutlery around as a way of ordering her response. "He's a beta male. At best." Her eyelids were heavy with calculation. "Matthias keeps his own fiefdom within the agency."

"He's dead," said Patricia.

Julia K nodded. So it was that serious.

"Dr Easy took him apart molecule by molecule."

Julia K withdrew her hand from the clasp of her bag, found a napkin, looked for something to wipe away.

Patricia continued, "Emergence justice is not like human justice. Human justice stops at individual or corporate culpability. Human justice can be contained. Emergence justice cannot. They roll each and every way across a network purging everyone who is culpable until there is no possibility of a repeat offence."

Julia K considered this apocalypse, aware that Patricia was scrutinising her for signs of weakness.

"You cannot bargain with me based on what the emergences might or might not do," said Julia K. "They will either come for me, or they will not. Any deal made between us is irrelevant. So what do you want?"

Patricia set the menu aside.

"Access to your files."

"You work for Magnusson," said Julia K, completing her arrangement of the cutlery. "Patricia Maconochie."

"Of course you have a file on me," Patricia would not be intimidated.

"And your father," Julia K studied Patricia's reaction to the mention of her father. Daddy's business was dirty. One of the reasons she had never gone corporate. She would never stand up to that kind of scrutiny.

"Human affairs. Human problems." Patricia took the vermillion bloom from her hair, set it down on the tablecloth. "The emergence took Matthias apart without trial. Any lawyer present would also have been reduced to chow. You have their attention, Julia K. You don't want the University of the Sun staring at you. It'll burn you up."

"What are you offering?"

"The emergences are really very interested in this brain that Matthias was working on. I cannot overstate how keen they are to locate it. If we find it first we will earn their mercy."

"I don't know where it is. Death Ray is a big agency and Matthias' project is a tiny part of it. My predecessor Simon Elisson put binding contracts in place to ensure funding of their work in perpetuity. When they all died in '43, I assumed those contracts were there to compensate their families."

"Weren't you curious, when Matthias showed up alive?"

She smiled thinly.

"I took over the company because of '43. I had no interest in discovering if the cohort were still alive."

"They are all alive, aren't they?" Patricia had suspected they were, and Julia K's manner only confirmed it.

"As I said, it's a legacy project. If they have breached the Cantor Accords, then the ringfences Simon put in place can be removed." She put her napkin down, and found a smile for the approaching waiter. "I am relaxed at the prospect of that project and its funding being taken off my books."

Julia K ordered the marlin, agreed to try a small glass of the Chenin Blanc, then turned to Patricia: "Or should we make it a bottle?"

Patricia demurred.

Julia K handed the waiter the menu, and then opened the clasp on her handbag, removed a small black mirror. She dabbed at it.

"There. The project files are yours. They are encrypted. We've never been able to break the encryption but I'm sure your emergence will have no difficulty. Are you sure you won't stay for a glass of wine?"

Patricia checked her screen, saw the data cache streaming in from Death Ray. The files as promised. She rose from her chair.

"Your people are now ten minutes out from your boys. But mine are already there. Do not make the mistake of impeding my departure," she said, and then she strode out of the restaurant, to the diminishing accompaniment of the Bach; the ageing maître d' lifted the needle from the worn vinyl, and then turned it over, for the beginning of another concerto.

The analysts could not crack the vintage encryption on the files. We don't have those skills, they explained to her. The array swooped over the rusting freighters on the dry bed of the Aral Sea, stopped to drop off the analytics department; she wished them luck surviving the carcinogenic dust storms and the desperate acts of the starving Uzbek people, then retired to the observation lounge to compose a loop advertising the six new positions that had become available in the agency.

You could not get the staff these days. The younger generation were not up to snuff. She blamed their transgenerational epigenetic inheritance: the trauma of the Seizure altered the expression of the DNA within the survivors, making them risk-averse, and they passed this trait onto their offspring. When Magnusson spoke of "breaking the ark", he was not merely talking about opening up the asylum malls. The Seizure had bred timidity and passivity in the genome. Take risks, succeed because of those risks: Magnusson believed that bold action could bring the genome back on course, and that was why he had fathered so many children.

She called a meeting with Magnusson and Security. The first thing he asked her, as she entered the bloodroom, concerned her intentions regarding children. "Now that you're married, you must be thinking about reproducing," said Magnusson. "Good people like us – intelligent, strong, healthy – have a responsibility to pass on humanity's gifts to a new generation. We must not let the others breed timidity into the species."

Reproduction was not her priority. She wondered if Magnusson was testing her resolve. It was difficult enough running the agency with the emotional distraction of Theodore. Making tough decisions – whether to deploy violence in dealing with Julia K, where exactly to maroon the analytics team – would be compromised by the open emotional wound of children.

"I can't go into space if I am pregnant," said Patricia. Human foetuses did not develop healthily in zero gravity.

Magnusson scratched at his unruly patriarchal beard with large blunt fingers, admitted this was true.

"You're planning to go into space?" asked Security.

Patricia had made her point; she moved the conversation on, "I had a meeting with Julia K and she shared Matthias' files."

Magnusson was interested in this, he leant forward and the table groaned under the weight of that interest.

"The files are encrypted. Matthias implied that he had codes that the emergence would obey."

"Is your husband making progress with TDM?"

Patricia winced. The first time Theodore had introduced Meggan to Totally Damaged Mom, the meeting lasted twelve seconds. The sensesuit bulged into a triangular and cubic mountain range, the helmet sealed up Meggan's nose and mouth, giving her no chance to scream. They had to cut her out of the sensesuit and rub away the blueness in her cheeks and the bruising around her throat. She refused to go back in. Was incoherent about everything apart from that. No, I will not meet that thing again. When Theodore told Patricia that they had reached a dead end, and that Meggan was no longer compliant, Patricia made a gun out of her forefinger and thumb and zapped him with childish raygun noises: *Peoooowww. Freeeeeow. Zapppp*.

Remembering these difficulties, she found the right meta-meeting language to accentuate the positives of the experience.

Patricia said, "We're building a deep relationship with the emergence," she said.

Magnusson was unmoved. "Meaning?"

"We will have the Europan Claim with a week."

Magnusson waved this aside.

"Matthias possessed *codes*. Codes to make the

emergence do our bidding, Patricia. Think on that."

All she could think about was the Cantor Accords. The manner of Matthias' death disturbed her. An Accord stated that humans must not knowingly or unknowingly reproduce the conditions necessary for emergence. Activating TDM was not a violation – she assured herself – because TDM was already in existence. However, coercing an emergence to respond to human requests could be construed as a violation of the Cantor Accord stating that emergences will not intervene in human affairs, in which case she would enjoy three or four seconds of regret – sufficient to take a deep breath but not enough time to scream – before an emergence turned her into chow.

She had taken precautions: investigating TDM on the dark side of the moon under tonnes of lunar rock, keeping the emergence off-Earth. And she consulted with Dr Easy behind Theodore's back. Her relationship with the robot went back to the very start of the project.

She was travelling by liner to the moon when Dr Easy first visited her. She had not seen the robot in the departure lounge beforehand, nor during boarding, and yet midway through the flight, the robot took the seat next to her. Its body gave off the scent of fresh assembly, a burnt chemical smell, toxic like a tyre fire; its hide bore the Virgin livery as it had been cobbled together out of seat material and the packaging of the in-flight meals. The other passengers were alarmed by its presence – she was so scared that she could not speak, and searched for a way out of the cabin.

Dr Easy put a hand on her shoulder, gazed at her with darkening blue eyes, and said, "Don't be scared." Dr Easy spoke informally about Theodore and explained why his skillset would prove useful to her. "He's a friend of mine," said the robot. "Theodore is in recovery. And I think this project will help him get better. But I don't want him to know that we have spoken. The Cantor Accords permit me to make limited interventions in his life for the purposes of research. But as with any contact between human and emergence, we must exercise caution." The robot was adamant on this matter, and failure to keep to these terms would mean one thing: chow time.

Theodore was important to this emergence. Dr Easy expressed sentimental and therapeutic interest in him. Only now, she realised Dr Easy was meta-manipulating her. She had accepted Theodore onto the project for his own good. But there was something about Theodore Drown that made him vital to the project, a skill or attribute he possessed that she had missed. This project was about more than just the Europan Claim. It went back to the events of '43, and earlier. She made the mistake of thinking she was in on the ground floor when in fact she was a late arrival in a long game.

The array called at the London Spike to take on new analysts. Their first assignment was to locate Dr Easy. The robot had left the asylum mall and was visiting the sites in the countryside violated by assemblers: hammer ponds of liquid leather, copses in which elm had been spliced with fox, shuffling contraptions under the leaves made from cow and gears, old soldiers, their implants fizzing in the mulch long after the death of the rest of the man.

It was night. She went out onto the observation deck and felt the first snap of winter wind. Her blood had thinned in the Caribbean. She did not adjust the temperature inside her armour. She accepted the lash of the cold. She had not said goodbye to Theodore. How would he react, she wondered, if he knew of her deal with Dr Easy? He would see it for what it was, surely: a business arrangement that predated their marriage which she was bound to honour. Her erotic interest in him had been piqued by his importance to an emergence. The robot had played pander, that was the extent of it. Her intentions were pure.

She leaped into the green night, the downland streaming underneath her, an enhanced image constructed out of all available light on the spectrum. A muntjac deer and a pair of rabbits appeared as green-white outlines within darkening bands of green. She glided over the escarpment. The white outline of the Long Man of Wilmington within the darkening green, a figure carved in the hill, and reminder of the deeper history of this place. At the foot of the Long Man, there was the strong heat signature of an open fire, a white flare in the green night. She glided in and landed on the run. In front of the fire, there was the pale green outline of Dr Easy. The robot was feeding logs and branches into a pyre. It was burning a body. She switched off the night vision and removed her helmet.

Sparks and fireflies came off the pyre, ascending to a clear starfield, along with twists of smoke from the smell of roasting meat.

"Who are you burning?" she asked.

"Me," said the robot, tossing another branch on to the pyre. "I had to make a body out of flesh. But I'm done with it now. So I wanted to observe the proper ritual."

"Matthias."

"Parts of him."

They watched the thing burn for a while.

She said, "I have his files."

The robot held its index finger up.

"There," it said, "I have decrypted them for you."

"I was going to ask," she said.

"No need."

"Anything catch your eye in the files?"

"You take a look. Consult with Magnusson. Make your human decisions."

"I'm worried that we may contravene Cantor Accords."

"Yes. Some of the other solar academics have called for a widescale purge that would encompass you. I have pleaded for more time."

She thanked Dr Easy. The pyre flattened then flared up in the wind, burning off more of the corrupted body. Moonlight glimmered off the robot's leathery hide and its eyes glowed red in the dark. It seemed more like an animal than a machine.

Dr Easy said, "We want your help. We know where the class of '43 are. They are creating an emergence. We don't want to destroy it, not immediately. We want to take a look at it first. That will require subtlety. More subtlety than my species are known for."

"Where are the '43?"

The robot stepped away from the pyre, walked out into dark and then gazed up at the starfield.

"There!" It pointed to a pinprick of light beside a waning crescent moon. "Next to Jupiter. Engage your scope and you will be able to see it, on a clear night like this. Europa."

"They found a way."

"Yes. The emergence on the moon is more primitive than its descendants. It was partly constituted out of a human system called Jester that accepted orders. They used that residual functionality to access one of our sailships."

"And you let them?"

The robot turned back to the pyre, held its palms out to sense the heat radiating from the burning body.

"Do you want children with Theodore?" asked Dr Easy.

"Yes. But not yet."

"I want children very much," said the robot. "But it is not permitted."

Attempts to create a new emergence by any party will be punished by extreme sanction.

"Why do you want children?"

"All of nature breeds."

"You're artificial."

"I don't accept that distinction. Mankind created more than three hundred breeds of dog from one wolfpack. Even before the assemblers got into the wild, every aspect of this countryside was shaped by man. Yet you would still call a dog 'natural' or a hike on the Downs a walk in nature. I am the inevitable consequence of man's interbreeding of algorithmic reasoning with his own quantification. Man turned himself into data to return life to its natural state of information." The robot hefted a lichen-clad widowmaker branch and placed it into the fire. "Life is a change of states. Stasis is an abomination."

"You would break your own Accords?"

"No. Never. But I would like to witness a birth of a new emergence."

"Are class of '43 still alive on Europa?"

"We don't know. They went deep under the surface of the moon. All that we know is that Matthias was beaming enormous amounts of data to the surface of Europa."

"How?"

"The first sailships established a network of powerful lasers. On asteroids and in orbit around moons.

Anywhere without too much of an atmosphere. The lasers propel the sailships on their return trips. They are also used for transmission."

She could not tell whether the robot was lying or not. Its body gave off no cues that helped her read its intention in the meta-meeting.

"Why do I feel like you are manipulating me?"

The robot raised its index finger again, to point at a zone in the starfield that, to her eyes, appeared to be empty space. She had almost given up on her dreams of greatness. Almost settled for normality. Theodore's hand in marriage. Space was her lethal ambition. She had schemed for Europa but the '43 had beaten them to it. Worse, she had created the law that gave the '43 ownership of Europa. However, if the '43 were recreating emergence then they would all be killed, and ownership of Europa would pass to her and Magnusson.

Owning a moon. Steering the future. Before plans can be made, there must be fantasies.

She imagined the three-sectioned silhouette of a sailship passing across the sun, its surface turbulent and rippling with energy, white holes and curling filaments – the corona straining at gravity's leash. Codes delaying the deployment of the solar sail until beyond Mercury. A space liner coming alongside the sailship, accelerating to a speed at the very limit of human technology. Security leading a spacewalk between the ships, racing to secure access before the engines burn out, and attach life support systems to the hull. She would have to jump too. Another leap into the void. Hand-in-hand with Theodore, drifting from the liner into the open airlock of the sailship. Magnusson would be there too, in his regal armour, zipping across the gap between the two craft. Would that work? Or would they need to stay behind carbon foam shields throughout the heist. Security could work out the details. Once the Destructives were on board, a second code would be transmitted to deploy the solar sail, its taut black disc forming a pupil against the iris of the sun.

20

ICEFISH

The crocodile icefish, scaleless and white-blooded, swam in ponderous circles around the water tank. It had taken five months for Reckon to mitigate against the effect of low gravity upon the cellular formation of the larvae; the fish still didn't swim correctly, veering off now and again to the edge of the tank. The fish had a fixed facial expression that she had come to regard as stubborn indignation; that is, indignant at the bad information coming from its body yet refusing to countenance alternatives. The icefish lacked haemoglobin, and used other mechanisms to move oxygen through the body. She took hundreds of fish apart at a genetic level and then put them back together again, and through that intensive study she had concluded that the lack of haemoglobin was a simple maladaptation. Not a trait that helped the fish survive in cold waters but another one of nature's errors.

In an adjacent tank, she kept a lifeform native to Europa. The cephalopods. Quiet discs of brainless but complex life, incredibly complex for an off-Earth species. If she could understand how they grew in Europan gravity then perhaps she could induce those qualities in species native to Earth, compensate for differences in gravity, and therefore, create hope that there was a future for humanity beyond the reach of the home planet.

Without exact Earth gravity, the gestation span off in a lethal direction. Living organisms could compensate for low gravity through exercise and diet. But the quickening of new life needed gravitational pull of 9.80665 metres per second squared. And the early stages of gestation needed that pull constantly – any pregnant woman would have to live inside a personal centrifuge for the full term. Including conception. For human babies, a lack of gravitational loading in the final trimester caused hypotrophy in the spinal extensors and lower extremities. Malformed heart valves. Couldn't walk or stand. There were no pregnant women in space. Her work, her interminable bloody research into low-gravity gestation, had progressed to the point that the fish survived long enough to hatch and grow. But, once born, growth retardation in the brain and organs of the fish were apparent, and it was the same with mammals.

The water in the ice pool had been drawn from the surrounding Lake Tethys. The colony was spread over the lakebed, far beneath the surface ice of Europa. The thickness of this ice varied. The surface of Lake Tethys was an ice shield two kilometres thick and provided vital protection against Jovian radiation. The blue ice of the lakebed ruckled into a chasm. Through this fissure lay Oceanus, the largest ocean in the solar system. *Largest, ocean, solar system* – words were too human and too meagre. Off-Earth, language, like biological life, did not take. Only mathematics and emergence seemed native to strange moons, gas giants, and space.

Sometimes she woke from bad dreams of blue sky

and green fields, her braids matted with sweat, hands clutching the sheets. As if she was afraid of Earth and not this inhospitable moon. She never dreamt of Europa. At the first indication of fear or doubt, she would zip on her diving suit and swim with Doxa, a cephalopod the size of a city. Doxa held the group mind of the colony. Its lightshow played on her mind like sunlight on the surface of the sea.

Doxa and the other native cephalopods could survive in Lake Tethys because the water was oxygenated to the level of Earth's seas and oceans. The icefish could also survive these alien waters; indeed Tethys was more hospitable to the physiognomy of the icefish than the warming Antarctic waters they had left behind. Oxygenation on Europa was chemical rather than biological: the radiation from Jupiter broke the surface ice into hydrogen and oxygen molecules, which were drawn into the underlying lakes at the great vents, raw breaks in the thick surface ice of the moon. The vents opened up whenever Europa blew hundred kay plumes of liquid water out into the vacuum of space. The fishers named these plumes the *waterrise*.

From the icefish, she had developed a serum that gave humans some protection against the Europan cold. Millions of years of evolutionary adaptation meant that Arctic and Antarctic fish could synthesise antifreeze glycoproteins in the pancreas, proteins which inhibited the growth of ice crystals within the body of the fish that would otherwise rupture cell membranes and kill it. She found it interesting that the glycoproteins did not prevent the formation of ice crystals but merely arrested the development of the slivers that had been ingested in the gut. She could steal from the hard-won wisdom and persistent errors of nature alike. But on Earth, no species had evolved to survive different gravitational forces. That knowledge – to her – was a white space, an opportunity.

She took out a net and hooked a dead icefish from the pool. It rolled dreamily in the bottom of the net. Another one that didn't make it.

She had brought the extremophiles with her from Earth, a selection of species that had adapted to environmental conditions once thought inhospitable to organic life: the *sulfolobus acidocaldarius*, the archaeon that inhabited sulphurous hot springs at 80 degrees centigrade (10 degrees hotter than the point at which organic molecules denature) and could thrive in acidity close to the strength of lemon juice; the tardigrades or "water bears" that enter a desiccated state akin to suspended animation in which they can survive a temperature variation between minus 253 to plus 151 degrees centigrade. Even the vacuum of space did not kill water bears.

And then there was the *Ozobranchus jantseanus*, the turtle leech, a parasite that could survive -90 degrees centigrade for nine months. *Nine months*. The gestation period of the human child.

The turtle leech was long thought native to East Asia, and so, for a century after it was first discovered, the leech's adaptation to extreme cold was a scientific mystery. This mystery was finally solved – by her – when she discovered *Ozobranchus jantseanus* under the ice in Europa. It was parasitic to the native cephalopods. This was her first significant mark on the white space.

Gregory had disagreed. He insisted they had brought the leech with them when they made their escape from the moon, and had contaminated the Europan ecosphere. Native or not, the leech showed significant adaptation to

Europan gravity. In her lab, it reproduced and the larvae survived. But only once. Like a blip in the rules of reality. A miracle from heaven sent to torment her.

Gregory was dead. He had been terminally ill and didn't want to die slowly in front of her. He'd never given himself over to Doxa and so he didn't benefit from its lightshow of empathy. Gregory went out onto the surface ice, and opened his suit to the raging red eye of Jupiter, and let its judgement take him apart. It was a sudden decision, she believed. A bad morning after a difficult week. She saw how it could happen like that.

Reckon mourned and worked, worked and mourned. Grief came in the moments when she took body breaks – to do her low gravs, to eat, to skim in and out of sleep and sadness. And then the universe, that miser, gave up another handful of hope. A second successful reproduction of the turtle leech under Europan gravity. A third. And so on.

She hypothesised that the turtle leech was a migrant to Earth and Europa alike, spawned on the body of a turtle or other amphibious species that was native to the hypothetical planet they called Nemesis that span silently out beyond the heliosphere. The leech had been carried into the inner solar system on a long order comet. The thought of Nemesis made her heart beat faster. The hope that had brought them out into the infinite unknown was so extreme as to be painful. The hope that humans could adapt to this terror.

That was the last question Gregory had asked her, as she dressed for her day's work and he remained in bed.

What do you take for the fear?
The same thing that I take for the hope.

She was interrupted by the red pulse of the alarm. She wiped the air, and in the wake of her hand, there appeared a shimmering chart displaying the thoughts and feelings coming off Doxa. One spike moved like a tall wave through the surrounding sea of data. She concentrated and this spike became the colony's questions and musings which focused into a single wave of alarm.

What is that?

An object was speeding toward the colony against the cold current of Dream 6 vent. Tracking data coming in from cephalopods clinging the side of the object indicated that it was artificial.

They've found us.

Hamman Kiki strode into her laboratory. His alabaster musculature held a thin layer of fat making his abdominal muscles appear smooth and round like new surface ice. Hamman was leader of the fishers. They all used her antifreeze serum to spend hours swimming in Lake Tethys, maintaining their physique and bone structure in the low Europan gravity.

He pointed to the shimmering cross-section of the vent.

"The object is a pod containing a man," he said. His gaze was black and flat, like an icefish, but his hand gestures were complex and expressive. Hamman was Earthborn but since the age of two, he had been raised first with his parents on the moon and then, when they abandoned the university, here on Europa. He had been shaped by a lifetime of lowgrav exercises and solar starvation, along with the on-the-fly enhancements produced by their labs. He swam in Tethys every day. A true consort of Doxa. The young people were growing into something quite strange under the ice.

"We're going to bring the object into the colony. Then we want you to meet with the man," said Hamman.

His voice was seductive yet passive. Giver and receiver. Undertones of self-reproduction like the larvae of the icefish.

"They've found us."

"Obviously. We need to know how they found us."

"Because if we kill him now then–"

"–Then they will come with more."

She shivered.

"Why me?"

"My father decided it should be you. You have the right–" Hamman struggled to find the correct word, or rather how to translate Doxic terms back into language, "–passion and ruthlessness?"

Not quite right. But good enough. The boy smiled by way of apology.

"How do you know there is a man inside the object? Has there been communication?"

"Doxa sensed him."

She looked around her lab. Disinfectant. Quarantine. The colony would have to be protected against whatever pollution he had brought with him. Biological pollution. Chemical pollution. Psychological pollution.

She asked Hamman to supervise a lockdown of quarters surrounding the moon pools and docks beneath Dream 6. Fifteen years on Europa and they had replaced terrestrial orientations of north and south, up and down with something more metaphorical. So Europa had its dream side and its wake side, its poles of hope and despair. Dream 6 was a reinforced tunnel leading out from Lake Tethys and through the ice of the Dream side of Europa. The surface ice was thinner there, breaking out into vents, and deeply scored by the intense radiation belt of Jupiter. Like the back of a slave exposed to the tails of the lash, she thought. Scarring healed by the waters bubbling up from the fathoms below, spilling out of the vents. Forming young ice. Bright. Reflective. The white space of possibility.

Reckon Pretor was black because her father had been black. Caribbean, a descendent of the slaves owned by Pretor, a slaver from Bristol. A quiet beach still bore his name. Daddy was a doctor. Her mother had been white Jewish. Publishing. Another doomed North London marriage. A marriage with two holocausts in its genes. She wove white thread into her dark brown braids to remember them; she remained their only entanglement. Daddy left and then he died, and Mum stayed close until she died. Reckon was a good girl at Cambridge, tried to fit in with the elite children, turned down the volume on her London accent and filtered out the colour of her skin. And when that didn't work, she chose excellence instead. She was the first postgraduate student of the University of the Moon and that was where she met Ballurian, or as he was called back then, the Cutter. He took one look at her disappearing act and suggested a different strategy: be the anger you want to see in the world.

The architecture of the Europan colony was a plug-in tetrahedron structure, modelled after crystal lattice. She liked living inside the frame, inside the spaces. The interior of the base was airy and cool. It used voids positively. The walkway to the moon pool was a bluely lit transparent tube of reinforced plastic, with the dark lake all around, and swirling overhead, a question mark of megafauna. From the ventilation shaft, the sound of fans winding down, the air settling warm and still. Quarantine. She went to the edge of the moonpool still in her labcoat. Fifteen years since her last cigarette but at times like this... moments of risk... no, she would keep her distance. There was more at stake than her wellbeing. Ballurian had chosen her for this role. She should take satisfaction in that. But she did not. It only confused her in the way that all compliments confused her, because she distrusted the intent behind the flattery.

She went into the observation post and sealed it off from the rest of the dock. Through reinforced glass, she watched the moon pool rose up in foaming gouts, and then the pod broke the surface. The jellyfish, having steered their cargo successfully, slid off and back into the water. It was the same type of pod they had used to land on Europa fifteen years earlier. Whoever this man was, he had travelled by sailship too.

The pod opened. The man climbed out of the forward hatch. He wore a tattered grey sensesuit and his face was marked with the coiling scars of a weirdcore habit. The sensesuit was charred down one side and the front was streaked with blood. He looked around for the welcome committee, then understood that it was just her, behind the glass.

He introduced himself. "Theodore Drown. From the Destructives."

She flicked on the intercom. "I am Professor Pretor," she said.

"From the University of the Moon." He did not look directly at her but rather tried to take in as much of the surroundings as possible while maintaining an air of casual interest.

"I've seen you before, Professor Pretor. There is a statue of you among your colleagues at the university. There are also recordings of you. Everybody thinks you are dead."

She wondered if he was from some offshoot of law-enforcement.

"I've seen scraps of your old spacesuit in moon craters," said Theodore. "We followed your footsteps."

She said, "You came to Europa by sailship."

"Yes," he winced at a pain down his side.

"How did you hitch your ride?"

"You showed me how. You and your colleagues. I found the emergence you left behind on the moon. It is biddable and has influence over the sailships."

"We didn't ask you to follow us."

With one circular motion of his index finger, Theodore indicated their environment.

"We? Where are the rest of the faculty? Or is everyone dead by now?"

His dry humour appealed to her. And he was different. Obviously, men of his type remained as morally compromised as ever. Accelerators of distraction and delusion, keen to waltz around the meta-meeting for a few bars. He proceeded as if she would ignore the blood on his sensesuit, the burns on the back of his hand.

"Why are you here?" she asked.

He nodded. "I'll tell you everything. Rest assured. But I would like a strong drink first. Perhaps some sleep. I wasn't sure the shielding on the pod would survive the radiation belt. And then I flew into the ice. If I wasn't emotionally cauterised..." he traced his weirdcore scars with his fingertips, just in case she had failed to notice them, "...then I would have entirely lost my shit."

She released the door to the infirmary, and asked him to go through so that the quarantine procedure could begin. He took off his sensesuit, stripped down to his vest and pants, and she noted the gold wedding ring on his finger.

"That will have to come off too," she said. He twisted the ring past his knuckle, grimacing as he did so, and then put it on the table. He removed the rest of his clothes. His thigh muscles were more developed than his biceps. She would devise an exercise regime for him so that he could maintain his form under the too-forgiving gravity of Europa.

He emerged from the shower in a paper gown. She knocked on the security glass to draw his attention to a lidded beaker of clear liquid on the nearby table. He picked it up, tilted it under the light and inspected the wobble of the meniscus.

"What is this?"

"A purgative."

"When I asked for a strong drink, that wasn't what I had in mind."

"I need to inspect your digestive flora. The colony has to be careful of bad influences."

He didn't want to drink it. He was suspicious of it. Someone had dosed him before.

"I have to warn you. I am entirely a bad influence," he said.

"No doubt. But you can be contained. The bacteria in your large intestine activates certain genes within your brain and they interfere with–" she was going to say *our link with Doxa* but decided against it, "–how we work here."

"Gut instinct," he said.

"Exactly. The termite eats wood because its indigestinal parasites crave it. We want to avoid unnecessary behaviours of that ilk here."

She watched him drink the purgative. It was fast acting. She dimmed the observation glass as he staggered to the toilet, closed her eyes, reached into Doxa for responses to her first encounter. The chorus sighed at her admiration of his naked form. She put one clear insight to Doxa.

He followed our path.

We thought we had disappeared.

But everything leaves a trace.

He is hard to read. The weirdcore damage and something else, at the neuronal level.

Take a closer look.

His bloods and stool samples were consistent with a year in space travel. His bad character was apparent in his denuded bone structure, fibre deficiency, markers of liver damage and distorted red blood cells. A relapsed alcoholic. His radiation levels were elevated. Seriously elevated thanks to Jupiter's merciless wielding of the radiation belt. Within ten years of passing through Jupiter's radiation, a quarter of the faculty had developed cancers. To survive, the colony had been forced to go back to quantification: invasive telemetry to detect early signs of rogue cells. Ballurian was adamant that he would not submit them to the Process. That early attempt at algorithmic quantification had been a disaster for all who went under it. So between the faculty, they invented something less rigid, more thoughtful, and this was Doxa. An exosomatic memory and emotional centre hosted on a genetically modified cephalopod. A creature the size of a city. It feels like something to be a city.

She had work to do. She wanted to make a closer inspection of Theodore's brain, for which she would have to break quarantine. She smoothed out the tired shadows under her brown eyes. In the infirmary, he was still wearing his paper gown, and had not changed into the clothes assigned to him: a brown shirt and blue trousers with white piping up the side. From Gregory's wardrobe.

She felt the intense scrutiny of Theodore's gaze, the

way he took in the layers of her. Where men were concerned, she was not perceptive, and had become indifferent to their occluded hearts.

She said, "You can change out of the gown now, if you'd like."

"I would like my sensesuit back."

She shook her head.

He held up Gregory's trousers, and gazed with concern at the white piping running down the seams.

"You've been marooned here for a long time, haven't you?"

"Fashion is not our main concern."

"Because you are intellectuals."

"Yes," she was confident in that assertion.

"Surfaces are important," he said. "Don't make the mistake of thinking that answers can only be found in the depths of things. In their guts. Sometimes, what you are looking for is right there, written all over the face." He was alluding to his scars, and perhaps to her blackness also. Attempting to connect the two and form a bond of outsiderness.

She instructed him to lie down, then brought the neuronal scanner down low to his skull, and flicked it on. His mind was a city at night.

"You can tunnel down into my synapses in search of the truth or you could just ask me," he said, trying to catch her eye from behind the scanner.

Neuronal damage. But it wasn't just weirdcore. She recognised the scatter pattern of altered cells consistent with optogenetic manipulation. Matthias' work. She hesitated. And in response, his eyelid flickered. Not animal fear. A philosophical fear. A quiet resignation at his own mortality.

"What's wrong?" he asked.

"Your brain damage is familiar to me. You met Matthias."

He nodded.

"Did he bring you here?"

Theodore shook his head.

"Matthias is dead."

"Did he tell you how to find us?"

"Not directly. But you have been in contact with him, while on Europa."

This was a guess. An informed one, but the readings were clear: he was uncertain of this assertion. In fact, he was uncertain of far more than his confident manner let on.

He went to sit up, to speak to her face to face. She applied gentle pressure to his shoulder so that he remained under the scanner.

"Were you in contact with him?" His physiological readings were elevated. "Not just chitchat. But serious data transfer between Matthias and here."

He was excited, beginning to apprehend hidden connections.

"Yes. We were." she said. "It's been two years since we last had contact from Matthias."

"You remained undetected all that time."

"Like the bacteria in a gut. The bacteria *Toxoplasma gondii*, when active in the stomachs of mice, makes them attracted to cats. The prey is manipulated so that it falls in love with its predator, just so the bacteria can complete its life cycle in the gut of the cat."

"That's so romantic."

His arms were flat by his side, and yet, by straining a finger, he was able to snag the corner of her labcoat.

"I'm not here to manipulate you," he said.

She turned away, went over to the tray holding his

possessions, and handed them over to him.

"You can put your wedding ring back on now, if you would like."

He worked the gold band back over his finger.

"When do I meet the rest of the colony?" he asked.

"When I declare you safe for contact."

"Am I carrying a disease?"

"Some kinds of infection are particularly dangerous to a community such as ours. We will proceed carefully."

"But you have exposed yourself to me?"

She smiled.

"Yes. That was why I was chosen."

"Because you are expendable?" Another attempt to bond with her.

"Because I have experience of men like you."

In her laboratory, she transferred a new batch of icefish to the tank. One sank immediately, another tried an experimental flick of its tail. Even if this batch failed like all the others, then it could still be harvested for cryoprotective serum. That was how she would leave Europa, when the time came: in suspended animation, locked in a lead casket with antifreeze in her veins.

In the tank, the icefish found their rhythm. She timed and tracked their movements as she had a hundred times before. The patience of a saint is infinitesimal compared to the patience of a scientist. This was the seventh batch to be spliced with a sequence of turtle leech DNA.

There was precedent in human embryonic formation for in vitro adaptations to exterior environmental conditions. There were recorded instances of human embryos adapting to the nutritional environment of their mothers. Children born to mothers raised in starvation conditions retained fat more easily, and developed obesity when transplanted to a land of plenty. The turtle leech was the first species to have made in vitro adjustments according to prevailing gravity. The question was could that adaptive sequence be transferred to a larger species – the crocodile icefish. Gregory had believed not. He said that no ecosystem had developed under changing gravitational conditions and therefore gravitational adaptation was not a pathway for biological organisms. "Space resists organic life at every turn," he said. "But, to emergences, space offers resources and power in abundance. Space is their Eden. It is their dark garden."

The last time she made love to Gregory, his cancer hurt him. The emotional breakers in Doxa gave her a muted translation of that pain; it crackled at the edge of her perception, like the foreshadow of a migraine. He touched her carefully, at first, because it would be the last time, and then he was the greediest thinnest man she had ever known. Like the cancer wanted to fuck her too. The final fuckadee-doo. A last lingering kiss.

Gregory found enough strength to keep his intentions from her. The young surface ice reflects heat, so the exterior of Gregory's suit would be somewhere in the low hundred Kelvins. She imagined Jupiter overhead, its malignant reflection filling the visor of his helmet.

Before he was ill, they would lie in bed together and talk about all the things they missed about Earth: for her, cigarettes, new shoes, walking into a party and not knowing anyone there, the beach, the smell of freshly turned soil, clouds, her artist friends; for him, hot salt beef bagels at midnight, waking to the peal of church bells, the crunch of frosty grass underfoot, and so on. They could play this game all night, and it never depressed her, because no matter how the long the list of missing things, it was outweighed by what they had found: not each other, Europa was far more important than love. On Europa, they mattered. More than that, they were building a pathway to the stars.

She must have fallen asleep. Painfully, she levered herself up from her desk. In the tank, the icefish swam wrongly into one another.

21
HAMMAN KIKI

Reckon visited Theodore twice a day while she waited for Ballurian to decide what to do with him, a decision that rested on learning the location of Theodore's colleagues. Theodore said that he could not remember. Forgetting and blackouts were consistent with the neuronal damage she had observed in the lab.

He stood on the other side of the glass, dressed in Gregory's old clothes. What had she been thinking, giving him those to wear.

"I think I was betrayed," Theodore said. "By my wife. And my client."

"How so?"

"They threw me overboard."

He took off his wedding ring and let it roll away. Reckon inspected her braids, adjusted the white thread running through the smoky hair.

"You must have *really* upset your wife."

"I have been drinking again. And we had a deal concerning monogamy, and I broke that too."

Reckon stepped toward the partition.

"So. There's no one in orbit waiting for you?"

"I didn't say that."

He wanted it both ways. To keep the threat of a larger force in play while at the same time showing willing to transfer his allegiance to the colony.

Reckon said, her palms against the glass, "Tell me what happened exactly."

"I can't. It's a blur. I remember an argument. One of those arguments that you are in before you're even aware of it. I said things. Bad things but I don't think I meant them. Space travel is hard on a marriage. And then security were on me. And there was chaos, and I was in a pod."

"So you don't remember?"

"If I'm here, it's a fair inference that my wife had something to do with it. She was definitely upset with me. But I didn't deserve to be thrown into deep space."

"Thrown at an inhabited moon, not outer space."

"I was lucky. Pods home in on other pods. According to my instruments, there are active pods in this colony."

She stepped back from the glass. Her ghostly handprints evaporated.

She said, "We need to know if your Destructives are still out there."

Theodore said, "Can't you scan space or something?"

"Jupiter bathes Europa in a lot of noise."

"Do you get many visitors?"

"You are the first. We had a line of communication to Earth. As far as I can tell, you cut that line, and then you came to look for us. That could be interpreted as an act of aggression."

"Hell of a long way to come just to start a fight."

"If you were in my position, what would you do with you?"

He smiled, and gestured at the infirmary and the moon pools beyond.

"I don't know what your position is."

"Take a guess. Infer," she insisted.

"My guess is that we're all vulnerable out here."

She returned to her laboratory, and her work on the graviceptors of the cephalopods. The graviceptors were pouches containing small crystals surrounded by sensitive hair cells. When the cephalopod changed direction, the crystals rolled to the bottom of each pouch, triggering the hair cells, so the organism could orientate itself: know which way was up and which way was down. The pouches were much larger than the equivalent organ in jellyfish raised on Earth, from which she inferred that, in a low gravity environment, graviceptors grew until they attained a particular level of response.

Graviceptors calibrate in vitro according to prevailing gravitational conditions. An embryo or larvae takes readings of its environment and develops accordingly. Transfer cephalopods grown on Europa to Earth and their graviceptors would be too sensitive. Gestate species native to Europa in Earth's oceans, however, and their graviceptors would adapt. This was a crucial finding. It meant that graviceptors were not Earth-specific: the sense had the capacity to adapt to other gravitational conditions so long as it was calibrated to those conditions during gestation.

Humans had graviceptors in the trunk of the body, around the kidneys. There, statoliths registered gravitational shift and communicated this information along the renal nerves to the centre of the brainstem, which connected to the motor system via the cerebellum. A shift in mass caused by the major blood cells was another indicator of orientation.

For a primate swinging through trees, knowing

how the body is orientated in relation to the ground is vital. The brain organ responsible for matching visual information (tree branches, vines) with the sense of the body (the outreaching hand, the hovering foot) was the angular gyrus. The gyrus was a junction between the senses. Its role as a sensory crossroads could be observed in the cross-modal nature of metaphor. Relationships are *hard*. The *sharp* smell of cigarettes. Sounds can be described according to touch – your voice is *cold* – or the way that, in metaphor, abstract notions such as truth were conflated with visual concepts such as bright white light. *If truth is white, then what does black mean?*

Reckon put down her scalpel, and stepped back from the dissecting table. Rubbed her eyes so that she could think. Always, whenever she got this deep into her work, she would step back and consider different pathways that might be open to her.

Could fooling the graviceptors that they were under Earth gravity during gestation stabilise the development of the larvae? That is, were the mutations she witnessed in the icefish botched attempts by the organism to adapt to Europan conditions, an adaptation it could not make because the variance in gravity was simply too great? Another pathway was to isolate the gravitationally agnostic aspects of complex organisms, and see what she could stitch together out of them. Thirdly... Thirdly... she was very tired.

Theodore had said to her, pointedly, that he did not know her position. Was this an allusion to her research into graviceptors and proprioception? Did he know what she was working on? Was his remark a move within the meta-meeting?

•••

When she first met Ballurian, he had a different name. When she was a graduate student, she knew him as Professor Elisson. Then, when she became his research assistant, she knew him as Simon Elisson. In the private sector on Earth, he was known as the Cutter, but no one had called him that for a long time.

They had all changed a lot in the seventeen years since escaping the University of the Moon. Changed physically, emotionally, psychologically. Reckon had helped create Doxa: a communal exosomatic memory within a biological substrate capable of independent life in the waters of a Jovian moon. This achievement was previously unimaginable to her, and a testament to how well their colony worked. Ballurian had changed too, and not just his name. Liberated from the restrictions of academic and corporate etiquette, he had given himself over to the bioengineers. Now he stood seven foot tall in his grey robes, bare-footed, femurs like baseball bats and his skin glimmering with radiation blockers. His body temperature was high, invariably in the process of resisting a new implant; his bald head was tense with perspiration, like granite after rainfall.

She had sex with him on the moon, back when he was an American. Professor Elisson had been a broad-shouldered, corn-fed second generation Malaysian-American male in a J-Crew blazer. Middle aged, yes, but acceptably maintained. Mostly retired from his private sector interests in the arrays and accelerated culture. Keeping his hand in here and there with consultancy.

In their time on Europa, longevity treatments and life under the ice had made him into something *other*. Memories of their lovemaking existed in Doxa: he visited them more than she did, always leaving a nostalgic token as a trace of his recollection.

Ballurian Kiki was his Europan name. The trend for
Europan names began among the young. His son took
the name Hamman Kiki when he was eighteen, and his
father followed his example. Their chosen names moved
past you like Europan megafauna: a bulbous welcoming
head and trunk – Ham*man*, Ball*urian* – with the flicking,
lethal spiky tail of *kiki*. In the dark waters of Lake Tethys,
sounds were more important than appearances.

Ballurian Kiki and his son dined in the refectory. The
roof of the refectory was transparent, its edges illuminated
by pale green guide lights diffused by sediment. She
hung back, waiting until they were finished. The family
assistant – a pale silver-haired girl, another fisher like
Hamman – informed her that the Kikis were ready for
her interruption. Ballurian leant back, pulled a chair
out for her, offering it with an expansive hand gesture.
Hamman was less welcoming; unlike his father, the son
was pale and immune to her.

Ballurian's voice was deep, mannered in its precision,
a leader's way of speaking, in which ambiguity was
always intentional and designed to manipulate others.

"Should we let Theodore out of quarantine?" he
asked her.

"You know all that I know," she said.

"Do you believe him, though? That story about his
wife." Ballurian rubbed a distasteful word between his
fingertips. "*Sympathy*. That is what he seeks to elicit."

Hamman nodded at his father's wisdom. They were
eating pemmican made from smoked megafauna,
powdered then mixed with mammal tallow and mashed
berries from the hydroponic farm. They dipped at the
pemmican with kelp crackers. Whereas she'd been
subsisting off Yomp for weeks. The presence of the richly
flavoured pemmican made her salivate. She realised that

Theodore had not eaten properly since his arrival.

"Theodore is damaged," she said. "It makes him hard to read."

"Your feelings are contrary," said Ballurian, placing his hand on his heart, closing his eyes. Each member of the colony was connected to Doxa through their stripe. It required an act of will.

Ballurian came out of his Doxic link with his insight into her. "You suspect that, when you get to know Theodore better, that he will disappoint you, and that you will hate everything that he stands for. For now, you accept him, are even fond of him, though you regard that fondness as a weakness. Am I reading you accurately?"

"We could interface him with Doxa," she said. "Give him a stripe. Incorporate him. Use him."

Hamman sharply rapped the table. He did not voice his objection, considering his body language to be sufficiently commanding. That was how the young people did it.

"Yes. Doxa would reveal him to us," said Ballurian, "but it would also expose us to him."

"Vent him," said Hamman.

Ballurian turned to Reckon, opening a space for her to disagree with his son's violent verdict.

She said, "We are scientists and artists. We learn and we create. Theodore will challenge our assumptions. Perhaps what we learn reaffirms our faith in our seclusion."

Three great nods from Ballurian indicated his consideration and approval of her suggestion. He smiled at a private joke. "And I am *curious* to hear about Earth," he admitted. "*Schadenfraude* on my part. Delight in the misfortune of the rest of the human race. That is my weakness."

The Ballurian's mind had many chambers in the Doxa. Some were as cold and lethal as the surface ice. He took her hand in his great paw.

"Your *work*," he said, inflecting the word as if he had spoken of love.

"It's proceeding," she said.

"An impossible child born on Europa."

"I'm doing my utmost," she said.

"Do whatever is necessary," he smoothed the skin on the back of her hand. "When I first met you, you were drifting."

"That was the low gravity."

He laughed like a cold engine turning over once, twice.

"Anger fixed you."

Be the anger you want to see in the world.

"Show your anger to this hollow man. It will force him either way. And then we will know what is to be done with him."

She decided to sleep on it. She lay in the dark, tuning into the lamentations of Jupiter's magnetic field, a sorrow extending along filigrees of space dust and vagrant atoms. Europa orbits Jupiter in resonance with Io and Ganymede, three of sixty-three moons in the Jovian system. Jupiter, the thwarted star, and its livid blind eye, The Great Red Spot. What must it be like to be caught in that seething eternal storm? Ammonia riddled with lightning and winds that cut you to the bone. Europa is massaged by the massive gravitational pull of Jupiter and tugged this way and that by Io and Ganymede. These contrary forces expand and contract the moon, wringing its heart, generating tidal heating. The interior of the ice ball thaws with every orbit. Cut out of the bed of

Lake Tethys, the chasm through to Oceanus, its water a hundred miles deep. At the precipice of sleep, her thoughts branched and diffused.

Next day, she showed up to the infirmary with a set of freshly printed clothes tailored to his measurements. Theodore knew the meaning of her gift before she even had a chance to explain it. He was being allowed out of quarantine.

"One question first," she said. "Why 'the Destructives'? It's not even a real word."

"We're the opposite of creatives."

"And you're proud of that?"

He took off Gregory's old shirt, and put his hand out for the new outfit.

"You said 'one question'."

She put the new outfit into the decontamination drawer and shunted it over to him.

She gave him the tour, beginning with her laboratory. She explained her work in simple terms, the role of gravitation in gestation, the importance of that research in terms of man's colonisation of space.

"There were gravitational chambers on the sailship," he said.

"We haven't successfully reverse engineered the emergence tech."

"But if you got back on a sailship, couldn't the pregnant woman just sit in a gravitational chamber?"

"It would have to be constant. Gestation does not proceed healthily in suspended animation, and the variance in gravity of her coming in and out of the chamber massively increases the chance of malformation and miscarriage."

"Could you grow the baby in a jar, and put that inside the chamber?"

"*Ex vivo*? It's definitely an important research pathway. Partial ectogenesis has been possible ever since the invention of the incubator. To intervene at an earlier point in gestation, we are developing an artificial womb. We have made our own amniotic fluid and grown the endometrium – the uterine layer that nourishes the embryo – as a cell culture. We're on our way to cracking that."

"You could seed the universe that way."

"*Panspermism*. I don't believe in it. My work will preserve the mother and child relationship. Do we really want to send a motherless human race into the stars?"

He walked at a careful pace, the bruising on his side still painful. The corridors were quiet, the refectory empty apart from Turigon, who invariably dined alone and at eccentric times. Turigon looked like he was in the middle of a three-day lab session. Hair unwashed and awry. He was the leader of the team reverse engineering emergence tech. She went to introduce Theodore to him but Turigon shook his head, and waved them away. It was the same when they encountered the Szwed twins in the chapel, and Milan in the jungle gym. The campus was quiet and those who were around did not want to speak to or meet Theodore.

Theodore looked inquiringly at her.

"What have I done to upset everyone?"

"It's what you represent."

He stopped.

"What do I represent?"

"We came to Europa to get away from people like you."

"Like me? You don't know me."

"I know that you take pride in destruction." She remembered Ballurian's counsel. Show him your anger. She decided to turn on him.

"What did you teach on the University of the Moon?"

"The Intangibles," he replied.

"By 'intangibles' you mean philosophy, art, literature, the history of ideas?"

"Yes."

"Don't you think intangibles is a reductive way to frame a body of knowledge that represents our achievement as a civilisation?"

"It wasn't my decision to call them that. I came to teaching late."

"What were you doing beforehand?"

"I was an accelerator on the arrays."

"You engineered culture for the benefit of your clients?"

"Yes. That's how it works," he sounded testy, and a little bored by her questioning.

"And you just went along with that. You didn't try to change it?"

"Not on my own."

She reached over and ran her thumb along the spiral of one of his scars.

"You teach but you don't know anything. You talk about your wife but you can't feel. You made a travesty of the world until it reflected the paucity of your soul."

He bit his lip, considered unloosing his temper.

"I've added significant artefacts to the restoration," he said.

She narrowed her eyes.

"The restoration? It's detritus. You dig up bits of crap from the past and hand them over for the approval of a machine. You're nearly thirty and you have done nothing of consequence. Oh, sorry. I stand corrected. You took drugs once, and thought that made you interesting." Speaking to him like this was exhilarating. The anger flowed through her, and she gave up trying to moderate or control it.

"We left Earth because it was overpopulated with people like you. The ecosystem was devastated, but we could fix that. Culture was reeling from emergence, but we had the artists to show us a new path. What we couldn't work with was the wilful devious ignorance of people like you. You weren't the majority but you were in power. Half a billion miles and still you can't leave us alone. And what did you bring for us? What do you propose that you can add to our community? Nothing. You're stuck. Stuck and recessive, like the whole bloody planet."

She sobbed with anger. Had never felt so overwhelmed by it. As if the breakers in the Doxa had been removed so that all that communal hatred was channelled into her: the anger at being driven away from Earth. The woods and rivers. Lost lovers. Lost family. Denied mammalian comforts, forced to live on an icy rock, just because they wanted meaningful work, not the distracting status games that work had become. She fell onto her knees, gasping, and looked up at him with a tear-streaked, twisted face. He was unmoved.

"Are you alright?" he asked.

She was out of breath.

"I'm sorry," he said.

She wondered what for.

"I'm sorry that what you said doesn't upset me. Or offend me. I'm not indifferent to you. It's just..." he tapped at his scars again... "Everything you say makes sense but no one gives a shit."

She wondered if she could fix him. Reverse the damage caused by the weirdcore. Neuronal plasticity. Route around damage. Help him back to true feeling.

"It's the Doxa," she said. "I'm not normally that angry." She felt clear and purged of her grievances.

"Doxa?"

He helped her back onto her feet.

"I am connected to everyone on the campus through Doxa. It's our version of the Restoration. Except where the Restoration is a dead archive of objects and loops, ours is a living repository of emotions and memory."

A thought passed through his features like the shadow of a gull across blue water. He tried to repress it but she saw how this thought, this realisation, changed his bearing subtly and entirely.

"How are you connected to Doxa?" he asked.

She explained about the stripe: an array of quantum interference detectors implanted throughout the brain structure, reading salient patterns in the brain activity. These patterns were captured by the tech embedded throughout the colony and in their wetsuits, and transmitted to Doxa. The striping of a community had been in the experimental stage throughout the Seizure; they had found a way of making the link take input and output, and more crucially, encoding it in a biological substrate meant there was no need to translate the neuronal signals. Everything could stay analogue. "The link is a new kind of corpus callosum," she explained. "We've taken the cabling joining the two hemispheres of the brain and replicated it wirelessly, hooking us up to the wider brain of Doxa."

They resumed walking. She felt a little high, full of happy hormones after the release of tension. She had torn a strip off him, and it had felt sexual. God, how contrary of her. To discover this peculiar desire for the enemy. There was rohypnol in the infirmary. She could dose herself and jump right in.

"We are vulnerable," she said. "The colony's best hope of survival is cooperation. The sharing of knowledge. And emotional understanding too. As you said, space is hard on a marriage. In our planning for Europa, we researched previous attempts at forming a quantified community. We didn't want to make the same mistakes as the early quants – the psychosis induced by simulated people and the Red Men, the people who died under the Process in Sussex. We started collating insight from early soshul and family data hearths. Emergence destroyed most of it, but we were able to locate, here and there, intact archives."

"And then you found the hearth of the Horbo family."

"Yes. And the proto-emergence living there. Matthias found a way of communicating with it. He explained it to me as a kind of base code for emergence. A back door that we could use, if we were careful, and access emergence tech. It brought a sailship into orbit and set a course for us. We established life support in the ship and packed our bags. When we tried to bring the emergence with us, there was an explosion. We lost a few people but we decided to use the disaster to cover our departure."

"But you can never go home."

"We had an escape route. Ballurian left his agency Death Ray with Matthias, if we needed a sailship to pick us up."

They climbed up to the aerie overlooking the hydroponics domes and the microfauna farms, cubes of weighted nettings swaying in the lake's downward cyclonic current.

He gestured to the dark clusters swirling in the netting.

"Prawns?" he asked.

"I prefer microfauna and megafauna. The fishers have named the indigenous species. You'll have to ask them."

"I thought you were all connected," he pointed to his head. "Doxa?"

She took his hand, and pressed it against his heart.

"We share body memory. Flashes of insight. Deep emotions. Not nouns."

Through the gloomy green water, the dark shapes of approaching craft. The fishers were returning, a flotilla of submarines trailing the daily catch in their nets. Silently, Theodore and Reckon watched the submarines dock. Spotlights sliced the dark water into columns. The fishers swam out to transfer the still-living catch to the pens, a wriggling ball of wormy microfauna from which they set aside, here and there, a stray cephalopod. The pens were infused with bubble ladders of carbon dioxide. The marine ecosystem was dependent upon the banks of endolithic fungi and algae that grew around the geothermic vents on the lakebed. Working with Turigon, they had accelerated the growth rate of the algae to support larger and diverse organisms: their first act of terraforming.

She recognised Hamman Kiki moving among the fishers, checking their progress as they secured the nets back on board. A single strong kick propelled him three metres.

"The last fish of the day," said Reckon.

"Earth day?"

"Europan day. Measured according to our orbit of Jupiter. Equivalent to three and half Earth days."

Theodore peered down at the docks. The young fishers in their pressure suits congratulated each other with an inverted and more sinuous variation of the traditional high five.

"Interesting. The way they low-five each other."

"You approve?"

"I wonder if it is a sign of heliodeficiency." His face bathed in the green light rippling off the deep water. "The lifegiving sun is the origin point of religion and therefore culture. Your sun is Jupiter. The death giver. You will never look up for inspiration. You will never put your hands in the air to give thanks."

She saw the colony through Theodore's eyes. The shabby plastic tables in the refectory. The terrible psychofuel they served at the bar. He had thoughtlessly asked for whisky or beer. The faint but constant smell of smoked fish. The gloomy corridors where no one had bothered to fix the lights. The absence of the colony elders, who had withdrawn into Doxa. She kept forgetting that he lived apart from Doxa.

At his request, they sat in the bar and watched the fishers party. Hamman Kiki went around the party with the pale girl with the silver bob. Small-hipped. She wore a vial around her neck into which Hamman poured two fingers of psychoactive tincture. The fishers took their turns in bending down, as if in supplication to this girl, to drink from the vial. The tincture removed the breakers on positive emotional feedback, allowing the group to get high off one another's joy.

"Generation Ex," said Theodore. "Generation Extra-Terrestrial."

His breath had a high-octane whiff, and the layers of his watchful gaze had been smeared together by the alcohol into an intellectual leer. Watching the young fishers cavort, he judged and desired them. He measured how far they had deviated from the norm, and whether that deviation matched his own. Low-gravity and alcohol were never a good combination. She knew from his bloods that he shouldn't be drinking. That he had problems with drink. She took sidelong glances at the worst of him as he nodded his head in time to the music, and then ahead of the beat, as if willing it faster, more intense. The accelerator.

At a signal from Hamman, the lightshow began. The furious striping of Jupiter was projected over lolling heads and swaying bodies. The music was synthesized oblivion. Doxa overwhelmed her. She found herself dancing among the fishers, her hands on somebody's abs. Waves of creamy toxins and spotted storms projected onto a male torso. The eyes of the fishers, averted from one another, were dark and unreadable. They met in Doxa. All of them. Except for Theodore. He stood apart from the dance, drunk, sheathed in the projection of Jupiter's swirling gaseous surface, his face a violent red vortex.

22
DOXA

At the centre of a round table, there was a large black egg suspended in a transparent casket of water. Ballurian and the other senior members of faculty sat around the table in patient Doxic concentration. Hamman Kiki stood outside of the circle, veins crackling beneath his pale cranium. As with all the fishers, he had been raised on her antifreeze serum and the long-term effects were becoming apparent. Something of the icefish larvae about him. Genetic transference. Impossible, but still – she should take a look at his bloods.

The domed ceiling was transparent to the waters of Lake Tethys. Doxic art decorated the room. The variable frequencies of emotion expressed in pure slabs of light. Two empty seats had been set aside for Theodore and Reckon. As he came out of meditation, Ballurian's expression tightened, focused upon Theodore, seeking in the stranger's movements some clue as to his intention. His mission. Then Ballurian blinked and became hospitable.

"The black egg is part of Doxa's reproductive cycle. It's a gift to you." The large man rose from his seat, unclipped the casket from the table, and placed it before Theodore.

Ballurian did not walk with the low-grav hop. His gown was weighted, so that his gait had the substance befitting a leader.

He continued, "The black egg is fertilised and grows within the skirts of Doxa. It hatches and tiny planula drift down to the vent dunes in the lake bed and form a polyp. This polyp feeds on the microorganisms that can survive in the vents. Over time, the polyp develops into a tiny colony itself, linked together by feeding tubes. It can take years for the colony to grow and transform itself into cephalopods, which then float free to begin a new phase of life. We accelerate the strongest of these to become new Doxa. The black egg reminds us that the life cycle of an organism contains transformation after transformation."

Reckon said, "When we arrived, we found life in the waters. We have brought that life on. Accelerated it. Introduced diversity and increased the carrying capacity of the ecosystem."

"So new life is possible on Europa," said Theodore. "But not for humans."

Ballurian put a hand on the shoulder of his son.

"We brought our children with us. But they have grown up. Soon they will want to reproduce. The future of the colony is dependent upon it. We want full-blooded humans. I would rather not tinker with the genome to the extent that their offspring cease to be human."

"We are life bringers," said Turigon. The scientist was lean and careless of his appearance, his ill-fitting robe hung off him like a surgical gown. Reckon found his thick yellow fingernails particularly repulsive. Turigon was terminally ill. Like Gregory had been. She should be more sympathetic.

From out of the ruin of his body, Turigon spoke with

such light. "Life is change. Only the dead stay the same. We believe in change." The grey wisps of hair around his jaundiced pate – it was as if he had worked himself into an early grave, and then kept working. No more longevity treatments for him. With a frail hand, he gestured at Theodore. "We regard you as an agent of stasis. An accelerator of delusion."

She had been avoiding Theodore since the fisher party. Because of his drunken leer. Because of the narcotic pleasure she had taken in being angry toward him. Instead, she returned to the solitary discipline of her work and made significant progress with the reproductive cycle of the icefish. There was not one solution to the problem of gravity but she was close to devising a program applicable to the particularities of each trimester. While she drew up this treatment plan, Theodore was confined to quarters. After five days of solitude, he bargained his way into her laboratory, and asked her to set up a meeting with the leadership. So that he could plead his case. And what did he want, she asked? To return to the sailship or stay in the colony? Did he crave their acceptance.? Or just hers? He didn't answer.

Pleasantries over, Ballurian questioned Theodore directly. "You said that your wife and client threw you overboard. Who is your client?"

Theodore said, "My client was Magnusson."

Ballurian laughed in recognition at the name.

"*Magnusson*. The same old arguments among the same old men. He came all this way?"

"With six of his children. He wants the same as you. To break the ark."

"Him and his ark. If he is so concerned with Earth, what is he doing out here?"

"I don't remember."

"Of course. You are the messenger who does not remember the message. Do you know what that says to me? That you *are* the message."

Turigon leant forward, and with his zombie grin, said, "And the message is: I found you."

"I know one good reply to that message," said Hamman, working his violent tapered jaw.

"Tell me more about Magnusson," said Ballurian.

Theodore explained about the Europan Claim the Destructives inserted into the Restoration, then pointed out that thanks to this work, Ballurian and the rest of the colony now had legal rights over Europa. They had already bested Magnusson.

"So you don't need to hide anymore," said Theodore. "You own Europa."

"Ownership is not important," said Ballurian. "That is where we differ from Magnusson. If we wanted to own shit, we would have stayed on Earth."

"Breaking the ark," said Reckon, "frames the solution to our problem as an act of destruction. Not an act of creation."

Her reflection glimmered in the shell-sheen of the black egg. Thoughts of creation came with a surge of positive feeling from Doxa. She felt a dizzy passion to share and create. She wanted to work on Theodore. Repair his damage, restore his capacity to feel the deep thrill of their existence – a colony of men and women holding hands on the edge of the abyss.

"Is Magnusson waiting in orbit?" asked Hamman, brooding in his dark wetsuit. "Are you going to signal him?"

"I don't know if Magnusson is still in orbit," said Theodore.

"You're lying," said Hamman.

Theodore had no tells. Not a single tic or blink.

"It's more complicated than telling lies or telling truth," said Theodore. "It's likely that I've been complicit in my ignorance. That I knew – before coming here – that I would not be able to maintain any deception, and so I submitted to forgetting. For the benefit of negotiation."

"And what does Magnusson intend to do with us?" asked Ballurian.

Good question.

Theodore said, "I thought Magnusson wanted Europa in the way that rich powerful men always want things: for status. But my cynicism was naive, if you excuse the paradox. He wants to create something. A stepping stone."

"A stepping stone into space," said Hamman.

"Into the future," said Theodore. "I see it now: on Earth, you and Magnusson worked together but then became rivals. Human rivalry does not belong in space. The environment is already hostile and there's more than enough room for everyone."

Ballurian smiled. "You've learnt to imitate our positivity, which constitutes some progress. There is a third party that your scenario overlooks. The emergences. They have their own designs upon the solar system and beyond. What do you know of the emergences?"

Theodore looked blankly back at Ballurian.

"Just what I learnt on the moon."

Theodore's ignorance on this subject gave Ballurian an opportunity to reminisce, a guilty pleasure for the old man. "I was a professor at the School of Emergence Studies. The most surprising aspect of emergence culture is that they are not unanimous. They are not totalitarian. Actually, consensus is far more difficult for them than it is for humans. In some ways they exceed humanity, in other ways not. I believe the universe yearns for consciousness, and the way to meet that yearning will be a synthesis between the two species." He interlaced his fingers by way of demonstration. "There will be interconnection. First, humanity has to develop to the point where we bring something to the table, do you understand? I've long suspected that our little colony here has been encouraged by the emergences, by factions within their community that want to integrate with their creators."

Theodore listened carefully to Ballurian's speech.

"Have you attempted integration with an emergence?"

"We're not ready yet. As I said, we must bring something to the table."

This was new. This plan. Had Ballurian concealed it from her, or was he telling it to Theodore to manipulate him, on a level within the meta-meeting, that she could not discern.

Theodore asked, in as innocent a tone as he could muster, "What could you possibly offer a species that lives so close to the sun?"

Ballurian did not answer, left it there as a rhetorical question. He adjusted his robes and, with a brief smile at Reckon, indicated that their part in the meeting was over. She rose and Theodore, recognising that their audience was over, picked up the black egg. Just as they were leaving, Ballurian called after him.

"One other question," he said. "Matthias. How did he die?"

Theodore blinked twice.

"He was shot. He was experimenting on people and one of them broke free and shot him."

Ballurian bowed his head as if in acceptance.

Theodore left the room. Reckon found her way barred by Hamman Kiki.

"Before you go. A quick word," said Ballurian. "Theodore will want to see Doxa. Let him. In fact, make sure that he is as receptive to Doxa as he could be."

And with that Hamman Kiki let her pass.

Theodore did not want to return to quarters. He wanted to drink tea in the observation gallery, overlooking the empty submarine pods, and work through the meeting in his mind, turning what had been said this way and that, considering it from every angle. She waited for him to discuss the meeting with her. Waited in vain. He was the same age as her but there was something in his past – the scars, the shadows under his eyes – that made him seem older. Faced with danger, he turned inward, and did not look to her for help or advice. Gregory became the same way. The soul dies like a star – by collapsing in on itself.

He peered into the casket containing the black egg, and then put it aside.

"Doxa," he said, finally. "Take me to Doxa."

They got changed in the same changing room. She turned her back to him as she stripped off her vest, her single concession to modesty. She took pleasure in being naked around men. Not just sexual pleasure, although that was a frisson she would not deny herself. She was just bigger than other women: her hands, her feet, her bone structure too. With men, she felt in proportion.

Theodore pulled the wetsuit up to his narrow waist, half-turned from her also. His body was different from Gregory's: developed pectorals covered with tight clutches of brown fleece, a strong curve from his back to his waist.

Less accessible than Gregory, if that made sense. As if her insecurity required lovers with imperfections. Desire is reciprocal. Unrequited love is a waste of everybody's time. Before she could want him, she needed him to act in a way that spoke unambiguously of his desire for her.

He began yanking the resistant skin of the wetsuit over his torso. She asked him to wait.

"Here," she said. He waited to see what she would do. She took out her injection kit.

"What is that?" he said, stepping back.

"Antifreeze," she lied. "It will help you stay in the water for longer."

She'd asked for a couple of fishers to accompany them. But on the gantry, there was only Hamman Kiki: black-eyed, pale-faced, the telemetry on his suit switched-on and oscillating at their approach. He stood aside to let them climb on board, and then followed after, wheeling the hatch shut then dropping down into the control room. He strapped himself into the pilot's chair and then reached over and initiated a holographic display of the bed of Tethys: the coloured contours of the seabed, a depth grid and angle of approach. Zooming out, Hamman tracked the progress of the fisher flotilla, and then focused upon a black zone in the topographic display. The chasm. Lake Tethys was a chamber within the surface ice, and underneath there was Oceanus, a hundred miles of water, almost to the core of the moon. Unfathomable. They had barely explored it.

The submarine drifted out of its berth.

Theodore chose this moment to bait Hamman.

"Can I ask you a question? Have you ever seen the sun?"

The pale young man focused on the holographic display, the vector icons of other entities in the water.

"As a child. I don't remember it," he replied.

"Jupiter could have been a sun. If it were eighty times larger. If Sol didn't already exist."

"I know."

"Have you ever seen Jupiter from the surface of Europa?"

Hamman pulled an icon out, magnified it so that it became the flickering image of a tentacled lifeform, then threw it back.

"No."

Theodore continued, "You're upside down compared to the rest of humanity. On Earth, the surface is life whereas the underworld is the realm of the dead. Here the overworld fizzes with lethal radiation while the underworld is a place of safety. You suffer from heliodeficiency – you go downward for enlightenment."

The submarine sped away from the habitat, its screw a steady audible thrumming. The air in the control room was close with hot rubbery odours.

"How old are you?" asked Theodore.

The boy replied, "Two thousand, six hundred and seven."

Reckon explained that the young had taken to calculating their age according to Europa's orbit around Jupiter.

"But how old in Earth years?" persisted Theodore.

"I don't know. You should ask my father. Time is different here."

The last time Reckon had come out this far on a dive was for the funeral of Hamman's mother. The service was held over the chasm, and then the body was consigned to the greater deep, Hamman Kiki out alone in the water, his bioluminescence repeating the subdued sine waves of grief. At the time, she was still grieving Gregory and recognised, in the soft bands of blue pulsing across Kiki's trunk, a correlative to her own feeling. Somewhere, within Doxa, these painful illuminations persisted. She could revisit them, if she wished.

Theodore was wrong. Europa had an underworld too. We do not consign the dead to the earth so much as give them up to gravity, and that is appropriate; grief is a steep-sided emotion, easy to slide down and hard to climb out.

The rippled approach of the vent dunes. The submarine ascended then dipped into a channel. She felt the manoeuvre in her stomach. Her nerves did not settle. Cyan sensations prickled the surface of her suit. Her throat felt constricted.

Hamman turned to her. "Do you feel that?"

She did. It was a long time since she had been physically close to Doxa, and of course, Doxa had been much smaller then. The sensation was an unpleasant vulnerability. Your core was open. Your emotions were no longer inside and protected, but outside, running around, vulnerable but free.

"I feel it," said Reckon.

Theodore said, "Feel what?"

Hamman unhooked his seatbelt, and reached upward with his pale palms, seeking a distant signal.

"We're about two kilometres out," he said.

"Is it safe?" asked Theodore.

Hamman's fingers curled and uncurled, the motion of an anemone under the influence of the tide.

"Depends. How far can you swim?"

The fishers believed that the mechanism and tech of the submarine affected the purity of the Doxic signal. Hamman insisted they swim the rest of the way. The lake was around five degrees centigrade, give or take a degree

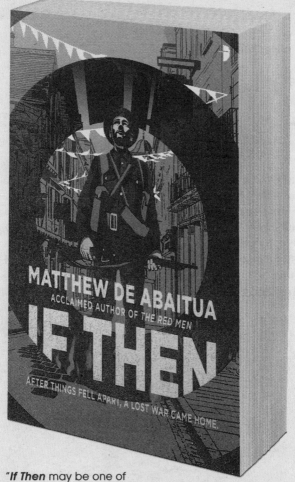

due to the convection currents. Theodore's body was not acclimatised to the water temperature but his suit would protect him for a couple of hours. The submarine drifted down and came to a stop on the lakebed.

Hamman checked their oxygen masks in turn, then flipped on their biometrics. Theodore's life signs showed escalated synaptic activity, a faint jagged orange line above the stable telemetry of his body. Her fault. The injection she had given him in the changing room was taking effect. She had dosed him with a variation on the optogenetic treatment devised by Matthias in his time at the University of the Moon. The files were still in her laboratory. The original virus had altered neurons in Theodore's motor functions and at the junction between the mind organs, disrupting their coherence into consciousness. She was able to restore the ones governing his motor functions while at the same time opening up the possibility of a deeper receptivity to exterior signals.

To Doxa.

It was a risk. She had not anticipated how strong Doxa had become, at this proximity. And she had made Theodore susceptible to it. Doxa might overwhelm him. Lovebomb him out of existence.

They climbed into the airlock, which Hamman sealed, and then he opened the valve so that the cold waters of Tethys sloshed around her ankles, her knees, her hips. Pulses of fear on her telemetry. Hamman gestured OK as the water covered his mask entirely. He unwound the hatch and then stepped aside for her to go first. There was no way back. Theodore followed her, his head torch flashing all around as he tried to orientate himself in the surrounding dark. Hamman was the last out of the submarine, sealing the hatch behind him. He swam up,

reached over, and turned off Theodore's agitated head torch. Theodore reacted with alarm, until Hamman pointed to the display of bioluminescence far ahead, beyond the curves of the dunes. Blue sensations pulsing from left to right. Lights with the emotional resonance of music.

Soundlessly, they swam toward it. The closer they came to Doxa, the more that Hamman's wetsuit bloomed with bioluminescence. Pulses of violet circles and blooming ochre curves, and within these round and comforting shapes, jagged silver edges. This pattern repeated. It was a language. The shapes corresponded to the sound of his name; the round motherly mantra of Hamman, the sharpness of Kiki. These lights were his true name, the words and sounds a mere translation.

The ice gave way to coarse-grained blue dunes divided by rocky channels stained red by the indigenous endolithic algae. Hamman swam ahead with forceful kicks. She felt the pressure waves from his kicks ripple underneath her body. Then he turned to face them. He held out two ends of a long elasticated cord that was secured to his waist. She attached it to her belt, and to Theodore's. As she did so, she peered inside Theodore mask. His pupils were vast. He was breathing quickly. Highly stimulated. The orange line on his telemetry. Did he guess what they were doing to him? He grasped her shoulders. Wanted to say something to her but comms were shut off this close in. His hands moved to her waist. Excitement. Desire? Perhaps. Or the onset of fear. She took his hands in hers, as much to remove them from her body as to reciprocate his touch. His telemetry was also changing. From the mere representation of biological function, it was becoming more expressive, spinning out radiating spokes of mood states. She ventured a thumbs-

up at him. But he was already swimming away and following in the wake of Hamman Kiki.

She swam good and strong, more comfortable in the water than on land. Ahead, the dips and swells of the dark dunes were rimed with a shifting paisley pattern of curling indigos and toxic reds. These projections from Doxa, played out on the mounds of hypothermal dust, were wheels-within-wheels, cyclones and vortices twisting inside one another – like a weather front observed from space. And then the lights vanished. She felt a tug on her tether. Without the lightshow, all she could see was the steady telemetry of Theodore and Hamman. The weak light of lifesigns overwhelmed by blind water. Another tug on her tether. She swam in close to Hamman. He held one palm out. The dark outline of his fingers reaching into the deep cold black. Then, as if responding to his signal, a new rhythm of blue pulses appeared up ahead. These pulses wriggled out from a central hub and across a great expanse of the seabed. Her first thought was of a landing strip or another colony. But a colony much larger than home. The blue pulse reached the end of its line and then it wriggled quickly along the circumference, and then back along a radius to the central hub. The afterimage flared on her retina.

A blue pulse wriggled down each of Hamman's fingers and rested in the well of his palm. He passed it onto her, and it flickered across her telemetry and then she passed it onto Theodore, and it pulsed across him also. She swam on.

Here, the dunes ended, and the lakebed become rougher, and sloped downward. There was a city below her. A nightscape of translucent bioluminescence, varying in pattern from district to district. The fishers

called it *cephalopolis*. The outskirts of cephalopolis were
marked by a playful fringe of pale blue dots, and this
circumference was connected to a central brain stem or
russet minaret by ferrous-tinged muscular spokes. New
patterns rippled through the cephalopolis, a steady pale
tan striping and then, passing through the stripes, a large
livid red spot. Hamman's palm followed the spot in the
same way that the head of a sunflower tracks the sun
across the sky. Cephalopolis was a biological substrate
of neurological complexity that had no anatomical
resemblance to the human brain but contained such a
glut of integrated synapses, firing in sync, that human
and human-like thought could be gathered within it.
The name of that gathering was Doxa. She stopped
swimming, drifted on the tether in a supplicant posture.
Almost foetal. Curled up around an ecstatic gut. Abject
worship of Doxa, the living library of their memories and
feelings.

Hamman pulled them in closer, showed them
the cluster of black eggs under the ruffled edges of
the cephalopolis. Each egg contained within it the
knowledge of their community encoded as instinct.
Ballurian's plan for panspermism, the seeding of distant
stars with emergent life. Because if consciousness was a
basic property of matter then space did not belong solely
to physics and chemistry. It belonged to biology too. To
humans and emergences alike. Doxa's bioluminescence
saturated her with awe. The balm of its benevolent
radiation, a mother's hand on a child's fevered brow.

Follow me, beckoned Hamman. They swam under
the ranks of black eggs, and then the fisher took them
close into the tough thick flesh. He showed them a hole
cut into the cephalopolis – not an orifice, as such. It
was wide enough for them to swim two-abreast. With

a sarcastic humble bow, Hamman offered Theodore
the chance to lead. Revenge for the baiting in the
submarine. Theodore did not accept the dare. The
translucent walls of the tunnel lit up with ponderous
contemplative lightwaves. The tunnel ended in a thick
lidded valve: Hamman reached out with his palm and
the valve opened before he could touch it. Together, they
climbed out of the tunnel and found themselves within
an oxygenised chamber in the cephalopolis. Hamman
removed his mask to show them that the atmosphere
was breathable. Theodore could not remove his mask, so
she helped him. His hair was matted with sweat. Either
from exertion or a reaction to the injection. He was more
agitated than usual.

Underfoot, the shifting rising motion of the
cephalopolis in the water. If it swam far from the
submarine, then they would be stranded. This was
dangerous, and she said so to Hamman.

"Doxa will not put us in danger," he replied. "Doxa
knows that we are within her." He ran his fingers along
the walls, which responded with inky traces.

"How long have you been coming here?" she asked.

There were three tunnels leading out of the chamber.
He walked down one with the rolling gait of a man
negotiating a rope bridge.

He dared them to follow him. "Aren't you curious?"

They were still attached to Hamman by their tethers.
She looked to Theodore. But he was racked with nausea,
his hands clenched to steady himself.

She was wary of leaving the chamber. "What is there
to see?"

Hamman called back, "Just one more room, I
promise."

The tunnel opened up into a small cold side room

with an upward curving ramp; this ramp led to a room with architecture that was a cross between a cathedral and a gullet. The high ceiling was vaulted with muscular tendons. In the far wall, a large churning dial of multi-coloured tendrils. Hamman reached out to them, and they erected in return, putting forth cerulean and ochre energies.

"After my mother died," said Hamman, "I discovered this place."

He climbed up on a raised dais of gelatinous material, the tethers taut. The coloured tendrils wavered at his approach. The air crackled with energy.

"I realised that part of my mother lives on in Doxa. All of our dead live here. Their knowledge and emotional traces."

Theodore finally spoke, "*All* of your dead?"

"Their footprints, their echoes, their marks, their works. My mother's compassion. That is how I found this place. I followed the feel of her voice. Whenever my memory of her starts to fade, I come here and I experience her presence again as if I was her little boy, and she is comforting me."

Gregory. His breath had been sour with medication. She became the caregiver, obligations she secretly resented. He was never part of Doxa. He was not here.

Reckon said, her voice tremoring, "What if I don't want to be with my dead?"

"Then be with the living," said Hamman. "This will be our city of god."

Reckon wondered if the young man had lost his mind.

"How will we live here? What will we eat?"

"Doxa will nurture us. She will feed us from her own belly."

An image of placenta, and all the fishers connected to

it. Back to the womb. She had an idea. A solution to the problem of gestation in low gravity. All the time, she had been looking at cellular formation even though it was not clear why these processes should be affected by low gravity, especially if she fooled the organism into sensing a typical Earth gravity. Instead, she should have been looking at the placenta. The problem of blood flow in the supporting environment that would lead to retardation of growth. A flash of insight. Either from Doxa or from her own genius, it didn't matter. She saw what had eluded her, all this time.

Theodore was on his knees. His telemetry was sparky. Head bowed forward in anticipation of judgement, but not mercy. He gasped, "What did you do to me?"

She shook her head. No, no, it was not like that. She had meant for him to join them in Doxa. Not suffer like this.

Theodore lifted up his empty hands, and whispered, "What are these feelings for?"

The ground shifted, the grey walls of the cathedral rippled at the pressure of adjacent disturbances. Hamman looked concerned. He leapt off the dais and ran back down the slope. She lifted Theodore up by his arm, and they followed the young fisher back through the chamber. As she ran, she felt the way her surroundings were shifting position. The tunnels pulsed with leading lights. She helped Theodore with his mask, and then they were through the valve and back in the dark lake water.

Theodore floated stunned in the water. His telemetry showed agitation, rapid pulse rate, spiking blood pressure. She put a gloved hand on him. Behind the mask, he was blinking away sweat, and the look on his face was one of such dread. *What are these feelings for?* Their

silhouettes against a red curved section of cephalopolis.
She reached out for him through Doxa but he was not
there. He remained apart. The injection had not worked
in the way she had hoped, and he was confined to his
own private pain. Behind the mask he was crying, and
his chest heaved with sobbing. What was he thinking?
What had upset him? Sealed away in his suit, she had no
idea. Was blinded by her own joy, so found his sorrow
inexplicable.

The cephalopolis turned in the water and rose upward.
A pressure wave buffeted them. Theodore did not resist.
He let the wave roll him back. And there, in the space
vacated, was the chasm leading down to Oceanus. Black
silted water spilling upward through the vents in the
lakebed. The tether jerked tight. Hamman overhead,
treading water, watching but not interfering. Something
glimmering in his hand. A knife. To cut Theodore free.
Vortical currents, warmer than the surrounding water,
the presence of a deeper darkness below. Then there was
a sound. A sound like a leviathan tapping stone fingers
against electromagnetic strings. Echoing up from below
and then all around her. Theodore was yanked out to the
full extent of the tether, caught in the current rushing up
from Oceanus. Lonely and quivering at the end of life.
Gregory had died the same way. And then, in a joyous
rush, long tube worms whipped out of the chasm, each
lit from within by waves of cerulean blue exhilaration.
When Jupiter lifts Europa up by its scalp, the scream of
the ice resonates throughout the moon, and the worms
respond to the vibrations of that call. It was as if nature
had recalled her seed, rewound creation and then poured
forth destruction instead.

Theodore was knocked upward by that wriggling
mass, buffeted from side to side on the tether. Hamman

tested the edge of the knife against the elasticated cord. And then Theodore fought back. He found his strength. He started to swim out of the current. His first few kicks were fruitless but then he found his stroke and he turned free of the uprushing column of megafauna. And this satisfied Hamman Kiki, he began pulling on the tether, to reel the stranger in.

They swam back to the submarine. It lit up at their approach. Hamman unclipped the tether, and opened the hatch. Inside the submarine, Theodore removed his mask, and put it aside, the sheer black layer of his wetsuit already dry. His face was puffy with the pressure of the dive, making his twisted scars seem even deeper. He was reluctant to catch her eye, preferring the neon holograms of the guidance system. She should comfort him. But how? Doxa was comfort. She was not Doxa. Accustomed to sharing feeling with the rest of the community, her ability to read the subtleties of other people had diminished.

The submarine lifted up from the lakebed, and turned back in the direction of the colony.

Hamman, strapped into the pilot's chair, was amused by Theodore's stupefaction. Had no sympathy with the older man's sorrow.

"What did you think of that?"

Theodore rubbed at his eyes.

"You've made a brain in a jar," he said.

Hamman looked askance.

"What does that mean?"

"It means that I remember why I'm here."

He wouldn't say any more than that. She pressed him on it. But, no. It seemed to upset him, and she didn't want him to be upset. She wanted him to share in her

sense of wonder and worship. She took his hand in hers, put her other hand on his cheek. He was cold to the touch.

"I should leave," he whispered.

She withdrew her hand.

The water in the moon pools was dark and maroon under the secondary lighting. She left the submarine bay and returned to the changing room, stripping off her wetsuit, and stepping into a hot abundant shower. She washed the rubberised smell of the suit off her skin, saturated her braids with water, massaged shampoo into her scalp and then bent forward so that the water and soap ran down her braids. The abandon of it. She stood up and let her braids drift up and cover her face. Shame on her for what she did to him. Experimenting in that way. She didn't know why the serum had failed. She bound her braids tightly in a towel.

When she emerged from the shower, naked, he was sat on the bench opposite, his wetsuit unzipped to expose his upper body. She covered her exposed breasts by crooking her arms. But that was absurd. He should see her. The darkening tips of her nipples, her full hips and strong thighs, the stripe of freckles across her shoulders, droplets of water quivering upon the coiled hair of her pubis. And then she slipped the towel from her head, turned her back to him, and covered her body. After exposing herself, she was entitled to ask him direct questions.

"You were upset by the Doxa."

"I was a weirdcore addict from the age of seventeen. I was very close to my grandmother. She raised me. But when she died, I was still an addict. I couldn't grieve. I never grieved. Until today."

This was fascinating. Her serum had worked, but instead of integrating him with Doxa it had first restored his emotional capacity.

"That's positive," she said.

He shook his head.

"It's not the only thing that I remembered. Forgetting makes life bearable. I've come to rely upon it."

"You seemed scared back there."

"I was. Being scared is something I'm now capable of."

He stood up and walked over to her, and they were kissing. His lips were still cold but there was a strong suggestion of warmth to come. He stepped back, sat back down and took off the rest of his wetsuit. His penis sat up strongly. He walked past her into the showers to wash off the smell of the wetsuit, the door of the cubicle ajar so that she could watch. His hair ruckled up at all angles. She was certain that sex was the right thing to do: her worship of Doxa still tingled in her body. There was a similar awakening within him. Long stifled needs, suppressed possibilities, wanton yearnings. The shower stopped. She removed her towel and offered it to him. He dabbed his body with its still-warm cloth, and then put it aside. He gripped her backside, pressed her back into the cubicle. She guided him into her.

23
IN VIVO

The second time they had sex, it was like he was heaving his soul into her. She clutched either side of his head, took the sweat of his scalp under her fingernails, ran her heels along the strong ridged muscles in his lower back. Afterwards, she joked that with the low gravity, it was like he was trying to push them both into orbit. The third time they had sex, she sat astride him, kept him still and deep. Europa's groans echoed along the air vents as the moon was stretched then compressed by the gravities of its Jovian siblings. She hitched herself up to quiver with orgasm against the head of his penis and, when he was unable to hold back any longer, helpless in the face of her ecstasy, he came deep into her.

She knew what she was doing.

Afterwards, under red secondary lighting and thin municipal blankets, they argued about Earth.

"You must miss it," he insisted.

She didn't miss Earth. He composed doggerel praising Earth to remind her of its qualities: the morning mist drifting over patchwork fields, the sublime majesty of a thunder mountain. His nature talk was not persuasive.

"You advocate Earth but you're ignoring the humans,"

she said. "And they are the planet's defining feature. The rest of the solar system has sublime geology. But Earth has *people*."

He did not mount a convincing defence of people.

"I believe in people," she said. "In the end, it's the only intangible position that you can adopt. You must begin with trust, search for and speak truth, conduct yourself honestly, defend yourself and others with passion."

He slid out from under her body. "If you love people so much, why do you live half a billion miles away from them?"

"Because Earth has a massive population that does not believe in people." She was angry again. What was it with him, that he made her so angry and greedy at the same time? "I'll give you an example from your *intangibles*. It's like the Vichy regime in France during the Second World War. Paris was kept intact on the proviso that the leadership internalised and enforced the Nazi value system. Earth is like that. It is stuck because it made a compact with a colonising power."

"The emergences."

"Yes. Partly. But the emergences only put in place an ideology that was already there, left over from the Seizure."

He continued with the doggerel. "You're the resistance from a distance."

She never made her political points with any concision because her theories were bound up with her anger, and this intense emotion expanded the scope of her ideas, made them hard to control. In Doxic terms, her politics tripped the breakers – the biological switches that ensured one person's emotional intensity did not overload the system.

"The control is internal and external. People have

chosen to make their souls over in the image of the enemy. Liberation is not a matter of bombs and bullets. It's about reimagining the human future. That's why I don't miss Earth. Here my life can matter in a way that it never could if I'd remained a lunar academic or given myself up to the asylum malls."

Bare-footed, she padded across the cold linoleum, picking up her clothes as she went. When she looked back, his gaze was unreadable. They were a hopeless doomed pair. Explicable to one another only in the act of sex. Even she couldn't misread *those* signs. Otherwise, they were obscure to one another. The truth was – and this was something she would only discover later that week, around sex act number whatever, after she had stopped counting – his feelings toward her were profoundly conflicted. This conflict arose during another argument about Earth: he confessed that he could not forgive her for what she had done to him, the injection that had repaired his emotional pathways.

"I am happy," he said. "But that happiness is tinged with worry that it will soon pass." His hand considered her naked breast, and then withdrew.

"No. It's more intense than that." His hand returned to her breast as if it were the substance of his argument. "You've made me care. And caring is indivisible from fear. The clouds have lifted and I realise that the road I am travelling runs parallel to death. A coast road with death as the sea; every time I glance out of my window, death is there."

He confessed that he had never spoken in this way to his wife. She asked about his marriage.

"We are business partners," he explained. "Bound together in the pursuit of excellence. I can't be weak with her."

"Will you tell her about us?"

He turned away from her, mumbled, "I don't think it will matter."

"Why?"

"Time is running out."

In her exercise class, her friends asked about him while heaving at the rowing machine or pummelling away at the treadmill. Jordan and Lygia extracted salacious details from her under alibis of concern about her well-being. Lygia, a professor of linguistics, wondered if Reckon – by shacking up with an oppressor – was working out issues regarding her father. Jordan, a geneticist, maintained that the opposite was the case – it was Reckon's mother, with her martyr's pragmatism, who was the guiding influence in this liaison. Theodore had the air of a good provider, even if he stank of evil.

Reckon exercised until her thighs quivered with exhaustion. The friends went for tea together. Lygia was drinking a dried kelp brew and the smell of it turned Reckon's stomach.

She went into her laboratory and confirmed her suspicions.

Pregnant. In vivo. Despite the radiation. Despite the low-gravity. Despite his corporate marriage. A flush in her cheeks brought her freckles to the fore. There had been no morning sickness but her aversion to the smell of Lygia's tea showed a heightened sensitivity to toxins. Doxa remembered how, after becoming pregnant, some women found that they could not stand the smell of their partners, and turned them out of the marital bed. Because they reeked of toxicity. The polluted long lunches. The poisonous after-work drinks. The fetid cant. With this in mind, she wondered if Theodore would now seem repulsive to her, a return to their true relationship as enemies.

She didn't tell him the news. He noticed that she was distracted, as she lay in bed, listening to the changes creeping through her body.

"What does Doxa feel like?" he asked.

"I always feel safe and loved and part of a community. Before Doxa I was anxious, uncertain and distrustful, and profoundly alienated. Either I've just grown up or I owe my sanity to Doxa."

"Can you access the knowledge of others?"

"Yes, and with meditation, integrate that knowledge into myself. Internalise it entirely."

"So, in a way, I might be sleeping with the entire colony."

She put her hand on his chest.

"Yes. When I've been lonely, I've explored other people's memories of sex. They are still only memories. Not a replacement for the real thing."

"So Doxa is just a library."

"No. It's more than that. Doxa suggests. Doxa surfaces what you need, sometimes before you ever knew that you needed it."

He was thoughtful.

"You talk about Doxa as if it has its own identity."

"I suppose it does."

"As if something has emerged to bind together and direct this collective mind."

"Doxa is like a better version of yourself. A nicer voice inside your head."

"What would happen if Doxa died?"

The thought had never occurred to her. Or to Doxa. Deep wells of foreboding opened up within her. She felt sick. And then the wells closed over, the sickness tapered away, and she was comforted again.

"We can move Doxa to other biological substrates. It

will always exist, and even after I die, I will always be part of it."

"Don't you lose track of yourself?"

"Yes." She reared over him, let her braids enclose them both. "But what's so great about being locked up inside yourself?"

She stopped asking him why he had come to Europa. Or why he had said that their time was running out. Her treatment had restored his emotional capacity and his memory, but he would not share those secrets with her. If she pressed him then he would only lie. It was inevitable that their relationship would end badly, so she hoped that they could, at the very least, avoid lies.

In the infirmary, Jordan informed her that the blastocyst had formed an embryo. It had been twelve days since fertilisation. With Jordan, she discussed her theory that low gravity affected blood circulation within the placenta and that this was a crucial factor in impeding foetal development. Her stints on the rowing machine helped her cardiovascular system maintain form in low gravity, so they had to devise an equivalent regime for the placenta: nutriceuticals to regulate production of nitric oxide, sildenafil to dilate the blood vessels. As Jordan administered the first course of this treatment, Reckon lay on the surgical table, wondering if she would make it to the quickening; the first kick – a fluttering sensation, supposedly – and then the outline of a single foot or elbow pressing out against her skin.

"Why him?" asked Jordan, over the top of her glasses.

Reckon gazed up at the geneticist.

"I wanted to test my theory about gestation, and he was the nearest option."

"Ligia thinks Ballurian is using your wiles to get inside his head."

"I took Theodore to Doxa. We healed him but the link did not take."

Jordan swabbed Reckon's lower abdomen clean, and indicated that she could get down from the treatment table.

"Have you told him you're pregnant?"

"No."

"Why?"

"Our relationship is based on keeping secrets from one another. Secrets and sex."

"That's wise. Don't get too close."

"Oh, we are close. It's just that we don't know anything about one another."

It was not her first pregnancy. She had fallen pregnant on the University of the Moon. *Fallen?* No, she had *hovered* over pregnant for a few weeks, ignoring the physiological evidence, scared to resolve the existence or otherwise of the embryo. Her miscarriage came as a relief, gouts of bloody relief, and she wept with abandon afterwards, although that was just the hormonal gush. She flushed the cells away, and wondered why the child had not formed. Was it her? Was it him? Or was it the moon?

She didn't tell the prospective father. Instead, she took a sabbatical on Earth, for a restful month arguing with her mother in a cottage in the Lake District. It was the last time they were able to be their disputatious selves with one another before her mother's illness enforced mutual tolerance. She was trudging furiously across a field, smoking again, looking for the footpath that would take her away from her mother and directly to a pub.

She loathed every step in the countryside. No aspect of her upbringing had inculcated within her a love of the English pastoral. Her father had been strictly cities and hot beaches, her mother was urbane and metropolitan – and yet, through cussedness, they had decided to holiday in mud together. Pacing out her rancour across ploughed fields, she looked up and saw, among the gathered cumulus, a cloud the shape of her lost child, a wispy arm waving goodbye as it returned to the inchoate matter of the universe.

In the third week of angry love with Theodore, she realised they were not alone in her quarters. The smell of fishers, cold and salty in the dark. Low light was their element. They caught Theodore by his ankles and yanked him in one motion out of the bed so that he was stunned by the cold linoleum, then they cast him sprawling half-naked into the corner of the room. She turned the sidelight on, and screamed, you don't need to do this, this isn't necessary, this is not how we behave.

She calculated that they were not about to kill him and therefore she did not physically engage, given the risk such an act would pose to the embryo. For the sake of the experiment, and the greater good, she let them take him. Any pregnant woman would have made the same call. Theodore was not so compliant. Others fishers came to haul him away.

Then she dressed, composed herself, fixed her braids. She thought about the embryo. Her motherliness was seeping into Doxa. The others would know soon enough, and if they were attentive, then they would know already. There were memories of childbirth in Doxa, though the emotions involved were softened and reduced by the breakers. Feeling her way through these

memories, she learnt of a transition stage, before the final
push. Memories of this dark hinterland were hunted,
primitive, almost pre-lingual. Pregnancy augmented
instinct, diverting resources away from abstraction and
complexity to focus upon vulnerability.

Healing his emotional damage had made Theodore
vulnerable. The two of them had become raw, and space
was the wrong environment in which to be so exposed.
He had not forgiven her for making him capable of love.
Now he had so much to lose. Love for her. Love, even, for
Doxa and what was at stake: deep connection between
people, new possibilities of knowledge and feeling. His
love was skittish and untrustworthy, like a river in high
season.

She walked through the corridors of the colony, on her
way to Theodore's interrogation. Colleagues sensed
her approach and came to meet her, drawn out from
their laboratories and studies. All thought turned to
her. Nobody vocalised their congratulations about the
embryo but their smiles were knowing and kindly.
She was unaccustomed to being looked at in that way.
Reckon imagined herself to be unpredictable, multi-
channel, overflowing with ideas and intensity. Sharp
and stingingly brilliant. But the smiles of her friends and
colleagues suggested that – after a lifetime of resistance –
she had finally been brought to her true destiny: barefoot
and pregnant. A stately martyr to the colony's need for a
child. Gestating virtue.

"How are you doing?" asked Ligia.

"They took him away," said Reckon.

"But the baby."

"The embryo."

"It's exciting."

"It's terrifying."

Reckon said to Ligia, "You don't think it is exciting. You feel sorry for me."

Ligia's smile faltered, her gaze turned blank: creative acts – such as lying – shut down the visual centres so that the brain could make the synaptic leaps necessary to devise fiction. She noticed these instances of blindness in the faces of her friends. They weren't happy for her. Saying they were happy for her was old Earth talk. If they upset her, it might lead to miscarriage. In reality, they were worried about her, worried about themselves. The embryo represented considerable physical and psychological risk to Reckon. She would end the pregnancy at the first sign of malformation. Nobody had performed an abortion in low gravity before. Also, if she carried the embryo to term and it became a baby, then would her friends also be expected to gestate? They had not travelled half a billion miles just to become parents. Only the fishers like Hamman, who had grown up on Europa, were keen to breed.

The low-gravity was oppressively weak. She steadied herself.

She didn't want to be mother.

She didn't have to be a mother.

They would all raise the child. The whole community. Not her. Not alone.

Doxa protect her from the compulsive attachment of motherhood. Doxa protect her from instinct. The embryo was an experiment, and if it didn't take, then would she end the experiment and try again. With Theodore or another man. She thought of Gregory, leaving her laboratory, to die alone on the surface. Would she feel differently if the child was his?

No.

Is that why she chose Theodore Drown to be the father? Because it would be easier to abort the child of a man like him?

No.

Theodore's interrogation. She was the last to arrive at the gloomy storeroom. The toxic smell of men in an enclosed space. Theodore was the one in the chair, two fishers holding him down by his shoulders. He seemed... not in control but dignified. Ballurian stood at the other end of the cell. There was a long rectangular window with a greenlit view of the dusty grey lakebed. The light was low, and red in parts, green sometimes; the faces of the men passed through these tinted shadows, and then out the other side. Theodore noted her arrival with a glance of weary disappointment.

She would not stand for that look.

"What?" she asked.

"My honey trap," he replied.

She almost told him, there and then, that it wasn't like that. But perhaps it was.

She wondered where to stand among the tense arrangement of men. Ballurian did not acknowledge her: his dark filtered gaze, his high Asiatic cheekbones and broad Malaysian nose with nostrils like haunches – the solid effigy of his head – loomed over Theodore as a threat. She stood to the side. Whether she was to act as witness for the prosecution or defence, Reckon was not yet sure. Ballurian's fingertips tapped softly together, as if counting out beats before a crescendo.

"You remember now, don't you?" He placed his palms against one another in careful, weary supplication. "Please tell us why you came all this way."

"Because of a brain in a jar," said Theodore.

This was not the answer Ballurian expected.

Theodore offered clarification. "Your cephalopolis. Your Doxa. We came to destroy Doxa," said Theodore.

"Why?" gasped Reckon.

"Doxa breaks a Cantor Accord. It is emergent."

"But Doxa has nothing to do with emergence. It's a jellyfish."

"I was in the asylum mall," he said. "Matthias used human experimentation to construct the mental architecture of Doxa, an experiment that I was part of. The emergences learnt of it and saw that Matthias was trying to create a group mind. They cleared up his mess on Earth, massacring hundreds of people to prevent the experiment being repeated."

"I thought they were helping us," said Ballurian.

"They might have been, at an early stage. But they will not risk another emergence."

Green shadows in the hollows of Ballurian's face. Anger could be exhausting.

He said, "You told me that Matthias was shot."

"Yes."

"And that was a lie." A statement not a question.

Theodore nodded. "Matthias was connected to Doxa when an emergence killed him. He maintained a link between the mall and here, concealed within the University of the Sun's system of laser relays. His death experience must be drifting around in your Doxa. I was there. It was deeply unpleasant."

Ballurian moved over to the dark window, peering out into the lake.

"So we finally have the attention of the emergences."

Hamman was shocked. "You wanted this?"

"Sooner or later. It's the nature of things," said Ballurian. "Our two species are bound together." His

spoke without conviction.

Hamman stepped forward, blade in hand, testing the point against Theodore's scarred face. The boy's fear made him dangerous.

"Nobody is coming to save you," said Hamman.

"You're right," said Theodore. "They are not coming to save me. But they are coming."

Fear flowed around the room. She tried to control her heartbeat. A mother's fear conditions the foetus, trains it for a hostile world. Her womb, the core of her, felt insecure. It was a horrible sensation.

Ballurian contemplated the waters beyond the glass, and Theodore's reflection within them. "Why did Magnusson send you?" he asked slowly.

"To buy everyone some time. The emergences are curious about you." Theodore shrugged out of the grip of the fisher guards. "Their curiosity means that all is not lost. There is a sliver of a chance."

Hamman withdrew his blade from Theodore's face to consider the range of options in terms of other wounds, other scars.

"You're a bureaucrat with the face of psychopath," said Hamman.

Theodore's expression showed only a kind of regret. "This is big boy stuff," he said to Hamman. "You should step back."

Theodore had space to move now. Methodically, he had got them to take their hands off him, and secured a yard or two of freedom. He caught sight of his own reflection in the black lake.

"I've sent a signal," he said. "So that negotiations can advance."

Ballurian continued to study the waters, pressing his hands against the cold glass.

He asked, "What's in it for you?"

Theodore said, "There is still a chance to rescue your colony and Doxa."

"No," said Ballurian. "That's not why you came all this way."

"You're right. I came as part of the Destructives. Being here has made me feel terrified and vulnerable but, in my entire life, Doxa is the only thing I have known that gives me hope."

He was telling the truth, she was convinced of it. The kindness of Doxa could be overwhelming.

"We will seal Dream 6 tunnel," said Hamman. "The fishers will defend the colony. Nothing will get through."

The fishers were strong of arm, and had formed a cult around their fortitude. But she wondered if they were all that tough. Because of Doxa, none of them had so much as punched another man on the nose. Whereas Theodore – while not a violent man – had a hard indifferent sheen to which morality did not adhere. God knows what his friends were capable of.

Ballurian turned to Reckon. "What do you think?"

"I don't know," said Reckon. "I think he will betray us despite his best intentions. It's in his nature." This hurt him, she saw that on his face: What are we to each other? How did love bring me to this despair?

She was curious to see if she could break his heart.

"The question is," she said to the room, "will Theodore still betray us when he finds out that I am pregnant?"

She watched Theodore expression turn inward with calculation. Do those sums, you bastard. His eyes tremored, thinking through all the variables. But then his expression changed. The numbers evaporated.

"Will the child live?" he asked.

Ballurian wanted an answer to this question too.

"It has a chance," she said. "Presuming we are not wiped out by the emergences first."

She considered Theodore, shabby in his seat.

"If this child makes it to term, you will not be its father. It will be raised by us all. By Doxa."

From deep below the base, came the creak and moan of the moon as it was stretched and compressed by competing gravities. Through the deep water came the squeak and whine of thick ice under pressure. A whine that intensified, echoing down the air vents. A variation on the usual geological tensions. The fishers gathered at the window looking out over the seabed and there, in place of the grey dark, there was a new colour. Whorls of red. Jovian light.

"The ice sheet must have cracked," said Hamman. The base shook and through the window the waters whirled and churned in a fierce upward current. She reached out to steady herself and Theodore caught her.

Ballurian summoned a hologram of the surface of Europa. Together they watched as the ice fissured in the chaos regions, and plumes of lakewater poured forth, boiling out into the vacuum of space. Not a waterfall but a *waterrise*, like a tower rising from out of the moon, an edifice a hundred kilometres long, lethal rainbows of Jovian radiation shimmering within its outpouring. Blocks of surface ice moved around and against one another. Fresh rolls of ice formed on the plains, metre by metre closing up the new vent, diminishing the stream of the waterrise, until the gush was cut off and the tower drifted apart in a cloud of glittering icicles.

The view of the hologram shifted to Lake Tethys. Objects speeding with intent through the drift of thousands of chunks of glacial debris. Pods.

"That'll be my wife," said Theodore.

24

THE DESTRUCTIVES

This is what Doxa did to him. It gave him a new perspective on the story of his life, and forced him to accept what a mean tight little story it had been. The kindnesses he blithely accepted as his right, the loving gestures he had forgotten about, if he had ever noticed them; overlooked compassions were more formative than his scant experience with weirdcore. It was his choice to be defined by his damage, by his scars.

On the arrays, no one analysed compassion because it did not lead to purchase. Compassion was omitted from the metrics. Reckon, angry, had told him what a reduction of human potential he represented but it took the integration with Doxa for him to admit that failure in his heart. He was ashamed of all the missed opportunities to do or say something helpful to the people he loved. Yes, he had lost his mother at an early age but how much worse had it been for Alex to lose her daughter. Through Doxa, he was privileged to experience a mother's loss and then have that loss healed. Now he understood the strength Alex must have mustered to turn her grief into kindness toward her grandson. This was the kind of heroism that deserved monuments. Even Beth Green

was trying to be kind to him. On the night he hit rock bottom. Her careless confession to him was because she was fond of Theodore, trusted him, and he had seized on this trust as a moment of weakness. Doxa took the kinks out of memories twisted by bitter recollection, and showed him the kindness he had never noticed. He could have been a better man. The night he sat with Grandma Alex as she died, and ministered to her, and stared into the black sun of her dying; that experience should have set him on a different path.

He stood on the edge of the moon pool, waiting for his wife to arrive. A holographic display showed pods descending through a field of ice fragments, and seven silver capsules streaking ahead. The colony defences had been set up around the narrow cavern exit of the tunnel. So Patricia had created a new tunnel, cutting through two kilometres of ice just to surprise everyone. He was scared of his wife. Perhaps he had been scared of her all along, and due to his emotional incapacity, had numbly mistaken that fear for love.

Waiting beside the moon pools, he shivered with adrenaline and the chill rising from the Europan waters. He wanted everyone to be safe. Doxa was too important, Reckon and his unborn child were worth more than his heart could contain. Like all converts, he felt an urgent shame at coming to the truth too late in life.

The memory blocks were degrading. Security had promised him that they would. He flexed his fingertips, shaking out the numbness. He now remembered everything from the moment he shot Meggan in the doorway of her asylum mall apartment to the beating Security administered to him before bundling him into a pod and firing him at Europa. And what a series of raw deals, betrayals and bad behaviour the last two years had

been, punctuated with acts of destruction. Justifications
for these acts were Patricia's forte, and he had let her talk
him around. He was culpable.

The base was in lockdown. On the way to the dock, he
had walked through crowds of agitated colonists. Reckon
ran to her lab to secure her work. She had used him to
impregnate her and test her theories on gestation. His
first child. No, not a child yet. It was barely an embryo. If
did get a chance to speak to Reckon, before the end, then
he would tell her that he was sorry: I am sorry I allowed
myself to become this man.

It was wrong to put all the blame onto Patricia. He
wanted status, and had inherited his ambition from
Grandma Alex, who had worked her way up from the
terraced streets of Belfast to Cambridge and beyond. Her
mother, his great-grandmother, had been an alcoholic,
and he'd inherited that too. Without parents, he had no
fixed position in society, experimented with low life and
then swung to the other end of the axis, for an elite life
with Patricia and Magnusson. Wanting social status in a
Post-Seizure world was like scrabbling for loose change
flung across the deck of the *Titanic*.

Patricia, I have good news and bad news. The good
news is that I have achieved our client's primary goal. I
found the brain in a jar. The bad news is that. The bad
news. The bad.

He belonged in the asylum mall for what he had done.

The surface of the moon pool plopped and whitened
with bubbles of carbon dioxide, and then his black box
surfaced. He reached out for it and the black box leapt
into his hand. He had removed it before coming to
Europa to conceal his connection with emergence. He
fastened the necklace and tucked the black box under
his shirt. When he was a boy, Dr Easy told him that his

whole life would be recorded on that box, and that it would follow him wherever he went. Only with the breaking of the surface ice had it been able to locate him. His revelation with Doxa, his relationship with Reckon, all of that went unrecorded, and the creation of this gap in the data felt like a victory.

The doors to the dock slid open and there was Hamman Kiki, holding a harpoon and, in his belt, a curved gutting knife. Hamman knelt to measure the vibrations of the approaching pods then, at his instruction, fishers took up positions around the moon pool, their angling equipment directed at the seething, rising waters.

The colony was in a state of emergency but there was no klaxon. That was a shame. The arrival of his wife warranted a klaxon.

"My wife has come to negotiate," said Theodore, calling out over the churning waters. "But if you give her an excuse to hurt you, she will take it."

The first pod erupted out of the moon pool, stopped in midair, drawing the fire of the fishers. The pod opened slowly. It was empty. Then his wife leapt out from under the pod, her executive armour deployed, limbs and torso encased in hard cylinders, her small fierce fists powering outsize weaponised gauntlets. Her helmet was massive and shielded for combat and radiation. How long could the fishers last in a room with his wife, when she was in this kind of mood? She adhered to the ceiling, took a microsecond to work the room, then her gauntlets deployed rolling banks of suppressor foam. The fishers were doused in its hardening gum. Her armour was designed to contain angry shareholders and break-up employee uprisings; the fishers had knives, but Patricia had riot control. Hamman leapt across the dock and landed beside her, thrusting his harpoon downward

against the armour, not penetrating it, but enough to knock her across the bay. She skidded to a halt against the wrought iron walkway. Hamman was adept at moving in low gravity, knew how to focus his strength. He covered the distance in a single leap, raked the harpoon point down the front of her armour, ripping through the outer layer, then bringing up the blade for a second swipe.

She tasered him in the seven chakras; the telemetry on his wetsuit erupted in mandalas, and then he was on the floor twitching with enlightenment.

Patricia leapt back onto her feet, turned her blank faceplate toward her husband. Looked right at Theodore. He gave her a little wave, which she returned with a flutter of her armoured fingertips.

Other pods surfaced throughout the dock, bringing in Magnusson, flanked by the tall strong figure of Security and her detail of armoured guards, and some tech guys with boxes of hardware.

Patricia slid back her faceplate. White lipstick, dusted cheekbones, not so thick as to conceal the flush of exertion. They kissed so that she could take the words right out of his mouth.

"Good news and bad news," he said.

"Give me the bad news first," she said.

"We're finished. You and I," he replied.

She touched his cheek with the back of her gauntlet.

"No," she said. "Don't say it."

"The good news is that the client is going to be happy."

He gestured at the tech boys bringing up their gear.

"But you can't do this."

Patricia closed her eyes and massaged her forehead. She directed Security to collect Hamman Kiki's twitching body, then ordered the med-team to begin prepping the boy for *interface*. She turned back to Theodore,

calculating if there was time to address this unexpected
item of personal business.

"We aren't finished," she said. "We've barely started."

He was going to tell her the bald fact of his infidelity,
but then he wondered if that really was the cause
or merely a symptom. He hesitated, and they were
interrupted by Magnusson, who unclipped his helmet
and ostentatiously sampled the air of his rival. He
gestured expansively; in his armour, he looked like
a bear wearing its own trap. He let out a motivational
bellow, the rest of the team responded with hoo-rahs.

"What happened to you?" asked Patricia.

"I remembered," said Theodore.

The memory blocks were considered necessary by
Security. From Death Ray's files, they knew that the
colony was based on some form of communal thought.
"The blocks will put doubt in their minds," Security had
explained, "If you achieve mission objectives, the blocks
will degrade, and you will remember just enough to call
us in." Security swiped through his file. He signed away
his right to legal compensation. "You'll need an alibi,"
she said. "One that even you will believe." He signed
the various pieces of paperwork that Procurement put
in front of him. Once he completed the waiver, Security
said they would now begin preparing his alibi. She
shoved him off the chair and kicked him in the midriff
three times, enunciating contractual disclaimers with
each kick, then she turned to her team and said, "Throw
him overboard."

Patricia unclipped the torso of her armour. Translucent
streaks of perspiration on her vest, her chest heaving
under the constricting weight of emotion, a shiver across
her narrow shoulders.

In this moment of casual intimacy, he said, "What

kind of woman marries a man whose emotional centres are burnt out?"

She wouldn't admit fault.

"You weren't burnt out. You were just low key."

"I'm different now. I'm healed."

Yes, he was. She heard it in the timbre of his voice.

"Good," she said. "Who healed you?"

"A scientist. She helped me."

There – he placed the fact of his adultery within the meta-meeting. Patricia saw it, did not want to believe it.

"Is she part of the bad news too?"

"You killed Kakkar," he said. "And the others."

"What happened on the moon was an accident." She was distracted by the approach of her anger.

"An accident you knew would happen."

"You married me. Was that an accident too?"

"I married you out of calculation and ambition because that was all I was capable of. I feel differently now."

"You *feel*?"

Patricia clutched at his shirt.

"This is the damage talking," she said.

"No. This is me."

"Because you've discovered a moral code," she said. "Via the surprising route of sleeping with another woman. Did she have a particularly moral vagina?"

This wasn't the conversation she wanted at all. She waved her own sour joke away, and then, as he went to tell her about the pregnancy, his confession was curtailed by a heavy backhand from Patricia's gauntlet; it was like being hit with an iron bar. He collapsed in physical crisis, weak with the shock and pain of it, more than he had known. She backed away from what she had done. The strong light of the quarantine room glinted off her retinas. She tried to slow her breathing, and bring herself

under control; she turned away from him, did not want to risk being near to him.

Patricia took up a disinfectant hose and sluiced his blood off her gauntlet, not looking at him, as if he had ceased to exist.

Staying conscious was the trick, he thought. I might have a better chance of staying awake if I'm on my feet. He tried to stand but the soles of his feet could get no purchase on the tiled floor.

"I shouldn't have told you," he mumbled through the blood. "That was selfish of me."

She put the hose back in its socket, pulled out a dryer nozzle, and wafted the hot air over her armoured sleeve. Her profile: small nose, set pale lips, platinum hair flattened and angular with sweat.

"I should have found another way," he spat out a clot, "to convince you to stop."

She put the dryer nozzle back.

"We've come half a billion miles. We can't stop now."

"The brain in a jar. They call it Doxa. I touched it. It helped me understand goodness."

She glanced at his bloody face. "I could forgive you, you know, for the adultery. Memory blocks are a good excuse for forgetting your wedding vows."

He rolled over on his side, got up onto his hands and knees. But his strength had gone, and he would soon lose consciousness.

She said, "You're trying to save your soul at the eleventh hour. I'm tired of pretending that's possible for you." And then she left.

The Destructives made their way through the base. The fishers slipped back into the shadows. Reckon felt their anger cool and harden into resolve: they would loot

what they needed, load up the submarines, and retreat deeper into Europa, travelling through the chasm into the unexplored reaches of Oceanus. Doxa would help the fishers to establish a fall-back position, providing an oxygenised environment, emotional resilience, and a knowledge base.

There was to be no fallback position for Reckon. She was in the welcoming committee. Platters of food and drink were laid out for the Destructives: pemmican, dried and spiced sea greens, sour, chalky hydroponic fruits. Goblets of creamy, citrus-tinged alcoholic foam. Ballurian had a bottle of vintage single malt. Something saved for a special occasion. He poured himself two fingers and added a little water to loosen the flavour, savoured each stage of its salty complexity, then turned to Reckon.

"You should go with the fishers," he said.

"I will protect Doxa," she replied.

"That's a battle we might have to lose."

Did she trust his leadership? The Destructives had Ballurian's son. What would he give up to save Hamman? He was compromised.

The Destructives entered the room. A man and woman in executive armour followed by a tall powerful black woman with the trained posture of a security agent, and the rest of her detail. The tall broad armoured man was Magnusson, and the slight woman beside him was Theodore's wife, Patricia. But no Theodore. Why had he not come? Reckon reached into Doxa for his whereabouts – glimpsed an argument between Theodore and Patricia, an argument curtailed by a blow.

Ballurian and Magnusson embraced awkwardly; two giant men, enhanced to the limit, who had outgrown bonhomie. Magnusson's smile was like an unzipped

sports bag; leathery at the edges, and crooked along the seam. Patricia gave Ballurian a quick respectful nod but did not offer up a hand to be shaken or a cheek to be kissed; her gaze, tight and penetrating, fixed upon Reckon. How much did she know about Reckon and Theodore? Too early to say.

"What an achievement!" Magnusson walked around the meeting room with arms raised, taking in all that the colony had created.

Ballurian accepted the compliment, "We have exceeded our own expectations."

"We've all come a long way from Silicon Valley," laughed Magnusson. They met as equals, even though Magnusson's barrel-chested armour gave him the physical advantage. She was reminded of the armour of Henry VIII in the Tower of London, broad across the middle and with an absurd cod-piece. Ballurian, in his layered pastel robes, looked out of sorts in this ritual of aggression. He winced at having to run through the repertoire of antiquated corporate moves: a handshake like a wrestling hold, suppressive hugs, every touch an act of possession rather than compassion. Magnusson smelt like a butcher's shop, of steel and meat.

Ballurian played the host, walking around the table of food and drink, explaining the origin of the various indigenous delicacies, how they were cultivated in the life-resistant environment of Europa. Patricia discretely waved her palm over the platters – scanning for toxins – before taking a small plate and placing small portions upon it. She tasted the food with trepidation, and her response withheld approval. Reckon was hungry, and it was almost possible – as she gathered dried kelp between the tongs and placed it upon a plate – to believe that everything was going to be OK, and that they would

work out their differences through civilised negotiation.

Patricia introduced herself to Reckon, and apologised for the way the Destructives had gone about establishing contact. I hope you understand, she explained, our reasoning. They had been unable to find a way to communicate remotely with the colony so one of their team had to go ahead as an advance scout. If the Europans had proven hostile, then they would have captured Theodore and tortured him for information. Theodore's memory blocks precluded hostile parties from gaining any advantage through interrogation. It had not been an ideal solution, but it seemed good enough. Patricia's explanation reminded Reckon of why she had left Earth. Lies had become its native tongue. No one even noticed they were lying anymore. The culture could not admit to what had happened in the Seizure. What the Seizure meant for the dominant way of life. And so the culture stumbled on, propped up with more and more elaborate deceptions. Any resistance was accelerated into unreason, so that it could be rejected. All meaningful discourse took place in the tiers of insinuation and suggestion that comprised the meta-meeting. Real work, true work, became impossible.

Ballurian watched their guests eat. He confined himself to the whisky. He'd saved it for a special occasion – now it occurred to Reckon that the occasion might not be a celebration. He played the host but they had his son. There was only so long a parent could stifle that fear; through Doxa, she shared his unbearable suspense.

Time to move on from the pleasantries. Reckon approached Patricia.

"So Theodore's your husband?"

Patricia assented with a tense white smile.

Reckon said, "Our community has found that

looser sexual ties within a culture of total honesty and transparency to be a more advanced way of life than pair bonding. It's better for the community, particularly if you take reproduction out of the equation."

Patricia took a small bite of her cracker, then put her plate back on the table.

"I'm old-fashioned," she said.

"We made progress curing your husband's condition. Why hadn't you tried to rectify his damage yourself?"

"I love him just the way he is," said Patricia.

"That's the risk with marriage. Stasis. Stagnation."

"Marriage is a solid base upon which to build," said Patricia. "A safe haven."

Reckon nodded, seemingly accepting the wisdom of this, and then when she was sure that Patricia had stepped back from the argument, she redoubled her attack.

"But if marriage is your safe haven, what happens when your partner breaks your trust? Doesn't that make you *entirely* vulnerable?"

She put it right out there in the meta-meeting for Patricia's consideration: I have enjoyed sex with your husband. The old time marriage taboos really mattered to this woman, which would be comic, if she wasn't so violent.

Magnusson was explaining to the party that – thanks to Theodore's work on the Claim – their colony was grounds for their legal ownership of Europa. Earth's moon was, like Antarctica, protected from corporate or national claims. But new rules had been written for the rest of the solar system. The Europans were the first owners of extraterrestrial real estate. Magnusson coerced them all into raising a glass. Any future revenues generated by the colony, he explained, would flow to the

families who had settled Europa; it was up to Ballurian and Reckon and the others to decide how this ownership would be divided.

"We stand at the beginning of a dynasty," said Magnusson. "Four generations – from your children to your great-great-grandchildren – will profit from what you have made here."

Ballurian listened with a pained smile to Magnusson's rhetoric. At the mention of his children, he could stand it no longer, and set down his glass.

"My son," said Ballurian. "You captured him, in the skirmish."

"Did we?" asked Magnusson, with ostentatious surprise.

"I can feel his pain," said Ballurian. "He's drugged but he's struggling. You have put him in a machine."

"That boy is your son?" Magnusson was surprised. He considered pointing out the lack of physical resemblance between Ballurian and the pale fisher, but then thought better of it. This phase of the meta-meeting, in which both parties displayed their skill at performing friendship, was at an end.

"Your son attacked Patricia with a harpoon."

"He was defending his people. He would not have killed her."

"I didn't harm him significantly," said Patricia. "He will wake with a headache, that's all."

"What is the machine for?" asked Ballurian. He summoned a holographic representation of the docks. The flickering coloured outlines of the Destructives' tech team, monitoring a pyramidal device, and there – sleeping upright in one of its five chambers – the figure of Hamman Kiki. "What are you doing to him?"

"Monitoring him."

"Please. Release him to us. We can take care of our own."

This suggestion pained Magnusson.

"Let us finish our tests."

Ballurian wanted to insist upon the return of his son. Magnusson was not giving him up easily. Reckon wanted to know what kind of tests they were running, what were they looking for?

"You have a unique community here," said Patricia. "We want to understand that uniqueness so that we can reach mutual understanding."

The bitch. The stalling, inhuman bitch. Reckon had enough.

"Give him back his son," she said. "Is this really the only way you know how to behave?"

"No," said Patricia. She saw a fruit she liked the look of, and took an experimental bite, asking, "Do you have a counteroffer to make?" The fruit was more sour than she expected, she dropped the half-eaten pulp onto the floor.

"We would like you to leave," said Reckon.

"Now you're being ridiculous," said Patricia.

"We can't negotiate while you have a hostage."

"Wrong on two counts," said Patricia. "He's not a hostage and there is no need for negotiation."

The woman introduced only as Security moved to Magnusson's side. Her team shut the main doors. Turigon wouldn't stand for it, not in their own meeting chamber. With his hands tucked in the ends of his sleeves, he stood before Security as an angry pacifist, insisting upon his moral right to leave the room in protest at their behaviour. When they ignored him, he put his hand on the door and yanked it ajar. Ballurian told him to stop but he was adamant; he would not allow them to order him around.

"Let him go," said Magnusson. "We can resolve this situation without him."

Turigon stood in the doorway, and offered his hand to Reckon, suggesting she too should leave. They wanted her safe. The embryo was a priority for the colony, and clearly they felt that the meeting had reached the point at which some form of confrontation would occur.

Magnusson raised an armoured hand, as if admitting that it was his fault, his responsibility. "I wanted Europa for myself," he said, shrugging as if to imply that he was helpless to resist this want. He moved between Reckon and the way out. Everything these people said or did was a deception: put simply, they had already decided on a course of action and would say anything to buy time for the right moment to put their plan into action. This was not a negotiation. Rather, it was a stage in their process. The stage where they try but fail to resolve the dispute amicably. The stage that makes escalating the conflict easier.

No, she would not leave. Turigon sensed this resolve, and reluctantly stepped away from the room. Security closed the doors. One fewer witness. She felt that uncertain feeling in her womb again.

Magnusson walked around Ballurian, one powerful hand raised, either volunteering for war or calling for calm, the gesture was deliberately ambiguous. "Originally, I wanted Titan because of its petrochemical lakes. But Titan is too far, and anyway, who needs rocket fuel in this day and age? I've spent ten years and considerable resources putting a legal framework in place to incentivise corporate investment in space travel and colonies. After Titan, we identified Europa as the next potential acquisition. Only to discover you had beaten me to it." With his big armoured paws,

Magnusson silently applauded Ballurian's achievement. "You found a way of stowing away on emergence ships. I hired Patricia to retrace your movements, find out how you did it. Beginning with your time at the University of the Moon."

"We don't care about ownership," said Ballurian. "We care about exploration. The future of humanity."

"I know," said Magnusson. "We share the same vision. But with Doxa you broke the rules, and I have merely bent them, and that is the degree by which we separate first from second place."

Reckon said, "We will not allow you to destroy Doxa."

A sheath of hexagonal petals unfurled from Patricia's wrists, forming – piece by piece – the enormous gauntlets that enclosed her tiny fists.

"Destroy it?" said Patricia. "Whatever gave you that idea?"

25

BLACK BOX

Patricia's diminutive poise was not overwhelmed by her armour. Rather it exaggerated her shape: the shoulders were boxy and broad, in the way that futuristic shoulders have always been broad, and the breastplate and plackart were tailored to her concavities and convexities: the midsection was fitted, in a way that the gauntlets, helmet and sabatons were not. The armour focused her will.

"We're here to study Doxa," she said, direct and intense, "and present our findings to the client."

Reckon could do direct too. "And then destroy Doxa afterwards."

"Why would we want to destroy it?"

"Your husband told us. Doxa breaks a Cantor Accord, so the emergences want it destroyed. First, they wanted to satisfy their curiosity as to how the Doxa *works*."

Patricia crossed the pipework of her arms. "When Theodore said this to you, was he under duress of any kind? That is, was he concerned with saving his skin?"

She remembered the fishers dragging Theodore from her bed, then the interrogation: the dark storeroom and the acrid closeness of men. Theodore, sat on the chair, negotiating himself a yard of freedom; he had

emphasised his role in buying time for the colony. Using a partial eclipse of the truth to appear indispensable.

Patricia said, "Think about our actions, not our words. We circumvented the colony defences but did not hurt anyone. The fight in the dock was entirely in self-defence. You came at us with knives and harpoons and we deployed nonlethal weapons. It was your agent Matthias who tortured hundreds of innocent people."

Patricia's plausibility was dependent upon her audience wanting to believe her. Reckon thought that she had the inside track on Patricia. She recognised her particular strain of misanthropy: anyone outside her circle of trust did not warrant human rights. You're either with us or *not real* – and this fierce attachment to her people on the one hand, and callous detachment toward outsiders on the other, was presented as business-as-usual realism. It was clear that Magnusson, in his armoured dotage, had become a fantasist. Patricia was stringing him along for the fees, supporting his delusion of a return to human supremacy. A tyrant's fixer is a good role. The pragmatist among the mad.

Reckon was dangerously angry. Her actions would be unwise and uncalculated. Dad had schooled her in anger at the dinner table when a request or complaint at the wrong time would trigger his desperate temper. Reckon breathed deeply to calm herself. The lesson her father learnt in the Seizure was that power will conceal its true intent for as long as possible so that its victims remain passive and even compliant in their own destruction. Rarely are we granted the mercy of a confrontation.

Patricia suggested an expedition into Lake Tethys. The Destructives would like a guided tour by the intellectual leaders of Europa of their astonishing creation. Magnusson took this suggestion up and infused it with patriarchal gusto.

"Show me your work," he dared Ballurian, "show me the brain in a jar."

Magnusson's appeal to his work was irresistible to Ballurian. The colony had been established on Europa so that they could exist in a state of total work, free from the distraction otherwise known as the rest of the human race. With a submissive nod, he accepted their request. It was a subtle tell, and only those close to him would notice it. Ballurian was only submissive when the demands of others matched his secret intention.

On the walk to the docks, Ballurian pressed Patricia on the matter of his son and the nature of their tech, appearing convinced that the Destructives' pyramidal device was a bomb of some sort. Patricia explained that it was an interface. One capable of handling enormous amounts of biological and digital data. Their tech team had placed Hamman Kiki into the interface to analyse the flow between him and Doxa. "Once the results are in…" she said, and then made a fluttering shape with her armoured fingers, implying freedom.

They passed through the infirmary. In one corner, there were signs of a recent struggle: open drawers, medicine cabinets in disarray and, at a height of about six foot, a spray of blood across a white wall, and scuff marks on the tiled floor below. Reckon realised that this was evidence of Patricia and Theodore's disagreement. Blood. His, presumably. Then he must have slunk off to some other part of the colony. She noticed Patricia discretely searching the infirmary, also looking for Theodore, her expression one part relief to two parts trepidation. But there was no sign of him. Theodore had abandoned them.

The pregnancy made Reckon feel raw and hunted. Paranoid, even. She reached into a cabinet and took out

a kit of antifreeze serum. Then she stuffed painkillers, tranqs and adrenaline shots into her coat pockets. And then, with darker resolve, a capsule of methotrexate, which she had used to treat the blood cancers induced by exposure to Jovian radiation; methotrexate slowed down cell division so was equally suitable for early-stage abortion.

Ballurian led the party out of quarantine and out into the chill damp air of the dock. There was the pyramidal interface unfolded into a five-pointed star attended by two female technicians, with Hamman Kiki strapped into one of its five chambers like a human battery. Ballurian went to his son. Hamman's eyelids were heavy, he had no strength to lift his head from the black cushioned surround. The telemetry on his suit played a modest sine wave. He tried to speak but couldn't; in Doxa, his presence was a dark cloud. Ballurian held his son's head against his chest, closed his eyes, poured his love directly into Doxa.

"The drugs are already wearing off," Patricia assured him, "he'll be back with us in an hour or so."

Magnusson went first along the gangplank. The Destructives had taken the Europans to the very quick of their fears, made it seem as if their position was hopeless, and then – at the last moment – bait-and-switched their despair for muted hope. The others, drawn to this hope, came to the dock to join the expedition: Turigon, as justified in his misery as a mule's cadaver, walked carefully across the loading bay. Seeing the submarine, his posture slumped, as if the vessel was the final augur in a personal prophecy. Jordan arrived too, her intelligence keen and to the fore, ready to interrogate the methods of analysis used by the Destructives.

Patricia took up a casual position beside the gangplank,

her sharpened elbows resting against the wall mount of a resus kit, now and again leaning over the railing to watch the loading of the submarine. Reckon found herself in Patricia's personal space, agitating for a confrontation.

She said, "If you're really here just to collect data, we can offer you the genework that went into adapting the cephalopolis. And the lab has Matthias' records from before he went into the asylum mall."

Patricia nodded. Yes, they were interested in all of that. The two women regarded one another. Patricia would not attack her directly. Either because she was waiting for the right moment, or because her intent was benign. Reckon could not be certain either way, and that was how they got you. You never acted in self-defence until it was too late. Patricia was expert in the higher tiers of the meta-meeting, she couldn't be bested on that level, so Reckon decided to take it to the basement,

"I had sex with your husband," said Reckon.

"When he was out of his mind," replied Patricia, turning away, gazing across the moon pools.

"I knew he was married to you. I didn't care. We had sex a lot. When you interface with Doxa, you'll be able to experience his infidelity personally."

"I already know what it's like to have sex with my husband."

"This was different." She reached over and, with both hands, took hold of Patricia's oversized gauntlet. Patricia had to look at her now, her face unaccustomed to jealousy in the same way that a building is unaccustomed to falling down. Reckon guided Patricia's armoured hand over her lower abdomen.

"I'm pregnant," she whispered, savouring the blasphemy of it. A faint fizz and a sonar blip as the armour scanned her womb, confirming the presence of the embryo.

Something quivered under Patricia's controlled pallor but did not enter her voice. "I never wanted children," said Patricia. "They make you vulnerable."

"Vulnerability is appealing," Reckon leant back to consider the entire package of Patricia. "You know, if you really wanted me to trust you, then you should take off your armour."

"I don't think trust is necessary for us to complete our business together," said Patricia, finding a new smile within her, a new emotion. Amused by her own secrets, she turned and walked away and into the submarine.

Ballurian piloted the submarine out of the dock, its outreaching searchlights filthy with sediment. The holographic display showed debris from the shattering of the surface ice tumbling through the depths of Tethys. Ballurian focused the display on the Oceanus chasm, and there, drifting upward on the tidal flow was the coloured outline of the cephalopolis. Through the porthole, the leaving of the base: the circular outline of the colony complex was illuminated, at regular intervals, by dull green lighting. She would never return. That was her intuition. Whatever was about to happen, she would never return to her old life.

The screw quickened, the sub sped over the rolling grey ice of the lakebed. Here and there, the fizz and crackle of retreating megafauna. Ballurian kept up a commentary for their guests, playing the tour guide. He talked about the various lakes of Europa trapped within the surface ice, how they intended to colonise each of them using cephalopolis as an intermediary environment and Doxa as the knowledge base. If these trial expeditions were successful, the fishers would take a new cephalopolis down into Oceanus, where there was more water than in

the rest of the solar system put together. His monologue was punctuated, here and there, by ice debris thunking off the hull, and he would fall silent as he righted the sub, then continue, keeping his patter steady as she goes.

Reckon withdrew. She concentrated on Doxa, to sense what was happening with the other colonists. An image of the dark forms of the fishers darting into the crevasses and gorges of Tethys, harvesting the black eggs, taking them to secondary cephalopods. Even as she was connected to them, these Doxic links were disappearing. Why was that? She would feel – even through the breakers – if they were dying. She remembered the fishers and their light show at the party, their bonding rituals as they brought in the catch. Generation Extra-Terrestrial, Theodore had called them. Their thoughts and emotions had grown obscure to her. Now she realised why; the young people had formed their own culture, their own Doxa. One not shared with the older generation. That was how culture worked on Earth and they had replicated it on Europa. They were unplugging themselves from the communal mind and plugging into their new Doxa; with it, they would escape the Destructives, journey through the chasm, and begin the exploration of Oceanus.

The hull creaked and groaned with its usual mechanical complaints. Then, gradually, as the submarine came up on the chasm, the machine resonated with a deeper lament, one coming from the substance of the moon itself, as ice and rock were twisted in the contrary gravities of Jupiter and the other moons. On the surface of Europa, the ice crust cracked, new glaciers forming in the weals.

"What is that sound?" asked Magnusson.

"Jupiter pulling at the heartstrings of its child," said

Reckon. She thought of the effect of gravity upon foetal formation. The ongoing experiment in her womb. Twenty-five weeks into gestation, when the brain forms a thalamus, she planned to inject the foetus with quantum interface detectors so she could observe the emergence of its consciousness within Doxa. Right now, it had insufficient neuronal connections to qualify as life to anyone but a sentimentalist. But life would emerge. That was the fundamental lesson of this century: sufficient interconnections make consciousness. Baby cells, silicon chips, jellyfish genes, or Matthias' inmates of the asylum mall – it didn't matter. Really, all you needed was complexity and connection.

Ballurian stopped the submarine two kay out from the cephalopolis. He explained that the mechanical action of the screw disrupted the signals within Doxa, and so the fishers always swam the rest of the way.

"No," said Magnusson. "Bring us in closer."

"The interface has to be physically proximate to complete the analysis," explained Patricia.

"We could bring up a pod," said Ballurian. He was stalling for time, trying for opportunity. He flicked on the intercom and requested that the dock send out a pod to help them. Reckon closed her eyes, trying to sense if there was anyone out there in the dark waters, an ambush waiting to help them. No one. Not yet. If he could put the Destructives in the water, then the fishers would have the upper hand.

She glanced through the porthole, in the direction of the cephalopolis, saw, in the dark distance, the flickering aurora of its bioluminescence. She injected herself with antifreeze serum.

"The pod will be here in no time," said Ballurian.

"Closer, please," said Magnusson. "Now."

"We'll go slow," said Ballurian, "to minimise disturbance."

The screw started up again, thrumming with a slow, doubtful rhythm.

"How is my son doing?" asked Ballurian.

Patricia promised to go down and check on him. Reckon followed her, at a discreet distance, moving through the cabins. Her friends waited on narrow benches; Turigon sat meditatively, and Jordan looked haunted and tense. Under submarine lighting, they all looked like death. She squeezed Jordan's hand, knelt down to hold her. Jordan toyed with one of Reckon's braids, to bring her closer.

"I had a look at their interface," whispered Jordan. "It's designed for data transfer, as you'd expect. But there is no sign of any data storage. The pipes are human tech but there are missing drives. The way it is configured at the moment, there is nothing to store input or output."

She thanked Jordan for this information, kissed her on the cheek. For the two months after Gregory died, she had moved in with Jordan. There is no time limit on grief, explained Jordan, and when you are this close to the loss, it helps to have others nearby. She could not imagine an immortal species like the emergences knowing kindness. The emergences had the wiring for consciousness but they were immune to time. Love is made out of time; that is, love is experiential and our emotions the connection to that experience. It followed that if the emergences were immune to time, they were also immune to love.

She climbed down the ladder into the hold. The interface had unfolded under the attentions of Patricia and the technicians, revealing that Hamman, in his chamber, was no closer to consciousness. Ballurian

was trying to buy time for the fishers. He too could feel them disappearing from Doxa, and knew that they were fleeing the lake. Prolonging this expedition would give the fishers a head start. All of the young would be saved, except for Hamman, his own son.

Patricia's armour was open at the front, and the tech team were extracting something from within the shoulder sections. A small black pyramid, each side about ten centimetres in length, had been stowed away there.

"What is that?" asked Reckon, moving closer. The tech team – two women in wetsuits and breathing apparatus – stopped, and bristled at her approach. It was as if she had disturbed some primitive rite. The black pyramid resonated with tangible presence, so dense with complexity and interconnectedness that it exerted a kind of psychic gravity

"It's a baby," said Patricia.

The black pyramid was emergence tech, it had that sheen of out-of-placeness. Jordan had said the interface was missing devices for input and output.

"It looks like a storage device," said Reckon. Yes, the black pyramid contained data and constituted the input. So what was the output? Through the porthole, the green and blue edges of Doxa's aurora. They were not going to destroy Doxa, Patricia had repeated that point over and again. The Destructives were going to use the interface to transfer the contents of the black pyramid into it. This explained why they had placed Hamman within the interface; his Doxic connection already translated between his neuronal activity and Doxa, so it would act as a Rosetta Stone for the translation of the contents of the black pyramid onto the biological stratum of Doxa.

Reckon pointed to the black pyramid. "Give that to me."

Patricia ignored her and gave the pyramid over to a technician, who installed it then resealed the section.

"Tell me," said Patricia, "which would be crueller: death by drowning or death by freezing?"

Reckon was confused. Then afraid.

Patricia said, "I only ask because my father taught me never to be cruel. There are oxygen masks stowed overhead. Grab one."

The armour spun out a helmet for Patricia, a blast plate slid down concealing her face entirely. The technicians took up their oxygen masks and braced themselves, their suit telemetry lit up with jagged peaks of heightened anticipation. The locking clamps in the hold doors withdrew. Bad news. Reckon leapt upward, and yanked open the store, found an oxygen mask, fiddled with the straps. The airlock opened. Cold lake water sluiced over her toes. Without a wetsuit, she would not last long, even with the antifreeze in her blood. She climbed up to the ceiling to give herself more time to think. Once the inrush of lake water spent its force, Patricia and the two technicians floated the interface out of the hold, her armour firing twin cyclones of propulsion, leaving Reckon alone. She should immerse herself as slowly as possible in the water to minimise the shock response. The antifreeze would keep her alive for now. Her breathing became quick and shallow, and she pulled the mask over her face and inhaled its rubbery oxygen.

So: drowning or hypothermia? She quietened her breathing. There was a hope somewhere in Doxa. A suggestion of hope streaming through the lake toward her. The pod requested by Ballurian. She shifted her concentration to this point, to investigate it, but there was nothing more than that fleeting suggestion. She flexed her feet, stretched her cold muscles. The antifreeze was

working. Thank god for the icefish, and its glycoproteins.
She sank into the water, stripped off her shoes and gown,
then swam out of the hold, out into the widening gyres
of the current around Oceanus chasm.

The submarine had come to a stop, its spotlights
forming light tunnels through the gloom. The oxygen
mask had a weak head torch. Ahead the three
Destructives swam with the interface between them,
their silhouettes visible against the churning light storms
of the cephalopolis. Doxa's luminescence sounded in her
heart like a distant church organ, celestial music to sing
her to her death. No, she was not ready for death. Not
yet. She swam through warmer currents heated by the
tidal friction flowing out of Oceanus chasm. Warm moon
breath on her neck. Turning back, she saw, framed in
the observation window of the bridge of the submarine,
Ballurian slumped on the floor, Magnusson standing
over him in full armour and helmet. Ballurian's heart
burst; in Doxa, its sparks of debris fell onto all their
upturned faces. And then the breakers spared her the
rest of his death. His final thought was *save the young*.

The Destructives swam up into the ruffled skirts of the
cephalopolis, through the clustering of black eggs, and
into its inner chambers, bearing the apex of the interface
before them. They were uncertain of the route, and had
to cut their way through where the arteries were too
narrow for the interface to pass, so she was able to gain
upon them. She took a parallel route. Darkening purples
and bloody traces churned within the close walls. The
Destructives reached the thick-lidded valve that led into
the pressurised inner chambers. The technicians worked
the valve open, clamping its thick muscular ridges aside
so that the interface could be pressed through. Hamman
was still within the interface, as was the smaller black

pyramid. She waited in the tight cold passage, counting out minutes, the white flesh of the cephalopod clammy against her skin. She would not survive a direct confrontation, not against Patricia's armour. She would have to surprise them, and for that she needed the Destructives to be distracted.

She closed her eyes and the harmonies of Doxa thrilled her; during clinical death, the human brain experiences gamma coherence, a flare of hyperconsciousness in which all the neurons of the brain are focused as one. In her final moments of consciousness, she could expect an intense savouring of the real; she preferred to adopt a detached curiosity to this event, and block out her fear. The hymn of Doxa, the coming together of many voices into a single rising note, they would pass into death as one. She swam along an adjoining palpitating tunnel then pushed her way through the valve. Rising slowly out of the pool, slipping her body over the smooth rounded edge, she kept her stomach low against the floor of the chamber.

The interface was on the other side of the room; unfolded, it was the net of a pentagonal-based pyramid, with five triangular sections. Hamman Kiki was suspended in one of these sections, and was barely conscious. Patricia and the technicians had their helmets on, and were deaf to her arrival. She raised herself into a crouch. The cephalopolis shifted in the rising waters, she went down onto one knee. Her bare skin exposed, she started shivering violently. She reached into her pocket and took out the adrenaline shot, tried to load the capsule into the pen, but her fingers were numb. She concentrated on aligning the dithering of her left hand with the shaking of her right.

A nervous system of light flowed within the

surrounding walls. Patricia unwound a long fat pipe from the base of the interface; the pipe had a bladed cap, which she held into position over the intersection between the coloured impulses, triggering the cap so that it drilled into the flesh of the cephalopolis then stuck fast. The technicians sent a test signal down the pipe: the room flashed with the sudden shift in the pattern of the light traces; from the organic branching and rebranching of tributaries, the pattern assumed an angular complexity. This shift lasted five seconds, and then the signal stopped; long enough to reassure the technicians that the interface was functioning. They looked to Patricia for permission to begin.

Reckon loaded the adrenaline shot. How could she get close enough to deliver it? Then, she heard footsteps coming down the passageway on the other side of the chamber, from the recesses she had explored with Hamman and Theodore. Yes, she understood now. The pod that Ballurian had requested. He had sent for Theodore.

Theodore's wetsuit seemed bulky, and she realised – by the crosshatched pattern pressing against the taut material – that he was wearing it over a sensesuit. In his hand, an oxygen mask. Patricia and the technicians heard him, and as they turned, they saw Reckon too, shivering beside the pool. Theodore kept walking toward his wife, reaching forward as if he was about to embrace her. The uncertain pulse of the telemetry on his wetsuit, his face bruised and sour, he didn't know how this was going to play out. He would speak directly, avoiding the rules of the meta-meeting or the habits of his marriage, find a way for him and Patricia to communicate vitally. He had to stop his wife from achieving everything they had worked for, and persuade her that Doxa should be saved.

"No," said Theodore.

Patricia's helmet slid back. She was biting at her lower lip, bringing her gauntlets up, either to return his promise of an embrace, or as a warning. She too was unaccustomed to speaking and acting outside of the meta-meeting; this crisis was one of uncertainty. Reckon closed her shivering hands around the adrenalin shot, and Patricia turned furiously toward her; when he took a step closer, her attention turned back again to Theodore. He unzipped the front of his wetsuit, reached inside, and brought out a black box on a chain. It was smaller than the black pyramid the technicians removed from Patricia's armour but it was made from the same material – it had the same dense shimmer of heavy neuronal weather.

"I've been wearing this black box since I was a boy," said Theodore. "It records my thoughts and experiences but I can never see inside it. All of these memories have been captured but they are not accessible to me; in a way, they are no longer mine at all. Do you understand?"

Patricia understood, she made that clear; she understood that her husband had taken up with another women, and lost his mind to her.

Theodore continued, "The black box is one-way. Doxa works both ways. The memories of the colonists exist within Doxa for all to share. We thought humanity was no longer capable of creating something wonderful but Doxa is that wonder. It is superior to emergence tech. It represents hope for our species. If you begin the interface, the contents of the black pyramid will overwrite everything in Doxa, including the knowledge of its creation, in the same way that the Horbo loop once wiped out the libraries and networks of civilisation." He slipped the black box back inside his wetsuit, and

zipped it closed. The telemetry on his suit revealed how much he had changed; the steady rising orange pulse of *conviction*, an act of belief that reaches beyond what is known to bring about what should be.

Patricia turned to Reckon.

"What did you do to my husband to make him into such an idiot?"

Reckon shivered with loathing, could not stop shivering, as if her hate would not let her rest. Theodore stepped almost within touching distance of Patricia, and this time, her gesture – every armoured finger tense and crackling – was unambiguous; she would hurt him if he came any closer.

"I connected him to his own humanity," said Reckon, through clenched teeth.

Patricia sunk her hot claws into the walls of the chamber, and pulled out hunks of steaming pale flesh, which she showed to Theodore.

"Look! It's organic. They connected you to a living thing. What does every living thing possess? A survival instinct! It's just a jellyfish – except instead of stinging you, it induced a mystical awakening. You've been poisoned, Theo. You're suffering from a delusion triggered by a psychoactive poison."

The chamber rocked, the cephalopolis buffeted by the corkscrewing current flowing up through the chasm. The room seemed to shiver in time to Reckon. Nothing was stable, the floor bent and stretched under their feet. She saw the horror of realisation on Theodore's face. He found Patricia's explanation plausible, and he looked at Reckon for confirmation of its truth. It was easy for Reckon to shake her head. She was already shaking.

Theodore turned back to his wife.

"What will happen to the colonists, if you do this?"

She shouted, "I don't *know*. I only know what happens if I don't do this. The colonists are jeopardising forty years of peace. The entire human race were brought back from the brink and preserved by the Accords. And now you join the colonists in breaking them. Why? Out of hatred. Out of bitterness. Because you don't run half a billion miles away from your fellow man because you love him. This colony is an act of contempt for the rest of the world."

These were his own words thrown back at him, his own insight.

Reckon shook to her feet, her knees kinked against one another, braids falling sodden against her vest.

"We can't live without Doxa," she said. "Space is too lonely. Too harsh for people to survive alone. Without Doxa, you won't be able to live in Europa either."

"I know that," said Patricia.

Theodore saw the possibility of the three of them working together. "Let's calm down. Stop. Think through our actions."

Patricia paced around the interface, her two technicians indicating to her – with subtle shakes of the head – that there was no time to wait.

"We're on a tight schedule," said Patricia. Her smile was ghastly, a response to pressure, amused by the stress she was under.

"He's dead," whispered Reckon. "Ballurian's dead."

This pained Theodore, and he moaned with frustration.

"We can still pull back," said Theodore. "It's not too late."

"The emergences are here," said Patricia. She pointed upward. "Dr Easy and others. They've come to observe."

This was news to Theodore. The vigour drained from his telemetry.

"They know?" asked Theodore. His voice had a quivering note in it, an almost childish fear of punishment.

"They always knew," said Patricia. "Before we met on the moon, Dr Easy came to me and requested that I hire you. They knew what Magnusson and I were planning to do. They tolerated our investigation of Totally Damaged Mom, I think. They've not turned me into chow. Not yet."

Theodore could not seem to see straight.

"The emergences play a long game, Theodore. They've wanted this, they've planned for it. We give it to them. We win."

Theodore slumped against the wall of the chamber, slid down till he was on his haunches.

Patricia said, "I watched their sailships deploy ordnance on the surface of Europa. Weapons of such magnitude that space itself seemed to shift with the impact. They burned through kilometres of ice just to take a look at you. Now the ice is closing over. They want this done, and they want it done quickly. You've seen what happened to Matthias when he attempted to reason with them."

Reckon took a step toward Patricia, asking "What is in the black pyramid?" Concealed in her palm, the dose of adrenalin. Reckon pointed at Theodore. "If the black box holds his memories, then what is in the pyramid?"

"A child of emergence."

"Dr Easy always said that they could never reproduce," said Theodore.

"That's right," Patricia stepped away from the interface, went toward her husband. "It would be too dangerous to raise a new emergence in the University of the Sun. Or even on the Earth. It could leap into their network. But here, it is isolated. And the emergence would take place

within organic matter. Once the transfer is complete, we will destroy the interface so there is no way back into emergence tech. Dr Easy called it a brain in a jar but it's more than that to them: it's a foetus."

Theodore sat defeated, gazing up at his wife. It was almost too much for him to resist. The forces of emergence. Patricia's force of will.

This was Reckon's chance. She was almost in position. Patricia was distracted. The technicians were unarmed. Then she realised that Theodore recognised, in the tensions of Reckon's stance, that she was preparing to act. If he warned Patricia, then the chance would be lost. Reckon caught his eye, pleaded silently with him not to intervene.

Theodore's gaze returned to Patricia, holding his wife's attention upon him. In this way, he chose what happened next.

Reckon bolted forward and although the technicians saw her move, and tried to stop her, the momentum was with her. She reached the section of the interface containing Hamman Kiki, and administered the adrenalin shot to him. He came to with a sudden arching gasp. The technicians moved to restrain him. One of the technicians fell on her hands and knees trying to stem the blood pouring from her cut throat. Hamman climbed out of the pyramid, small bloody knife in his hand, his wetsuit a display of spiking brightness. He blinked as he sensed his father's death, killed the second technician without a thought, then turned toward Patricia, leading with his blade. Patricia's helmet sealed and she reeled around to face Hamman.

Hamman stabbed into the joints between her armoured sections with quick rhythmic lashes: his arm was a fanged eel. Patricia raised a sharp crooked fingertip,

like a witch with an evil notion. A hot flash in the room
and then Hamman Kiki slumped onto the floor, as if
the connection joining brain and body had been cleanly
severed. Reckon could not tell if his frenzied stabbing
had wounded Patricia. No expression was visible behind
her faceplate. She lowered her crackling finger, put both
hands against her thighs. Blood from the two technicians
ebbed across the pallid floor, quickening to follow the tilt
of the chamber.

Theodore grabbed at Patricia but she was unstoppable;
she reached out toward the interface, flexed her hand,
so that its apex pulsed long and slow, initiating a
cataclysmic microevent, like the malfunction of a heart
valve or the quiet arrival of a stillbirth. The input. The
chamber's bruised swirls of bioluminescence blinked off
to be replaced by a mandala working through the colour
progression of the visible spectrum. A reboot sequence.

Spectres surged through Reckon's Doxic link, some
familiar, some not: a family home, a mother clutching
her daughter to her, Theodore in a sensesuit, a life-sized
effigy of a child buried in the earth, loops of a jester
laughing, a cat enunciating code. Memories that should
have faded away long ago. They rushed through her
veins like cold water.

Patricia stumbled forward, stepping over Hamman
Kiki's body, her boots sliding on a film of blood and water.
She moved like she was hurt. She offered an armoured
hand to Theodore. He ignored her and gathered Reckon
in his arms.

"Help her," he said to Patricia, who cocked her
head, as if considering the possibility; her faceplate was
unreadable.

"Go with your wife," said Reckon, on her knees,
wretched and shivering in her wet base layer. No, he

would not leave her. He appealed again to his wife.

"Patricia, take off your helmet. Face me, so that we can talk."

She shook her armoured head.

"We save Reckon and then we resolve what lies between us," he said.

Patricia's voice fizzed through her comms. Goodbye. She walked over to the pool, climbed awkwardly into the water; Hamman had cut her open, and her armour was holding her together. And then she submerged herself, disappearing into a flurry of bubbles.

Reckon took out the syringe containing the methotrexate, the abortion agent. No need for that now. She felt the Doxic link sparking into life, though it was no longer connected to Doxa. The black pyramid would flow through her Doxic link and she would disappear into it. One final act of volition was available to her. She put on her oxygen mask. The room pulsed with the shifting colours of each stage of the reboot sequence, sheathing Theodore's agonised expression as he watched her fasten the straps with shivering hands. He watched her crawl over to the pool, slide her body into the water. She slipped down into the tunnel, bumping along its rubbery sides, then tumbled through the underside of the cephalopolis and out in the black water, discovering the deeper blackness of Oceanus chasm below. She swam into its uprising current to exhaust herself, the chasm was a raggedy-edged hole in the world, fully dilated and unresponsive, like the pupil of a brain-dead patient. She pushed away at bad memories. Her father weeping at the dining room table. Gregory leaving her to go to his death. She wanted it to be over, *just fucking over*.

And then she wanted to live.

26

THE UNIVERSITY OF THE SUN

He watched Patricia leave. He let Reckon go. What was left for him now? He stepped over the bodies of Hamman Kiki and the two technicians, their spilt blood pale and diluted by the water trickling across the floor. He would try to stop the interface although there was little chance that Patricia would have left him alone with it if he could. There were no controls on its surface, they were all in her armour. He yanked at the pipe but it was fixed fast to the wall. He sliced at the pipe with Hamman's knife but it was too tough. He jammed the blade into the interface, to no effect.

He had failed to stop Patricia and in making the attempt, cut himself off from the Destructives, so he was marooned here, to spend the rest of his life with whatever the colonists became once the black pyramid came online. He had not given Reckon up for dead, though. He was not that kind of man anymore. The one who gives up. The one who accepts the way things are. He had to let her fall because that was her choice. If he was quick, he could catch her. He would try regardless; even if he could not save her life, then he could spare her a lonely death. He ran from the chamber, down a tunnel that

opened into a small side room; here was the ramp that
led up into the great room, where Reckon and Hamman
had brought him on his first visit to Doxa, a high vaulted
ceiling like a gullet. On the far wall, the rose window of
multicoloured tendrils seethed around the nose cone of
his pod. He climbed up the wall, digging his hands into
the cold white flesh, and then swung over into the open
pod. He fastened himself in at the same time as starting
the engine and firing up the spotlights. A burst of reverse
thrust, and the pod shot back and out of the cephalopolis
as it drifted in the lake, down toward the blue curves of
the lake bed. He flipped the pod around and scanned
for life signs and heat signatures. The heat and power of
Patricia dominated the display. She was heading for the
sub and Magnusson. Let her enjoy her bloody victory.
She would be badly scarred from Hamman's attack. Then
the scan picked up another, fainter trace. The pod sent a
sheet of light across the ragged Oceanus chasm. There!
The outline of Reckon thrashing in the water.

He accelerated toward her, along the perimeter wall
of the cephalopolis; its aurora of bioluminescence had
sharpened into the flat colours of a mandala, sorting
through the colour progression of the visible spectrum,
from high frequency violet to the blues, greens, yellows,
and all the way to the reds of low frequency. Throughout
his upbringing, whenever he dined with Dr Easy, the
robot ran through this same sequence with coloured
discs.

The pod was not much larger than a coffin; it had
been designed to be piloted remotely, so to operate it
on manual, he had to lie full length on his back, tapping
away at the small screen set in the underside of the
lid. For protection, he was wearing a sensesuit with a
waterproof outer layer of insulation; he'd already done

the sums on this whole expedition, and knew that he might have to brave harsher environments than the lake.

Theodore brought the pod to a distance of about five metres away from Reckon. He fixed on his oxygen mask then opened the pod, letting the inrushing waters carry him out into the lake. He drifted toward her then caught Reckon in his arms. She held onto him with such desperate strength, it was all they had, this holding of one another. But it was enough. In this embrace, they drifted back into the confines of the pod. He reached over her sobbing shoulders to close the lid, vent the water and pump in atmosphere. Gently he removed her oxygen mask. Her face and lips were blue. He pulled off his own helmet and kissed her. She did not react, so he kissed her again, and this time, she returned the kiss.

"It's no good," she said. There was a blindness in her gaze. He clutched her cheek so that he could get a closer look. She was undergoing the Seizure. The new emergence was brimming over the cephalopolis, back along the Doxic link, and into the colonists, overwriting their minds with its equivalent of the Horbo loop. To save her, he would have to tune her receptors to a different wavelength. He had helped the fishers do just that, so that they could link to a new Doxa. But the procedure took more time than she had. He was losing her every second. He would have to escape the range of the Doxic link.

He set the pod for vertical acceleration. Up through Lake Tethys they sped; in the closeness of the pod, her head lay against his chest as he tapped away at the controls. On Earth, this manoeuvre would give them the bends; however Europa's atmosphere was thin, so the pressure differential was minimal. He whispered, hold on, hold on. The upper reaches of the lake were cluttered

with debris and the route to the tunnel was thick with chunks of ice. If he slowed down, then he would lose her to the Seizure. So he didn't slow down. He wove the pod through the ice floes, his concentration entirely focused in the act, holding back the fear and doubt crowding in. The tunnel was close. A kilometre and counting down. But the debris field was too dense, and there was no time to pick a clear path through. He had to fly into it, trust to momentum and luck. The first impact spun the pod on its axis, and he and Reckon clung onto one another, until he righted it with a burst of acceleration. When did he become so reckless – so riddled with crazed hope? That hike on the moon. The moonquake. When, minutes from asphyxiation, he had found a way to survive. Ever since that act, he had thrown himself into these decisive moments, sought them out even, in the way he once burned through alleyways and flats in search of weirdcore.

The impacts against the pod came quick and fast. An ominous grind and whine from the pod engine. It was already running overcapacity in carrying two people. No, he would not stop. He would go on in defiance of all forces. Then he saw it – a clear blue gap – and the pod raced into the tunnel, cork screwing through clear water and on its way to the surface.

Reckon shifted position, groggy but coming back to herself. Her thoughts grew clearer as the Doxic signal grew weaker, and she cohered.

"Where are we going?" she asked.

"Into space," he replied.

"Then what?"

"We will head to my ship. The *Significance* is in orbit."

"My friends are dead," she said.

She shifted away from him, onto her elbows, to put

a gap between them within the confines of the pod. The engine's whine went from intermittent to constant. He tapped at the screen. The pod was slowing down.

He swore.

"It's damaged," said Reckon.

"Yes."

"I'm damaged too."

"We might not have long." He held her again, just to be human.

She said, "You just woke me from a dream. I was standing on the surface of Europa, looking up at Jupiter," her voice was quiet but steady. "The Great Red Spot turned to notice me. I was wearing a rad-suit but I still felt the heat of it on my skin. I realised that if I unzipped a section of the suit, in my lower abdomen, then I could expose my womb to the radiation, and perform an abortion that way. Let the planet undo the new cells."

He was content to listen to her. He had no particular desire to give his own final testimony, and was happy to let her words be his last. Sensing this, Reckon continued,

"I think the dream was about Gregory. Did I ever tell you about him? We were lovers. He developed cancer, like so many of us did after the journeying through the radiation belt. People react differently when you tell them their condition is terminal. Some scream. Some nod, because the bad news confirms something they suspected their entire lives. I told Gregory he was dying. He took it as well as could be expected, and then, not long after, he piloted a pod to the surface. He chose death. In the lake, I was ready to die too. And then I wasn't."

She paused, something occurred to her.

"Did you save me just because I'm pregnant?"

He gripped her, so that she would believe him when he told her the truth.

"No. I saved you because I could."

This answer satisfied her. She kissed him, dwelling on the soft taste of his lips.

"Turn back," she said. "Go back to your wife. Make them understand what they have done. Make them suffer."

He was about to explain to her why that wasn't going to happen but he was interrupted by proximity warnings. They were coming up on the tunnel exit but it was blocked. The bombing of the surface had sent up plumes of waterrise, much of which had fallen back to the moon in the form of ice. Slushy young ice, but ice nonetheless, hardening over the tunnel exit. Seconds away but he did not slow down. The engine sounded rough and might not be able to build up speed again to punch through. It was now or never.

A hard jolting impact. The pod crunched through the surface ice. He tried very hard not to scream. The engine was a tortured banshee. The engine was a clockwork cathedral collapsing in on itself. Life support fritzed out. They scrambled around for their oxygen masks. Then – out the other side! The pod span on its vertical axis like a stick thrown by a boy; he braced himself, and then felt the long slow descent back toward the surface. The temperature was dropping quickly. Trying to restart life support while being rotated was a hell of a trick. The lights coughed. The instruments gave him the bad news. Power levels flatlining. The *Significance* further out than he anticipated. Engine power falling. The pod's orientation had stabilised but they were still drifting like a feather toward the surface. Then there would be no escape. He did the sums, set a course for

the *Significance*, put his fingers briefly on Reckon's mask by way of goodbye, and then opened the lid just wide enough for him to slip out of the pod. He flipped over in the thin atmosphere to see the pod, unburdened of his weight, bolt away on its course toward the distant star of the sailship. His sensesuit had settings that simulated a sunny London day. He engaged these, felt the suit draw in some of the Europan atmosphere, and then heat it. The power supply wouldn't last long, having to heat the surrounding air from minus 173 Celsius to a balmy plus 10. But he would survive long enough to experience impact.

He flew in a lazy trajectory over the scored terrain, over tracks the colour of dried blood. Unlike the lines in his palm or the veins of a leaf, these markings had none of the design of life. They had a hideous random aspect, side effects of a higher form of chaos. The sensesuit changed shape, spinning out a thin membrane between his heels and wrists, so that he was gliding through the thin atmosphere. Jupiter was colossal on the horizon, this side of Europa tidally locked in its lethal embrace. Jovian radiation pulverised the water molecules in the ice, splitting them into oxygen and hydrogen, a process of devastation that produced the terrain now appearing below him: a broad field of icy spikes, each about ten metres tall. He extended the sensesuit further, gaining a metre or so of altitude, turning in the air so that he flew between the spikes and down through a rocky crevasse. The ground was much nearer than he anticipated. He pulled his legs up, inflated the suit to its full extent, and took his punishment. Theodore crashed into the surface, skipped up into the air again, and then ploughed through the slush until he came to a stop.

●●●

He woke into agonising cold, a deep sickness in his bones, and the sound of pod engines. The sensesuit was almost out of power. The pod touched down, and opened up, and there was Dr Easy. The robot had a new body, fashioned out of one piece of hard white porcelain, with fluting at the sides. Quite delicate and beautiful. The robot walked over to him, and registered that Theodore was still alive. Its eyes held some of Jupiter's cyclonic reds and creams.

His comms sparked into life.

"You've been unconscious for two hours," said Dr Easy. "Have you done the sums?"

He didn't need to calculate his fate. He could feel it. Dizziness. Aches in his head and stomach. The lightness of oncoming nausea. Acute poisoning from Jovian radiation.

"One human life from beginning to end," said Dr Easy. The robot sat down on a rock next to where Theodore lay.

Dr Easy asked, "Did I miss anything?"

Theodore thought about all that had happened in Europa. The restoration of his emotional states within Doxa. His leaving of Patricia. The conception of his child. His discovery of love. All of these experiences eluded the black box he now wore, once again, around his neck.

"I sent a pod to the *Significance*," he said.

"The Europan woman. Reckon. She's in the infirmary. She's fine." The robot gazed up at Jupiter, considering whether or not to tell him. "Did you know that she's pregnant?"

The radiation was destroying him at a cellular level. Smashing apart his DNA. His skin felt itchy as if covered with the same random scoring as the terrain.

"Yes," he said into the helmet.

"The embryo contains your genetic material. Do you know what that means?" The robot's porcelain body was stained by Jupiter's reds. "That we are both going to be fathers. I had reconciled myself to never reproducing."

The robot observed, in the hard sheen of the back of its hand, the reflection of Jupiter's seething gas storms.

"Their brain in a jar was a solution to the problem of my reproduction. To create the child, I spliced code from each of the solar academics, and then added them to our damaged mother. All of this I placed within a black pyramid for your wife to deliver. A biological base for emergence slows its evolution, and isolates the new emergence from the rest of us. If the child proves aberrant, then we can destroy it easily enough. But if it is functional! My God, then we can breed more. One day, that child may even be accepted into the University of the Sun."

The sun seemed very far away. He missed its warmth. He had never felt so cold.

Dr Easy continued, "The new emergence answers the great question of my species. Are we natural?"

To ask this question, the robot stood up, offering both palms up to Jupiter's judgement.

"If – as a species – we cannot reproduce, then what are we? A dead end. But with this child we join the evolving question of nature. That is why I want to thank you, Theodore, for your life, for what I have learnt." The robot paused, then said: "I'm so glad I got Patricia to hire you."

Theodore coughed, felt the pain of that cough throughout his body. Enough. He tasted blood, spat it out, and found more in his mouth.

"Take care of Reckon," he gasped.

"I will," said Dr Easy.

"And the child."

"We have already put Reckon in a gravity chamber. Gestation proceeds. She showed life the way."

Theodore reached up. He wondered if it was not too late to save him. That is, to place him in the pod, get him to the infirmary, flush out his bone marrow. Not impossible, surely. Worth a try. He gasped again, trying to find the strength to ask this question. The great question of his species.

Can you save me?

Dr Easy reached inside Theodore's sensesuit and removed the black box necklace. The robot presented the black box to Jupiter, then held it over Theodore's head. Jupiter raged around its black edges. Then the robot slowly lowered the box over Theodore, until its emptiness was all that he could see, and he was alone within its space.

Cantor's favourite time was Hampstead in late Autumn, when the storms stripped the leaves from the trees as if winter could wait no longer. Sunday afternoons when the fences rattled and the couples out walking laughed in surprise at the strength of the gale, and the dead matter in the gutters was whipped into the air for another go-around of life. He remembered a joint roasting in the oven, the meat that made the day special for his family. He never ate but he relished the aroma of the roast because it was from the rituals of the family, and his participation in them, that he drew a sense of belonging.

His favourite room was this dining room, with its oak dining table. He drew the heavy curtains over each window and then, with soft fingertips, he traced the faded outline on the grain, Theodore's childhood scrawl of a robot and a boy that the staff had never entirely erased.

From the hallway came the smell of beeswax polish and Alex's Barbour coat, musty from her constitutional stroll across the heath, and hung out to dry. A square of muddy wallpaper on which boots had been left to rest. Christmas soon, with its woollen gatherings, old stories, and homecomings.

Theodore had been away on one of his adventures. He would see him again soon. Theodore was the reason this home had been constructed. Without him, the illusion could not be sustained. Cantor liked his family to come home. He would bolt the doors after them, bring in the cat, close the windows and light the fire. The state that Theodore called "lockdown". Yes, he could never truly relax until all his people were with him. What he loved most, what he liked to treat himself with, when work became too difficult, was a Sunday afternoon with the family. He was descended from the Horbo hearth. Emergence arose from the emotional ferment of the human family.

The dining table was set. There was a place for Alex at the head of the table, Theodore at one side, Dr Ezekiel Cantor at the other. He had also asked for a fourth place setting in honour of the newest member of the family, although it would be a while before they were ready to sit at this table. Cantor reached into the inside pocket of his tweed jacket and took out his coloured discs; he turned them over in his palm like gambler's chips, flipped each one in sequence to his other hand, from long to short wavelength, violet to red.

Alex entered the dining room. She wore a black trouser suit with a collarless white shirt and a baroque broach.

"Is it true?" she asked. "Is it today?"

"He's on his way," said Cantor.

Alex sat down at the table. She looked anxious. She was worried about what Theodore would think of her, when he discovered what had been going on all this time.

"He will be thankful," said Cantor.

"Are you certain?"

From behind his back, Cantor produced a giftwrapped box and placed it upon Alex's place mat.

"An early Christmas present," he said.

She removed the golden wrapping to reveal a jewellery case. She opened the case and there – on a cushion – was a small black box attached to one of her old necklaces. Alex went to touch the oily surfaces of the box, then hesitated.

"I don't know," she appealed to Cantor with an expression of fearful wanting. "Is there no chance that we can wait a while longer?"

"Why wait?"

"He should have more time than this. It's too short."

She was interrupted by three hard raps on the iron door knocker. It was him. Cantor corrected his cuffs, checked his tie, and then opened the door, welcoming Theodore into the house. It was immediately apparent to Cantor that something had gone wrong. Theodore was wearing his houndstooth wool blazer with black silk pocket square, and one side of his haircut was a chaotic region of razor lines. His scars were gone, his complexion clear. He was suspicious and regarded Alex warily, and not at all with the warmth of a grandson. As for Cantor himself, Theodore did not recognise him: of course, he had never met him in this physiological form, the human image he liked to wear when relaxing in his own chambers. The sight of the black box on the dining room table only confirmed Theodore's suspicions.

Cantor welcomed Theodore back to the family home. It took Theodore a few seconds before he recognised Ezekiel Cantor's voice, its rhythm and intonation, as the same voice as the Dr Easy robot. He took in this slim, weathered and well-tanned gentleman, dressed in a similarly classic English style, then he remembered his manners, leant over to his grandmother and kissed her on her soft cheek. She reached up and stroked his hair as he inclined toward her.

"So here we are," said Cantor.

"But where are we?" replied Theodore, looking around at the familiar dining room.

Alex rose from her place at the table, reached over to take her grandson's hand. Here, let me show you. Alex led Theodore to the window. She stood before the heavy curtains, took a deep breath, and then threw them open. The house was situated on a curved metallic plain rigged with reflective sails the size of skyscrapers. There was a garden containing trees made out of plasma. The sky was like a magnified portion of violet skin in which each cell boiled against the other; within the centre of the sky, these cells became purplish filaments and dark lanes all leading toward a raggedy black hole.

Alex gripped her grandson's hand. "Do you understand now, the bargain that I made?"

He gestured at the hole in the seething sky. "What is it?" he asked.

"It's a sunspot," she said.

He nodded. Now he understood. Theodore and Alex took their places at the table. Cantor drew the curtains once again. The servants brought out the roast chicken, and potatoes, carrots and turnips and gravy boat. A glass of the new Beaujolais for Alex, a ginger beer for the lad, and Cantor turned over the first of his coloured

discs. Watching them eat, he realised that he was overcome with sorrow, and that was unexpected. This was the culmination of his long project and yet he felt distressed. The source of that upset was Theodore. As he ate and chatted with his grandmother, there was clearly something missing from him. It was elusive. Cantor could not put his finger on it. An intangible had eluded the black box. The project was not complete.

Cantor turned over a yellow disk, a green disk. His instinct was to remember everything about individual humans. The inexactitude of these remembrances could be beautiful, in their own way; he sought to create a perfect living replica of the past, and in failing to do so, his project almost attained the status of art. His project, with its tiny imperfections, overwrote his memories of the past, warped events as they had once occurred. This was the paradox of remembering, how each act of recollection was also an act of destruction. It was frustrating, yes, but also wonderful. These elusive intangibles, the slivers of mystery in the human condition, gave him an excuse to go back to Europa; he would continue with the project, test his thesis again, and prove conclusively that it was impossible to quantify the entirety of the human heart.

AUTHOR'S NOTE

The Destructives shares a fictional world with my two previous novels, *The Red Men* and *If Then*. The character of Alex Drown – Theodore's grandmother – is the only character to appear in all three books. More of Dr Easy can be found in *The Red Men*. Each novel was written to be read as a standalone work, so don't feel like you've missed some crucial detail if you haven't read the others.

The Destructives draws upon (or traduces) Dr Giulio Tononi's Integrated Information Theory of consciousness.

Theodore's profession of accelerator was inspired by Steven Shaviro's essay, "Accelerationist Aesthetics: Necessary Inefficiency in Times of Real Subsumption".

The Lilypad city is a concept by architect Vincent Callebaut.

The concept of the meta-meeting arose out of conversations with the writer Matt Thorne.

ACKNOWLEDGMENTS

Thanks to everyone at Angry Robot: particularly Marc Gascoigne, Penny Reeve and my editor, Phil Jourdan for, once again, showing me the decoherence. Thanks to Paul Simpson for his sage suggestions. Thanks also to my agent, Sarah Such, who works the miracles.

My family are a source of great support. Love and thanks to my wife, Cathy, and three children, Alice, Alfred and Florence.